D0949811

Defending Britta Stein

A Novel

RONALD H. BALSON

ST. MARTIN'S PRESS
NEW YORK

First published in the United States by St. Martin's Press, an imprint of St. Martin's Publishing Group

DEFENDING BRITTA STEIN. Copyright © 2021 by Ronald H. Balson. All rights reserved. Printed in the United States of America. For information, address St. Martin's Publishing Group, 120 Broadway, New York, NY 10271.

www.stmartins.com

Library of Congress Cataloging-in-Publication Data

Names: Balson, Ronald H., author.
Title: Defending Britta Stein : a novel / Ronald H. Balson.
Description: First Edition. | New York : St. Martin's Press, 2021. |
    Series: Liam Taggart and Catherine Lockhart ; 6
Identifiers: LCCN 2021016353 | ISBN 9781250274809 (hardcover) |
    ISBN 9781250274816 (ebook)
Subjects: GSAFD: Historical fiction.
Classification: LCC PS3602.A628 D44 2021 | DDC 813/.6—dc23
LC record available at https://lccn.loc.gov/2021016353

Our books may be purchased in bulk for promotional, educational, or business use. Please contact your local bookseller or the Macmillan Corporate and Premium Sales Department at 1-800-221-7945, extension 5442, or by email at MacmillanSpecialMarkets@macmillan.com.

First Edition: 2021

10 9 8 7 6 5 4 3 2 1

*To the people of Denmark who stood up to tyranny and
embodied the principles of Danish unity
And
To Monica, with whom I sail the seas*

Defending
Britta Stein

CHAPTER ONE

———— ⬡ ————

CHICAGO, 2018

Judge Obadiah Wilson peers over his reading glasses at the two attorneys who stand before him, and he smiles. His smile is perceived as warm but menacing. It is an up-or-down moment and only one of the lawyers will go away happy. He is about to rule. "I must admit," he says in his sonorous baritone, "that you two have given me quite a bit to read and digest." He points to a stack of papers on his bench. Wilson's pronouncements are carefully crafted, and delivered with a touch of an East Texas accent.

The eminent jurist has served the county judiciary for the better part of his forty professional years. Though age has bowed his solid frame a bit, his majestic bearing remains keen. Now serving as the presiding judge of the Cook County Law Division, he leans forward and says, "Do either of you have anything more you wish to add to this considerable record before I deliver my decision?"

Attorney Catherine Lockhart's hands are clasped before her. She stands poised and confident with just the hint of a smile. The thirty-eight-year-old attorney has appeared before Judge Wilson many times and she knows his routine. His invitation to supplement the record is disingenuous. He does not want further argument; he's ready to rule.

If experience is any guide, he's already written his opinion. "No, your honor," she says. "Defendant will rest upon the briefs."

The bony, angular man to Catherine's right is nervous. He twitches and shifts his weight from one foot to the other. Mustering up a bit of drama, he clears his throat, lifts his chin and says, "If your honor would like me to reiterate the considerable flaws in the defendant's motion, I'd be most happy to comply, but I am satisfied that I have presented our position in a persuasive and compelling manner, and I am confident of the outcome." His stilted response broadens the smile on Catherine's lips. He resembles Ichabod Crane in a three-piece suit.

Judge Wilson stifles a short chuckle. "Hmm," he says from deep down in his chest. "Well, perhaps not as compelling and persuasive as you had hoped, Mr. Coggins." Wilson shifts his gaze to Catherine. "Defendant's motion is granted, and this case is dismissed. Ms. Lockhart, you are given twenty-one days to file your petition for attorney's fees and costs. Judgment will be entered accordingly. I've prepared a written opinion; you can pick it up from my clerk. That will be the order." With a smack of his gavel, Judge Wilson rises, steps down from the bench and leaves the courtroom.

As Catherine stands at the counsel table gathering her papers and sliding them into her valise, a familiar voice addresses her from behind. "Nice work, Ms. Lockhart."

"Hello, Walter," she replies without turning around. "I thought I noticed you sitting in the back of the courtroom. What brings the eminent Walter Jenkins to Wilson's morning motion call?"

As always, the founding partner of the firm of Jenkins and Fairchild cuts a stylish appearance: custom-tailored suit, monogrammed shirt and designer tie. His shoes are polished to a mirror shine and every styled gray hair lies in place. He is a force in the Chicago legal community. He is also Catherine's former boss and a close friend.

"Whenever I happen to be in the courthouse and find myself with a bit of extra time," he says, "I'll duck into Obadiah's domain. You never know what pearls of wisdom will roll off the old man's tongue. He's one of a kind, Catherine. A dying breed. Besides, it's great theater." He tips his head toward the bench and nods. "But today, however, I come on a mission. I tried to call you and your office told me you would be here.

It's actually a matter of some urgency to me. Do you have time for a cup of coffee with a tired old litigator?"

"With you, Walter? Always."

At a small table in the corner of the first-floor coffee shop, and after an exchange of small talk, Walter sets his cup down and changes his expression. Catherine knows the look. He is troubled. "Are you acquainted with an establishment called The Melancholy Dane?" he says.

Catherine nods. "I believe so. If that's the restaurant and bar up in Andersonville, I've been there once or twice. I seem to remember there were drawings and pictures of various *Hamlet* stage productions pasted all over the walls. It has a Shakespearean theme, in a noisy tavern sort of way."

"That's true. Other than the *Hamlet* posters, did you happen to notice the old black-and-white photographs of Mr. Ole Henryks, the restaurant's owner? They're on the wall behind the bar."

Catherine shrugs. "Not that I remember, but I know who he is. I know he's involved in civic affairs and he frequently appears on local TV. Bushy white hair. A happy-go-lucky personality. I seem to recall he was making cocktails behind the bar when we were there."

Walter concurs. "Right. His son, Nils, runs the business now, but Ole's still around. He's getting up in years, but he'll come in to greet his regulars and shake a martini or two. Anyway, behind the bar are these three black-and-white photographs. They are pictures of Ole Henryks and his family taken seventy-five years ago in Copenhagen during the Nazi occupation. One of them shows Ole and his father standing in the harbor in front of a fishing boat. Ole is only too happy to tell anyone who will listen that in 1943, as a young man, he and his family helped Danish Jews flee to Sweden aboard those fishing boats in order to escape deportation to Nazi concentration camps."

"I didn't know that. So, he's a certified hero?"

Walter twists his lips. "Personally, I can't say, but that's been Ole's repute for many years. In fact, next month, Ole is scheduled to be inducted into the hall of fame of the Danish-American Association of Chicago, not only for his participation in several Chicago charitable and civic causes but in recognition of his heroism during the war. There was a fair amount of press when the honor was announced. The *Tribune* ran a full-page article complete with photos including that black-and-white of Ole and his father in the harbor."

Catherine sips her coffee and gives a slight nod. "I saw the page in the *Trib*."

"Ole has quite a following. Many people think the world of him."

Catherine is puzzled. "Are you trying to hit me up for a donation?"

A laugh erupts. "Goodness no. As I told you, I'm here on a mission. A serious legal matter. Fits right into your book of business. While there are many who laud Ole and sing his praises, there is at least one person who doesn't think very kindly of him. Quite the contrary. This person has been vilifying him by spray-painting nasty comments right on the outside wall of Ole's restaurant."

A slight grin comes to Catherine's lips. "Seriously? Spray-painting insults about a tavern owner?"

"They've been on the news, Catherine. Haven't you seen them?"

She shakes her head. "I'm afraid I missed that. What do they say?"

"Liar. Traitor. Betrayer. Nazi collaborator." Walter taps his finger on the tabletop. "You get the idea. They are not humorous in the least. Someone is taking direct aim at Ole's character. Ole believes that this individual is writing slanderous insults in order to sully his reputation in advance of his induction."

"Perhaps it's an effort to have the association change its mind?"

"If so, it's not likely to happen. The association is solidly behind him. The words are cruel, and they are exacting a heavy toll on poor old Ole, or so I hear. He's in fragile health to begin with. Hell, he's ninety-five. I saw a TV interview the other day and Ole was clearly out of sorts; red-faced, shaking, jaw quivering."

"That's a shame. Does he have a clue who's behind this?"

Walter shook his head. "I don't think he does. At least, not yet. Ole told the TV reporter that it was probably some old German soldier trying to get even."

"That doesn't make much sense to me."

"I agree. The remarks are always painted in the middle of the night. Ole's son finds them when he comes to work the next day. He quickly removes them, but by then it's too late. Someone has tipped off the TV stations and videos are shown on the morning news. The statements are always painted crudely, in a shaky script."

"Doesn't the restaurant have security cameras?"

"It didn't. It does now."

Catherine leans back in her chair with a puzzled expression. "Walter, I don't know anything about Ole, his son or The Melancholy Dane. And I surely have no knowledge of whoever is spray-painting derogatory remarks on his building. Why did you seek me out today? What's the urgent mission?"

"Ultimately, the person who's painting these words will be caught and charged. Likely very soon, now that there are cameras. And it won't be enough to prosecute her for misdemeanor property damage. No. Ole will want to be vindicated and repair the damage that's been done to his reputation."

"Oh Walter, surely some crackpot spray-painting insults on a building isn't going to damage Ole's standing in the community. He's been a fixture on the North Side for fifty years—a happy, jovial tavern owner."

Walter shakes his head dismissively. "Jovial no more. He's distraught. Discouraged. He doesn't even want to come into the tavern."

"Well, that's a shame, but it's understandable. He's ninety-five. People that age can be emotionally fragile. Still, Ole must realize that his lifelong reputation is secure. No one is going to believe insults spray-painted on brick walls in the middle of the night."

"Don't be so sure. Because the accusations are so bold, so brash, so outlandish, it's human nature to permit them some degree of credibility. Why would someone paint these? What's behind it? People will think maybe there's something here? Could any of this really be true? Is Ole really a Nazi collaborator? People love to gossip and a story like this spreads like wildfire. Ole thinks so and he doesn't know how to stop it."

"Well, Walter, as you say, this vandal will soon be caught and arrested. A conviction will certainly put an end to this matter."

Walter pulls on his lower lip. "Hmm, I'm not so sure. Neither are Ole or his son. I've spoken to Nils. Once the perpetrator has been identified, arrested and charged, Nils will urge his father to file suit to clear his name."

Catherine nods, finishes her coffee and sets the cup down. "Okay. I acknowledge that this is an unfortunate circumstance that has befallen Ole Henryks and that a lawsuit is likely on the horizon. Now, do you want to tell me why you came to see me this morning?"

After a pause, Walter said, "Because I'm pretty sure I know the identity of the perpetrator."

"And it's a woman?"

Walter furrows his forehead. "How did you know?"

"A moment ago, you said it wouldn't be enough to prosecute *her*."

A smile creeps across Walter's face and he claps softly. "That's why you're such an excellent cross-examiner; you don't miss a thing. I've given you one side of the story, and now I'm going to give you the rest. At my firm, we have a young attorney, Emma Fisher. She's a brilliant young woman who graduated at the top of her class and has recently passed the bar. We hired her three years ago when she had just begun law school. Talk about self-assured, she made an appointment at that time, sat right down in my office and told me she was about to commence her legal education but knew that there were lessons that could not be learned in a law school. She had researched my firm and decided that Jenkins and Fairchild would be an essential component to her legal development."

Catherine is amused but impressed. "That took some guts."

"Indeed, it did. She has that kind of drive. She reminds me of the young Catherine I met years ago. Well, the other day Emma asked to meet with me in private. I had no idea what to expect. Behind closed doors, she told me, in confidence, under the umbrella of attorney-client privilege, that she had reason to believe that her ninety-two-year-old grandmother was the person painting on the walls of The Melancholy Dane."

Catherine is shocked. "A ninety-two-year-old woman? Spray-painting in the middle of the night? Is she sure?"

Walter nods. "Fairly certain. Emma thinks it's only a matter of time until her grandmother gets arrested."

"This gets stranger by the minute, Walter. Are you going to represent Emma's grandmother?"

Walter leans forward and speaks softly. "Well now, here's the rub. I would like to, I really would, but Jenkins and Fairchild has represented Ole Henryks personally and The Melancholy Dane as a corporate entity for years. I told Emma that I was constrained from delving too far into the dispute and I stopped her from giving me all the details, but I heard more than I should. Quite obviously, there could be a conflict."

"Could be?" Catherine says. "There most certainly *is* a conflict. The identity of the perpetrator was revealed to you. Emma's grandmother is committing criminal and tortious acts against *your* client. She is defacing Ole's building with slanderous statements, she is directly attacking his reputation and you know her identity. Don't you have an obligation to communicate that knowledge to your client?"

"I'm not sure, because the information was revealed to me in a confidential setting. It was a privileged communication. It's probably de minimus in any event because Ole will quickly find out on his own, if he hasn't already. The cameras have been running for a couple of days. But still, you're right, I possess information crucial to a client."

Catherine pauses to consider the ethical enigma. "Emma asked to see you to secure legal representation for her grandmother, is that not so?"

"I believe that was her intention, though the conversation did not proceed that far."

Catherine is surprised her former mentor has fallen into an ethical web. "She came to you in an effort to obtain legal representation and she provided information in that privileged setting. You shouldn't have taken that information to begin with, but since you did, you can't disclose it. You're going to have to bow out of this dispute entirely. You are totally conflicted from representing either Henryks or the grandmother."

"No argument here."

"Is that why you contacted me this morning, to get my advice that you need to step away from this matter?"

"No, I don't need your advice. I know the rules. I fell into a rabbit hole."

"Then tell me, Walter, why am I here?"

"Because I'm going to ask you to do something. Of all the lawyers I know, you're the only one I trust to make sense out of this mess. I sat there yesterday listening to Emma and I heard more than I should have. Far more than I should have, but I was fascinated. Emma loves her grandmother, and she came to me for help. She doesn't want to see her grandmother charged with a crime or sitting at the defendant's table in a high-profile lawsuit. When she asked to speak to me, she didn't know that the firm had represented Ole and The Melancholy Dane. She was hoping I could help her grandmother and resolve the matter out of court. As she was speaking, I thought perhaps I could bring about some type of compromise. I like Emma, and I sat there listening to her and I let her go on for too long."

Catherine's eyebrows narrow. "A compromise solution? Did it also occur to you that maybe Ole and Nils wouldn't want a brokered solution? Maybe they want Emma's grandmother prosecuted and punished. Maybe they want a very conspicuous lawsuit for defamation to show the public that the statements on the wall are false. Besides, how do you compromise what's already been done? How do you un-ring a bell?"

Walter wears a pained expression. "We're talking about a ninety-two-year-old woman doing some pretty bizarre things. I thought if I could get the woman to stop, maybe apologize, I could move forward with a peaceful resolution and help Emma's grandmother. Maybe it's a mental health issue, who knows? It's some pretty crazy stuff. Maybe Ole would see it that way."

"Okay, I get it. You tried to be a peacemaker. But Walter, you crossed the line getting involved at all."

Walter cringes. He is freely willing to concede his errors. "I know, but I asked Emma to talk to her grandmother and determine whether she'd go along with a peaceful solution. I even offered to try to set a meeting in my office with all concerned. Kind of like a settlement conference. I thought whatever might be on this woman's mind, perhaps we could clear the air. I asked Emma to reach out to her grandmother and see if she'd be willing to meet."

"And . . . ?"

Walter firmly shakes his head. "Nope, not a chance. Emma's grandmother, by the way her name is Britta Stein, rejected the proposal outright. Turned me down flat. She says she knows exactly what she's doing, she's not going to stop and she's not going to meet with any 'hotshot lawyer who represents a lying traitor.'"

A laugh bursts from Catherine. "She said that about you? The ninety-two-year-old woman?"

Walter nods sheepishly. "She said that."

"Okay, so now they've installed cameras and they're going to catch her, and then what?"

"Nils has already contacted my office. He spoke to Howard Foreman yesterday. They will want aggressive legal action."

Catherine tries to cover a coy smile. "You're in a pickle, Walter. What are you going to do?"

"Not a damn thing. What can I do? I can't handle this case." He shrugs. "Ole will learn Mrs. Stein's identity soon enough and then he'll ask us to represent him, and I'll have to turn him down. My firm can't sue Britta Stein."

"So that's it? You want me to sue Emma's grandmother? Seriously?"

Walter slowly swivels his head. "No, Catherine, that will not be necessary. Ole won't have any trouble finding a lawyer to sue Mrs. Stein. They'll line up like kids at an ice cream truck."

Catherine spreads her hands. "Then why am I the only one you trust with this matter, and what are you trusting me to do?"

"I want you to sit down and talk to Emma. I want you to consider defending Britta Stein. From the short visit I had with Emma, from the bits of information that I learned, I'm sure there's something here; I can feel it. Behind those painted statements there is a story. As they say, turbulent waters run beneath a placid surface. There's a viable defense, I know it. Call it the sixth sense that comes to old trial lawyers. You would know—we're two of a kind."

"*Old?*"

He grins. "I didn't mean that you are old. I meant to say you have the *soul* of an old trial lawyer, even if you don't have the miles. I'd like you to sit down with Emma, talk with her awhile, maybe with Britta Stein as well, and see if you get the same vibrations."

"Oh, Walter . . ."

"Don't turn me down yet. Talk to Emma. She's a very sharp young lady, and the things she told me about her grandmother, well . . . there's a story there." Walter slides a business card with a phone number written on the back.

"Walter, please . . ."

"Talk to Emma, Catherine. I think you'll sense it too. You're perfect for this case. You'll thank me." He stands and reaches into his pocket. "I'll get the coffee."

CHAPTER TWO

———— ∞ ————

LIAM TAGGART LIES on the floor of his living room with Ben, Catherine and Liam's two-year-old son. They are busy building a castle with plastic bricks. The evening news is playing on the TV and the announcer is recounting the circumstances of an arrest made earlier that afternoon.

"Wow," Liam says, "would you look at that. The Fifth District booked a ninety-two-year-old woman for spray-painting insults on the wall of The Melancholy Dane." He chuckles. "They perp-walked that old lady into the Belmont station. Cuffed. Can you believe it? That's our CPD for you. 'We Serve and Protect.' The streets are immeasurably safer now that this dangerous ninety-two-year-old and her lethal spray can are in custody."

"Liam," Catherine calls out from the kitchen, "would you pause that program for me?"

"Seriously? The news report?"

With a dish towel in her hand, she walks into the living room. "Back it up, please, Liam. That's the woman Walter was telling me about." As the report continues, the screen displays a grainy nighttime video of a woman in a long overcoat scrawling "Nazi Agent" on an exterior brick wall.

The female reporter, standing outside the police station, suppresses a smile and says, "The alleged offender, a senior citizen, Mrs. Britta Stein, has been charged with violating a Chicago municipal ordinance entitled 'Criminal Defacement of Property with Paint.' You can't make this stuff up. We're told that violation of the ordinance carries a fine of seven hundred and fifty dollars."

Liam chuckles. "They perp-walked that old lady into the station on a seven-hundred-fifty-dollar graffiti misdemeanor."

"That's the least of her worries," Catherine answers quietly. They watch as another news reporter interviews Sterling Sparks, identifying him as the attorney for the restaurant's owner, Ole Henryks. Known to be overly dramatic, and often accused of trying his cases on the six o'clock news, Sparks has earned the sobriquet "Six-o'clock Sparks." He leans over and speaks directly into the reporter's microphone. His eyebrows are furrowed, his lips are curled, and he delivers his responses in angry bursts of righteous indignation.

"Mr. Henryks is outraged and saddened by the false and defamatory statements that have been plastered on his private property by this troubled person," Sparks declares. "Mr. Henryks is baffled; who would do such a mean thing? He initially assumed that it must have been some kind of prank by neighborhood punks who have no conception of the hurt such meanspirited words can cause. It isn't bad enough that these nasty comments appear on the walls of his establishment, but that the insensitive media has broadcast them for the whole city to see. Maybe the whole country! Mr. Henryks is a strong man, a good man, but he's ninety-five years old and these words hit him like a sucker punch in the gut, and they've taken their toll on his physical well-being. He's under a doctor's care. We're talking about a man who lived through the Nazi occupation of his homeland. Do you understand?"

The reporter interjects, "I think it's pretty well-known that Mr. Henryks immigrated here from Denmark after the war."

"Right, and it's no secret that back in his home country, Mr. Henryks was regarded as a *war hero*. That's why the nasty lies painted on his restaurant are so hurtful. Today we learned that the words were not pranks painted by neighborhood youth, but by a *grown woman* as part of a purposeful campaign to destroy the man's reputation. I will tell you this right now, whatever this wicked woman has in mind, we're going to put a stop to it and hold that woman legally responsible!"

"You just referred to Mr. Henryks as a war hero," the reporter continues. "The latest sign reads 'Nazi Agent.'"

Sparks is ready for the question. He reaches down and pulls out a copy of a photograph. There are three people in the picture—a tall man and two younger men, all standing side by side before a large fishing boat. The boat itself has a small cabin on the bow. It appears to be docked in a slip, along with several other fishing boats in a commercial harbor. "Do you see this?" Sparks says. "This is a picture of Copenhagen Harbor in World War II. This photo hangs proudly behind the bar at The Melancholy Dane. That's Ole and his father. You better believe that 'hero' is the correct description for Ole Henryks. His family helped to rescue hundreds of Jews from the gas chambers. Maybe thousands. Ole and his father snuck Jewish families out of Denmark in their fishing boat in the middle of the night. Risking their lives, I might add. He's a certified hero."

The reporter nods empathetically. "Well, notwithstanding those slanderous comments on his wall, we understand that Mr. Henryks is going to be honored next month by the Danish-American Association of Chicago."

"You're absolutely right, Erin. He'll be inducted into a prestigious hall of fame! I just hope he regains his health enough so he can attend and accept the honor." Sparks pauses and appears to suppress his emotions. "This should be one of the happiest moments of his life . . . ," Sparks shakes his head, ". . . but along comes this depraved woman, for reasons known only to her, and viciously attacks his reputation with a succession of slanderous, vituperous epithets." Sparks raises his chin and waits for the media to digest and appreciate his savory oratory. Pure Six-o'clock.

"Does Mr. Henryks know this woman? We are told her name is Britta Stein."

Sparks responds dismissively. "Know her? Absolutely not. He's never seen her before in his life. He has no idea why she would choose to attack him in such a vicious manner."

"Then I assume Mr. Henryks intends to press charges?"

"Are you serious? Of course he does, and that's not all. Mr. Henryks's good name has been assailed and it must be redeemed. The only way to do that is in a court of law. I am announcing that first thing tomorrow morning, I will file a lawsuit against Britta Stein for defamation, and we will seek compensation for all the damage and injury she has brought upon my client. We will ask the court to award him a civil damage award of five million dollars. This woman must be taught a lesson."

"Five million!" the newscaster says with the hint of a smile. "Do you think this elderly woman has that much money?"

"Whether she does or she doesn't is entirely beside the point. The measure of damages is what a man's good name is worth, not how much money the criminal defendant has. Five million is probably a small fraction of the value of Mr. Henryks's reputation, which he has earned by a lifetime of service and good deeds. I assure you that he will be vindicated in a court of law!"

"Well, thank you for talking to us tonight, Mr. Sparks."

Liam shakes his head and utters, "Good luck defending this case, Mrs. Stein."

Catherine stares at the screen, backs up the video and replays the newscast. "There's something here, Liam. Walter felt it and so do I." Catherine fishes through her purse and pulls out the business card Walter gave her a few days ago. "I'm afraid I'm about to do something really stupid," she says. She dials the number on the back of the card. "Maybe I'm the crazy one."

"Hello?"

"Is this Emma Fisher?"

"Yes," she says tentatively. "Who's calling?"

"My name is Catherine Lockhart. I'm a friend of Walter Jenkins. I met with him a couple of days ago, and . . ."

Catherine hears the young woman's sigh of relief. "Oh my God, thank you so much. I was so hoping that you would call me. Mr. Jenkins speaks so highly of you and he said that if anyone could help my grandmother, it would be you."

"Walter is very persuasive. Would you be able to bring your grandmother to my office tomorrow afternoon, say about three o'clock?"

"You'll take her case?"

Catherine hesitates. She takes a breath. She's about to jump into deep, unknown waters and she knows it. "Well, let's not get ahead of ourselves,

Emma. Walter thinks I should talk to you, and I respect Walter's judgment. Have they released your grandmother yet?"

"I was just getting ready to go pick her up. I'm certain we could be at your office tomorrow at three. Thank you so much."

Liam shakes his head in bewilderment. "Cat, what in the world are you doing? Have you lost your mind?"

She nods. "Oh well, maybe. Or maybe I really do have the soul of an old trial lawyer."

CHAPTER THREE

CATHERINE LOCKHART'S FOUR-ROOM storefront law office is on Clark Street a couple of miles north of Chicago's Loop. She has what is commonly referred to as a neighborhood practice—wills, trusts, real estate transactions, criminal defense, personal litigation matters—all in sharp contrast to the high-profile, institutional clients she served when she worked for Walter Jenkins.

At precisely three o'clock, a young woman with curly black hair, large expressive brown eyes and a bounce in her step opens the door to Catherine's office. She holds it open for her companion, an elderly woman in a wool suit with fashionably styled white hair and perfect posture.

"You must be Ms. Fisher and Mrs. Stein," the receptionist says. "My name is Gladys Valenzuela. I am Catherine's assistant. It is nice to meet you both. Catherine is expecting you. Please follow me back to the conference room."

Catherine enters the conference room moments later with a brown file folder, which she lays upon the table. Emma extends her hand. "I'm Emma Fisher and this is my grandmother, Britta Stein."

Catherine warmly takes their hands. "It's a pleasure to meet you both." She gestures to her file folder. "I asked Gladys to run down to the courthouse and pick up a copy of the lawsuit that was filed against you today,

Mrs. Stein. As you no doubt recall, Mr. Sparks threatened to file it first thing this morning."

Britta sits erectly in her chair. She does not seem at all nervous. She nods her understanding. "I haven't seen the lawsuit yet," she says matter-of-factly. "I bet it's a doozy."

Catherine lifts her eyebrows. "Yes, I'm afraid it is a doozy, Mrs. Stein. It alleges that on six separate occasions you trespassed upon Mr. Henryks's property for the purpose of defacing his building by painting scathing insults concerning Mr. Henryks, harming him in his good name, his business, his health and his reputation."

"Hmph," Britta interjects. "Reputation indeed."

"Bubbe, hush," Emma says. "Let Ms. Lockhart finish."

"On each of the six occasions, the complaint alleges that you intentionally wrote false and defamatory declarations on the outside walls of his restaurant. Further, that your illegal and tortious conduct followed the announcement that Mr. Henryks was to be honored by the Danish-American Association."

"Honor?" Britta says. "He deserves no such thing." She dismissively brushes away the accusations as though they do not affect her. "Who are they anyway, this make-believe association? As far as I am concerned this Danish-American nonsense is just an excuse for young men to congregate for the sole purpose of drinking beer. For them to bestow an honor upon a traitor only means that the members of the association have been hoodwinked. I'm sure it must be the younger ones; they wouldn't know any better. They probably want an occasion to honor a popular personality and have it shown on TV, as if that would bring them some credibility. Silliness, is all . . ."

Catherine taps her finger on the lawsuit. "Let's focus on the complaint-at-law, shall we, Mrs. Stein? Are the allegations correct? Did you intentionally paint those words on the side of Henryks's building?"

"Yes, I painted those words on the side of his building. And of course it was intentional. I don't see how one could possibly paint those words unintentionally. But, Ms. Lockhart, the words were not false nor were they defamatory. The words were and are true."

"Why, Mrs. Stein? Why did you go over there and paint those words at all?"

Britta lifts her chin. "I am a Danish lady; I can't abide the charade. He is no hero. He is nothing but a liar and a coward. Worse, he's a traitor."

Catherine turns the pages of the lawsuit to the page listing the painted statements, which she reads one at a time. "Liar. Informer. Traitor. Nazi collaborator. Nazi agent. Betrayer. Is the list correct? Did you write all of those?"

"He is a liar and a traitor and all those things and more, and I'm not the least bit sorry that the truth is there for all to see."

Catherine sits down. "Mrs. Stein, this lawsuit is not to be taken lightly. It charges you with 'defamation per se.'"

Britta shrugs. She is impassive, as though they were talking about someone else.

"Defamation per se means that the words you have used accuse Mr. Henryks of criminal conduct, crimes of moral turpitude and of coalescence with the Nazi Party. As such, the words themselves are innately harmful." She lays her pen down. "And actionable in a court of law, with serious consequences."

"What about the First Amendment?" Britta says. "My freedom of speech."

"Freedom of speech is not absolute, Mrs. Stein. You are not free to use words that wrongfully defame another person." Catherine extracts another document from her folder and places it on the table. "This is an order of protection; a temporary injunction which was entered this morning against you by Judge Obadiah Wilson. It strictly prohibits you from coming within fifty yards of The Melancholy Dane or Ole Henryks's residence on Lake Shore Drive."

"Nobody notified me of any court hearing," Britta says defiantly. "How could a judge enter an order against me if I wasn't even there? What about due process?"

Catherine rolls her eyes. "It's a temporary injunction. The order was entered ex parte, in your absence, because it was presented as an emergency to prevent you from committing further unlawful conduct. The language of the order recites that a video of you spray-painting on Mr. Henryks's building was shown to the court."

Britta looks at the order, sets it down and scoffs. "Fifty yards! Does that mean I can't take a taxi down Clark Street or Bryn Mawr? I guess if my taxi driver decides to drive along Lake Shore Drive, the both of us are going to jail, right? Does Ole Henryks now own the streets? Such nonsense. I will go where I choose. It's a free country."

"Bubbe!" Emma pleads. "Listen to Ms. Lockhart. You can be jailed for willfully violating an injunction."

"She's right, Mrs. Stein. I wouldn't test Judge Wilson's mettle. You can be sure that Mr. Henryks will immediately call the police if he sees you anywhere near his establishment or his condominium building. A willful violation of an order of protection could subject you to fines or even punitive incarceration. And I know Judge Wilson. He's not one to fool with."

"Listen to your lawyer, Bubbe. Don't go anywhere near The Melancholy Dane or Henryks's apartment. You don't need to paint any more signs; you're bound to have accomplished what you set out to do. The whole world knows what you think about Mr. Henryks."

Britta leans forward and raises her index finger. "It's *Hendricksen*, not Henryks. He even lies about his name. I wrote the truth." Turning to Catherine, she says, "You called the order temporary. Does that mean it expires? There are additional statements I have in mind."

Emma's head flops forward. "Bubbe, Bubbe. No! No more painting!"

Catherine slowly shakes her head. "Definitely no more painting. Believe me, you've done enough. More than enough. The order is temporary because you weren't there. Judge Wilson scheduled a hearing for all sides next Thursday to consider whether the injunction should be extended, and I'm fairly certain it will."

"You'll go with her to the hearing, right?" Emma says. "I mean, she needs to take a lawyer with her, doesn't she?"

Catherine holds up her palm. It's a stop sign. "She does, but Emma, we're getting ahead of ourselves. I told Walter I would agree to *meet* with the two of you and we would talk. There is a lot to consider before deciding how a lawyer can defend a case like this. Or whether I am the right person to defend your grandmother. I don't have a handle on this. Mrs. Stein, you must have expected that there would be serious consequences when you painted all those harmful statements."

Britta clamps her lips. She inhales deeply through her nose. Finally, she says, "Consequences? You mean the kind of consequences where

people learn the truth about an evil person? Those kind of consequences?" Tears fill her eyes. "I pray for those consequences, Ms. Lockhart."

Emma gently lays her hand on her grandmother's arm. "I think that
Ms. Lockhart is referring to the criminal charges and the five-million-
dollar lawsuit against you, Bubbe. What is my grandmother going to do
about these charges, Ms. Lockhart?"

"I don't think she has much of a choice. She'll pay the fine and she's
going to have to defend herself in the civil case in some way. Ole Henryks and Sterling Sparks are not going to disappear. They want vindication. Henryks wants his reputation repaired. He wants his pound of
flesh and he's hired the right lawyer to pursue it. Sparks is an aggressive
publicity hound. That's why they call him Six-o'clock. I think you can
look forward to months of contentious hearings and depositions. Sparks
would like nothing better than to play out this drama in front of a jury
and the evening news. He'll call numerous witnesses who will all say they
heard about or read about the statements which caused them to question Mr. Henryks's character. Henryks will claim that his reputation has
been irrevocably damaged. I'm sure that Henryks's doctor will testify that
Henryks has suffered and continues to suffer extreme and pervasive
mental and physical trauma. It will be a bitter battle. A nightmare for
you, Mrs. Stein."

"Bubbe, what she's saying is that the lawsuit will be very stressful for
you and, no doubt, very expensive."

Britta stares straight ahead. "I can handle the stress," she mutters. "I've
been through worse." She opens the clasp on her leather purse and takes
out her checkbook. "I don't have a lot of money. I can give you three hundred dollars to get started."

Catherine shuts her eyes. When she opens them, she is smiling. It is
a warm smile that one would show to a child who has acted in a simple
but unrealistic manner. Catherine gently reaches over and closes Britta's
checkbook. "I appreciate your offer, Mrs. Stein, truly I do, but money
is only a secondary consideration. As Emma correctly pointed out, the
most important thing for you to consider is your health. You are ninety-
two years old. I've seen much younger people lose their balance in such a
contentious proceeding. Mr. Sparks's attacks can and will be very cruel."

"What are you suggesting, Ms. Lockhart?" Emma says. "You said she has no choice but to defend herself."

Catherine reaches out and pats Britta's hand. "Look, Mrs. Stein, the lawsuit is really not about the money. They know you don't have five million dollars. There may be another way to resolve this; a nonmonetary way. Mr. Henryks may be amenable to a consent decree. If you agree to publicly apologize, admit that your accusations were in error, and agree never to insult him again, maybe he would drop the suit. Or agree to a judgment of a small amount, perhaps one hundred dollars."

Britta's jaw begins to quaver. Her eyes widen. "Error? But there was no error, Ms. Lockhart. Why should I apologize to Hendricksen for writing the truth? I'm sorry, but there's no way I'm ever going to do that. I grew up in Denmark during the war. I was there. I know what ordinary people did, and I know what Hendricksen and his family did. Ordinary people were the heroes, and the Hendricksens were not. Quite the contrary. They were no better than the Nazis; maybe worse, because they helped the Nazis. Ole Hendricksen can file his lawsuit, and he will soon learn what a true Dane will do in times of adversity. A true Dane will stand her ground and fight."

Emma squeezes her grandmother's hand. "I know there were terrible tragedies that happened to the Danish people and to our family, Bubbe. Nothing can reverse that. I respect your resolve, but I don't want to see you get sick. Henryks is not worth it. You should listen to Ms. Lockhart and let her try to settle the case."

Britta's jaw is set. "Emma, the truth is always worth it. I'm not going to quit and I'm not going to apologize. I'm sorry if that means you won't take my case, Ms. Lockhart."

Catherine is moved. Rarely do her clients show such dedication, and there is something about Britta's steadfastness that appeals to Catherine. "I think I understand you, Mrs. Stein, and I'll take your case. But you have to help me here. How do I make a defense for you?"

"Isn't truth a defense to a lawsuit for defamation? Aren't I allowed to speak or write the truth no matter how hurtful it may be?"

Catherine nods and answers softly, "In theory, yes, you are, Mrs. Stein. Truth is an absolute defense to a suit for defamation."

Britta gives a sharp nod of finality. "Then we will prevail."

CHAPTER FOUR

LIAM SCRATCHES HIS head. "You took her case? You actually agreed to defend Britta Stein in an unwinnable defamation case? Do you have some secret desire to be a punching bag?"

She shakes her head. "It's not unwinnable, Liam. It's defensible. Britta swears that all of her statements are true."

Liam closes his eyes. "Oh, of course they are. Every one of them. Why wouldn't they be? Traitor? Nazi collaborator? Nazi agent? I suppose she's given you solid evidence that proves each of those statements is true? You can *prove* them in a court of law with competent evidence?"

Catherine winces. "Well, not yet. I was kind of hoping that you'd help me with that."

"Mm hmm. I should have figured. Honey, this case is going to bury you. It'll eat up your productive hours and your days. It'll cost a fortune. Sparks is a ruthless adversary who loves nothing more than playing to the TV cameras. He'll litigate you to death with multiple pleadings, motions, discovery demands and depositions. The trial itself will last for days. Can Britta afford to pay you anything? Can she even cover the out-of-pocket costs?"

Catherine bites her bottom lip. "I don't think she has that kind of money, Liam. She offered to pay me three hundred dollars."

Liam snorts. "Tell me the truth, Cat. She cast a spell on you, right?

Because I can think of no other basis for you to take this on. I know you feel sorry for her, and I know she's going to need a lawyer, and I don't blame you for wanting to help her, but you seriously can't believe you can take this case all the way to trial and win."

"What am I supposed to do?" Catherine shrugs. "Britta won't withdraw her statements or consider a compromise."

"What are you supposed to do? You're supposed to decline the case."

"I can't do that. Where would that leave Britta?"

Liam rubs his forehead and turns to face her. "Then let the case go to judgment. He's going to get a judgment anyway. So what? It's uncollectible. She doesn't have five million dollars, she probably doesn't have any substantial assets; she's judgment proof. So why defend it at all? Let it go."

Catherine's response is sharp and quick. "Because that's not who I am, and you should know it by now. Confessing judgment is out of the question. Sparks would bury her in citation proceedings and force her into bankruptcy just for spite. Whether she has any personal assets to protect or not, a bankruptcy would devastate her. If after all my efforts there's a judgment entered against her, then so be it, but I will have done my best."

Liam is proud of his wife and he wraps his arms around her. "I'm sorry, Cat. I shouldn't second-guess you; I just don't want to see you get banged around."

"She's a good person, Liam. She passionately believes in what she's doing. I believe in her too. You can call me foolish, but you weren't there; you didn't talk to her. When Walter met me for coffee the other day, called me an 'old trial lawyer' and told me about this case, he said I would be perfect for it. That's the word he used. Perfect. And now I think he's right."

"I know you respect Walter, and I know you value his opinion. And I'm sure it was flattering to hear Walter say that he thinks of you as one of the club, but . . ."

"Liam, you can stop right there. This is not about flattery. Walter knows my background. He knows we represented Ben Solomon and Lena Scheinman, both Holocaust survivors, and that if anyone would be sensitive to the plight of a World War II survivor, it would be me. He thinks there's a case here, and that I'm the right attorney to handle it. And now that I've met Britta, so do I. What if Henryks was not some Danish war hero like he boasts? What if he *was* a Nazi?"

"Why has she waited all this time, Cat? She's lived in Chicago for six decades. He's been on TV several times. Why does she choose to confront him now?"

"Possibly because he's about to be honored by some Danish association and she wants to set the record straight. She seems very principled."

Liam grimaces. "Cat, I'm just trying to point out the impossible hurdles of defending this case. Mrs. Stein, a ninety-two-year-old woman, goes after a ninety-five-year-old man, and not just any ninety-five-year-old man, but one whom everyone loves. And she does it just to set the record straight?"

Catherine nods sharply. "Yes. That's right."

"I think a lot of folks would say why doesn't she just leave the man alone, let him have his accolades and go off to some nursing home?"

"A lot of folks didn't meet with her today; I did. It's not just about setting the record straight. It's something else. Something much deeper. I believe that something Henryks did years ago harmed Britta or her family."

"What did he do?"

"I don't know yet, but there's a personal connection here, I'd bet my bonnet on it. To witness Henryks being honored as a hero is something she cannot abide. Maybe after all these years she sees an opportunity for redress. Her motives are pure, I'm sure of it, and I need you to believe in me, to stand behind me." Catherine has tears in her eyes.

Liam holds her tightly. "Of course I believe in you. Always have, always will. I'm just trying to protect you from a crash and burn."

"I don't need you to protect me. I need you to support me."

"One hundred percent. So, it's your belief that something happened to this woman years ago, something terrible, and Henryks was involved or responsible, right?"

Catherine nods. "She didn't exactly say that, but sitting in my conference room, with those two women, I could feel it. She seemed so genuine. Walter had sensed it too. Liam, no one would sneak around in the middle of the night and paint such horrible statements unless they were impelled to do so."

"No one in their right mind?"

"There's nothing wrong with her mind. She's a wealth of knowledge and her recall is sound. There's a lot of facts sitting in her memory; I just have to dig them out. She told me that after the war, thousands of Danes were arrested and charged as collaborators. To her memory, many were sentenced, some to death. According to Britta, Ole Henryks was a collaborator."

"He was charged?"

She shakes her head. "He was not."

"Why not? Was he exonerated, or did he just vanish?"

"I don't know. That just might be a job for the world's greatest private investigator. By the way, at one point in our discussion, Britta called him Hendricksen."

Liam lifts an eyebrow. "Hmm. Did he change his name?"

Catherine shrugs. "I don't know. He could have, or it could have been changed by an immigration officer at Ellis Island. It might indicate a desire to hide his true identity."

"Ultimately, you know where the answers to these mysteries lie, don't you? They're probably three thousand miles away in some Copenhagen office or museum."

Catherine nods.

"Well, I've never been to Copenhagen," Liam says with a whimsical smile. He raises his index finger, winks and says, *"But . . ."*

Catherine sighs; she knows the joke. "I know, but you kinda like the music."

"Exactly. Well, I'm all in, honey. I'll help in whatever way I can. When does the case come up in court?"

"Next Thursday. There's a hearing to extend the temporary restraining order. I'll go but I won't contest it."

"Why not?"

"In order to contest the order, there would have to be an evidentiary hearing. Britta would have to take the stand and subject herself to Sparks's cross-examination. And to what end? There is no denying that Britta spray-painted the wall. It's on video. I'm not going to bring Britta into court; not now anyway. Just to walk into the courtroom she'd have to weave her way through a pack of hungry reporters. It would be a zoo."

"Do you really think the media will be there for a routine motion?"

"It's Sterling Sparks, Liam. He will have alerted the media; that's his style. I'm afraid there will be nothing routine about this case. It's going to be a battle every day."

"All right, I get it. Let me know what I can do."

"I have a meeting at the office with Emma and Britta at nine a.m. tomorrow, and I'd like you to attend. I want to get you involved from the very beginning. There will be a lot of work to do in a short period of time. Consider this; I have to prove that six of the most dead-on slanderous statements, spray-painted on the private property of a person who is about to be honored as a war hero, are all nondefamatory. Why? Because the statements are privileged. And they are privileged because they are true."

"Is that all?"

Catherine smiles proudly. "That's all."

"Are you ready for the massive attention?"

Catherine leans back on the couch and bites her lower lip. "Liam, just think of it; this case is so impossible, so high-profile, it'll be the case of the year. And I'm going to win it."

CHAPTER FIVE

❦

"THANK YOU ALL for coming in so early this morning," Catherine says as the group assembles around her conference table. "There is a lot to be done. In order for us to build an effective defense for you, Mrs. Stein, each of us will have to work very hard."

"You can start by calling me Britta."

"Of course. Britta, I'd like to introduce my husband, Liam. He's an excellent private investigator and researcher. I've asked him to sit with us during your appointments, if you don't mind. As this case heats up, there may also be security concerns. One never knows in an emotionally charged case."

"Welcome aboard, Mr. Lockhart," Britta says. "I feel safer already."

Catherine perks up. "Yes indeed, welcome aboard, Mr. Lockhart," she says with a wink.

Liam starts to correct Britta, thinks better of it, smiles and dismisses it with the wave of his hand.

Catherine continues, "I anticipate that Mr. Sparks will ask the court for quick deadlines, so we may have far less time than normal to prepare. I'm going to pass out assignments to each of you this morning, and we're going to dive right in. In a tight schedule, we will need to gather facts quickly."

"Sparks doesn't impress me as the type who likes to work hard," Britta says, "so why would he move for quick deadlines and put the pressure on himself? What's bad for the goose is bad for the gander, is that not so?"

Catherine sees a light go on in Emma's eyes. The young attorney understands perfectly. "I think I'll let Emma answer that question for you," Catherine says.

Emma turns toward her grandmother. "The man who brings the law-suit, the plaintiff, has the burden to prove his case by a preponderance of the evidence. He is required to introduce sufficient proof of each of the elements of his complaint, whether by witness testimony, documents, videos or other physical evidence. If he fails or falls short, his case may be dismissed by the judge without even getting to the jury. Normally that burden requires substantial pretrial time for the plaintiff. But in your case, Bubbe, much of Henryks's burden has been lifted. You can't deny that it was you who painted the words."

"I wouldn't."

"Right. It is undisputed that you painted all the signs on Mr. Hen-ryks's property. And it is undisputed that the words you painted are se-rious enough to be actionable. Sparks doesn't need days of proof. All he needs is the video and your admissions."

"But the words are true, Emma. And Catherine said that truth is a defense to a claim of defamation."

"She's right, Bubbe, but that defense is ours to prove. A trial is all about shifting burdens—who has the burden of going forward with the evi-dence. In a defamation case, asserting that the statements are true must be raised in a pleading known as an affirmative defense, which places the burden of proof on the defendant. Now *you* have the responsibility of go-ing forward with the evidence. If you fail, your defense will be dismissed. In other words, you must prove, by a preponderance of evidence, that Henryks was a Nazi collaborator, a Nazi agent, a traitor, a betrayer, and all those things you wrote." She glances at Catherine for approval and receives a nod and a smile. "As Catherine said, we have a lot of work to do and probably a short time to do it."

"That doesn't seem fair," Britta argues. "Isn't there something we can do to make sure we're given sufficient time to prove the statements are true?"

Catherine shrugs her shoulders. "The anticipated rejoinder to such a request is that you should have had the proof before you went out and painted those statements."

"We do have some proof. I'm an eyewitness. You have my memory, clear as a bell, and I will so testify."

"And that is important, but unfortunately, we'll probably need more than that. If it's just your word against his, it may not carry the day. When and if Sparks moves to accelerate the case, I'll strongly object, but given your age and that of Mr. Henryks, the judge is likely to do it anyway. So, the sooner we all start working, the better off we'll be. As I said, each of us will have an assignment. Britta, yours will be the most important. You will have to search that memory of yours and tell me everything you know about Henryks; every detail. Your narrative will supply the road-map for us to gather as many supportive facts as we can to prove he was a Nazi collaborator."

Britta sits back and lifts her chin. "I'll tell you whatever you need to know. Hendricksen is exactly what I said he is, of that there is no doubt. I can still see him goose-stepping behind the Germans down Fredens-gade as early as June 1940. Ole and his friends were even giving Nazi salutes as they marched with the soldiers. He liked the idea. His parents even bought him high black boots."

"Britta, if he's ninety-five today, he would have been seventeen in 1940. We're going to need a lot more than a teenager marching in a parade and mimicking Nazi soldiers. The terms 'traitor' and 'collaborator' have le-gal meanings. We have to provide proof to support those accusations. The bar is set quite high."

"The proof is there, I guarantee it," Britta responds. "I only mentioned the parade to show that Hendricksen chose sides from the very begin-ning. Believe me, between 1940 and 1945, the Hendricksens committed several traitorous acts. They shamelessly betrayed the people of Den-mark."

Catherine nods. "Okay. We'll need to find witnesses, pictures, doc-uments, tribunal records, all that sort of thing. We know the Nazis were thorough recordkeepers; perhaps there's something to be found there. Liam, this is where you come in. Find out what you can about Danish collaborators. Britta said that thousands of Danes were tried as collabo-rators after the war and some were convicted. See what court or tribunal records can be accessed, both from the Danish courts and the Allied war trials. Are there transcripts? Can we access them? Do we know the identities of those organizations that collaborated? Would they have records of their members? See what we can pull out of the Nazi records. Will we find any mention of Henryks?"

"Hendricksen," Britta says. "Their name was Hendricksen. I doubt you'll find any Henryks."

"Hendricksen, then. Perhaps we'll find the name Hendricksen in some archival records."

Liam leans forward. It is obvious he has a threshold question on his mind. "Britta, I need to ask you something, and please don't take offense. Is it possible that Ole Henryks is not the same person you knew as Ole Hendricksen? I mean, it's been over seventy years. You knew him as a boy. You saw him marching with the German soldiers. But now he's ninety-five. I'm sure he doesn't look the same as he did in 1940. How can you be certain that the man you see today is the same person you re-member from your childhood? Don't you think that might be a reach?"

Britta answers quickly and confidently. "I was fourteen in 1940 and nineteen when the war ended. I was not a child. I have a clear memory, and if that isn't enough, the photograph of Ole and his father that ran in the *Tribune,* the one they say he boldly displays on the walls of his tavern, removes any doubt. I recognized his father and I recognized Ole. So no, Mr. Lockhart, it's not a reach."

Catherine glances across the table at Liam and suppresses a grin. "Knocked the world's greatest detective back on his duff, didn't she, Mr. Lockhart?"

Liam smiles as well. "I guess she did. Actually Britta, it's Taggart. Liam Taggart."

"Oh!" Britta says with a bit of embarrassment. "I'm so sorry, I just thought . . ."

"It's no big deal. I think I'd like to start off by researching Mr. Hen-ryks. How and when did he come to the U.S.? What has he done be-sides run a restaurant? Who are his friends and associates? And what about this Danish-American Association of Chicago? What members sponsored him for the hall of fame? On what basis? There are lots of questions in my mind, and if you have any of that information, or know how to get it, I'd like you to give it to me."

Britta purses her lips. "I'm afraid I do not know any of the members of that association. I have no connection with them. As far as Ole Hendricksen is concerned, the knowledge that I possess concerns his life in Denmark, and it all would be prior to his entry into the United States. I'm sorry."

Catherine shifts in her chair. "And now for you, attorney Emma Fisher. I need help researching and drafting a motion to dismiss Henryks's complaint, and I'll also need help in drafting our affirmative defense. Walter raves about your legal abilities and I'm delighted that he's loaned you to us. Please start researching immediately."

Emma smiles broadly. "I'm ready."

"All right, Team Britta," Catherine says enthusiastically, "let's all get started. I will meet with Britta right here every day and we'll drag out every detail she can remember. Let's all keep each other in the loop as we go forward. Keep me informed of anything you come across that you think might spark a memory in Britta's mind."

Britta turns her head toward the wall. Her lips are quavering. She dabs at her eyes with an embroidered handkerchief. Her chest heaves as she tries to conceal her sobs. Catherine waits for her to compose herself. Britta runs her tongue across her lips and takes a deep breath. "I know I don't often express my feelings very well, that is my flaw, but I'm so thankful that you've agreed to take me on as a client. I know this wouldn't be an easy case for any lawyer, and lord knows, I am not an easy client. I know the challenges are formidable, and there is no economic upside for any of you. And yet . . . all of you . . . are so willing, so determined to help me, I just don't know what to say."

Catherine smiles. "You don't have to say anything. Sometimes it's not about the money. Sometimes we get involved in cases because we know it's the right thing to do. I suppose it's the same reason that you felt impassioned to paint the truth on Henryks's walls."

"When I learned that Ole Hendricksen, that absolute fraud, was going to be honored, inducted into some so-called hall of fame, it made me sick," Britta says sternly. "What is this Danish-American Association of Chicago? Who do these members think they are, that they're entitled to anoint a Danish war hero? Denmark had *real* heroes, people who deserved to be honored, people like my father, my sister and my brother-in-law. I'll be damned if I'll stay silent while Hendricksen holds himself out as a war hero. They might as well pin a ribbon on Hitler."

In Catherine's mind, all of this serves to confirm the decision she has made. "Britta, I want to know about those real heroes. I want to know about your family. I want you to tell me everything you can remember about those heroes and also about the traitors. We're going to start working as soon as I return from court tomorrow."

As the meeting is breaking up, Catherine pulls Emma aside. "How familiar are you with defamation law?"

She wrinkles her nose. "Second-year tort class. About as much as one could learn from a survey course. We covered the major decisions." She shrugs. "Considering our case, I would say not nearly enough."

"As I mentioned to you earlier, I think our best move is to file a motion to dismiss the complaint, or at least parts of it. I doubt the motion will be granted, but it will buy us time. My memory tells me that calling someone a liar is the expression of an opinion and is not actionable. What about the other statements? What grounds do we have to ask Judge Wilson to dismiss part or all of the complaint?"

"Do you want me to prepare a memo?"

Catherine shakes her head. "Ordinarily that would be great, but we're short on time. Given the likelihood that we'll face a compressed case management order, a memo will take time we don't have. As soon as you've completed your research, I'd like to get together and work on the motion."

"I'll get right on it."

CHAPTER SIX

———— ◦◦◦◦ ————

CATHERINE STEPS OFF the elevator onto the twenty-first floor of the Richard J. Daley Center. Built in 1965 and located at the corner of Clark and Randolph Streets in Chicago's Loop, the thirty-story courthouse is distinctive for its rust-colored patina, and for the controversial Picasso statue in the plaza. The wide hallways with their walls of windows and marble benches provide ample room for last-minute negotiations. It is often said that more business is conducted in the hallways than in the courtrooms themselves.

As soon as Catherine enters the hall, she realizes that her expectations were correct. This will be episode one of the Sterling Sparks Show. There are several groups of reporters congregating outside Judge Wilson's courtroom even though the doors will not open for another thirty minutes. *They should put up a warning sign,* Catherine thinks. *Circus in Progress.* She gazes across the hall and recognizes CBS's Vera Paulson talking with her cameraman.

Donning a blank expression, Catherine strolls over and innocently asks, "What's the big occasion this morning, Vera? Is there something going on? The pack looks hungry."

"Six-o'clock has a case on Obadiah's call," Vera responds. She wears a Cheshire grin. "It's the one where the wacky old woman painted signs on the walls of The Melancholy Dane."

Catherine places her hand on her chest in a mock gesture. "Really? I understand it's up this morning on a routine motion to extend a protective order. Does a wacky old woman demand the attention of all four networks?"

"Are you kidding?" Vera answers. "The public loves this case. They eat it up. Besides, my anchor wants a statement from each of the attorneys for his evening broadcast. He wants video."

"Obadiah doesn't allow cameras in his courtroom."

Vera shrugs it off. "Then we'll get what we can out here in the hall. By the way, I love your suit."

"Nordstrom. Where's Sterling, I don't see him?"

"Hasn't shown up yet. You know Sparks; he'll make a grand entrance, deliver his morning press briefing and give us a slew of good quotes. He could fill an entire segment. Do you have any idea who represents the old woman?"

Catherine smiles. "I guess you'll find out soon enough. It's me, Vera."

"You stinker!" she says, biting the corner of her lip and quickly motioning for her cameraman. "Give me something, Catherine," she whispers. "Something juicy and exclusive before these other vultures get to you."

Fashioning quotable comments is not Catherine's style, but she nods conspiratorially, leans over and whispers into the mic, "Always remember, there are two sides to every story."

Vera scoffs. "Oh, hold the presses. Thanks a lot for nothing. Tell me one thing, are you going to plead a mental disability, diminished capacity— you know, not legally responsible for her conduct?"

"She's as sane as you or me, Vera."

Vera chuckles. "Well, speak for yourself, my dear. I don't go sneaking around with a spray can in the middle of the night."

At that instant, Sterling Sparks steps off the elevator and struts toward the courtroom door. The reporters flock to him, shouting questions, pushing their foam-covered mics into his face. In a majestic pose, Sparks holds up his hand for silence. "Easy, folks, you'll all get your chance. One at a time, please."

Looking for a sentimental lead on the lunch hour news, a reporter asks, "Tell us, Mr. Sharp, how is Mr. Henryks holding up? We've heard this is affecting his health."

Sparks lowers his gaze and smiles at the reporter. The flamboyant lawyer is in his happy place. "It's Sparks, honey, but some will say I'm sharp. Unfortunately, Mr. Henryks is not well, not well at all. This terrible ordeal has taken a heavy toll on a fragile elderly man." Sparks scans the crowd. "Can any of you even remotely imagine what it would be like to be called a Nazi collaborator? Can you imagine anything worse? And then can you imagine what it would be like to have it spray-painted on your private property and then broadcast on television for a million people to see? I mean, all of you are in good health—strong young reporters. Imagine the toll such an ordeal would take on a ninety-five-year-old man." Sparks closes his eyes, presses his lips tightly together and shakes his head. "It's so sad. So wrong. I can only say that Ole Henryks is holding up the best he can. Of course, he's under close medical supervision at all times. Twenty-four/seven."

Catherine feels the bile rise in her throat, mumbles "Academy Award," turns and walks away.

THE COURTROOM SEATS are filled with reporters, shoulder to shoulder. The overflow stands two deep along the walls. Anticipation grows, the corner door opens and a giant of a man steps into the courtroom, his black robe unbuttoned and flowing. As he mounts the steps to his elevated bench, he draws a deep breath through his nostrils. He gazes out at his packed courtroom and slowly shakes his head. He has presided over his share of headline cases and has little patience left for the theatrics. Finally, he turns to the side and nods to his courtroom deputy, who slams the gavel and loudly proclaims, "All rise. This branch of the Circuit Court of Cook County is now in session pursuant to adjournment, the Honorable Obadiah J. Wilson presiding. Please be seated and come to order. And silence your phones."

"I suppose we should get right to the main event," the judge says to his clerk. "Call Six-o'clock's case."

The clerk announces, "Case number 18-L-20998, *Henryks v. Stein.* Motion to extend a temporary restraining order."

There is a rattle of papers and an undercurrent of comments as Catherine and Sparks approach the bench. Wilson wrinkles his forehead and announces to the gallery, "This is a Cook County courtroom, not a sports arena. I will insist on proper decorum at all times. Take all the notes you want, but if it comes to my attention that an audio or video clip of this morning's proceeding has made its way onto the nightly news, I'll consider that direct contempt and the violator will find himself or herself standing before me the very next morning. You don't want to be that person." Then he peers down at Catherine and smiles. "Ms. Lockhart, it's nice to see you back in my courtroom so soon again. I take it you will be representing the defendant, Britta Stein?"

"Yes, your honor, I filed my appearance this morning and I will be seeking twenty-one days to file Mrs. Stein's initial responsive pleading." Wilson nods, begins to make a note in his judge's notebook, and is about to speak when Sparks interrupts.

"May it please the court," Sparks says. "Plaintiff objects to defendant's request."

In one of Wilson's patented facial expressions—furrowed eyebrows, squinted eyes and a broad smile just short of breaking into a bold laugh, he says, "So, it's going to be that kind of day, is it? You object to the defendant's request to file an appearance and respond to your lawsuit, Mr. Sparks? Are we going to bar her from having a defense at all? Are we no longer in the United States of America, *Mister Sparks*?"

"No sir. I mean yes sir, we are in America, but I don't object to her right to file a response. I object to twenty-one days." He hands a set of papers up to the judge. "This is the plaintiff's motion to accelerate the case for trial."

"Your honor," Catherine says, "defendant has had no notice of such a motion. I have just filed my appearance and we are here on a hearing to extend a protective order. Twenty-one days is not an unreasonable amount of time to file my initial response."

"Oh, yes it is," Sparks snaps. "In *this* case it is. My client is ninety-five years old and thanks to the criminal conduct of the defendant, he is now in very poor health. I can see right through Ms. Lockhart's tactics. Why, I'd do it myself if I were her. Delay and delay, file motions, kick it down the calendar and pretty soon one or both of these nonagenarians will have passed on. I demand an immediate trial setting." For emphasis, Sparks slaps his hand on the podium.

Wilson curls his lips. Sparks is in hot water. "Do that again, Mr. Sparks, and I will have you removed."

"Yes, sir. Sorry."

"You demand?"

Sparks tips his head from side to side. "All right, I mean I humbly request. My client deserves his day in court and if Ms. Lockhart has her way, he won't live long enough."

The judge turns his attention to Catherine. "He has a point. How long do you really need to file an answer to the complaint?"

"Your honor, the defendant has a right to prepare and present a thorough defense. As much as Mr. Sparks may disapprove, due process requires that we be given sufficient time. The rules grant me the right to file a motion to dismiss, which I intend to do."

Wilson rolls his eyes. "Naturally."

Speaking in an even tone, Catherine continues. "I would expect the motion to be fully briefed by both sides and given its due consideration. Depending on the outcome of my motion, I wouldn't be surprised if there were further preliminary pleadings and motions like every other case in this building. There will be depositions and pretrial discovery. Just because the plaintiff is in his nineties doesn't mean that we abandon the Illinois Code of Civil Procedure. An immediate court date is out of the question."

"You see?" says Sparks, turning his head briefly to the rear of the courtroom to acknowledge the reporters. "It's just like I said. A motion here, a motion there, and pretty soon we're three years down the road without a trial."

Wilson reaches up and scratches his head. "Ms. Lockhart, I have to tell you, I've seen the closed-circuit video. Mr. Sparks played it for me the other day when I granted his protective order. Is your client going to deny that it is she in the video with the spray paint in her hand?"

"No sir. She won't contest that it was she who painted words on the building wall."

"Is she going to deny that she trespassed on Mr. Henryks's property?"

"Well, she was standing on a public sidewalk. Most of the time."

"And the six painted signs, Ms. Lockhart, all of that accusatory language, was that her handiwork?"

"I believe it was."

"Then truly, I'm at a loss to see why Mr. Sparks's motion to accelerate doesn't raise a valid concern. Why should we prolong the discovery process? Enlighten me, Ms. Lockhart. Why do you need time?"

"My client is being sued for defamation. Five million dollars, I believe. Mr. Henryks alleges that the words painted on the walls of The Melancholy Dane were false and defamatory. Some of the words—liar, for example—are statements of opinion and cannot constitute defamation. I will move to strike them. As to the balance, Mrs. Stein will deny they are defamatory and affirmatively assert that each and every one of the remaining statements is true, and thus privileged."

A rumble of muffled chatter skitters through the courtroom. The deputy bangs the gavel. "Quiet, please. Silence in the court."

Judge Wilson pulls on his lip. "You intend to prove that Mr. Henryks was a Nazi collaborator and a traitor to his country? Seriously? In *my* courtroom?"

"Yes sir, I do."

Wilson takes a deep breath. "Well, I sure get the assignments, don't I? A war crimes case in Obadiah's courtroom. Do you have such proof, Ms. Lockhart? Do you have the proof that he was a Nazi collaborator?"

"I'm not prepared to discuss the evidence at this time, your honor, but rest assured, I'm working on it."

"Exactly!" Sparks shouts. "She doesn't have any proof; she doesn't have anything. She wants years of delay to manufacture facts that don't exist, hoping that the case outlives the participants. But from my client's perspective, the longer this case sits unresolved on the court's docket, the longer these defamatory statements are allowed to float around in the winds of Chicago, the more they will be bandied about online, in the papers and on the streets. Until these defamatory statements are snuffed out once and for all, Mr. Henryks's injuries compound. He deserves the right to have this court issue a judgment clearing his name at the earliest possible time. Justice is served by bringing this matter to a prompt conclusion. We demand, I mean I request, that this case be set for trial immediately! Justice must be served!" Sparks swivels around and smiles at the gallery, as if pausing for his standing ovation.

Wilson takes another deep breath through his nostrils and rolls his eyes. "Give it a rest, Mr. Sparks; there is no jury sitting here. Not yet." Then turning to Catherine, he says, "Ms. Lockhart, I have to admit, he makes a persuasive argument. To call these words mere opinion would be a gross understatement. They contain accusations of the most extreme and odious nature. The longer they are allowed to linger, the longer their perceived legitimacy remains unadjudicated, the more they generate discussion. Mr. Henryks is entitled to snip these accusations in the bud, if he can. I'll give you until next Wednesday to file your motion. Mr. Sparks, you will have two days to brief your response."

"Two days?"

Wilson smiles. "I'll give you two months if you like. Do you want more time?"

"No, no, two days. That's all I'll need."

"Good. Then I'll see everyone back here a week from Monday. Nine a.m." He nods to his clerk. "Call the next case."

The clerk, wearing his irritation like a face mask, waits while the rush of reporters stampedes out the door to make their phone calls.

CHAPTER SEVEN

—∞∞—

A WEARY CATHERINE enters her office in the early afternoon to find Britta Stein sitting alone in the conference room. "I'm sorry to be late for our meeting," Catherine says. "No sooner did I finish with Mr. Sparks this morning, than I had to cover an emergency hearing in another case. I tried to call you, but your line was busy."

"I took the phone off the hook," Britta replies. "I had a few unruly callers."

Catherine is at once concerned. "Have you been getting threatening phone calls?"

"Not exactly threatening. I would more accurately characterize them as disturbing. There is no shortage of filthy-mouthed people in our city."

"My goodness, Britta. Have you called the police?"

She shakes her head. "What can the police do? It was just a handful of meanspirited people swearing at me—no doubt part of Hendricksen's tavern crowd. I'm sure it's nothing to worry about. They're crank calls."

"I don't like it, Britta. You never know. Some people may be crazy enough to act out. The police might be able to trace those calls. What do they say?"

"Oh, if you'll excuse my French, I'm the Jew-bitch from hell. How dare I dishonor such a wonderful war hero? It's too bad the Nazis didn't gas me when they had the chance. The restaurant wall should be painted with my blood. That sort of thing."

"Those are not crank calls; those are threats. We need to report them. I'll have Liam get on it."

"It doesn't matter, I'm not answering my house phone anymore. I'm only using my cell phone."

"Nevertheless, I'm going to talk to Liam about increasing security at your residence."

"I live in a secure building on Marine Drive. There are thirty-seven floors and a full-time doorman at the front entrance. I'm perfectly safe."

"The world is full of crazies, and one of them may seek to do something other than scare you with a phone call. Did you come down here today on your own, or did Emma bring you?"

"She dropped me off, but I'm very capable of traveling on my own, thank you very much. I know how to take a taxi. I do very well. I've been getting around quite nicely for ninety-two years. You needn't worry about me. *I* was the one who was on time this afternoon."

"Point taken. But be careful. I'm still going to have Liam report it." Catherine takes out her yellow notepad and picks up a pen. "Let's get started. I'd like to begin by getting a general understanding of your life in Denmark before the war. Tell me, what was it like growing up Britta Stein?"

"Well, back then I was Britta Morgenstern and life was pleasant. Copenhagen was a delightful place to grow up. It was peaceful, liberal and tolerant. The financial center, where my father worked, was vibrant, centrally located and an easy trip for him to ride his bicycle to and from work. I'm sure you've seen pictures of Danish businessmen riding their bicycles in their suits and sport jackets. They still do." She smiles at her memory. "There's a Danish word for our general feeling of well-being; it's called 'hygge.' It's like taking a deep breath of fresh air on a sunny afternoon.

"My family lived in an apartment in the center of the city—the first floor of a three-story walkup. There was my mother, Nora, my father, Joseph, and my sister, Grethe, who was three years older than me and my best friend. When things unraveled, as they did in the forties, and when I was unable to process what was happening in the world around me, it was Grethe who kept me centered. She'd sit down and talk to me in terms that I could understand."

"How did Grethe know what was going on?"

"Well, for most of those years she was at the university and a good student. She was very smart. Between the two of us, Grethe was the studious one; a voracious reader and a girl with boundless curiosity. She'd corner Papa and have long detailed discussions about what was happening. She relished the fact that Papa was so highly placed and well-informed. He was in the administration, you know. He worked for Denmark's taxing authority and was an elected member of the Folketing—the Danish Parliament."

Catherine jots a few notes. "I'm afraid I don't know much about Denmark's political structure. Doesn't Denmark have a queen?"

Britta nods. "Queen Margrethe II. We are—I mean Denmark is—a constitutional monarchy. Not unlike the U.K., but with several political parties. Since no single political party ever achieves a majority, they must form coalitions in order to select a prime minister. The Danish constitution provides that the monarch is the titular head of state, and the queen or king has limited authority. Parliament makes the laws and the leading member of the majority party normally becomes the prime minister. My father worked in the Finance Ministry during the terms of Prime Minister Thorvald Stauning, a Social Democrat, and his successor, Erik Scavenius. King Christian X was the ruling monarch in the forties."

"Your father sounds very important."

"Well, he certainly was to Grethe and me. He was tall and strong and devoted to his daughters. And to my mother, of course. For Grethe, he was the fountain of knowledge, but for me, he was pure adventure. He loved to sail, and even when I was very little, whenever I saw him take out his sailing parka, I would run to him and beg him to take me along. I loved it."

"Did Grethe love to sail as well?"

"Oh no. She hated the water. She got seasick. My mother wasn't crazy about it either, even though Papa named his boat *Queen Nora*. Papa and I would pack a lunch and spend the afternoon on the body of water between Denmark and Sweden called Øresund. Those were the happiest days of my life."

"Sounds lovely. Your family was Jewish; what was that like in prewar Denmark?"

"Well, I didn't think being Jewish was anything unusual. We practiced our faith, but you wouldn't say we were deeply religious. I think I would characterize us as assimilated. Jews were well integrated into Danish society. Denmark was not a particularly religious state anyway. Not like Poland or France or Spain. The prominent religion was Lutheran. Two hundred years ago, the Danish constitution established the Folkekirken, the Danish People's Church. The majority of Danes identify themselves as Lutheran. There has been a Jewish presence in Denmark for four hundred years." Britta shrugs her shoulders. "I never felt excluded from anything that I wanted to do because I was Jewish. It was never an issue at school. At the beginning of the war there were less than eight thousand of us in a country of almost four million. Compare that to Poland, which had three million Jews, fully ten percent of the country, yet we know there was pervasive anti-Semitism in Poland. If there was an anti-Semitism movement in Denmark, it was insignificant and not apparent to me. Of course, there were always exceptions."

"Henryks?"

"Hendricksen. I don't remember the Hendricksens being openly anti-Semitic. Ole was a member of a club and they all wore blue shirts. Not to school, of course, because uniforms were prohibited. There were political parties and there were groups and clubs. They had different dispositions, but I don't recall any groups that were openly anti-Semitic. Not in the prewar years. Ole's father was a day-worker down at the harbor. He'd sign on as a laborer whenever a fishing boat needed an extra hand. According to Ole, he was rough. Grethe told me that in discussions among her classmates, Ole would complain that his father drank too much and knocked him around. His mother worked long hours at the market.

"Although Denmark was generally a prosperous country, the Hendricksens were not. I suppose they felt more or less disenfranchised. In the thirties, during the depression years, Denmark suffered along with the rest of Europe. In the early thirties, it was basically the malcontented people in central Europe who were a tuning fork for Hitler's hate campaign. They would look for someone to blame for their misfortune, and Hitler was offering up a scapegoat. But Denmark was relatively prosperous, especially as the decade was drawing to a close, and there was little audience for Hitler's prattling. I know of no anti-Semitic movement for the Hendricksens to jump on. Denmark just wasn't like that."

"So you were acquainted with the Hendricksens?"

"Oh yes. I knew the two Hendricksen brothers. As I said, Ole was three years older and I didn't know him very well. He was in my sister's class. William was a year older than Ole. They were never serious students and always found themselves in one sort of jam or another. It was mostly petty stuff. Pranks. But they could be meanspirited. My sister always said they were the sort to kick a puppy. And it wasn't just Grethe who felt that way.

"Getting back to your original question," Britta says, "I never felt like an outsider because of my religion. My family worshipped at the Great Synagogue on Krystalgade, a very old and very grand synagogue, built in 1833. In 1933, when I was seven years old, my mother dressed Grethe and me in brand-new outfits and we all walked down to the Great Synagogue for the hundredth anniversary. It was a gala celebration. King Christian X attended the ceremony and delivered a congratulatory address." Britta sits back and smiles at the recollection. "Like I said, it was very pleasant growing up Jewish in Copenhagen." She pauses. "Until it wasn't."

Catherine rises to answer the intercom and returns with a smile. "Your amazing granddaughter has just arrived. She says she's finished with her research. So, I'm afraid we're going to have to break for the day. I really need to talk to her. As you know, we're under some pressure; our motion is due to be filed shortly. If you wouldn't mind, we'll pause the narrative for today and we'll pick it up right where we left off next time."

CHAPTER EIGHT

—⊸⊸⊸—

EMMA SETS TWO thick file folders on the conference table. "Goodness," Catherine says, "that's a lot of research in a short period of time. Walter wasn't wrong when he sang your praises."

Emma blushes a little and waves it off. "I logged some late hours, that's all. It felt like I was back in law school at finals time."

"Excellent. Our goal is to file a motion to dismiss all or part of Henryks's lawsuit. Let's start with a general overview. Is Henryks's complaint legally sufficient? Did Sparks set forth the basic elements of a claim for defamation?"

"Without a doubt," Emma says, and she proceeds to count out the elements on her fingers. "The complaint alleges that Britta made a series of false statements about Henryks, that these false statements were communicated to a third person or persons, in our case to the general public, and that the publication caused damage to Henryks's reputation. Given that she accused him of being a 'Nazi collaborator,' a 'Nazi agent' and a 'traitor,' the statements are considered defamatory per se, and Henryks's injury is presumed."

Catherine is impressed with Emma's presentation. She nods her approval. "Your grandmother and I are very lucky to have you, Emma. And I can see the close relationship when the two of you are together."

"We've been together almost all my life," Emma says. "My father was out of the picture when I was very young, I don't even remember him. My mother worked every day, long shifts in the hospital. Bubbe would stay with me. When my grandfather died, she moved in with Mom and me. She practically raised me. You could say she became my primary caretaker. Now, I guess the shoe's on the other foot, but the time I spend with her is precious to me." Catherine smiles with the suspicion that there is an interesting story about the two of them that may or may not come out in the course of the representation.

"Getting back to Henryks's complaint," Emma says, "since my grandmother doesn't deny she made the statements, Sparks achieves a prima facie case without calling a single witness. The case will rise or fall on the strength of our affirmative defense."

Catherine nods. "I understand that 'traitor,' 'Nazi agent' and 'Nazi collaborator' are defamatory on their face. But what about 'liar,' 'informer' and 'betrayer'? Can't they constitute mere name-calling? Is it possible to eliminate those statements? Shouldn't we move to strike them from the complaint?"

Emma spreads her hands. "What's the point? Nazi collaborator, Nazi agent and traitor are enough to get the case to the jury without any other words. Judge Wilson is not going to dismiss the case because a few of the words might happen to be name-calling. Why does it matter if he strikes some of the words? It doesn't make the case go away and we don't really achieve anything. And, by the way, I'm not so sure that informer and betrayer are merely name-calling."

"Meaning?"

"Taken in context, they can refer to criminal activity. Why don't we just get our affirmative defense on file, allege that the statements are all true, and proceed to defend the case?"

"Three reasons," Catherine says. "First, any of the statements that are stricken lessens our evidentiary burden at trial. For example, we won't have to prove Henryks is a betrayer or a liar. Secondly, if Wilson strikes a portion of the complaint, it will be a victory, albeit small, in the court of public opinion. For at least a portion of the morning, we will have gone on the offensive and succeeded in obtaining a ruling in our favor. Thirdly, and most importantly, filing and briefing a motion to strike buys us time, and we need every minute we can get. So, do we have grounds to strike any of the words?"

"Maybe liar. I think all the others would survive."

Catherine is not convinced. "Emma, when we talk about traitor, informer and betrayer, aren't those really statements of Britta's opinion? Aren't they protected by the First Amendment? When we comment about someone in the public spotlight, aren't we allowed to state our opinion without liability? Isn't that a recognized privilege? Can't I express my opinion that the president is a failure or that he's lying or that he is incompetent?"

"You can because he is the president. He is a public official. The Supreme Court has held that a public official cannot recover for a false and defamatory statement unless he can show that the person who made the statement did so with actual malice, which means that the person knew that the statement was false before he made it. Sorry, Henryks is not a public official. He's a tavern owner."

"But didn't the Supreme Court expand the doctrine to include people who were *public figures* as well as public officials? Isn't Henryks at least a public figure?"

Emma shakes her head. "Henryks wouldn't qualify as a public figure either. A public figure is someone who voluntarily thrusts himself into a particular public controversy, and as such, he invites comments and opinions about himself."

"What could be more controversial than what's going on right now?"

"Henryks didn't exactly thrust *himself* into this controversy, did he? My grandmother was the one who thrust him by spray-painting those derogatory statements."

"Hmm," Catherine says, "but I would like to include traitor, informer and betrayer in our motion anyway. What do we have to lose? If Wilson denies it, we're no worse off. We'll move to strike them, notwithstanding. Let's draft our motion. We can file it in two days. What would you think about—"

Their conversation is abruptly halted by the crashing sound of broken glass and the squeal of automobile tires. Catherine rushes to the reception room to find the front window shattered and an angry Gladys pointing to a dark red brick on the floor. On the brick is a painted message: "Death to the Jew-bitch."

BY THE TIME Liam arrives at the office, there are two CPD patrol cars, lights flashing, blocking off the northbound lanes of Clark Street. Liam jumps out of his car at the end of the block and darts for the door but is stopped by a uniformed officer. "Hold on, fellow. Nobody's going in right now."

"That's my wife in there," Liam frantically declares. "That's her office. Is anybody hurt?"

The officer shakes his head and steps aside. Inside, a plainclothes detective is taking a statement from Gladys while an evidence technician is examining the brick.

"Mrs. Stein told me she has received threatening phone calls that caused her to shut off her landline," Catherine says to the detective. "She now uses her cell phone exclusively."

"What do these, uh . . . so-called threatening callers say?" The detective's tone and expression convey a decided lack of interest in Catherine's response, as though the question was required, and he couldn't care less about the answer. His attitude peeves Catherine.

"Excuse me," Catherine says. "The *so-called* callers spew anti-Semitic threats. They say that the Nazis should have killed her, that the wall should be painted with her blood. They call her a Jew-bitch. I wouldn't refer to them as 'so-called' threatening callers. Do you understand this is all about The Melancholy Dane and the lawsuit?"

The detective looks up from his notepad. "Look ma'am, she didn't report any of those alleged calls, did she? I mean, we have no record. It doesn't sound to me like she felt too threatened." He shrugs. "As to whether or not this has anything to do with her dispute with The Melancholy Dane, do either of you have any reason to believe that Mr. Henryks is involved in any way with either the prank phone calls or this mischievous window breakage?"

Catherine's anger intensifies. She places her hands on her hips. Her face is red. Her voice gets louder. "Prank calls? You call them prank calls?

Mischievous breakage? Is that how the Chicago Police Department now chooses to refer to hate crimes, Officer Martin? Are they *mischievous*?"

Martin tries to hide a smirk rising in the corners of his mouth. "Hate crimes? Really? This was nothing but a brick. Given what your client wrote on Mr. Henryks's restaurant, I think the message on the brick was pretty tame."

Liam realizes that the matter is rapidly getting out of hand. He steps in front of Catherine, holds her back and says, "Death to the Jew-bitch? That's tame to you? Don't you dare minimize this act. You and I both know it's directly tied to the signs on the walls of The Melancholy Dane. It's retaliation and you should be concerned that it could escalate to more serious acts than threatening phone calls and criminal damage to property. You just asked Ms. Lockhart if there might be *any reason* to suspect Ole Henryks of being involved. Well, I can think of six graphic reasons."

"Sir, I asked her a fair question. Does she have any evidence that ties the phone calls or the brick to Mr. Henryks? I doubt that she does. I know Mr. Henryks. I've been in his restaurant many times, and he's just not the type to go around threatening old women or throwing bricks. I'd say that your client is much more threatening than old man Henryks."

"Given your mindset, detective, you have no business being assigned to this case."

"Tell that to my captain; he's the one who sent me over here. If he wants to consider it a hate crime and pull me from this case, well, that's up to him." The detective closes his notepad, turns to Catherine, touches the bill of his cap and says, "Have a nice day, ma'am."

Catherine sits down hard, her face in her hands. "Can you believe it, Liam? The officer thinks it's a prank. 'Death to the Jew-bitch.' And he asks me whether this has anything to do with Henryks."

Liam shakes his head. "That's not exactly what he said. He asked if you thought Henryks was *involved* with the threats."

"*Pranks,* Liam, he said pranks."

"I know. But I'm sure that Henryks didn't drive over and throw that brick."

"There are plenty of people who would. He has followers. He's a popular man, especially among the cops."

"Where's Britta?"

"She's not here, thankfully. She's at home." Catherine tips her head toward the rear of the office. "Emma's in the conference room."

"How is she?"

"More angry than upset. What are we going to do now?"

Liam places his arm around her. "You made the report. From now on we're going to be extra careful. You're going to keep your door locked. I will join you and Britta here at the office whenever you do your interviews."

Emma walks out to join them. "I have a thought," she says. "Why don't we call the media, have them come out and take pictures, and report what's happened. So far, the press reports have been one-sided: favorable for Henryks and very harsh to my grandmother. Everyone pities poor Mr. Henryks. Maybe the public should see the other side. With a court case coming up, we'll need jurors with open minds, won't we?"

Liam looks at Catherine and smiles. "You have a very bright assistant here. I think she's right on the money."

But Catherine shakes her head. "I don't try my cases in the media. Besides, Sparks would counter with a barrage of interviews. He's much better at manipulating the media than I am."

"Cat, there's nothing to manipulate, you have two clear episodes of criminal intimidation and hate crimes. The public should know. Emma's right; let them keep an open mind."

Catherine is resolute; she won't consider it. "I can't prove that Henryks was behind any of this; not the phone calls or the brick. If we call in the media, give them an interview, put it all out there, with the obvious implication that Henryks is somehow behind it, it'll backfire. We have no evidence who did this. The public might see it as a distraction, a ploy to divert attention away from Britta's spray-painting escapades, for which there is ample evidence, including her admissions. Certainly Sparks would see it that way."

CHAPTER NINE

※

BRITTA'S NARRATIVE RESUMES two days later. Catherine and Emma finished preparing their motion to strike portions of Henryks's complaint and they are due back in court in three days for a hearing. Catherine's front window is now covered with a plywood board.

Worried for her safety, Liam offers to drive Britta to and from the office. Britta respectfully declines the offer since Emma accompanies her each day anyway. "Bubbe is more comfortable when I am with her," Emma says. "She has made me promise to sit by her side throughout the ordeal. It's kind of unusual for my grandmother, because she is such an independent person."

"I feel so badly about your window," Britta says, staring at the plywood. "It turns out I am a greater liability than you thought. I regret I got you into this, and I would understand if you changed your mind and—"

Catherine's hand shoots up. "Don't go there, Britta; I'm not changing my mind. It's only a window, and if anything, these threats have strengthened my resolve to see this case through to its conclusion."

"Thank you," Britta says in a whisper.

"Now let's get back to the narrative. When we were finishing our last session, you said that growing up Jewish in Denmark was very pleasant *until it wasn't.* I want to talk about that last phrase. I take it you meant until September 1, 1939?"

Britta shakes her head. "September 1, 1939, was the day that Germany invaded Poland and started World War II, but that was not the date that anything changed for me. Denmark was a spectator. We were not at war. Nevertheless, it was a shock to my parents when they learned of the military invasion of a peaceful country, especially one with a large Jewish population. They knew what had happened in other countries that were overrun and occupied by Germany. My mother had a cousin in Prague.

"I knew my parents were troubled, but I was in middle school and other issues occupied my attention. Poland was many miles away, and my school was only a few blocks away. I was excited about starting a new year. My sister, Grethe, was more attentive to the war than I was. Other than the fact that our teachers gave mention to the international crisis, I remember the fall of 1939 as ordinary in every sense."

Catherine has a bewildered expression. "I know you were young, but you're a bright woman and I am puzzled by what you recall as being ordinary. Germany was commencing what became the worst war in human history. Hitler's racial hatreds were well-known, and he was exporting his racism into the occupied lands. You had a cousin in Prague!"

Britta nods. "My mother's cousin; I didn't know her well."

Catherine presses the point. "Denmark shared a border with a belligerent state that was methodically devouring neighboring states, and your family was Jewish. Why weren't you frightened? I think I would have been, even as a teen. Are you remembering all this correctly?"

"Why are you challenging me?"

"That's my job. You'll be challenged far more aggressively by Sparks."

"Well, I'm telling you the truth as I remember it, and I don't remember being frightened. I suppose I should be embarrassed or ashamed by my lack of awareness, because clearly, I was not aware. At least, not initially, and not in the fall of 1939. I went to school; I saw my friends. The war had not come to Denmark and we didn't expect it to. Really, other than the invasion of Poland, nothing was happening in Europe anyway. England and France had declared war, but there were no battles. Not until much, much later.

"Throughout the fall of 1939, there was no palpable terror in the Copenhagen Jewish community. If there was, I didn't notice it, and my parents didn't discuss it. Denmark was not an enemy of Germany. Indeed, we conducted a considerable amount of commerce with Germany, as did the other Scandinavian countries. The war was someone else's business, just like the First World War. At least, that's my recollection."

Catherine remains skeptical. "I hear you, but you were Jewish and living in Europe. Hitler was aggressive and unpredictable. It was no secret how the Nazis treated Jews in occupied lands. And he could have had Denmark on a whim."

"Hmm," Britta utters. "And ultimately, he did, didn't he? But I'm giving you my memory of Copenhagen as it was in 1939. Remember, I was thirteen years old at the beginning of the war. I wasn't oblivious to European affairs, but I wasn't worried either. And I think a lot of people were like me. If you took a walk down the street you wouldn't sense any anxiety. Things were normal in Copenhagen. There was no war in our city."

"Hygge," Catherine mumbled.

"Exactly! But we sympathized with Jews in occupied countries. I attended Sunday school each week and we'd take up collections to be sent to synagogues in Berlin and Vienna. We learned about Kristallnacht in 1938 and random arrests of Jews and we were told about the German boycott of Jewish businesses. We heard stories about the storm troopers and the detention camps and we prayed for the victims, but we lived in Denmark, and Denmark was a safe zone. Jews came to Denmark from other lands because it was safe. They came by land and by sea, mostly from Germany, Poland and eastern Europe. Many migrants went straight to the farms, training to be *chalutzim*, farming pioneers in Palestine.

"Everyone thinks of Denmark as a nation of islands, maybe because Copenhagen is located on the island of Zealand, but the country is comprised of a large peninsula called Jutland, and hundreds of islands in the Baltic Sea. Jutland shares a fifty-mile border with northeast Germany. It's a simple drive from one country to the other, and many Jews came to Denmark along that route."

Catherine notes it on her pad. "You recall feeling safe because you lived in a safe zone. But the other day, you said life was pleasant *until it wasn't*. Let's go there."

Britta gives a short nod. "We lived in a safe zone, or so we thought throughout the fall of 1939. Denmark was a neutral state; we hadn't fought a war since Napoleon roamed the continent. While all of central Europe was embroiled in the First World War, Denmark, Sweden, Holland and Norway sat it out. They remained neutral and prosperous. All during that war, Denmark did a robust manufacturing, farm and dairy business, shipping to both sides. Danish fishermen couldn't catch enough fish to fill the orders. So, the average Dane thought, Why would either Hitler or England seek to bother us when we were providing each of them with food and other supplies? As it turns out, we were overly complacent, and we were fools."

"But apparently not your father?"

"My father was wise and well-informed. Not only did he receive intelligence briefings as a member of Parliament, but he would obsessively listen to the radio. In our front room, we had a Philco console radio; a beautiful walnut piece, a full four feet high, that my mother kept polished to a shine. He would listen almost every night, not only to Danish broadcasts, but also to those emanating from Germany and the BBC. Long before Germany overran Poland, my father was convinced that Hitler's ambitions were likely to start another conflict in central Europe. He listened to Hitler's rantings. My father paid attention."

"Let's return to the phrase 'until it wasn't.' When did things change for you? When did it become dangerous?"

"Given Hitler's undisclosed ambitions, I suppose it was dangerous all along, but things changed for us on April 9, 1940. That day is fixed in my memory. It was a sunny Tuesday morning, and I was on my way to school with my classmate, Brenda Gutman. We were in the eighth grade, and that particular morning, we were eager to get to school because there was to be a musical assembly and each of us had a part. There was no reason to believe that our national security was endangered. There had been no threats made to Denmark from any belligerent. Hitler hadn't even mentioned Denmark in any of his broadcasts, and although Europe was in a state of war, there were no battles pending in any of Denmark's neighbors.

"As we neared our school, we saw hundreds of armed German soldiers in brown and green uniforms, with round helmets, black boots and belts. There were bayoneted rifles resting on their shoulders as they marched in formation down our thoroughfares. They weren't shooting anybody; the march was a show meant to terrify us, and it did. We saw a Nazi tank parked at the entrance to the public square. Brenda and I froze. 'What are we supposed to do?' she said. 'We have an assembly in an hour, and I've been practicing my part for weeks.' Then we saw the other kids running away from the school. I looked at her, she looked at me, we turned around and dashed for home. I needed to see my father. He would know what was happening.

"Suddenly the sky was full of planes; huge bombers making dreadful noise, like a forest of bumblebees. They were dropping paper leaflets, thousands of them, like giant snowflakes, and the air was filled with them. I grabbed one. In large bold letters it said 'OPROP,' which meant 'Attention.' It then went on to say that Winston Churchill was a warmonger and Germany had come to protect Denmark from the British attack. The leaflet clearly warned the Danish people not to resist the occupation. 'Do not take up arms. Lay your weapons down.'

"I burst through the door to our apartment and yelled, 'Papa!'

"My mother walked into the room. Normally a woman in complete control of her emotions, she was beside herself. 'He's not here, Britta. He went to an emergency meeting at the statehouse. He said to stay home and not go anywhere until he returns.'

"It was several hours later when my father arrived. His head was down, his shoulders were slumped. I remember thinking I'd never seen him looking so exhausted. Now in retrospect, I realize I had never seen him so disheartened. Denmark had surrendered to Germany. 'Turn on the radio,' he said. 'King Christian is going to address the country in a few minutes.'

"'What happened to us?' my mother said in a tremulous voice. 'What are all these Nazi soldiers doing on our streets? Has Germany invaded us like it did to Poland? Are we at war?'

"My father tightened his lips, shook his head and gently placed his hands on her shoulders. 'They have certainly invaded us, there is no other way to look at it, Nora, but we are not at war. We have capitulated. Without firing a single shot. They gave us a six-hour ultimatum to surrender. Six hours, but it took only three. At seven-twenty this morning, the Danish government surrendered to the German Reich.'

"My mother slumped down into a chair. 'Oh, my Lord,' she said, and the tears began to flow.

"'We had no choice, Nora. The German foreign minister warned that if we did not immediately surrender, the Luftwaffe, which is presently flying hundreds of bombers in our skies, would annihilate Copenhagen. Resistance would have been futile. There will be an agreement that the king will sign tomorrow.'

"My mother wailed. 'We are Poland. We are Austria. We are doomed.' She reached for Grethe and me and held us tightly. Then she frantically commanded, 'Pack a bag, children—socks, underclothes, dresses, shoes. Hurry!' Then to my father, she said, 'We will go to your boat in the harbor, Joseph, and you will sail us to England where we will be safe. Take us off the continent and away from that madman before he puts us in train cars.'

"He hugged her as she shuddered and he shook his head. 'The harbor is closed, Nora,' he said softly. 'There are German war boats. Even so, such a trip would be hundreds of miles on frigid sea. No, now is not the time to panic. They have made assurances. They are not going to kill anyone or arrest anyone. The Reich government has given their word that they have no interest in conquering Denmark. They insist that they will remain friends and allow us to run our country as before.'

"My mother was beside herself. 'Their word? Are you serious? No interest in conquering? And that's why they have thousands of Nazis on our streets and bombers in our skies? Because they are our friends? Are we all fools? Do we not know who the Germans are? Those Nazi soldiers you see, are they here to pay a social call on their *friends*? Have you lost your mind, Joseph? Write to Cousin Rachel and ask her what the Nazi *friends* have done in Prague.'

"'Please stop, Nora. I've been in meetings all day. The Germans insist that they are not interested in conquering or ruling Denmark. We are to become a protectorate. We have surrendered our external sovereignty only. We have agreed not to form alliances with any other countries. Germany assures us it has no interest in interfering in any of our domestic affairs. Denmark will retain its police, its judicial system and its government. We have agreed to supply milk, produce and farm products to Germany, as before. They have promised to leave our culture alone, that it will be life as usual in Denmark. Nora, our army has laid down its arms. Don't you see we had no choice?'

"'And all these German soldiers; what is to become of them?'

"'Unfortunately, many of them will remain. They will be granted housing in buildings that will serve as barracks and they will build bases for their operations in other countries, principally Norway.'

"'A protectorate? Protect us from whom? The only country we need protection from is Germany.'

"'We will be declared a German protectorate to guard us against a British invasion and occupation.'

"My mother violently shook her head from side to side. 'And when do all the Jews register and get their armbands? When do they paint *Jude* on the windows and declare a day free of Jews?'

"My father held up his hand. 'It won't happen. That was a sine qua non to our acceptance of their terms. They will not impose their racial laws, nor will they interfere with how Denmark treats its Jews.'

"'And you believe that, Joseph? You, of all people, a Jewish parliamentarian?'

"My father paused, and softly said, 'I believe I have no choice. I will never put my trust in the Nazi state, but at this time, we must go along with the agreement.'"

Catherine nods solemnly. "Your father was a wise man." She lays down her pen and closes her folder. "We've done a lot of work today. It's late. We'll pick it up again after court on Monday."

"One more thing, if I may," Liam says. "When you lived in Copenhagen, were you at all familiar with a magazine called *Kamptegnet*?"

"Battle Sign?" Britta furrows her forehead and shakes her head. "No, not at all. Should I be?"

"I don't know. Apparently, it circulated in Denmark." Liam shrugs. "I've come across it, and it's something I'm following."

CHAPTER TEN

OBADIAH WILSON'S COURTROOM is packed again, even tighter than it was before. As the judge steps up to the bench, he stops to view the room, grumbles and shakes his head. "This is too much. If you don't have a seat, please exit now. All you people standing, you'll have to leave. It's a fire hazard, not to mention a distraction to the legal process in my court-room. There is serious business going on in here and it's not for your entertainment." There are loud complaints as disgruntled standees file out the door.

When the last of the stragglers has exited, the clerk slams the gavel and calls out, "Case number 18-L-20998, *Henryks v. Stein*. Defendant Britta Stein's motion to dismiss the plaintiff's complaint." Sparks, in a light gray suit, tightly fitted, lavender shirt and multicolored tie, approaches the bench. His long black hair is combed back and gelled in place. He turns to nod at the remaining reporters. Judge Wilson looks down at Catherine and says, "All right, Ms. Lockhart, it's your motion. I've read the briefs. I understand your position. Is there anything more you wish to add?"

Catherine knows the routine. She shakes her head. "No, your honor."

"All right then, I'm ready to rule. As much as I've considered the arguments you've made—"

Sparks breaks in, "Just a minute, Judge. I would like to supplement my position at this time. I have something more to say."

"Hmph," Wilson scoffs. "I'm sure you do. Any opportunity to strut your stuff, am I right, Mr. Sparks?"

"I just want my opposition to Ms. Lockhart's motion to be clear on the record," Sparks says with a shrug.

Wilson lowers his eyes and sighs. "Has anyone ever told you that when a judge is leaning in your favor, it's best to—"

"To shut up," Sparks answers quickly with a snap of his fingers. "Are you leaning in my favor?"

Wilson exhales loudly and nods. "Ms. Lockhart, there is no possible way of construing 'Nazi agent,' 'Nazi collaborator' and 'traitor" in any way but defamatory. They are incapable of innocent construction under any circumstances. While I considered your argument that 'liar,' 'betrayer' and 'informer' might carry some degree of ambiguity, or may under some circumstances be regarded as opinions, they are so closely connected to the other unambiguous defamatory phrases as to render them actionable."

Now Catherine voices her opposition. "Your honor, Mr. Henryks is a public figure. He's on TV all the time, he's a well-known personality and he's about to be inducted into a hall of fame. In such a case, he is inviting comments and opinions about him, even though some may be unfavorable."

Sparks speaks up. "Nonsense! Mr. Henryks is only a public figure because the defendant has—" He stops abruptly as Judge Wilson is wagging his finger at him. "I know. I should shut up when I'm ahead."

Wilson nods reluctantly. "One would think so. To the extent Mr. Henryks is now a center of attention and at the forefront of this particular public controversy, he is there because Mrs. Stein has put him there. He is there involuntarily."

"He is being feted as a war hero," Catherine argues, though she is now certain that her arguments are falling on deaf ears. "Surely that invites public discourse on his war activities."

Wilson gives her a look that says I'd like to help you, but I can't. "He did not thrust himself into the public arena, Ms. Lockhart; it was done by others. I rule that he is not a public figure."

Catherine isn't finished. "What about 'liar'? Isn't that a mere statement of opinion?"

Wilson lifts shoulders in a minor shrug. "I don't see that it will make much difference in the grand scheme of things, but I'll grant your motion to strike 'liar' from the complaint. Otherwise, as to all the other statements, your motion is denied."

"Your honor," says Sparks, "I would like—"

"That is my ruling, Mr. Sparks. In case you didn't realize it, you have won this morning."

"No sir, I wasn't going to address the motion. I have two other concerns."

Wilson shuts his eyes. "What are they, Mr. Sparks?"

"We all know what Ms. Lockhart is going to do now. She's going to file an answer admitting that her client painted the words, and she's going to file an affirmative defense, no doubt asserting that the defamatory remarks are privileged."

"And you want me to order her to file her papers promptly, am I right?"

"Yes, sir; that's the first part."

"And?"

"I want you to order her to divulge to this court, right here and now, what evidence she will have to show that there is any truth to the wild assertions which will be made by her client in the affirmative defense. Right here. Right now. What evidence is she going to have to support such a pleading?"

Wilson has a perplexed look on his face. "Well, that's not how the game is played, Mr. Sparks."

Sparks puffs his chest; he is at center stage now, talking to a room of reporters as well as the judge. "If Ms. Lockhart has any proof, even the slightest scintilla of proof, from seventy-five years ago, that Mr. Henryks was a Nazi, I demand she come forward right now and disclose the evidence. She'll have to do it eventually. Mrs. Stein has cast a stain upon my client, I submit to you, without a shred of evidence. I don't know what bone she has to pick with Mr. Henryks, what ancient vendetta, but she has no proof to back up any of her wild insults, I guarantee it. If I'm wrong, then show it to me right now. It's not fair for my client to live under the cloud of these heinous accusations when there is not a chance in hell that they will be proven. At this moment of his life, when he is about to be honored as a hero, he should be free of such baseless condemnation. Where is the proof? I demand it!"

"Hmm," Wilson says. "Quite an oration, Mr. Sparks. I guess there's a good reason that you have such a descriptive nickname. Of course, I'm not going to order any evidentiary showing at this time, and you know that. But I do see your point. There is a stain on Mr. Henryks's reputation, at least temporarily. Whether that is his fault or not is a matter to be sorted out at a later time. But whether there is any evidentiary support for those statements is indeed a matter that concerns me at all times. I will caution you, Ms. Lockhart, if you file an affirmative defense asserting that the statements made by your client are true, you will need to plead exactly how and why such statements are true. Illinois is a fact-pleading state. I will not abide with a pleading full of conclusions. Each of Mrs. Stein's statements, whether it's 'Nazi agent,' 'traitor' or 'Nazi collaborator,' must be pleaded with specific facts. What did Henryks do? When did he do it? What did he say? To whom was it said? What facts make him a traitor? Or a collaborator? If you do not plead specific facts, I will dismiss your affirmative defense and grant judgment to the plaintiff. Are we clear?"

Catherine nods.

"I will give you thirty days to file your pleading which recites those specific facts. Court is adjourned."

CHAPTER ELEVEN

———⦇∞⦈———

"YOU DO UNDERSTAND that we are in deep trouble, don't you, Cat?" Liam laments as they wait for Britta and Emma in the office. "You have thirty days to allege specific facts about Henryks and thus far Britta hasn't given you any. She's only scratched the surface with her narrative about her family and life in Denmark. She hasn't focused on Henryks at all."

"That's not fair; I asked her for the total picture. I want to know what happened in Copenhagen during the war. If I don't have an understanding of the setting, I won't be capable of presenting the facts clearly to a jury. I need to know in what way and under what circumstances Henryks's acts were traitorous or collaborative or I won't be an effective advocate."

"Only thirty days, Cat. If you want my opinion, you'll have to move Britta along. What makes Henryks a traitor? What did he do? When did he do it? Impress upon her the need to know right now. Facts, Cat. To quote the incomparable Six-o'clock: 'Right here, right now.'"

Catherine twists her lips and shakes her head. "I don't need all the facts right now, I need them in thirty days. But I'll nudge her. She'll get there eventually. At some point, I'll need you to find witnesses and physical evidence, but not yet."

"Only too happy to comply, my love, but speaking selfishly from my own point of view, if you're going to ask me to go out and round up documents, witnesses or other physical evidence to corroborate the things Britta's going to say, then I need to have sufficient time. I might have to go to Copenhagen. That being said, if I don't have time, you'll be stuck with Britta's word against Henryks's. Like it or not, you need to rush her."

"You know me, Liam, that's not how I operate. I know time is tight, but if we jump ahead too quickly, I'll miss something important. Context and circumstance are paramount in this case."

"She's a bright woman, Cat. Give her some credit. Let her know that we need the details. Emphasize the urgency. She'll respond."

Catherine hesitates, then rejects the suggestion. "There is a time demand, but there is a danger inherent with rushing an interview. If I let her pick and choose the details, it's bound to come back to haunt me. I learned early on in my career, from Walter Jenkins himself, that you can't let a client sort through facts and disclose only those she deems helpful. Clients will filter information based on how they think their case should be presented, and they'll leave out the negative facts. Then we've set ourselves up for a surprise when our opponent introduces undisclosed facts in an 'Aha' moment. Every case has good and bad facts. Negative facts can be managed if you put them out there yourself and spin them in the most favorable light. It's much better than scrambling to clean up a messy surprise."

"So, you think that a thorough narrative is going to bring out both the good and bad facts? You could run out of time."

"I do. She's methodical. Going through Britta's narrative at her speed may take a little longer, but it may be the only way to get everything. I'll prod her along as best I can."

"Okay, you know best."

Catherine perks right up and smiles brightly. "Could I have that in writing, please? You know, the part where Catherine knows best? Also, what in the world were you talking about when you asked Britta if she knew about Camp Tennis?"

"Ha. *Kamptegnet.* It means Battle Sign. It was a right-wing magazine published in Denmark during the Nazi occupation. I came across it while researching Danish anti-Semitic groups. It was a nasty publication, patterned after *Der Stürmer,* the Nazi newspaper that displayed grotesque cartoon drawings of Jews with misshapen faces. I'm hoping there's a connection between the two publications."

"Britta maintains there were no anti-Semitic organizations in Denmark. She said it was religiously tolerant society. No Nazi sympathizers. To quote her, 'Growing up Jewish in Denmark was very pleasant.'"

"It may have been for her, but that doesn't mean there weren't any anti-Semitic groups. I've come across several of those groups, and many of their members were prosecuted after the war. Right now, I'm trying to find out if either Henryks or his father were members of Denmark's National Socialist Party."

"There was a Denmark National Socialist Party? You've learned that?"

Liam nods. "Yeah, the DNSAP. It was a minority political party. It held two percent of the Parliament seats. There were other fringe organizations, paramilitary groups that supported the Nazis and sought to undermine the Danish government, but before the war they were minimal. The question is whether Henryks participated in those groups. Did Ole or his family assist the Nazis in furtherance of their agenda, either before or during the occupation? Were they informers?"

"And you have information on the members in those groups?"

"Nope."

"Remember, not just Henryks. You have to research the name *Hendricksen* as well."

"I know, but I'm running into roadblocks. My research takes me only so far and then I'm stymied. Much of what I need can't be found online. I'm afraid the answers lie elsewhere, deep in Danish historical records. It's daunting. There's just too much. I need a guide. That's why I contacted Dr. Robert Lundhill, professor emeritus of Nordic history at the university. He's agreed to meet with me this afternoon."

"Good work. I'll handle Britta's interview without you today. How did you find out about Lundhill?"

"My friend John Lawrence knows him."

"John Lawrence, the golfer?"

"Golfer and scholar. He's friendly with Dr. Lundhill, and that's the only reason he's agreed to meet with me. Lundhill is a renowned historian who has written extensively on the Scandinavian countries, and he doesn't normally give interviews."

"Maybe he's come across the name Henryks in his research; wouldn't that be lucky?"

"He hasn't. Neither Henryks nor Hendricksen. I had to tell him about the lawsuit up front. I didn't want to be sneaky in my request to interview him, and he appreciated it. He already knew about the lawsuit anyway. There's another good reason for me to seek out Dr. Lundhill. Although Britta is very thorough, we're only getting what she remembers about what she observed, in other words, her teenage perception. She saw the occupation through her schoolgirl experiences."

"GOOD MORNING, EVERYONE," Emma says in a lively tone as she and Britta enter the room. Britta is dressed for spring in a light blue cotton suit and a soft red beret. She smiles and sets her straw purse on the table. "I hope we're not too late."

"Not at all," Catherine says, "right on time. Are you ready to have your memory prodded?"

Britta is not sure how to take that. "My memory is just fine, thank you. It doesn't need any prodding; it's there at my command. Fully cooperative."

"All right, then. When we broke last week, you had just finished telling us about the day the Germans occupied Denmark."

"That's right; April 9, 1940. As I said, it was totally unexpected, and everyone was shocked; my father, King Christian, members of the cabinet, all of them. Imagine waking up to see Wehrmacht soldiers marching through your streets in formation like they were in Berlin marching down Unter den Linden. There would have been absolute panic in Copenhagen had it not been for King Christian X. He came on the radio with an elegant address and told everyone to stay calm. He said the Germans did not come to kill us or rule us. We had not been conquered. Denmark had signed a cooperation agreement with Germany, and the agreement promised that there would be no interference with our daily activities. Our domestic affairs would be managed by the Danish government just as before."

"I thought you said that the king had limited authority."

"Well, he did, but he was the titular head of the country. His legal influence was mostly ceremonial, but the people loved our king. He was a symbol of the Danish spirit. He would ride his horse through the streets of Copenhagen almost every day." Britta's eyes brighten and she smiles at the memory. "He'd wear his royal tunic with golden epaulets and rows of shiny brass buttons, his leather britches and black boots. He'd sit high in the saddle and smile and wave at everyone as he took his morning ride. Children would follow him on their bicycles. People would come out just to wave at him.

"On this Tuesday morning, when the German soldiers swarmed our city, not only did he reassure us with his radio address, but he took his morning ride. It was an affirmation of normalcy. It was reassurance. He was still the king, and we were still Denmark. Do not fret.

"Grethe, who had gone out to see the king, ran back to get me. 'Come, Britta,' she urged, grabbing my arm. 'We have to go to the park. Everyone is going.' We ran all the way to Copenhagen's central park, Fælledparken; a beautiful park with acres of trees, a pond with swans and a children's playground. Many a night my parents would take us to stroll and enjoy the serenity. There were wonderful evening concerts and a dance pavilion. How we loved that park," she says wistfully. "I still do, you know. I miss it terribly." Something comes to her mind and it derails her. For a moment, she pauses to spend time with her memory. She reaches down, pulls a handkerchief from her purse and dabs her eyes. "And I miss Grethe more than you can imagine."

Catherine smiles. "It does sound enchanting, Britta. I'd love to see Copenhagen myself one day." She gives Britta a moment to get settled and then says, "All of your descriptions of life in Copenhagen paint a lovely picture, and I wish we had the luxury of spending more time talking about them. But we don't. I don't mean to rush you, but we have a deadline and we should get on to where Ole Henryks or his family come into the narrative. We can't lose sight of the fact that we have a drop-dead date in less than four weeks. We have to get to the point where Henryks collaborates with the Nazis."

Britta sniffles and flicks away a tear. "Yes, of course. I understand. But you see, what I'm telling you is so important, because here, on the day the Nazis invaded Copenhagen, with their tanks and their troops and their armored vehicles flooding our streets, my sister came home to fetch me, and we joined our people who gathered in the park to sing patriotic songs. Thousands of us on the great lawn, all together, just to sing. Can you understand that? We knew who Germany was, what it had done to Poland, Austria and Czechoslovakia. We knew what a warmonger Hitler was. Yet there we stood, my sister and I, and we sang Danish songs with our people. I held my sister's hand and she squeezed mine. Tears were visible on her beautiful face. Tears of pride, Ms. Lockhart. She was pure Denmark. They had crossed our borders and entered our world, but our spirit was unbroken. Our king rode his horse and we sang in the park." Britta tightly closes her fists. Her shoulders shudder and tears fill her eyes. Emma reaches over to place her hand on her grandmother's arm.

"Our people never lost their identity. You must understand that, because the unity of our spirit was the reason we were able to rescue our Danish Jews. No other occupied country did that. Only Denmark, and only because we were united. Three years later, when the deportation order came down, Denmark stood tall in solid defiance just like we did on that April morning." She pauses and points her arthritic finger at Catherine to make her point. "Except for Ole Hendricksen and his ilk. They were traitors and they betrayed us." With that, Britta gives way to her tears.

Emma reaches over and puts her arm around her grandmother's shoulders. "Bubbe, it's all right. We do understand."

Catherine pours a glass of water and sets it on the table. The room is silent. Britta reaches for the glass, but her hand is unsteady. Emma holds it out for her, but she declines. Britta struggles to get back on track, but it is apparent that her forward progress has stalled. Emma finally says, "Ms. Lockhart, I'm afraid this is all very emotional for my grandmother. I think it would be best if we stopped for today."

Catherine agrees.

CHAPTER TWELVE

—⁂—

LIAM ARRIVES AT the campus quadrangle, walks past several conclaves of students and enters the History Building. Dr. Lundhill's office is on the third floor. The elderly historian is seated behind a large oak desk covered with piles of papers. A pipe rack with five beautifully carved wooden and meerschaum pipes surrounding a golden tobacco jar sits to the side as a paperweight. Dr. Lundhill doesn't smoke anymore, his health and campus policy prohibit smoking, but now and again he'll hold an unlit pipe between his teeth. Behind him is a wall of books, many of which display titles in foreign languages. His windows overlook the quadrangle, although reams of reading material stacked on the windowsills obscure the view. The professor, a short stocky man with a mop of white hair and bushy white eyebrows, motions for Liam to be seated.

"Thank you for agreeing to see me," Liam says. "I appreciate fitting me into your busy schedule."

Dr. Lundhill raises his eyebrows and nods an obligatory you're welcome. "Mm hmm," he intones. "It is not my practice to provide assistance to someone engaged in a lawsuit. My duties here at the university and my scholastic endeavors are my primary focus. While your project is intriguing, I must tell you that I will not take sides in your litigation, nor do I intend to become a witness. As long as I have your assurance that you won't involve me in your court case in any way, I am willing to assist you as a resource. I'll answer what I can, and if I can't, I'll try to point you in the right direction."

"Thank you, Doctor, that's all I ask. As you know, my wife represents Britta Stein, who is accused of—"

"I know all about the case. I read the newspapers. I watch the newscasts."

"Then before we get started, I'd like to ask you if you are personally familiar with Ole Henryks or any member of his family?"

"I am not. I'm aware that he owns a restaurant and bar. I've eaten there on a couple of occasions, but not recently. It was rather bland tavern fare, but a jolly place."

"Would you have come across Ole Henryks in any of your research or studies? Or perhaps his father, Viktor Henryks? I am told they may have gone by the name of Hendricksen."

The professor considers the question and then says, "Not that I recall."

"Mrs. Stein is defending a defamation suit by insisting the statements she made about Henryks are true."

"I am aware of that. So is everyone who owns a TV."

"Right. Then you know that she accuses Ole Henryks of collaborating with the Nazis during the war. Thus far in our office interviews she has focused on the—"

Dr. Lundhill holds up an index finger. "You should be careful what you say to me, Mr. Taggart. I am not covered by the attorney-client privilege, nor am I covered by the attorney work product privilege. I am not part of your defense team. If you repeat what Mrs. Stein told you or her attorney in confidence, it would lose its privileged character."

Liam smiles. "Yes, it would. And I will be very careful, but in our interviews so far, she has just been giving us background on the Jewish community and a brief overview of the events of April 9, 1940. She strongly insists that prior to the invasion, Danish Jews were never singled out or subject to discrimination by Danish society. She says that they were always treated equally and fairly. Is that your understanding?"

"It is."

"But when it comes to April 9, 1940, her memory has boundaries. She was a fourteen-year-old child who remembers waking up, going off to school and seeing German soldiers marching through the streets. She said that it was a complete shock to everyone, including her father, who was a member of Parliament. I know the Nazis acted swiftly and without notice, but it's hard for me to believe that Denmark was totally surprised by the sudden invasion. Maybe it was a surprise to a child. German soldiers just don't suddenly materialize out of nowhere. If you wouldn't mind, I'd like to begin by getting a better understanding of exactly what happened in April 1940."

The professor nods his head and pulls on his lower lip. "Mm hmm. I'll try. Your client is not wrong. She may have been fourteen years old, but her description is fairly accurate. Denmark did not anticipate a German invasion. Denmark had a history of remaining neutral in European conflicts. In fact, in May 1939, a little more than three months prior to Germany's attack on Poland, Denmark and Germany signed a nonaggression pact. To all intents and purposes, there was no reason for the Danes to fear Germany on April 9, 1940.

"Two days earlier, on April 7, 1940, German Generalmajor Kurt Himer, chief of staff of the German 31st Corps, secretly boarded a plane bound for Copenhagen. He was dressed in civilian clothes with no outward indication of his rank or station. His uniform was sent by separate courier. In his pocket, he carried a sealed envelope addressed to the German Ministry in Copenhagen. It contained an ultimatum to be delivered to the Danish foreign minister at the commencement of Hitler's Operation Weserübung, Germany's planned invasion of Denmark and Norway."

"Britta told us that the Scandinavian countries had always been neutral and intended to stay that way. Why did Germany decide to attack?"

"Hmm. Geopolitical. It was all about shipping channels, and to a lesser degree, it was defensively necessary. Germany was dependent on a continuous supply of Swedish oil and iron ore which was transported overland through northern Norway to the Atlantic and then shipped south along the western Norwegian coast. If Britain were to occupy Norway, or bring the Norwegians into a joint defense pact, the route for Germany's essential supplies would have been cut off. For the Reich government, occupation of Norway was a must."

The professor unrolls a map and spreads it out on the desk. "The invasion of Norway was not an easy matter. As you can see, from Hamburg to the Norwegian shore would be several hundred miles over the North Sea, vulnerable to British air and sea attacks. However, proceeding on land through Denmark would provide a safer and quicker passage. Germany intended to establish bases in northern Denmark as amphibious and aerial embarkation points. Thus, the occupation of Denmark was largely a consequence of geography.

"April 8, 1940, was Denmark's last day as a free nation. Generalmajor Himer arose and walked down to the harbor to carry out his preplanned surveillance. Was the harbor free of ice? It was. Could the Germans safely land troops by naval transport? They could. The weather was warm that April and the harbor was quiet. He transmitted his findings by secret code to the German command and German troops were on the move.

"The next day, April 9, Himer rose at four a.m. At four-twenty a.m., he instructed the German ambassador to call the Danish foreign minister, Peter Munch, and demand an immediate meeting with the heads of Danish government. At the quickly assembled meeting, Himer informed the foreign minister that German troops were already moving into Denmark. He falsely told Munch that the occupation was necessary to protect Denmark from an imminent British attack; Denmark would become a German protectorate. Unbeknownst to the Danish government, German forces were already on Danish soil and just after dawn, a coal freighter sailed into Copenhagen harbor and docked at Langelinie Pier. It was not carrying coal, of course. The holds were filled with thousands of German soldiers who disembarked and began occupying the city.

"The Danish government asked for time to consider Himer's ultimatum. The request was granted—six hours. Either agree to the protectorate, or the Luftwaffe, which was currently in the air over Copenhagen, would unleash its bombs.

"Of course, the Danish delegation protested. They insisted that they were not Germany's enemy, that there was a joint nonaggression pact and that they intended to stay neutral. Predictably, their protests were rejected. Himer assured Denmark that Germany did not want to annex or even govern Denmark. They would sign a mutual collaboration and cooperation agreement. They would peacefully coalesce. There would be no interference with domestic affairs. The agreement would specifically

provide that Germany would not impose any of its domestic policies, including its racial laws, upon the people of Denmark. Germany knew
that would be a stumbling block, and so it was never an issue. There were
only seven thousand Jews anyway, a small minority.

"Himer insisted that German forces would be present only to protect
Denmark and to provide safe passage for the German troops bound for
Norway. Given no choice in the matter, Denmark agreed three hours
later. So, it is quite likely that young Britta Stein, her father and the rest
of Copenhagen would have been shocked to see German troops marching through the city when they woke up on the morning of April ninth."

Liam looks up from the notes he is taking. "Mrs. Stein remembers
that life went on as normal in the months following the occupation."

The professor tips his head from one side to the other. "I suppose that's
true to some extent; but after all, they were an occupied country. If anything, the German occupation was a boon to the Danish economy. German soldiers had money and they liked to spend it. Danish restaurants
and businesses were happy to serve them. Commerce with the German
occupiers was brisk and commodious. German troops had been told that
they shared a common racial ancestry with the Nordic countries, that the
Danes were their little Aryan brothers, and that they should be treated
well."

"Really?"

"There are some writings to suggest that Hitler regarded the people
of the Scandinavian countries as the purest Aryans. To him, they would
eventually be breeding stock for Germans."

Liam curls his lips in a sour expression. "I'd like to discuss that subject
with you further," Liam says, "but I'm under some pressure to discover
information about organizations of Danish collaborators and sympathizers, those who aided the Nazi cause."

The professor nods his understanding. "There were organizations
that collaborated, sympathized or furnished information to the Nazis;
no doubt about it. Some were small and others much larger. Indeed, as
the war progressed, there were factories in Denmark that manufactured
weapons for Germany. Those were what we might call the corporate
collaborators. For example, the Globus factory in Copenhagen manufactured V2 rockets that were sold to Germany and used to bomb England.

The Riffel Syndicate manufactured machine guns in Copenhagen and sold them to the Germans." The professor rubs his mustache. "That is, until both of those plants were blown up by the Danish resistance. If Henryks collaborated with the Nazis, it's likely he would have been a member of one of the smaller anti-Semitic groups."

"In her interviews, Britta told us that there were no anti-Semitic groups in Denmark either before or during the war. She seemed to think there was very little sympathy for German racial policies in Denmark."

"I'm afraid she was naive."

"That could very well be. I've come across a newspaper and I mentioned it to Britta, but she had no recollection. Are you familiar with a newspaper called *Kamptegnet*?"

"Of course. It was filth. Aage Andersen, a virulent anti-Semite, owned and ran that publication. He was a member of the National Socialist Party of Denmark. In fact, he ran for president of the party in 1935 and lost. Because he had written so many vicious statements about Jews, the party considered him to be a liability. After his rejection, he went on to found the National Socialist Workers Party, and after that the Danish Anti-Jewish League. In 1938, two years before the invasion, Andersen was sentenced to prison for his antireligious statements. So you see, there were anti-Semitic enclaves, although they only appealed to a small minority of the Danish population. What is your interest in *Kamptegnet*?"

"In one of the editions, there is a notation that it was printed by the Hendricksen Printing Company."

Dr. Lundhill shrugs. "That may or may not be helpful for you. Hendricksen or Hendersen are not unusual names in Denmark, and Andersen might have paid one or several companies to print his rag. It didn't mean they shared his philosophy. Keep in mind, *Kamptegnet* was an underground publication and its malicious content broke the law. It printed a stream of anti-Jewish rhetoric straight from Germany. One famously quoted *Kamptegnet* line was 'No peace on earth as long as even one Jew is alive.' Straight Nazi filth. It's unlikely any reputable printing company would have risked its license by being closely identified with a Nazi publication. Still, times were tight. Money is money. An occasional small side printing job would have paid some bills."

"Small printing job? It was a newspaper."

"It never had much of a circulation. A few thousand at best. It was patterned after Julius Streicher's Nazi trash, *Der Stürmer*. In fact, much of the content, the articles and pictures were supplied directly from Streicher to Andersen. *Kamptegnet* was a low-budget concern, but it survived throughout the war thanks to a monthly supplement of 8,000 krone supplied by the Reich minister to Denmark."

"Hendricksen Printing Company appeared on two separate editions I was able to get my hands on," Liam says. "Perhaps they printed other editions and formed a closer relationship."

"I suppose, if indeed it was *your* Hendricksen. Was Viktor Hendricksen the owner of the Hendricksen Printing Company?"

"I don't know. That's another matter I've been unable to ascertain from Chicago."

"There would be records in Copenhagen. I can give you a number of sources should you choose to travel there." The professor glances at his watch. "I'm afraid I have a class starting in ten minutes. I'm sorry, but I really must go now."

CHAPTER THIRTEEN

———— ∞∞∞ ————

"In the spring of 1940," Britta says at the next session, "my sister was seventeen and in her last year of high school. Grethe had a large circle of friends; she was immensely popular, and she was well-respected. She was elected to the student council, and she was also the school's delegate to the Danish Union of Student Councils. She had a handsome boyfriend and a million girlfriends. I was always in awe of my sister.

"Before the Nazi occupation, teenage life was easy and relatively unrestricted. The streets were safe, crime was negligible and, like young people everywhere, Danish kids looked forward to the weekends. There were movies, sports, clubs and of course the dances. Big band music coming out of America was popular at the time. Benny Goodman, Glenn Miller. Swing music. 'Jumpin' at the Woodside,' 'In the Mood.'" Memories play out in Britta's mind like a scrapbook, and she has a nostalgic smile. "'Doin' the Jive,' that was my favorite," she says.

"My sister loved to dance; you should have seen her. High-waisted skirt, a little above the knee, that would swing out and twirl when she danced, mirroring the movement of her long blond hair. There was a popular hall in Copenhagen, the Palace, where the older kids could go. I loved to dance too, but I was only fourteen, and I wasn't allowed to go to the Palace. And I didn't have a boyfriend.

"Then came April 9, the invasion, the Cooperation Agreement, and everything changed. German soldiers, rifles slung on their shoulders, walked casually on the sidewalks and congregated on the corners. War planes flew overhead on their way to bases in the north. Nazi motorcycles, trucks, jeeps, and strange vehicles they called half-tracks, rolled down our cobblestone streets. The European war was heating up. Within the next several weeks, Germany would invade and conquer Belgium, Holland, Luxembourg and France. Their conquests seemed boundless and unstoppable. Europe was Germany's for the taking, and Denmark was a staging area for their northern ambitions.

"Even though Denmark's government was operating as before, everywhere we looked there were green and brown uniforms, and everyone knew the Nazis were here to stay. And there was nothing we could do about it. Though they did not actively interfere with our daily activities, it was devastating and demoralizing to us.

"My father, like most Danes, didn't trust Germany, and by logical extension, didn't trust the soldiers in our streets. We had all heard stories about the German military and their brutality in Nazi-occupied countries. We were told to stay away from the soldiers. Don't talk to them, don't confront them. Our parents set rigid rules, strict curfews. Come straight home from school and stay home. In truth, my father didn't want us going out at all. I could live with it, but not Grethe. She was nearly eighteen, and she was in a relationship. Lukas was twenty-one. He was tall and very thin, but with big shoulders. He had floppy blond hair and big ears, which I teased him about. He was an athlete, a world-class runner, and whenever he competed, Grethe and I would be there on the sidelines screaming for him. He had qualified for the 800 meters and the 4 x 400 relay in the Olympic Trials and was due to compete in the 1940 Tokyo Olympics. Unfortunately, the Olympics were canceled in 1939 and did not resume again until 1948. But Lukas had won several medals in university events and was one of the best athletes in Denmark. And he was plain crazy about Grethe. Who wouldn't be?

"Lukas was in his second year at the University of Copenhagen, studying chemistry. Grethe was finishing high school and was going to enter the university in the fall. You can imagine how well a curfew went over with her. No dance halls. No Lukas. She and my father locked horns; there was shouting, screaming, slamming doors and threats to leave.

Mama would be crying and pleading. Father was trying to reason with her, but Grethe wanted no part of the new rules.

"My father wasn't entirely wrong. German soldiers were everywhere. They dined in the restaurants, sat in the cafés and strolled about in the evening. They were Nazis and my father saw them for what they represented. But Grethe and her friends saw them differently. They didn't feel threatened. The soldiers weren't hassling anyone or arresting anyone. They were young, friendly and sociable, and they walked the streets with swagger and a smile. They knew that Denmark was a cushy assignment, they had been told to be nice and they didn't want to screw it up. They called their service in Denmark *Sahnefront,* which is German for Cream Front; easy, smooth and lots of dairy products. Their brother soldiers were fighting in Poland, France, Belgium or on the eastern front. So the soldiers in Copenhagen weren't interested in causing any trouble or creating an incident.

"Teachers warned us as well. Don't confront the soldiers. Don't talk back, especially if they give you an order. But the German soldiers weren't authorized to give orders to civilians. They were there to be garrisoned, to ensure Denmark's neutrality and provide for safe passage to the troops attacking Norway. Danish police still patrolled the streets and maintained law and order. As the days and weeks passed, uniformed soldiers could be seen shopping in the stores, playing soccer in the park, going to the theater and being quite friendly with locals. They were even seen dancing in the dance halls."

"Did that mean that Denmark's attitude toward the occupation was changing?"

Britta starts to answer, catches herself, thinks for a moment and finally says, "The answer is yes, it was changing, but on divergent paths. At some point, the attitudes of young people began to sharply split from those of our parents and their generation. We began to feel the loss of Danish pride. We felt that Denmark shouldn't have rolled over so easily. We began to resent the humiliation, the disgrace of being an occupied country. Signing an agreement giving up our national autonomy without firing a single shot? A protectorate? Like we were little children? There was no way the youth of Denmark would approve of such domination. It was a blow to our national identity. Our generation needed a reason to feel good and it wasn't going to come from our parents. And I believe that was the start of the resistance. Soon after the invasion, reports began to roll in about the fighting in Norway and we cheered for the Norwegians. They were brave. We wanted to do something brave.

"We listened to reports coming out of Norway. We learned that on April 9, the same day that King Christian and the Danish government were handed the German ultimatum, a similar demand was handed to Norway's King Haakon. Same terms; either surrender your autonomy to Germany under a cooperative agreement or be annihilated. But unlike Denmark, King Haakon and the Norwegian Parliament rejected the ultimatum. They refused to become a Nazi protectorate. They refused to allow German soldiers to occupy their country. Germany immediately attacked, but the Norwegian army fought back. They stood their ground. They even sank a German ship carrying a thousand soldiers. They fought bravely, and to the young people of Denmark, they became our heroes.

"Although our regular radio stations were a little cautious about criticizing Germany, we were able to follow the battles in Norway on the BBC and on Danish rogue radio stations. We rooted for Norway. British battleships came to Norway's aid in the coastal cities and we cheered. King Haakon was able to escape to Britain and establish a government-in-exile. We were so proud of them; Norway was fighting, and our parents and our leaders had capitulated without a fight."

Catherine shakes her head. "That was pretty foolish thinking, Britta. We know what happened to Norway."

"True. Heroes or not, Norway was unable to hold off Germany for more than a month, and for that they paid a heavy price. Reprisals were swift and brutal. Norwegian soldiers were captured and executed on the spot. Resisters were hanged in the streets, or shot, their bodies left for others to retrieve. 'You see,' our parents said to us. 'Do you still think we were weak or cowardly?'"

"Did the young people think that Denmark should have fought the Nazis? Was that realistic?"

"No, of course not. That would have been foolish. Military resistance was impossible, but we felt some opposition should be shown to the continued occupation. Someone should stand up and declare that we are Danish. We have pride. We refuse to lie down and accept a life of subjugation. We argued that the Cooperation Agreement was a fraud. Cooperative governance of Denmark was nothing more than a paper illusion; our so-called independence existed at Hitler's sufferance. For the youth, for our generation, we were ashamed, and we felt there were things that we should do."

In Catherine's mind, the clock is ticking, and it is time to steer the conversation. She holds up her hand. "Britta, I have the feeling that we're straying a bit. We need to focus on Ole Henryks, on how he was a traitor, how he became a Nazi collaborator. We need to stay on subject. Norway's resistance is heartwarming, but we're losing track . . ."

Hearing that scolding, Britta stiffens. "I am not losing track! Everything I'm telling you is about heroes and traitors. Norway inspired us to resist. To organize. To form partisan resistance cells. Some of our young people formed secret clubs to create havoc for the occupiers. Some of the kids would flatten tires on Wehrmacht jeeps, or cut telephone wires to German offices. Einar Andersen threw a dead skunk through the window of a German barracks. Ultimately, the organized resistance grew, and the acts of sabotage became far more serious. Don't you understand? The youth of Denmark were heroic, but sadly, not all of us. Some were cowards, some were opportunists, and some were informers; like Ole and William Hendricksen."

"Okay then, what did Henryks do that made him a collaborator? It has to be more than marching in a German parade."

"Don't worry, I'm getting there. My point is that there were many in Denmark who not only detested the German takeover but who were willing to do something about it. And it began with the young people, Grethe's generation, who refused to accept their parents' complacency. Initially, the resistance was no more than mischief. Fires were lit beneath German vehicles. Paint was flung on the wall of a German office. Rocks were thrown through windows. But in the years that followed, the resistance grew in intensity, and by then it wasn't just the youth."

"Did Henryks join any of the youth groups that were committing acts of resistance?"

"Hendricksen, you mean. I should say not. Ole was in a group that wore blue shirts, as I told you before. I believe they were called the Blue Shirt Club or the Blue Storm. I don't know what their professed purpose was, but it wasn't for Danish liberty. His family felt no shame. I told you, they were flat-out collaborators."

Catherine sets her pen down on the table. In her mind, she knows she must accelerate the narrative. She reaches over and gently places her hand upon Britta's. Britta's skin is smooth and cool. Translucent. Her ancient hand lacks substance; it is thin, discolored and a road map of veins. Catherine can feel tremors. "Please help me, Britta," she says kindly. "We've spent considerable time talking and as far as I can tell, we're not getting close to the specific proofs we need. I'm sorry that I'm forced to be blunt, but it's hard for me to imagine why all this background is so important."

"Do you want the whole story or do you want selected pieces? I thought you wanted to know."

"I do want to know, but I can't imagine . . ."

Britta knows that in this matter, Catherine is her only friend, and she must make her understand. "I know it's hard for you to imagine, Catherine, because at that moment when Hitler decided to rip up the agreement and send his Gestapo to capture us and send us to our death, the terror we experienced is clearly outside anything you can imagine. I am also sorry to be blunt. There were heroes and there were traitors. There were those that stood up for us and those that turned us in. In the court of law, you are not only my pathfinder, you are my voice. When you speak for me, I want you to feel the story of Denmark; feel it in your heart and in your soul. Then you will know why it is so important to expose a man like Hendricksen. In this regard you must trust me. Stay with me a little longer, my young friend, and feel what I feel. Come with me just a little farther and then it will be possible for you to imagine things, like a young girl hiding in a locked storeroom, where it's dark and musty and she's there with her parents and a little baby. She's there because outside, there are wolves, snarling, drooling, growling. Cowards, traitors, soulless informants have directed the wolves to the location. She dare not make a sound or leave to use the bathroom. She prays the baby will not cry. Her life depends on it."

Catherine is silent. Her lips are closed and she breathes quietly through her nostrils. Her eyes are being opened.

Britta continues, her head held high. "Imagine a young girl lying in a hospital bed even though she is not sick. There is an oxygen tent covering her head and a sheet pulled up over part of her face. The wolves are circling the hospital, searching for her. On occasion, one will enter the hospital ward, walk slowly down the aisle and scan the patients with his steely green eyes. He is hungry. He bares his teeth and they are sharp. Some informant has told this wolf that the young girl is there, but he does not see her. Yet. As the wolf passes, the young girl can feel his breath, but she must lie perfectly still with eyes closed, pretending to be near death.

"Imagine you are all alone, just five years old, and someone you don't know, a strange woman suddenly grabs you by the wrist and dashes off into the night, pulling you toward the sea. It is dark and cold, you are out of breath and you stumble, but you know you must outrun the wolves."

Britta looks at Catherine, past her eyes and into her heart. "Sounds terrifying, doesn't it, Catherine, and I know it is hard for you to imagine such a dark and hideous nightmare. Or the fact that it wasn't a nightmare at all. You have no point of reference to fathom the terror that overwhelms a young girl. The fear is beyond anything you have ever experienced. But if you stay with me, Catherine, I will bring you to an understanding. There were heroes, there were cowards and there were flat-out traitors."

Emma reaches over to pat her grandmother on the arm. "Bubbe, don't come down hard on Catherine, she's only . . ."

"Don't, Emma," Catherine says softly. "Bubbe is right. I have no idea. None of us do." Catherine stands. "When I speak for you, Britta, I will try to do so with the same conviction. We'll do this at your speed. I apologize for pushing you. Why don't we all take a quick breather."

LIAM AND CATHERINE walk out to the reception room. Catherine raises her eyes, flicks away a tear and shakes her head. "She was right, you know. I have no idea. Was I a monster to push her? To doubt her?"

Liam places his arm around her shoulders and brings her to him. "Don't ever think that. You're a lawyer and you're trying to do your job. Keeping her on target is the right move. You're trying to serve your client's interests."

"How does it serve my client's interests when I discount her intelligence? She knows what the court order says. She knows we need specific facts and that we are under a deadline. In truth, she's doing exactly what I want my clients to do; she's giving me the whole and not just pieces."

Gladys suddenly interrupts. "Liam, I don't know if it's important, but I've been seeing this dude walking back and forth in front of our office. He's got a paper bag in his hand. Sometimes he stops in front of our window like he's going to do something nasty, but someone else will come along and he'll scoot away like an alley rat. Whatever he's doing, it ain't right."

"How many times have you seen him?"

"A few, but I'm not always looking at the window, you know?"

"Is he out there now?" Liam asks.

"I'm not sure, I don't see him."

"Let's go take a look."

They walk out and peer up and down Clark Street, but Gladys shakes her head.

"I don't see him now."

"Can you describe him?"

"Caucasian, medium height, medium build, no facial hair. He's in a tan jacket and a red baseball cap pulled low over his head. Brown hair, I think. He's got a weaselly look about him, I ain't lyin'." Gladys shrugs. "Sorry. I'm not much help, I'm afraid."

Liam smiles. "You did well. Let me know right away if he comes back."

THE GROUP REASSEMBLES and Catherine picks up her notepad. "Britta, let's go back to where we left off," she says, and then she smiles. "Not the part about the wolves. I get that. I want to talk about the resistance. I have two questions. The first one intrigues me. I want to know what happened when Einar threw the skunk into the German barracks."

Britta chuckles at the memory. "We all thought it was pretty funny, I must admit. I think it must have happened in July, about three months after the invasion. It was very warm, and the German soldiers slept with their barracks windows open. One of our friends told Einar that he had killed a skunk, and Einar got the idea of tossing it into the German quarters. He got up at four-thirty and rode his bike carrying the skunk in a cloth sack. When he got to the barracks, he pulled the skunk out of the sack, dropped it through the open window and pedaled away as fast as he could. Apparently, the sleeping soldiers didn't discover it right away because it wasn't until an hour later that they came pouring out of the building. Several of Einar's friends lay in hiding across the street. The kids all scattered and met up later for a laugh."

Catherine, Emma and Liam are struck by the humor. "I had never heard that, Bubbe," Emma says between her bursts of laughter. "That's precious."

"Einar had dashed home and jumped into his bathtub," Britta says. "He was afraid the stink would give him away. He did a good job of cleaning up, but Maryanne, his girlfriend, wouldn't hug him or kiss him for a whole week."

"That's a wonderful story," Catherine says. "Here's my second question—it's more serious. How did your father feel about the rebellious students and their pranks? After all, he was a member of Parliament, which had accepted Germany's ultimatum not to resist."

"Well, he didn't approve, but let's be fair, my father, like the other parents, was worried that the kids might be captured and disciplined. Maybe even jailed. The Danish police were charged with enforcing the law. If they abandoned their duty, the Nazis would take over. It was dangerous. 'Foolhardy,' my father said."

"Liam!" Gladys yells from the other room. "That creep's out front again. He's lookin' around, peeping in the window and taking something out of his bag. I think he's gonna throw something. I'm going after him."

"Damn!" Liam says. "I have to catch that girl."

"Gladys'll get hurt," Emma says.

"No," Liam answers, "Gladys can take care of herself. I'm worried about the guy." He jumps out of his chair and dashes for the front door. The man takes off down Clark Street with Gladys fast behind him and

Liam behind her. They catch up to him two blocks away. Liam grabs him by his upper arms and pins him against a wall.

The man squirms and tries to break loose, but Liam's grip is strong. "What the hell, man, leave me alone. Who the hell are you?"

"What were you doing outside my office?" Gladys says. "What was you about to throw?"

"I wasn't throwin' nothin', you crazy bitch. I don't know what you're talking about. What office? Let me loose."

"Let me ask you that question again," Liam says, squeezing his arms. "What were you doing outside our office?"

"Look, I got a right to be on the sidewalk anywhere I please. I don't give a shit about your office. Now let go of me 'fore I call the cops."

"Maybe I do that for you," Gladys says. "Where's your paper bag, smartass, and don't hand me any bullshit, like you didn't have one."

"I don't know," he snaps. "I must have dropped it somewhere."

"What was in it?" Gladys says, her face inches from his.

"Like it's any of your business, bitch."

Liam looks at Gladys, smiles and raises his eyebrows. "You know, buddy, I ought to let this Puerto Rican girl bust your ass. And don't think she can't. What was in the bag?"

"It was my lunch. Now let me go before you end up in more trouble than you can handle."

Unfazed, Liam tightens his grip. The man winces in pain. "Really. You working for the Mafia now, tough guy? Who sent you?"

"Your mother, after I finished with her."

One straw too many. Liam grabs a fistful of the man's jacket lapel, lifts him in the air and slams him back against the brick wall. "Who. Sent. You. I'm losing my patience."

The man swallows hard. "Look man, let me go, okay? I got paid a hondo to look in a window and tell him what I saw. That's it, okay?"

"You didn't answer my question. Tell me who? Who paid you?"

"I don't know, I swear. Some guy. Paid me a bill to tell him who was sitting in an office. That's it. I swear."

"What was in the bag?"

"Nothing. My lunch, I'm telling you. I dropped it when you and this crazy bitch was chasing me."

Liam spins him around, lifts his wallet out of his back pocket, snaps a cell phone picture of the driver's license and says, "Mr. Rivers, you tell Six-o'clock Sparks if I ever see you hanging around my wife's office again, I'm gonna break both your arms. And then I'm coming after him. You got it?"

The man shrugs himself loose, straightens up, turns and walks away, mumbling a string of profanities. Liam starts back to the office when he spies a paper bag lying on the sidewalk. Inside is a can of spray paint.

CHAPTER FOURTEEN

———⌖———

RED AND WHITE streamers crisscross the ceiling. Paper flags of Denmark—white cross on a bright red background—flap and rattle from the light fixtures. Helium-filled balloons are tied to weights on the tabletops. The lights are bright, the music is pumping and the combined noise of multiple conversations in the overcrowded room all serve to ramp up the decibel level. The Melancholy Dane is celebrating "Ole Appreciation Night." Revelers stand shoulder to shoulder, elbow to elbow, drinks in hand, hoisting them high, laughing, singing and toasting the evening's honoree. Behind the bar, a string of colorful metallic letters spell out "We Love You Ole."

A large cardboard sign is taped to the front window of the tavern reading, "Come One, Come All. Ole Appreciation Night. Show your support for our Hero. Festivities start Wednesday at 7:00 p.m. Special Guest—Retired Danish Major Jens Knudsen."

Street parking places are gone by 5:00 p.m. and two network TV trucks occupy the spots in front of the building. The bartenders on this special occasion are Nils Henryks and a group of lively young women in tight "We Love Ole" T-shirts. They can't fill drink orders fast enough. Ole stands near the bar shaking hands and receiving tributes. While the tavern has hosted many a large party in the past, it hasn't seen one rise to this level since Ole turned ninety and drinks were on the house.

At precisely eight o'clock, Sterling Sparks drains the last of his whiskey and says to the man next to him, "It's showtime." He weaves his way to the front of the room, picks up a microphone and steps up onto a chair. He waves his arm for quiet and announces, "On behalf of Ole Henryks and the entire Henryks family, I thank you all for coming this evening." He swivels around to face Ole, points a finger and says, "I guess you can see how many people love you, Ole." The crowd cheers. Sparks nods enthusiastically and blows a kiss toward the bar. "This man has spent a lifetime radiating friendship and camaraderie." Sparks pauses. "And courage!" More cheers.

"Most of you know Ole because you met him here at the TMD. Always a smiling face. Always happy to serve you a drink and share a story. You know the saying, 'No one is ever lonely at the TMD!'" More cheers arise, followed by the spontaneous chant, "Ole, Ole, Ole." Sparks bids the room be quiet. "Some of you know him from the Danish-American Association of Chicago where Ole is going to be inducted into the hall of fame. Some of you know him from the charities that he supports. No matter how you know him, you all share the same opinion; he's a first-class gentleman." The crowd roars in support.

"Tragically and sadly, as most of you already know, Ole has been attacked by a deranged woman who is trying to spread lies about him. She has defaced the walls of this restaurant with vile epithets." The crowd responds with a chorus of boos. "Maybe some people can ignore such slanderous attacks, you know, they can let them bounce off their shoulders like they don't matter, and say, 'Consider the source.' Maybe some people can paint over the words and think, 'I'm not going to let some meanspirited person get under my skin, because they don't count.' Vile insults can bounce off the shoulders of some people, but Ole isn't just some people. He's an emotional guy. He cares! All of you—the TMD regulars, friends, neighbors—you all know that Ole's not just *some people*. He cares!" The crowd cheers. Sparks solemnly nods his head. "He cares, and when someone speaks ill of him, he takes it in, and it hurts him. Bad.

"Of course, it's no secret that Ole and his family are war heroes. You all know that. They risked their lives to save others from the Nazis during World War II." Sparks points to the wall behind the bar. "Right there, that's a photograph of Ole and his father, taken at the very harbor where they saved hundreds of lives in 1943. Proof positive!" The crowd lifts their glasses and cheers, "To Ole!"

"I want each of you all to find a moment tonight to come over and look at that picture, and then keep it locked in your memory. Think about that picture when someone asks you if you read about the nasty statements that were spray-painted on the TMD walls. Tell that person straight out, 'It's a lie!' Look that person in the eye and set that person straight. Say proudly, 'I don't care what that demented woman had to say or write, I *know* Ole, and he's a hero to me!'" Cheers. "To Ole, to Ole!"

"Now folks, we are smack dab in the middle of this court mess, and I will tell you that things are going to get nastier before they get better. You're going to hear more slanderous statements from that Stein woman. She's going to say them out loud *in a public courthouse*! They're going to come out on TV, you'll read about them in the paper, or maybe some friend of yours will ask you if you heard about them. I want you to tell them, 'It's all bullshit! Ole's a hero!'"

The crowd begins to chant, "Bullshit, bullshit, bullshit!" followed by "Lock her up, lock her up!"

Sparks raises his hand. "We were informed just the other day in front of the Honorable Obadiah Wilson, that Mrs. Stein intends to counter our lawsuit with the outrageous and impossible defense of trying to prove that her filthy lies are really true." The crowd yells, "Bullshit!"

"It's a fact," Sparks says. "She intends to plead, under oath, that the vile statements she painted are true, even though she has not an ounce of proof; can you believe it? Of course, when she painted those words, she boxed herself into a corner. She has to say they're true because that is the only defense that's open to her. She has to *prove* her lies are true or she will go down in flames." Sparks smiles and raises his voice. "Five million dollars' worth of flames, folks. Five million! We all know there is absolutely no truth to any of her bullshit, so . . . Down. She. Goes!" More cheers and raised glasses and chants of "Down She Goes" are followed by another round of "Lock her up."

Sparks waves his hand from side to side. "I know they say that anything can happen in court, but don't you worry about a thing, folks. Sure as my name is Sterling Sparks, I'll take care of Mrs. Stein. You can bet the house on it." He nods and smiles in response to the applause. "Folks, I only have one more thing to say." He looks around the room, makes a long theatrical pause and shouts, "The next round's on me!" The crowd roars and pushes closer to the bar.

While the bartenders are dishing out the drinks, Sparks looks around the room and nods to the TV reporters he knows. One of them, a tall, shapely dark-haired woman in a tight knit dress, saunters over and says, "Hey Sparky, wanna give me a quick Q and A?"

Sparks leans over, gives her a kiss on the cheek, slides his arm around her narrow waist and gives her a squeeze beneath her rib cage. "Aw Janie, you're trying to take advantage of a weak man; you know I have a soft spot for you."

"You do, huh?" she responds coyly. "Then how about you give me a couple of your classic quotes to play at ten o'clock."

"I don't know, Janie. There's a lot of reporters here. If I start reciting my poetry they'll crowd around and take the focus off of Ole. You were here," Sparks says with a glib shrug. "There were lots of classic quotes."

"But you didn't give any exclusively to me." She sighs.

"This is Ole's night. Let the man celebrate."

Janie pouts. Her lower lip protrudes. "Sparky," she whines, "come on. For me."

Sparks takes a quick look around, gives her another squeeze and says, "All right, for what it's worth." He leans in and speaks quietly into her recorder, "Ole Henryks is a Chicago treasure. The city's impresario extraordinaire and a certified hero. Mrs. Stein picked on the wrong guy and I'm going to make sure that she has a bad day in court. I intend to press ahead for a quick trial."

"That's all?" Janie says.

Sparks winks. "For now."

Janie plants a kiss on Sparks's cheek, leaving him a dark red souvenir. "Thanks, Sparky, you're a doll."

Sparks smiles, walks over to a middle-aged man in a military-style shirt and says, "It's your turn, Jens." Then Sparks lifts the microphone, asks for quiet and says, "Ladies and gentlemen, may I present Major Jens Knudsen, a decorated Danish military major, now retired and living in Chicago. When the major learned about this event, he called me and insisted on coming and giving a testimonial. If anyone would know about Danish heroes, it would be Major Knudsen."

The major, a stocky, broad-shouldered man with a salt-and-pepper crew cut, accepts the microphone. "I guess I've known Ole for many years, ever since my aunt and uncle started bringing me to this restaurant when I'd visit them as a kid. My uncle and Ole would share fabulous stories of Copenhagen back in their day. They talked about the resistance, they talked about fighting the Nazis, they talked about saving lives. Oh, those were the days. My uncle, Ole and their buddy, Henning Brondum, were like the Three Musketeers."

The crowd turns its attention to Ole, who nods and smiles. "Henning, ya, we had a club. There were others. My friend Kai Nielsen. It was good times; when we were young. We went fishing; Henning had a boat."

The major continues, "And they were patriots, right?"

"Oh, ya."

"I never tired of hearing them tell their stories of courage and heroism. Brothers-in-arms. If my uncle was still alive, he would be here tonight to tell you what a stand-up guy Ole was and is!" Loud applause fills the room.

"Now my uncle is gone for twenty years, rest his soul, but whenever I want to feel close to him, I'll come over and ask Ole to share a story with me. I can tell you one hundred percent, from my personal knowledge and my uncle's knowledge, that Ole is a Danish treasure. A war hero! He fought those Nazis. And speaking for myself, I hope that Stein woman, like Mr. Sparks says, goes down in flames for all to see. I want Ole vindicated, and I know that Sterling Sparks is the man to do it."

The major returns the microphone to Sparks, who smiles and nods to the crowd. "If anybody would know about Ole, it would be Major Knudsen," Sparks says loudly. "Let's all give a big hand for the major." Loud cheers and applause. "Now folks, before we go any further, and before Ole has to have his hot milk and cookies and toddle off to bed," Sparks pauses to snicker at his joke, "I know you all want to hear from the man of the hour."

The crowd begins to chant "Speech, speech," and Sparks hands the microphone to Ole Henryks, who is shaking his head and trying to wave it off. "Speech, speech!" Henryks blushes, takes the microphone, swallows hard, starts to speak, turns his face to wipe away a tear and finally says softly, "I don't know what to say." He takes a breath. "Thank you all for coming here tonight. It warms my heart, it truly does. I don't know why this woman would want to write such dreadful things about me. I never did her any harm. I don't even know her. I didn't collaborate. I wasn't a Nazi. I worked my ass off during the war in a manufacturing plant owned by my wife's family. They made machinery. I worked long hours and I didn't have time to get into trouble. I loved Denmark." He looks at Sparks and his lips quaver. "Why did she do this, Sterling?" His voice breaks. "Why, Sterling? Why does she want to hurt me, I never did anything to her?" Henryks begins to weep and Sparks takes the microphone. The room is silent.

"Don't you worry," Sparks says with his arm around Ole's shoulder, "we'll take care of Mrs. Stein. You see all these people here tonight? They all came because they love you; and that's what counts. Turn up the music! Let's party!"

The music once again fills the room and pumps up the crowd. Nils Henryks walks over to Sparks and takes him aside. "Thanks for all you did tonight, Sterling. This evening is a beautiful tribute. My dad will remember this night forever and so will I." Sparks brushes off the comment. "No, I'm serious," Nils says. "But I'm worried about his health. This case is taking its toll on him. Isn't there anything you can do to make it go away? Sooner rather than later?"

Sparks nods. "Well, I got the judge to give us an insanely short schedule. I'm speeding it up as fast as I can. Lockhart has to file her defense in three weeks, giving us detailed descriptions of her proof. She won't have it. Obadiah will strike her defense and enter judgment for us shortly thereafter."

Nils pats him on the shoulder. "Great. I can't thank you enough."

Sparks shrugs a shoulder in a gesture which says, "No big deal." He struts off, walking through the crowded room. Many slap him on the back or shake his hand. While he's soaking in the compliments, a skinny man in a red cap makes his way over to him. "I got to talk to you," he says. "I didn't get the job done."

Sparks shakes his head in disappointment. "Yeah, I figured. I didn't see anything on TV. Too bad. What happened?"

"I got caught before I could spray anything."

Sparks is instantly disturbed. He pulls him aside. "What do mean you got caught? Who caught you? The police?"

He shakes his head. "Nah. The big Irish guy; the lawyer's husband. Chased me down the street with this crazy Puerto Rican broad and smacked me up good too."

"You didn't go in the middle of the night like I told you to, did you?"

"No, I messed up. I, uh, I had a conflict that night. I was otherwise detained. So I went the next day in the afternoon."

"Damn, Eddie, what did you say to Taggart?"

"Nothing really. I ditched the paint before he caught me. I didn't tell him nothing. Just that I was looking in the window. No worries; he doesn't know shit. But I'm sorry, I didn't get to paint the message on the window."

"He doesn't know who you are?"

"Not a clue. It's all cool."

"Did my name come up at all?"

"Hell, no. They don't know nothing about you. I just thought you should know that I didn't get the job done like you wanted. I guess I owe you a bill. Or I can try tomorrow night, if you want."

Sparks pats him on the shoulder. "Don't worry about it, Eddie. I don't want you going back there, but I have another job for you. One that's just as important."

"Thanks, man. This time I won't let you down, I promise."

"Come see me next Thursday; I'll fill you in."

Eddie nods and angles off toward the bar.

As Sparks heads for the door, he stops and turns around to view his handiwork; a room full of potential jurors, all in love with his client. "Pretty damn good night," he says quietly. "I wonder how much of this will make it to the ten o'clock news?"

He leaves The Melancholy Dane and walks out onto Wrightwood, where Janie is leaning against his car.

CHAPTER FIFTEEN

———⌘———

STERLING SPARKS'S EXPECTATIONS are on the money. Each of Chicago's four network news stations runs a segment on the well-attended fete at The Melancholy Dane. Several video clips are shown, including portions of Sparks's speech, Major Knudsen's testimonial and a full fifty-five seconds of Ole Henryks's tearful expressions of appreciation.

In a short clip, newswoman Jane Turner asks Sparks, "Does Mr. Henryks have any idea why Mrs. Stein wrote those statements?"

"I will provide the only plausible explanations: this doddering old woman has somehow confused Ole with some other person she knew or read about long ago in her younger years. To be frank, in her present condition I don't think Mrs. Stein could identify Santa Claus out of a lineup of Chicago aldermen."

Catherine and Liam are seated on the couch watching the newscast. They rerun it over and over, pausing it to watch the video of Henryks sobbing. They lock eyes. A palpable doubt is creeping in and taking hold. Liam says, "Do you suppose that it's possible? Could she have confused Ole Henryks with someone she knew years ago? Perhaps the boy she once knew as Hendricksen? Could she have misidentified Ole Henryks?"

"Could she?" Catherine sits back. "Hell, anything is possible."

"Henryks is really convincing. That was no act, Cat. No actor is that good."

"You could say the same thing about Britta. I've been sitting with her, listening to her for hours on end. I have to believe she is telling me the truth. I can't be that bad a judge of character."

"Cat, I don't think she's lying, I'm sure that someone named Hendricksen betrayed them or informed on them years ago, but this could simply be a case of mistaken identity. I don't think she's doddering, or senile, or demented, but to tell the truth, I don't know how well I could identify people from seventy-five years ago."

"She has a damn good memory. She narrates in extraordinary detail."

"I'm not talking about her ability to recall facts; I'm talking about her ability to facially recognize a person whom she hasn't seen in seven decades. And there's something else. Yesterday I went down the National Archives office on South Pulaski. You can research immigration and naturalization records there. All the Ellis Island stuff. By name and date. You may remember that I researched Eliot Rosenweig's immigration twelve years ago in that office."

"I remember. What did you find yesterday?"

"There are seven Hendricksens listed as immigrating to the U.S. during the relevant years. Only one of them came from Denmark, and that was in 1922. And his name was Asger Hendricksen. So, no Ole Hendricksen. But I did find the record for Ole Henryks, who immigrated to the U.S. from Denmark in 1947 with his wife, Margit."

Catherine clenches her fist. "You see! She's right. That's Ole Henryks! He would be the right age."

Liam does not share her excitement. "That doesn't solve our problem. We know that Ole Henryks immigrated here from Denmark. I was looking for Hendricksen."

A sly smile forms on Catherine's face. She has an idea. "What was Margit's maiden name?"

Liam shakes his head. "I don't know if it wasn't listed or if I just didn't look. Her name in the registry was Margit Henryks. Do you think that Britta knew a Margit somebody?"

"We're going to find out."

CHAPTER SIXTEEN

———✦———

"'Where are you two going?' my father asked Grethe and me," Britta says the next morning. "It was four o'clock on a September afternoon, and I had just come home from high school. It was the first month of the school year, and he expected me to be in my room getting busy with my studies, as he liked to say. In truth, I had just started my homework when Grethe burst into the room and said, 'Put your book down, Britta, and come with me. My friends and I are going to the Annex.' I had no idea what she was talking about or what the Annex was, but she was excited, and if my sister wanted to include me with her group, she didn't have to ask twice. We were about to leave, and that's when my father stopped us.

"'We're going to the university,' Grethe answered. 'There is an important program today in the Annex Auditorium. Professor Koch is giving a lecture, and everyone is going.'

"He looked at me askance. In his mind, it was reasonable for Grethe to attend a program at the university, but why me? 'Please let me go,' I said. 'Everyone is going.'

"'Is this part of your curriculum?' my father asked. 'Is it mandatory?'

"Grethe shook her head. 'No, it's open to the public.'

"'Hmm. A public lecture at the university and my high school student is eager to go?' My father knew something was up.

"'Everyone is going,' I repeated."

Catherine also picked up on the incongruity. "I thought you just said you had no idea what Grethe was talking about."

Britta responds with a slight shrug. "I didn't, but I wanted to go."

"You say this was during the first month of school?" Catherine asks.

"September 18, 1940. Like you, my father was skeptical. 'Britta, since when does my active little sailor choose to sit in an auditorium and attend a university lecture on a sunny afternoon?'

"'Papa, please,' I begged, 'everyone is going.'

"'Do you even know what the lecture is about?' he asked. He had me there, and I hung my head, but he yielded and pointed a warning finger at Grethe. 'Home before dark!'

"Once out the door and on our way, I asked Grethe if we were really going to a program at the university. Why was she so excited to go to a noncompulsory lecture in the late afternoon? Why would anyone go to school if they didn't have to? 'You'll see when you get there,' she said. 'Professor Koch speaks directly to us, Britta. To you and me, to the youth of Denmark. He understands our confusion, our shame, our collective humiliation in the midst of this German takeover. He talks about democracies and the cause of freedom. He talks about passive resistance. He talks about revival of the Danish soul.' Now I was beginning to lose interest, but as long as Grethe's crowd was going, I wanted to tag along.

"Throngs of young people were already in the university quadrangle when we arrived. We joined one of three long lines stretching from each of the auditorium's massive wooden doors. To me, it was a majestic sight. The University of Copenhagen is very old, more than five hundred years old, and sits in the center of the city. The architecture is Danish classic; large brown and red brick buildings with light stone accents, gabled roofs and arched windows. There were expansive grassy areas between the school buildings. And in the middle of this stately setting were thousands of teenagers and young adults, all coming together to listen to the words of a modern-day prophet."

Catherine nods. "It does sound impressive."

"The physical setting overwhelmed me. It was like looking into the past; I could see ghosts of ancient professors in their long dark robes and cloth hats rushing off to class hundreds of years ago. Standing there in line, this crisp, sunny fall afternoon, I felt envious of Grethe; she was enrolled here, she belonged. I eagerly looked forward to the time that I would study there as well. Sadly, that was not to be.

"By the time our line reached the door, the auditorium seats were all taken, and students were sitting on the floor or standing along the walls. Suddenly the room grew quiet, the side curtain ruffled, and Professor Koch stepped out onto the stage. As he made his way to the lectern, the auditorium burst into loud applause. He shook his head as if to say the applause was out of place and undeserved. The most powerful activist in Denmark was a modest man. I remember that evening so well, for it changed our lives."

"Wait a minute," Catherine says. "All these students stood in line just to hear a motivational speaker? You make him sound like a rock star. Professor Koch must have had quite an appeal."

"No doubt about it. It built rapidly. The students loved him, and in a way, he was a rock star. In 1940, Hal Koch was only thirty-six years old and devilishly handsome. He was a professor of church history."

Catherine's bewilderment increases. "A professor of church history changed your life? You and Grethe were both Jewish. Did you remain Jewish?"

"Yes, of course. The movement wasn't about religion."

"Yet the two of you, not to mention the thousands of other young people, were head-over-heels to hear a lecture by a professor of church history. I can't imagine."

Britta presses her lips together in a playful smile. "Is this another of those circumstances that you can't imagine? So many new revelations for you, young Catherine. For us, in 1940, Hal Koch was a force, and he was just getting started. Grethe and I were there because the hall was filled with our contemporaries, many of whom had heard the professor in a classroom setting. This was the first of his many public lectures. His reputation would grow quickly across Denmark, and he would develop an enthusiastic following. Word got around that his was the voice that refused to accept submission.

"On this September afternoon, Professor Koch raised his hand to the packed auditorium and in an instant the hall was silent. We sat still for a few moments while he surveyed the crowd. The only sounds were those of birdsong out on the lawn. Professor Koch tipped his head toward the door and smiled. 'She's singing for us,' he said. Then he leaned into the microphone and began by proclaiming, 'Our land and our people have become a plaything for great powers.' I could feel my heartbeat. There were quiet echoes and amens as though he was preaching in a church.

"'Violent forces threaten our entire existence,' he said, and he went on to explain that by existence he meant the Danish spirit. I have read and reread that speech just to remember that inspiring day. I see my sister sitting beside me on the floor near the corner of the stage, her eyes wide, her mouth open. From time to time, she would reach over and squeeze my arm so hard it left marks, saying, 'Didn't I tell you?' As she had predicted, Professor Koch was speaking directly to our souls. Grethe was mesmerized; much more so than I, I must admit. That lecture went on to define the rest of her life.

"His delivery was smooth and confident, and when he said, 'If you have felt that there is now only one thought that awakens with us in the morning, that follows us through the actions of the day and fills our minds when we turn in in the evening, then you know a little about what the Danish spirit is,' the entire auditorium rose to shout that they understood.

"That first lecture was printed in the *Copenhagen Journal* the next day and in the *Lederbladet,* the monthly publication of the Union of Danish Youth. It became the foundation stone of Denmark's resistance against the Nazi occupation. Professor Koch's second lecture brought even greater crowds and he began to do two lectures a day."

"Did you and Grethe continue to attend his lectures?"

"She did, but I could not; many of them were during the school day and in other cities. Grethe tried to attend as many as possible. In the fall of 1940, Hal Koch traveled around the country to almost every town or village, sometimes giving several lectures in a day. He spoke to farmers, factory workers, teachers, shopkeepers, fishermen and, of course, students. A groundfire was growing and he was the wind.

"After a few months, my father learned that Grethe and her boyfriend, Lukas, were cutting school to travel with Professor Koch. They had become part of his staff. Grethe hadn't told him she was missing school and Papa found out by happenstance. Never before had she been deceitful, and it upset my father. He called her into his study for one of his 'fatherly talks.' Did she realize that her studies were suffering? Did she realize that active resistance was against the law and could result in her imprisonment? Did she realize the danger?

"She replied that she hadn't missed that many days, she was current in her studies and was not involved in unlawful activities. She was but one of Koch's many followers, and happy to be included in a wave that was changing Denmark. It was a young people's movement. Grethe saw her generation as the ones anointed to rescript the failures of their parents. 'It falls to us to save Denmark's honor,' Grethe said, but my father shook his head. He admired her youthful passion and her dedication to the cause, but as a father, he feared for her safety. Justifiably, it turns out.

"Trying to make her see reason, my father warned, 'Never forget that Germany is a brutal, vindictive adversary, and Denmark is a tiny country. We are a bug that the Nazi boot can squash if the bug makes noise. We are treading water here in Denmark, hoping to wait out the war, but don't think for a moment that our inaction is weakness. It is caution. Germany could shut us down tomorrow.'

"Then came the bombshell. Grethe revealed her plans. 'Lukas and I are going to work for Professor Koch. We're going to join his advance team and help him set up for his lectures. We'll be going to the venues and providing for promotional and same-day activities. I want you to know that we may be on the road for several weeks at a time. I've made arrangements in two of my classes to submit a research paper in lieu of my attendance.' My father was heartbroken. This was not the vision he had for his older daughter. He expressed his opposition in the strongest terms. Did she understand that Nazi Germany was now in total control of central Europe? Did she not understand that Denmark's peaceful occupation was accomplished by a fragile agreement, and that open rebellion would not be tolerated?

"Grethe scoffed. 'That was no agreement, Papa, it was a surrender. It was appeasement on the scale of Neville Chamberlain's "Peace for our time." Bah! We sold our soul for a momentary pause in Hitler's quest for world domination. But I do agree with you in one respect; it is a fragile agreement, no sturdier than a sparrow's treetop nest teetering in the wind, which can be blown away in the snap of a Hitler tantrum.' My father shook his head, but in truth he was proud of her. 'We can regain our spirit,' she said. 'That is why we need Professor Koch. He's wise, he's careful; he talks about the Danish spirit but does not counsel open rebellion.'

"In the end, my father realized he was fighting a losing battle and he relented, subject to a few restrictions he knew he could not enforce. In practical terms, what could he do? She was eighteen and a woman on a mission. I'm sure he envied her dedication, her passion, her brilliance, her unbridled enthusiasm. Most of all he envied her freedom, unbound by responsibility to a constituency. My father loved Denmark every bit as much as Grethe, but now as a member of Parliament, his hands were tied. 'I must work for the safety of our people,' he would say, 'and right now that means cooperating with the German Reich.'"

Britta stops to pour herself a glass of water. She is tiring. Her hands are shaky, and Catherine thinks she has noticed a twitch on the left side of Britta's face. She helps her with the pitcher. "Are you all right?" she asks.

Britta nods. Catherine seizes the opportunity to change the subject. "Britta, when you were growing up, did you know a girl named Margit?"

Britta thinks for a second, twists her lips back and forth, and finally says, "I knew a Margit Simmons."

"Tell me about her."

"She was a year older than me. Same school. Popular girl. A little full of herself, by my standards, but okay."

"Did she go out with Ole?"

Britta furrows her forehead. "Unlikely. She was out of Ole's league. She was from a wealthy family. I don't think she would have been interested in a scruff like Ole Hendricksen."

"What if I told you that she married him?"

"I would be shocked. But who can account for taste? Maybe she was in trouble, maybe she needed to get out of Denmark; who knows? Did she actually marry him? Is that true?"

"Ole immigrated to the U.S. in 1947 with a wife named Margit."

"Was it Margit Simmons?"

Catherine shrugs. "What do you know about Margit's family?"

"I know that they had money. The Simmonses owned some type of manufacturing plant. I think it was called Simmons Machinery Works. I remember they made a lot of money during the war. Margit had her own car."

"Do you know what sort of machinery the Simmons company was manufacturing?"

Britta shakes her head. "No idea."

Catherine jots some notes and nods her head in satisfaction. At that moment, Gladys knocks and comes into the conference room with a plate of warm cookies and a pot of coffee. "You folks have been working pretty hard, I thought you might need a little break," she says with a proud smile. "Got these fresh-made cookies at Mrs. B's Bakery. Nothin' better in Chicago."

Britta perks right up and says, "Oh, my, that's just what I need."

"All right," Catherine says, "let's take a cookie break."

CHAPTER SEVENTEEN

⸻ ⬡⬡⬡ ⸻

"Before our break, we were talking about Grethe and Lukas," Catherine says.

Britta nods. "Throughout the spring and summer of 1941, Grethe's absences became more frequent, and her stays were for longer durations. She would send me postcards from Aarhus, Odense, Svendborg and towns I'd never heard of, many of them hundreds of miles away. Always the same upbeat messages. 'Hal was brilliant tonight.' 'Hal was spellbinding.' 'Large and enthusiastic crowd today.'"

"I don't understand why the German administration permitted him to hold these lectures," Catherine says. "He was clearly preaching resistance against the Nazis."

"Remember, the Cooperation Agreement allowed Denmark domestic control. The Nazis weren't censoring. If anyone was calling for insurrection or open rebellion, that would have been contrary to the Cooperation Agreement and also Danish law. As such, it would have been illegal, and the Danish courts would have prohibited such a movement. Koch never urged anyone to break the law; he was a nonviolent man preaching passive resistance. That said, many of Koch's followers had formed resistance groups; they called them clubs. At one point, there were seven hundred clubs in Denmark. Not all were nonviolent."

"Was Grethe a member of a resistance club?"

Britta answered with her eyes and a slight nod of her head. "Not at first, but Danish pride flowed through her veins. It was just a matter of time until she and Lukas joined a club. It was risky business. The Germans monitored Koch's lectures and even sent spies to attend. They kept notes on what was said and who attended. No doubt they made note of Grethe and Lukas.

"In 1940 and 1941, Germany was complying with the Cooperation Agreement, not because they felt it was a contractual obligation or because they had given their word. We'd seen what Hitler's word was worth. They complied because the arrangement was working for them and they didn't want to disturb it. Denmark was a staging area where German troops were garrisoned. They were there to protect their shipping channels and prevent Britain from gaining a foothold in northern Europe.

"From time to time, Koch's lectures riled up his followers and inspired local protests, which on occasion blossomed into acts of sabotage. In those cases, the German authorities would demand that the Danish police quell the disturbance and arrest the protagonists. That was the established chain of command. If it was necessary to conduct a trial, the offenders would be tried in Danish courts. All in all, it was an uneasy collaborative process, but it was working for both sides.

"In mid-November 1941, Grethe and Lukas were in the village of Kolding, where Professor Koch gave one of his most inspiring messages. 'You are in the Kimbric Peninsula,' he shouted, 'the cradle of Teutons; the Grotons. We are the Danes!' His speech was hitting home. As with many of his lectures, it was grounded in biblical morality. 'Can we look at ourselves today and say that we are practicing civic virtue? Are we following the Golden Rule? Are we our brother's keeper? If we answer affirmatively, are we not required to reject tyranny?' As it so often occurred, hundreds stood and shouted. Many were moved to tears.

"That night in Kolding, a group of young people, fired up by the lecture, left the program intent on damaging German vehicles and installations. Foolishly, Grethe and Lukas were swept up in the excitement and followed along. They made their way to a German communications center where several of the young men attempted to set a fire. Grethe would later concede that although she and Lukas did not participate in the arson, their presence was a mistake, a gross error in judgment. She said she had no prior indications of such destructive plans. As the fire began to blaze, the group was quickly surrounded by Danish police and taken off to jail. According to Grethe, the arrest scene was a contentious affair and some of the police became abusive. One of the officers grabbed Grethe and was roughly handling her. Lukas was alerted by her cries. You must understand how deeply Lukas loved Grethe. He rushed to her aid, ready to take on the entire police force. Two of the officers rebuffed him and pushed him down. Lukas didn't go down without a fight. He threw a number of punches but was quickly subdued. As he was being held in restraints, the officer who had accosted Grethe walked over, pulled out his club and slammed it on Lukas's wrist, breaking the bone.

"My father was working in his parliamentary office when he received a phone call. The caller identified himself as the precinct commander at the Kolding police station. With that sixth sense that fathers have, before another word was uttered, he said, 'Is she all right?' The commander said she was physically well, but she was in custody. There had been an incident at a communications facility and several young people were being detained. Kolding officials were trying to placate the Germans over minor fire damage. Given that Grethe was the daughter of a member of Parliament, the commander was inclined to offer special treatment. He would let her go, but only if my father would personally come and pick her up.

"Naturally, my father dropped everything, and one hundred fifty miles, two ocean causeways and three hours later, he pulled up to the police station in Kolding. The commander took him aside and said, 'If you wouldn't mind my passing along a word of caution, your daughter has involved herself with a dangerous crowd. They're a raucous bunch. They get all heated up by this professor character and they run off to cause mischief, some of it serious. I'm not one to say that your daughter's heart is in the wrong place, I'm sympathetic, but we must take care not to upset the current state of affairs, if you know what I mean. The Germans are losing patience with these rebellious youngsters. They are pressuring us to do something.'

"A few minutes later, he brought Grethe out. She was contrite, in that she regretted her actions of the previous night, but she was not sorry for being a member of Koch's inner circle. She was proud to be a self-professed resister. My father begged her to come home, and reattend her classes.

"'You're throwing away your gifts,' he said, 'don't you see that? You're going to be a brilliant physician, but a conviction for arson or criminal damage to property could very well kill your chances of getting a medical license. Don't jeopardize your future. As a doctor, you'll be helping Danes for the rest of your life.'

"Grethe was a hard sell. She was devoted to her cause. 'From where I stand, I can't see the rest of my life,' she replied. 'It's too far away and Nazi flags are in the way. Denmark is my future, but only if Danes unite to reject Nazi ideology. That is what Hal preaches; a united Danish spirit, undiluted by Germany's racism.'

"'Does Professor Koch preach rioting? Is that his method for achieving Danish unity?'

"Grethe shook her head. 'I was foolish tonight, I told you that. I shouldn't have gone off with that crowd. It won't happen again.'

"My father started to walk Grethe to the car when she stopped short. 'I can't leave without Lukas. He's still in the lockup, and he's only there because of me. You have to get him released. Please, talk to the police commander.'

"They met with the commander in his office. He told them that releasing Lukas presented a more serious problem; Lukas struck one of his officers. He was facing charges of resisting arrest and assault of a policeman. 'He's only in trouble because he was protecting me from one of your abusive officers,' Grethe said. 'The fat one with the mustache and the greasy hair. He thought the arrests gave him permission to grope a woman. He had his hands all over me. That's when Lukas came to my aid. He pushed the officer away, but others came and they threw Lukas to the ground. I think they broke his wrist. I want to file a complaint.'

"The commander took a deep breath. He didn't like what he was hearing. Apparently, there was a history with this particular officer, and the commander didn't want to process another complaint. An imbroglio connected to his precinct was the last thing he wanted. Especially involving the daughter of a member of Parliament. He asked Grethe and my father to wait while he checked the story with the other officers.

"A few minutes later the commander came out with Lukas, and my father drove him to a clinic."

"Grethe was lucky," Catherine says. "The commander might have faced discipline because of favorable treatment."

"Generally speaking, the Danish police resented the German presence, especially the Gestapo, and they were prone to bend the rules and look the other way if they could. Before he left Kolding, the commander took my father aside and advised him that the Gestapo had agents at all of the Koch lectures.

"According to Grethe, the ride home was more of the same. Did she understand that if this rebellious attitude spread, if there was general civil rebellion in Denmark, then Hitler would immediately disavow the agreement, overrun the country and impose his Nazi rule? 'Imagine the consequences to Jews and other minorities,' he said. And in that regard, my father saw the future.

"Once back home, my father wrote to Professor Koch on official Parliament stationery. 'Please be mindful of the delicate and precarious situation in which Denmark finds itself. The children who follow you and later commit acts of sabotage or property damage are placing themselves and their country at risk.' The professor replied promptly. He assured my father that he was counseling *passive* resistance, not criminal activities, and he would talk to Grethe as well as the other students he knew to be leaders of the movement."

"And did he talk to Grethe? Was she embarrassed by what your father did? I know if my father wrote a letter to my law professors, telling them what to teach and what not to teach, I would have been devastated," Catherine says with a grin.

"After receiving the letter from my father, Professor Koch made it a point to talk to Grethe about the delicate balance between the unity of the Danish people, the universal embodiment of Danish honor, and outright civil disobedience which would have the effect of encouraging the Nazis to police the state. I could tell she was mildly put off, but she respected my father and what he did."

Catherine squints one eye. "Why do I think that Grethe and Lukas didn't follow their advice? They continued their involvement in the resistance movement, didn't they?"

"Oh, yes they did, and the result was tragic."

CHAPTER EIGHTEEN

⸺ ∞ ⸺

"No sooner did my father return from bailing Grethe and Lukas out of trouble than he faced a political uproar over Germany's insistence that Denmark become a part of the Anti-Comintern Pact. Germany and Japan originally signed a treaty in 1936, promising to work together to denounce and defeat communism in the international community—thus 'comintern.' Its primary purpose was to isolate Russia and to lessen its world influence. It was a five-year treaty, so in November 1941 it was time for renewal. Germany and Japan were members of the Axis, fighting on the same side in World War II, and they wanted more partners.

"In late November, Erik Scavenius, Denmark's foreign minister and principal liaison with Germany, called Papa to a meeting. When my father walked into the room, he saw Cécil von Renthe-Fink, Nazi Germany's commander and official spokesman. 'Berlin is requesting that several nations join as signatories to the renewed Anti-Comintern Pact,' he said. 'Including Denmark.'

"Scavenius could not make such a decision on his own. 'I shall take it up with the prime minister and the cabinet, but I don't think they will go along,' he said. 'Denmark is a neutral country. It will not take sides.' Von Renthe-Fink responded, 'I'm sorry if you thought that was merely a suggestion. We will need your answer by tomorrow.' Scavenius and Prime Minister Stauning convened an emergency meeting of the cabinet. As

Scavenius predicted, the cabinet members refused to sign the pact, stating that it would violate Denmark's long-standing policy of neutrality. The meeting was a stormy affair, with Scavenius urging cooperation. Angry words like 'appeaser' and 'placater' were thrown about. My father seemed to take Scavenius's side. He feared that a negative response would anger Germany. And he was right.

"The next day, Scavenius conveyed the cabinet's decision to von Renthe-Fink. Denmark would not sign the pact, nor would it attend the ceremony. The next day, Germany responded by saying it is 'unable to comprehend a Danish rejection.' Berlin demanded that Denmark reverse its decision before the end of the day.

"The cabinet members reconvened and the argument went on for hours. It was finally decided that Denmark would partially agree. It would sign the pact, but only with an addendum of exceptions: 1) That Denmark would not have to go to war with the USSR or any other country, 2) that any anticommunist activities in Denmark were limited to police action only, 3) that there would be no legislation against Denmark's Jews, and 4) that Denmark would remain neutral in the war and would not join the Axis treaty.

"Von Renthe-Fink contacted Berlin and came back with the surprising message that Germany would 'consider' the terms, but that Denmark had to commit to coming to the signing ceremony or else Germany would cease its 'peaceful occupation' and would no longer be committed by the promises given in the Cooperation Agreement. For emphasis, the German forces in Denmark were put on full alert.

"That night, my father came home to announce that he would have to go to Berlin with Scavenius to attend the signing. Now my father faced his toughest challenge. My mother put her foot down. 'No Jewish husband of mine is stepping foot in Berlin! Send somebody else!' He tried to explain that he had a duty to go, that there would be delegates from ten other countries, that he was sure there would be no international incidents and that no one in Germany knew what religion he was. But Mama was not appeased. She stormed away, walked into their bedroom and slammed the door.

"Early the next morning my father stood by the front door waiting for the taxi that would take him to the train. His suitcase was packed, and his briefcase was strapped over his shoulder. Grethe and I stood with him. My mother was still fuming in her bedroom. The taxi sounded his horn, and my father picked up his suitcase, kissed me and Grethe and started to leave when my mother came running out of the bedroom and threw her arms around him. She hugged him tightly and buried her face into his chest. In a tearful voice she pleaded, 'Please don't go.' My father answered, 'I *have* to go, Nora.' She had tried one more time but failed. She nodded her concession. 'Then please don't do anything foolish. Don't leave the delegation, and don't go on any walks by yourself, not even to buy a cigar.' 'I won't,' he said, 'I promise.' She backed up a step, brushed the front of his coat with her hands and said, 'Please come back to me, Joseph.' 'I promise,' he said, and he left."

"Did he have to do anything to identify himself as a Jew?" Emma asked. "After all, it was 1941 in Berlin. Jews were required to register and wear yellow stars."

Britta raised her eyebrows. "My mother asked him the very same question, and he said no, he had diplomatic immunity from Germany's internal laws."

Emma shook her head. "When did Adolf Hitler ever care about diplomatic immunity?"

"Well, Hitler wasn't in charge of this meeting, it was his foreign minister, Joachim von Ribbentrop, and diplomatic rules were to be observed. The train ride took ten hours, with a stop in Hamburg. According to my father, Berlin's central train station, Lehrter Bahnhof, was a beehive of activity, with military presence everywhere he turned. He felt like eyes were on him every minute. There were numerous uniformed soldiers, but it was the dreaded SS that sent chills down his spine."

"How did he know which ones were the SS?" Emma said.

"He said the SS had brown uniforms with black ties and black hats with a skull-and-crossbones symbol. And of course, the jagged SS emblem on the lapels. The delegation was taken straight from the train station to the magnificent Hotel Kaiserhof. Every room had its own bathroom and its own telephone extension. My father's room overlooked the busy Wilhelmplatz. According to him, Berlin was a city of stark contrasts. The streets were alive with polished black automobiles and carriages. Men were handsomely dressed in long wool coats and trilby hats or bowlers.

Women were fashionably styled in long dresses and wide-brimmed hats. Boys hawking newspapers shouted from the corners. Everything seemed to be in motion. But it was also the picture of a city at war, the epicenter of the military. There were huge red Nazi flags hanging from the buildings. There were uniformed troops in formation, and parades of men in brown uniforms. On rare occasion, he would spot Jews with yellow stars affixed to their coats, averting their eyes from other pedestrians, looking straight ahead. It was the center of the hornets' nest and it had an ominous feeling.

"When the Danish delegation arrived at the hotel, they were met by von Renthe-Fink with a stark warning: Germany had changed its mind. It didn't like the addendum at all. 'Who does Denmark think it is?' said von Ribbentrop, and he summoned them to a meeting at the Reich Chancellery. In his imposing office, von Ribbentrop sat at the head of a long polished table. The tall, thin minister of foreign affairs, with his white hair combed to the side, sat in full uniform: black tunic with gold buttons, brown shirt, black tie, swastika patch on his left arm and oak clusters on his collars. His demeanor was stern and uncompromising. Scavenius was in a bind. He had strict instructions not to change a word. Von Ribbentrop was furious. 'To hell with Denmark.'

"'But Denmark is a neutral country,' Scavenius pleaded. The Reichsminister spat out a short burst of laughter. 'Neutral, until we decide otherwise.' He pointed at my father and Scavenius and said to his adjutant, 'We should take these recalcitrants into custody.' Then my father heard the word 'Jude.' Indeed, von Ribbentrop was well-aware that Papa was a Jew.

"After some very uncomfortable negotiations they agreed to a compromise. Denmark could have a watered-down addendum in the form of a separate agreement, not a part of the Anti-Comintern Pact. Scavenius was warned that no one was to know about the agreement.

"That night, their last night in Berlin, there was a knock on my father's door. It was the Gestapo and they demanded to see my father's papers. He said, 'I am on a diplomatic mission.' They said they knew all about his diplomatic mission. Papa handed them his passport. They wanted to know what train he would be leaving on the next morning. Papa told them and they said they would keep his passport and return it to him at the train station. My father protested, he said he was a member of the Danish diplomatic mission, and they had no right to take his passport. They took it anyway.

"The next morning, my father met with Scavenius, who called von Renthe-Fink. He said he knew nothing of the problem or why the Gestapo would have confronted my father or taken his passport. He suggested that they proceed to the train station anyway. At passport control, my father told the agent that two German officers had taken his passport the prior evening. The agent said he couldn't let him through without a passport and asked him to step to the side while he continued to process Scavenius and the other diplomats. My father stood there until he heard the final boarding call. He said to Scavenius, 'They are keeping me here, Erik. Tell my wife what has happened, tell her I am all right, and tell Prime Minister Stauning to file an official protest.'

"'That won't be necessary, Herr Morgenstern,' said a cold voice from behind. My father turned around to see the Gestapo agent with the passport in his hand. 'Have a pleasant journey, Herr Morgenstern,' he said and handed the passport to him.

"When they got back to Denmark, Scavenius was berated by an outraged cabinet. 'How dare you let von Ribbentrop push our delegation around? How do you let him tear up our addendum? How do you sign a pact with Germany and Japan without our specific limitations? Denmark is a neutral country that doesn't sign blanket agreements to pursue other nations.' Scavenius could only hang his head. 'You weren't there,' he said. 'I felt like I was facing a declaration of war. Would any of you have taken the responsibility for a German invasion?'

"Of all the years my father served in government, this was the one time I thought he might resign. He stood up for Scavenius. 'Members of the cabinet, you are wrong,' my father said. 'Germany would have ripped up the Cooperation Agreement and unleashed a full-scale occupation.' My father was the most honorable man I've ever known."

CHAPTER NINETEEN

———⊶∞⊷———

EMMA STEERS HER white Toyota up to the curb and parks directly in front of Catherine's office. She walks around the car and bends low to help her grandmother from the passenger seat. It is a windy morning and Britta grasps her wide-brimmed straw hat. Today she wears a dark blue suit over a white silk blouse with a bowknot collar. Emma is taken by how fashionable her ninety-two-year-old grandmother always keeps herself. Her makeup is expertly applied, never pasty or powdery like other grandmothers Emma has known. Her nails are freshly manicured and polished in a cherry red. Emma keeps a strong grip on Britta's elbow as they make their way across the sidewalk to the office door.

As they enter the office, Gladys loudly announces their arrival over her shoulder, "Catherine, Mrs. Stein and Emma are here." Then to Britta, she says, "Oh, how pretty you look today, Mrs. Stein. I love your hat." Britta smiles and feigns a curtsy.

Once settled, Catherine opens her file, folds back the pages of her yellow pad to find her place and says, "So, your father has returned from Berlin. What happens next?"

"As I recall we are now into the winter of 1941–1942. Given the harsh winter weather in the Nordic countryside, Professor Koch's traveling lectures were more or less on hold. He spoke only at the university. We all returned to school; Grethe and Lukas to the university, and I, to my second year of high school. So, in a way, it was a return to normal for us."

"Was it really normal, Britta? Had the situation changed in Copenhagen? I mean, you still had German soldiers on the streets. The war in Europe was intensifying. What do you mean by normal?"

"Poor choice of words," Britta says. "Remember, Denmark was not fighting in the war. We were technically an occupied country, but existing day-to-day under the Cooperation Agreement. In many ways, it mirrored our neutrality in World War I. The Cooperation Agreement allowed us to pretend that we were still independent. To our south, all Europe belonged to Hitler from the Baltic to the Mediterranean. But that winter the war had expanded to the Pacific and brought in America as well. So, to answer your question, life returned to normal for my sister and me.

"It was later that spring, when I learned that Grethe and Lukas had joined, or I should say, formed their own resistance club. One night, well after midnight, Grethe came home and I asked where she had been. She could have said 'Mind your own business, Britta' but we were very close. She confided in me that she and Lukas had formed their own club, the Holger Club, with several of their friends. I swore to keep it confidential."

"They called it the Holger Club?"

Britta nods. "My sister loved mythology, and especially Nordic legends. Holger Danske was a mythological figure, and a great warrior who dwelt deep in the catacombs of the Castle of Kronborg. According to Danish legend, when the time comes that Denmark is threatened, he will arise from his slumber, unleash his fury and save the nation. So, that is why they named their group the Holger Club. Grethe continued to attend Koch's lectures in Copenhagen, and I suspected she was getting more and more involved in resistance activities."

"Is that what she told you?"

Britta shakes her head. "Obliquely. She didn't want to tell me too much, both for my sake and hers. But she was staying away from home more often, coming back in the wee hours of the morning, and her shoes were often scuffed or muddy. If I showed curiosity, she'd wag a finger at me to tell me to stay out of it. That way, I didn't have to lie to my parents.

Whenever they would question her, she'd give lame excuses—her study group ran late, she fell asleep at the university library, she was out with Lukas, any of which could have been true, but I had become adept at reading Grethe's face. I knew they were false alibis.

"Other groups of young people had also formed their own enclaves, their own clubs, and expressed themselves in different ways throughout Denmark. Some published leaflets, some held rallies, some hosted bonfires, and others engaged in acts of sabotage. I heard of one group of young boys in the north who managed to set fire to a railroad yard and destroy German supplies and armaments. There was never a shortage of rumors. We didn't have the internet or Facebook or any of that modern stuff, but we did have what we called the 'did-you-hears.' Did you hear what the Churchill Club did in Aalborg? Did you hear what happened in Odense? Did you hear about the bridge in Randers; well, it's not a bridge anymore. There seemed to be a person-to-person network which was quite efficient even without a World Wide Web. I know that Grethe kept up very well with resistance activities."

Once again, Britta's narrative is broken by the sound of squealing tires and a shout from Gladys, who yells, "You son of a bitch. Liam, we got trouble."

Liam and Catherine dart out to the reception area where Gladys is standing at the door. "Some bastard drove by and threw something at our office," Gladys says, "but whatever it was, it hit Emma's car and not our windows."

The projectile happened to be a sack of red paint, which splattered the front of Emma's white Toyota. As the group gathers on the street staring at the car, Catherine dials the police. Emma is in tears. Britta hugs her granddaughter and whispers, "It's all right, sweetheart, it's just paint. And think about this: an innocent man wouldn't try to scare us away, would he? It proves our point. What we say about Ole Hendricksen is the truth."

"Henryks might not have done this," Liam says, "but I know a guy who would, and I have his address." Then, turning to Catherine, he says, "Why don't we call in the media now? It's time. When Rivers is arrested, and he will be later today, he won't take the heat for Sparks. He'll flip in the blink of an eye. The public is not going to like it when they find out that Henryks or his lawyer are deliberately trying to intimidate a little old lady."

"A little old lady?" Britta says with a scowl.

Catherine is still hesitant. She shakes her head to dismiss the thought. "Liam, you know that's not how I operate. I don't try my cases in the press. But when Rivers is arrested and charged with criminal damage to property and maybe intimidation, and if he flips on Sparks, the press will be all over it. Then I'll be happy to give an interview."

"If that happens, will the case go away?" Britta says.

"Only if Henryks is directly involved. If this is a publicity stunt by Sparks, and if Henryks didn't know about it, then the court will give Henryks time to find a new lawyer, and the case would continue."

Britta smiles. "That's good."

Britta's comment draws a bewildered look from Liam. "Good? That the case would continue? You think that's good?"

Flashing lights fill the room as a CPD squad car arrives.

Despite Catherine's reluctance to involve the media, the story gets picked up by NBC. They have film of Emma's car with paint on the left front quarter panel. A reporter who interviews the investigating officer learns that there have been other incidents: threatening telephone calls with racial slurs made to Britta's home phone, and a brick with a hateful message written in red paint thrown through her lawyer's office window. Catherine receives an inquiry: will she and her client sit for an interview? Catherine consents to be interviewed, but she will not allow Britta to appear or be questioned.

"WE ARE HERE this afternoon with attorney Catherine Lockhart, who represents Mrs. Britta Stein. As we see in this video taken earlier today, Mrs. Stein's granddaughter's car, which was parked outside Ms. Lockhart's law office, was splattered with a large amount of red paint."

Catherine nods. "That's correct."

"We understand from the police reports that this is the third time intimidation has been directed against you or Mrs. Stein in the past few weeks. Is that right? Would you call them acts of intimidation?"

Catherine nods. "Intentional acts or communications of one person that place another in fear of injury or harm do constitute intimidation. That's right. In this case, the conduct can be considered *ethnic intimidation* because the acts included specific reference to Mrs. Stein's religion. They are, quite simply, hate crimes. She received a number of threatening telephone calls, a brick was thrown through my office window with a religious hate message on it, written in red paint, and then, this most recent act of violence, again with red paint."

"It's general knowledge that Mrs. Stein is being sued by Ole Henryks over a series of defamatory statements *she* painted on the walls of The Melancholy Dane last month. I believe that she has *confessed* to painting those statements, am I right?"

"Well, I wouldn't use the word 'confess.' I would say she acknowledges that she did paint each of the words."

The interviewer is put off by the response. "Really? What's the difference?"

Catherine realizes her answer is terrible. She is not in a court explaining the technical difference, she is on a television news program shown to millions of ordinary folks who will now think she has given a slippery answer. It's a graphic reminder why she doesn't like TV interviews. "I concede the difference is slight and a bit technical," Catherine says, "but a confession connotes accepting the charges and admitting your guilt. Britta is not guilty of defamation. As you know, she maintains that the statements are all true."

"Well, whether they are or they're not, I guess that remains to be seen," the reporter says with a glint in her eye, "but as far as guilt is concerned, your client has confessed to spraying the walls in violation of municipal law. Wouldn't you call that a confession?"

"Yes, I suppose I would."

"You suppose?"

Who is this woman, and what is her agenda? Catherine thinks. *This is certainly a pointed interview.* "You are right; she has confessed to the misdemeanor of spray-painting on a wall. I was concentrating on the larger issues."

"Do you or Mrs. Stein have any idea who is behind these acts of intimidation? We learned that the police, on the basis of a tip, went out to an address earlier today only to find a boarded-up building. Do you know what that was about?"

"Not really," Catherine responds, and thinks, *Well, so much for Mr. Rivers and the blink-of-an-eye that he'll flip on Sparks.*

"Surely you don't accuse Mr. Henryks of *personally* placing the phone calls, throwing a painted brick or splashing paint, do you?"

Catherine says, "I have no idea who is committing these acts," and immediately regrets the answer.

With a small snort, the reporter says, "So it *might be* ninety-five-year-old Ole Henryks dashing over to your office in the middle of the day, heaving a heavy brick through the plate glass window and taking off down the street? Could it be?"

"I doubt that very much."

"Me too. Let me ask one more question. I note from the court records that you were given thirty days to provide the court with specific details about Mr. Henryks's so-called collaboration. Am I right?"

"That and others." *Another bad response. When will this be over?*

"Oh, when you say others, I assume you mean Nazi agent, betrayer, informer, traitor?"

"That's correct."

"Well, by my count, it seems that you only have sixteen days left before the pleading must be submitted to the court. Surely, you're already prepared to come forward with the required statement of facts. I wouldn't be a bit surprised if Mrs. Stein's pleading was all prepared and ready for filing right now. Do you suppose we could get a little preview? Could you tell our listeners and, more importantly Mr. Henryks, some of the factual support you will submit to show that Mrs. Stein's accusatory statements are true?"

"No, I'm afraid not."

The reporter's lips curl into an O, and she projects an expression of surprise. "I'm a bit confused. You're not prepared to come forward with the evidence right now, or your pleading is not yet prepared for filing, or you're just not going to give us a preview? Or, perhaps, they're not true."

"They are true, and the pleading will be filed in accordance with the court order."

The reporter leans forward. "Does she really have the evidence, Ms. Lockhart? Can she prove her case?"

Catherine puts on a confident smile. "She is a defendant; it is Mr. Henryks's burden to prove his case." *Another terrible answer,* she thinks. *But what can I say? Oh well, in for a dime, in for a dollar. I might as well finish strong.* "I will say this in answer to your question: Mrs. Stein will file her affirmative defense on the appointed date, and you and Mr. Sparks and Mr. Henryks and everyone else may rest assured that it will contain overwhelming factual support for each and every statement made by Mrs. Stein." Catherine stands and unclips her microphone.

"Well, thank you, Catherine Lockhart, for your time, we'll all look forward to seeing Mrs. Stein's pleading. This is Jane Turner reporting for NBC News."

Why in the hell did you do this, Catherine says to herself as she leaves the building. *What made you think this was a good idea?*

CHAPTER TWENTY

⸺⸺⸺

"TELL ME AGAIN why we're having dinner at Café Sorrento," Catherine says to Liam, and immediately catches herself. She realizes she said those very same words at the very same dinner table in the very same restaurant one year earlier. "I asked you that question right here a year ago, didn't I?"

Liam nods. "And I said, 'Because we love the food,' which was only a half truth. And from there it was off to Tuscany to save Aunt Gabi's vineyard."

Catherine smiles wistfully. "God, I wish I was going off to Tuscany tomorrow! Britta's case is making me crazy. I am so stressed. I made a total fool of myself on NBC today. Jane Turner has it in for me. I don't get it; I never met the woman before. What's with the sneak attack? Why would she do that? She'll get Sparks on, and he'll be prepared and do a much better job; he's a media hound."

"Okay, to answer your first question, we're here tonight because we *do* love the food and for no other reason, except that you deserve a night out. No work tonight, no stress tonight."

The restaurateur, Tony Vincenzo, a stout man dressed in a striped tuxedo vest and white shirt with rolled-up sleeves, a pencil behind his ear, comes up to the table with a bottle of Brunello di Montalcino. As he pulls the cork out, he smiles broadly and says, "My Aunt Gabi sends you all her love. I only wish I had a bottle from Ada's Vineyard to open for you. The one she calls Meditation 1997."

"Best wine I ever tasted," Catherine says.

"Tell Aunt Gabi we miss her," Liam says.

"And when my current litigation is over," Catherine adds, "we're jumping on a plane and heading straight back to Tuscany. Be sure to tell her that."

Tony nods and pours two glasses of the deep red wine. "Is that the litigation where you're defending the old lady who wrote all those terrible words about Ole Henryks?"

Catherine exhales and pops Liam on the shoulder. "You see? That's what people think."

Tony shrugs. "Mr. Sparks was just on the TV with Jane Turner. He really lit into your lady. Bad interview for Mrs. Stein."

"How many bottles of that wine do you have?" Catherine says.

Tony laughs. "Finish your lawsuit and go see my Aunt Gabi."

Catherine's chin is resting on her palm. "Liam, I suppose I need to see that interview. Tell me the good news; we forgot to record the ten o'clock news."

Liam sadly shakes his head. "Nope, I'm afraid I did record it."

Midway through the meal, Catherine puts her hand behind Liam and pulls him over for a kiss. "Thanks for tonight. Thanks for knowing me so well."

"Ah, does any man ever know a woman? They are God's great mystery."

"Oh, is that so?"

"Without a doubt. Men are allowed to play on the perimeter but are never allowed to enter the complexities of a woman's being."

"Liam, the great philosopher. And what about men?"

"Simple beings. As deep as a piece of paper." Catherine laughs and Liam flexes his muscles. "But strong like bull."

Tony brings a plate of cavatelli Contadina with crumbled sausage, sets it down and stands back proudly with open arms. "For you, special tonight. Buon appetito."

After a pause for the serious business of gourmandizing, Catherine says, "I sure wasn't prepared to be harpooned this afternoon. That woman . . ."

Liam covers Catherine's hand. "Let's forget about the interview. At the end of the day, it means nothing. It will have no effect upon the case whatsoever."

"But she was right. I am not prepared to file an affirmative defense, not even close. She saw right through me. Britta hasn't given me a single piece of evidence that I can use against Henryks."

Liam sits back. A thought has come into his mind. "How did she know? These interviews—yours and Sparks's—were set up because NBC had film of Emma's car outside your office, right?"

"Yes."

"So, how did they know about that? We didn't call NBC. I suggested we bring in the media, and you rejected it out of hand. So how did Turner know about the car, the brick, the phone calls?"

"I have no idea. Emma drove her car to the body shop right after the police left. When did NBC take that video?"

"It had to be before the police came."

Catherine and Liam swivel their heads and look directly into each other's eyes. "Sparks!"

"He alerted Turner," Catherine says, "and she sent a crew to film the car."

Liam slams his hand on the table. "He knew that Rivers was going to throw the paint. He paid Rivers. Sparks orchestrated the interviews."

"That slimy bastard. What happened to Rivers?"

"He gave me a bad address. Probably years old. Sparks played us to get himself on the ten o'clock news."

"We'll have to watch that interview when we get home."

They sit in silence for a few moments. Then Liam says, "Let's focus on Britta and her narrative for a second. Why isn't she giving us the evidence on Henryks? Why is she stalling? She's aware of our time constraints."

Catherine shrugs. "As my mother would say, 'That's the sixty-four-thousand-dollar question.'"

His elbow on the table, Liam rests his jaw on the back of his hand.

Catherine laughs. "Ha. I'm having dinner with Rodin. What are you thinking, my great philosopher?"

"I'm wondering, what does Britta have to gain by stalling? You've told her any number of times that she has to speed it up. But she doesn't. It's deliberate. There is a reason that she insists on telling the entire story—her sister, her father, Koch, the Danish spirit, von Renthe-whatever—even though it is all collateral and keeps us for hours in the conference room without letting us conclude our preparation. Why?"

"She told me she wants me to fully appreciate the story so that I can be her voice."

"I'm sure that's partially true, but I don't think that's the whole reason. Why else?"

Catherine shakes her head. "I have no answer."

LIAM'S CAR IS parked on Taylor Street, a couple of blocks west of the restaurant. The night is warm, there is a slight breeze blowing from the southwest and Liam has his arm around Catherine as they stroll through Little Italy. Both of them feel the glow of the wine. They hear the sounds of an accordion playing Italian music from the windows of Tavola Siena. Catherine stops suddenly and turns to face Liam. "Emma," she says. "Emma sits in on every interview, and it has been at Britta's insistence."

"And?"

"Britta is narrating a memoir for Emma's benefit. Oh, she'll get around to Henryks in due time, but I think she wants Emma to know everything about the history of her family."

Liam is perplexed. "Emma told us that Britta practically lived with her since she was a little girl. She's had twenty years or more to tell Emma about her family."

Catherine shrugs. "Well, maybe she never has. Not in its entirety. I doubt that she's ever gone into it in that much detail. She's ninety-two. Maybe it's now or never."

Liam smiles and nods. "I believe you are right. That makes perfect sense. A memoir for Emma." As they pass another couple, Liam points to Catherine and says, "This is my brilliant wife."

The couple giggles and walks on.

"There is something more, Liam," Catherine says. "There is a deeper story; one which Britta intends to disclose to Emma, but only in her way and at her time. And I sense there is some urgency here. I can feel it."

"What is the deeper story?"

"I don't know."

"WE HAVE WITH us tonight, famed Chicago attorney Sterling Sparks," Jane Turner says. "I asked him to come here to respond to the comments of attorney Catherine Lockhart, whose interview was given earlier on this station. So now, we will have both sides of the controversy. I always want my reporting to be fair and balanced. Welcome, Mr. Sparks."

"Thank you, Jane. We all appreciate a journalist who wants to hear both sides."

"What a setup," Liam says. "Played us like a grand piano."

"Ms. Lockhart told us that her client, Mrs. Britta Stein, has received several threats, including death threats, all because of the litigation."

Sparks is seated comfortably in a bright blue blazer, patterned shirt, open at the collar. His legs are crossed. He sports a paternalistic smile. "Well, that is very sad, but I suppose it's understandable. You can't go around painting violent slurs about Chicago icons and not expect there to be a strong reaction from the people that love him, though I want you to know that I don't condone those acts at all. One criminal act does not justify another."

"Ooh, I detest that man," Catherine says.

Jane gazes at Sparks like a teenager at a rock star. "You know, I gave Ms. Lockhart the opportunity to reveal some of the evidence that she intends to disclose against Mr. Henryks, I thought maybe we'd get a sneak preview, but she didn't really give me anything."

"And what does that tell you, Jane?"

Jane shrugs. "Maybe she doesn't have anything to give me? Maybe there is no evidence to back up all those nasty statements."

Sparks raises his eyebrows. "I should say 'no comment' but I've already said it in open court; there is no evidence. You can't supply proof for that which does not exist. These statements were nothing more than the misguided rants of a befuddled old woman. Unfortunately, they caused a great deal of damage. The fact that Chicago has now turned against this woman is the predictable consequence of her spiteful conduct."

"Turn it off," Catherine snaps. "I can't watch any more of this crap."

"Wait," Liam says, "he's got a picture."

Sparks hands a black-and-white photograph to Turner, who displays it for the camera. Though black and white, the photo depicts a long, narrow wooden boat. It has a center mast with a short boom. The sail is triangular and meant to supplement the long oars on either side of the hull. In the front of the boat there is a crude cabin covering the hold. The boat is docked. There are no individuals pictured. The boat bears the identification BC2342.

"This photo was given to me by Ole just a few days ago," Sparks says. "He dug it out of a bunch of old records. As you can see, it is a very clear photo of a fishing boat called the *Perlie B*, which belonged to Ole's father, Viktor Henryks. It was named for Viktor's mother, Perlie Bjorn."

Taking her cue, Jane says, with dramatic emphasis, "So interesting! Tell us, Sterling, why did you bring that photo here today?"

"Ole has been accused of being a traitor and betraying his people. He has been publicly insulted; called a collaborator, a Nazi agent and an informer. You have in your hands direct proof that Ole was not any of those terrible names. He was what he has always professed, a man who risked his life to save others. When the Gestapo was rounding up Denmark's Jews to send them all to the concentration camps, Ole and his father risked their lives to rescue Jewish families. Over and over again, in the dark of night, they would lead Jewish families to the *Perlie B*, hide them in the lower quarters, and sail them across the icy Baltic waters to Stockholm. They would drop them off on the sandy beaches and return for another group. The *Perlie B* is legendary. Does that sound like a collaborator or a Nazi agent?"

The reporter shakes her head.

"They were heroes, Jane!"

"How come we haven't seen this picture before?" Jane says with an astonished look. "I would think it is something Mr. Henryks would want everyone to see."

"I guess you'd have to know Ole. He's proud of his Danish heritage and what his family has done, but he is not a boastful fellow. This picture was hidden away in some trunk in his basement, and he figured it was time to bring it out and put all this controversy to rest."

Jane nods and holds up the picture. "This would appear to be proof positive."

"Oh, give me a break," Catherine says. "It's a picture of a boat."

Jane faces the camera. "This afternoon, when I asked Ms. Lockhart for proof—just a sneak preview—she wouldn't, or couldn't, give me any answer at all, but here in my hands, is proof positive that Ole Henryks did heroic things."

"I'm going to throw up," Catherine says.

Liam shakes his head. "This scenario of fishing boats transporting Jews all the way to Stockholm doesn't seem right to me. I don't think that's the way it happened. I think it's time that I pay another visit to Professor Lundhill. He can straighten this out."

CHAPTER TWENTY-ONE

"BRITTA IS NOT coming in today until two o'clock," Catherine mentions to Liam over breakfast. "Emma called last night and left a message on the office voicemail to let me know. Britta has a doctor's appointment this morning that she forgot to tell us about."

Liam shrugs and places a plate of scrambled eggs in front of their son, who sits back and makes a face. "C'mon, Ben," Liam says, "you can't have McMuffins every day."

"Why not?" Ben answers. "It's good."

"I don't feel like this appointment was prescheduled, Liam," Catherine says, pouring a glass of orange juice for Ben.

"That's because you are a suspicious person," Liam says with a smile.

"For one thing, Britta doesn't forget much. For another, Emma called close to midnight and she sounded anxious."

"You're not reading that into her voice?"

"And for another, I've noticed that Britta has been a little unsteady lately. Her hands shake when she holds a cup. Sometimes she breathes heavily."

"She's ninety-two years old, Cat, cut her some slack."

"So, I called Emma this morning to ask her if anything was wrong, but she only said that her grandmother had an appointment that she forgot about. I asked what type of doctor."

"Nosy."

"Well, she wouldn't tell me. She said her grandmother is very private about her medical affairs."

"As she has a right to be."

"I'm worried about her." Catherine sets down her coffee and starts to leave the room. "Ben, eat your eggs. I put cheese in them, just like you like them." Ben shrugs and covertly slides his plate over to Liam.

"DID EVERYTHING GO all right at the doctor's this morning?" Catherine says.

Britta is momentarily distracted. She's having trouble removing her hat. The hat pin is tangled in a lock of hair. Emma stands behind and helps her. "I'm very sorry," she says. "The doctor's appointment totally slipped my mind. As I was getting ready for bed, I suddenly remembered, and I phoned Emma to call your office and let you know. I hope it wasn't a terrible inconvenience."

"Not at all. Are you're feeling okay today?"

"Fit as a fiddle."

Liam looks at Catherine and raises his eyebrows in an I-told-you-so expression.

"Britta, last time we were together you were telling us about your sister," Catherine says. "She and her boyfriend had formed the Holger Club and she was staying out till the wee hours of the morning, presumably involved in resistance activities."

"That's mostly right. She was spending a lot of time with Lukas, but to be truthful, I knew it wasn't exclusively club business. She was nineteen, he was twenty-two, and they were in love. Mad about each other. The seriousness of their relationship was supposed to be a secret, but I think my parents knew."

"Why would she want to keep her relationship a secret? Grethe was a grown woman."

"I think that family stability had something to do with it. Grethe was still living at home, still sleeping in her girlhood bedroom. She was going off to school every day, albeit to a university, and the family routines, established over many years, remained constant. We would get up in the morning, take turns in the bathroom and my mother would have breakfast waiting on the table. We would have a sit-down family dinner, especially on Friday nights. In the summer of 1942, I don't think Grethe was ready to confront my mother with such a big announcement. And, by the way, Lukas wasn't Jewish; he was Lutheran."

"Was that a stumbling block for your parents?"

"My mother would have preferred a 'nice Jewish boy,' as they say. My father didn't care. My parents socialized with several friends who were in mixed marriages. Assimilation was common in Denmark. But, whatever her reason, Grethe chose to defer what would soon become obvious. For the time being, the comfort of the established Morgenstern routine remained undisturbed and that was the way Grethe wanted it. Besides, the business of the Holger Club demanded a lot of Grethe's attention, and that was one reason that Grethe was putting her announcements on hold."

"Did your father know what was going on with the Holger Club? You have painted a picture of a very astute man," Liam says.

Britta smiles. "I'm sure he did; he seemed to know everything that was going on. More often than not, a tacit understanding would unfold; he would suspect, he wouldn't necessarily approve, he might express his concern, but he would choose not to interfere. That was certainly the case with the Holger Club.

"Under the pretext of studying world affairs, Grethe had taken to listening to the BBC broadcasts at certain times each evening. She would sit in front of the radio with a pad of paper and a pencil. In fact, she was really getting coded messages. I'm sure my father figured that out.

"The BBC shortwave broadcasts contained messages from British intelligence to resistance groups. At some point during the evening's regular broadcasts, they would sound four chimes—actually, the first four notes of Beethoven's Fifth Symphony—followed by 'This is London calling.' That was the cue that a coded message would follow. Sometimes it was for Grethe's club, other times for other clubs. If we heard, 'Greetings for Holger. Listen again.' That was meant for Grethe, and she would pay attention until her message was sent."

"What type of message?" Liam asked.

"Usually it was a geographic clue. If the broadcaster said, 'The weather is balmy tonight in Aylesbury,' Grethe would go to the atlas and look up the town. If it was so many miles northwest of London, then Grethe would figure out where the contact point would be in Denmark."

"And you think your father was aware?"

Britta leaned her head back and laughed. "Ha. Joseph Morgenstern was nobody's fool. He'd hear the broadcasts, he'd see Grethe taking notes and getting ready to leave. Then he'd look directly at her, shake his head, point his finger and caution her to 'Please be careful tonight.'"

"But he never did anything to stop her?"

"No."

Catherine holds up her palm. "Britta, I've learned to pick up on some of your nuances. Maybe I'm a little like your father. A few minutes ago, you said 'And that was one reason that Grethe was putting her announcements on hold.'"

Britta nods. "Right."

"What were the other announcements?"

Britta stops for a moment to consider her next move. The undisclosed material would follow naturally in her narrative. It was chronological. But Britta is reluctant. She has never revealed that information to Emma and she is unsure that the time is right. Her hands are folded on the table before her and she stares at them as though they might give her a signal. She knows it should have been discussed years ago, and she has avoided it. Now she regrets letting it lie dormant for so long. She is sure that Emma doesn't have a clue. She unfolds her hands and places her palms flat on the table. She nods her head in accord with her inner voices. She will open the door, but only a little at a time.

She takes a breath and responds to Catherine. "The other thing. Yes. The matter first came to my attention in May 1942, I believe," Britta says with the assurance that she has finally made up her mind. "Grethe had been home on a regular basis for a few months. Before that, she and Lukas had been traveling off and on with Professor Koch. Grethe's presence at home served to reestablish and reinforce our closeness. Once again, I was enjoying her company and her counsel. I had always respected my sister, but since she had taken a leadership role with Professor Koch's movement, my admiration had increased. It was a joy to spend time with her. Those evenings that she didn't go out, which were few and far between, we'd talk late into the night; our rooms were next to each other.

"Since the time we were little girls, we would have breakfast together and head off to school—our schools were usually in the same direction—and we had resumed our routine." Britta draws a deep breath. "So, now we come to that morning in May 1942. The other thing. Grethe was lagging behind; she wasn't getting dressed, and I went in to tell her to hurry up or she'd miss breakfast. 'I can't eat today,' she said. 'My stomach is in knots.' Her face was rosy, her breathing was quick, and in the middle of the sentence she ran into the bathroom to throw up.

"I worried about her all day, but when I came home, she was sitting on the floor in front of the radio taking notes. I asked her how she was feeling, and she waved it off. 'I'm fine,' she said, but she still looked peaked to me. A little while later, Grethe came into my room, shut the door and asked if I would take a message to Lukas. 'Why don't you call him,' I said. 'The bookstore has a telephone.' She was in no mood for my suggestions. 'I can't use the phone for this message, Britta, or I would. It has to be in person. Please, Britta, it's important.' I asked her if this had something to do with the Holger Club, was this a secret mission?

"She laughed. 'All you have to do is take a message to Lukas at six o'clock. He'll be at the Viking Bookstore.' It was owned by a friend of Lukas's family and Lukas was the bookstore manager. My heartbeat quickened. It was my first foray into Grethe's world of espionage."

Catherine is intrigued. She leans forward. "What was the message? Was it in writing? A sealed envelope?"

Britta shakes her head. "Oh no, nothing was ever put in writing. The message, which I had to repeat back to Grethe three times, and which I did not understand at all—I still remember it—was 'Southwest coast number three.' I arrived at the bookstore a little after six and I was told that Lukas had gone to the Three Bells Bar across the street."

"Were you old enough to go into a bar alone?"

"No. Three Bells was an English-style bar; dark wood, brass, stained glass windows. People looked at me when I walked in. What was a sixteen-year-old doing in the bar? One man asked me if I was looking for my father. I said no, I was looking for Lukas Holstrum. He pointed to the back.

"Lukas was easy to see—over six feet, with a mop of blond hair—very handsome, have I said that? He was standing with two other men. When he saw me, he walked over and put his arm around me. 'What are you doing here, Britty?' he said. 'Where's Grethe?'

"'She's not feeling well. She told me to give you a message.' Before I could say another word, Lukas held up his hand and sternly shook his head. 'Not here.' We walked outside and I gave him the message: 'Southwest coast number three.' He nodded and said, 'Tell Grethe I will pick her up in an hour, at seven o'clock. It's a three-hour ride. Tell her I need her tonight. We're going alone.'

"I returned to the house, eager to tell Grethe that I had accomplished my clandestine assignment. My heart was pumping, and I couldn't wait to give her Lukas's message.

"Grethe listened and shook her head. Her face had lost some of its color and she was weak. It was obvious that she didn't feel up to going. I offered to go in her stead, but she firmly rejected the suggestion. Our parents were out for the night and I went into the kitchen to make a sandwich. A little while later Grethe came in. She had on a light jacket, and she had my jacket in her hands. 'Britta, I need help. I'm a little wobbly tonight. Can you come with us?' She didn't have to ask twice."

"Did you know what was going on?" Catherine says. "Didn't you think you would be in trouble with your parents?"

"I don't know what I thought. They weren't home. I put on my jacket, we went outside, and we got into a car that Lukas was driving. He looked at me and then at Grethe. He understood. 'Don't worry,' Grethe said. 'Britta's solid as a rock.' I felt very proud.

"The ride was difficult for Grethe. We had to stop once for her to get out of the car. Lukas was so kind to her and held her close, even while she was sick. He loved her so much. Finally, we arrived at a large open field near the coast. Lukas gave each of us a flare and we stood in a triangle, fifty paces apart. At ten-thirty, Lukas gave a signal and we lit the flares."

Emma is hanging on every word. She is enthralled. "How did you feel, Bubbe? Were you scared?"

"Lukas was a confident young man. He was strong, smart and always in control. I felt perfectly safe. It was cold and damp and I was worried about Grethe, but I did what I was told. I stood there with the bright red flare.

"Soon we heard the hum of a single-engine plane. It was a dark night, a new moon, and the plane had no lights. I couldn't see it until it was almost on top of us, but I could sure hear it; it was noisy. When it was overhead, a package was pushed out of the plane, a small parachute opened, and it was carried by the wind to the east of us. We had to run quite a ways to get it. It was a heavy wooden crate, too heavy to carry back to the car. Grethe and I stayed with the crate while Lukas went to fetch his car."

"What was inside?" Emma asks. There is a look of wonderment on her face. Her Bubbe was involved in the resistance. She looks at Catherine. "The things she never told me!" she says.

Britta shrugs nonchalantly. "I never knew the contents. Whatever it was, it was heavy. We drove back to Copenhagen and Lukas stopped at the apartment to drop us off. He hugged me and thanked me profusely for my 'invaluable help.' I looked up at him and said, 'Does this make me a member of the Holger Club?'

"'Full-fledged,' he said with a big smile, and he drove off to take the crate to its final destination. Grethe and I quietly walked into the apartment. 'I hope I get a boyfriend like that someday,' I said to her."

Emma smiles wistfully. There's a touch of sadness. "I never knew my Aunt Grethe, and that's a shame. I would have liked to have known her."

Britta lifts her eyebrows in what seems to be a confirmation, but Catherine is used to reading a witness's expression, and she has come to know Britta pretty well. To Catherine, the raised eyebrows say that there is more that you don't know, a deeper story to be told, and it will be told, but not right now.

It is late in the afternoon. Emma points to her watch and tips her head in Britta's direction. Catherine nods and rises. "I think that's enough for this afternoon, Britta. We don't want to overdo."

"One thing before we break," Liam says. "If you wouldn't mind, Britta, would you search that fabulous memory of yours and write down the names of the members of the Holger Club? First and last names. And to the extent you know them, could you also write down the names of people who were in other resistance clubs?"

Britta nods. "I'll try, but it was so long ago. I assume that none of them are still alive."

Liam smiles. "But I know one girl who is. And as the saying goes, when we assume . . ."

Britta chuckles. "Okay. I'll do the best I can."

"Even if they're not still alive, they may have families who remember and can fill in the blanks. It might get us closer to Henryks."

CHAPTER TWENTY-TWO

"Thank you for agreeing to see me again," Liam says as he takes a seat on the uncomfortable wooden chair next to Professor Lundhill's carved oak desk. Though the weather is pleasant, the windows are shut, and the professor is wearing a cardigan sweater.

"I'm afraid I don't have much time for you today, Mr. Taggart," he says, shuffling the papers on his desk in a seemingly random manner. "You asked to see me on rather short notice."

"I'm sorry, Dr. Lundhill, but our clock is ticking as well. I'm working hard to establish some connections, but I've run into some brick walls in my research and I don't think I can go much farther here in Chicago. I've exhausted what sources I can access online. I'd like to make plans to go to Copenhagen. Do you think there are sources that would help me there? Basically, I would like your advice on places for research or people that I might consult."

The professor nods. "Indeed. There are multiple sources for research in Copenhagen. I can make a list for you. I'll even suggest a few contacts. When are you planning to travel?"

"Next week."

The professor scoffs. "Next week? Do you always act so precipitately, Mr. Taggart?"

Liam smiles. "Only when Judge Wilson puts us in a vise."

"All right, I'll work on it over the weekend."

"Thank you very much. Do you have time for a quick question or two?"

Professor Lundhill grimaces and raises his eyes, but spreads his hands in acquiescence. "If you really are quick."

"When we interviewed Britta Stein this week, she told us that groups of teenagers were forming clubs and taking it upon themselves to resist the Nazi occupation. They cut phone wires, vandalized jeeps, started little fires and even threw a skunk into the German soldiers' barracks."

The professor agrees. "That is well-known."

"She said the resistance movement grew in intensity as the war progressed and became quite effective in disrupting the German occupation. Is she right?"

"Also true. Are you doubting her credibility?"

Liam tips his head from side to side. "She's ninety-two. Everything happened a long time ago. Maybe I'm prone to discount her version of the events as they occurred because she was a teenager during the occupation. Her perception was filtered through the lens of her teenage eyes and I am concerned that some of her recall is factual and some might be fanciful."

"Thus far she has been fairly accurate."

"She's very focused on the activities of her sister and her boyfriend. She says they formed a club called the Holger Club."

"I'm not familiar with that group, but there were many such clubs."

"Britta mentioned one group that blew up rail cars filled with Nazi munitions."

The professor firmly nods his head. "The Churchill Club. They caused appreciable damage. Perhaps their boldest act was when they blew up several rail cars filled with machine parts, airplane wings and iron ore, all headed for Germany. Again, Mrs. Stein is correct. Is that all, Mr. Taggart? I really must be on my way."

"Did British intelligence drop crates of materials by parachute to those clubs? Were the drops announced through broadcasts on the BBC?"

Lundhill sighs. "SOE. British Special Operations Executive, also known colloquially as the Ministry of Ungentlemanly Warfare. It was an organization set up at a Baker Street address to conduct espionage, sabotage and reconnaissance in occupied Europe. It would have arranged to drop weapons and explosive devices to resistance groups on Danish soil. The coded messages were indeed broadcast on the BBC. She is correct again. Now, Mr. Taggart . . ."

"One last question, sir. We've been shown a photograph of a little Danish fishing boat with numbers painted on the bow."

Lundhill nods. "Those were probably Copenhagen Harbor registration numbers. They had to pay a yearly tax."

"So, would there be records of who owned those boats, or who paid the taxes?"

"I'm sure there were at the time, but it was seventy years ago."

"We've been told that the boat in the Henryks photograph was used to save Jewish lives during the occupation, and—"

Lundhill waves his hand from side to side and interrupts. "That is a subject that requires much more time than we have today."

"I understand that, sir. My question is only whether or not these boats would have shuttled Jewish refugees from Denmark to Stockholm."

Professor Lundhill stiffens. "Stockholm? Hardly. That would have been hundreds of miles through dangerous waters. They shuttled them fifteen to twenty miles across the Øresund to western Sweden. Still, it took courage to make that ninety-minute journey in 1943. Now I must be off."

CHAPTER TWENTY-THREE

———— ∞ ————

"It wasn't long after my first foray with the Holger Club that we received an alarming message," Britta says the next morning. "There had been an explosion at Professor Koch's home. Thankfully, the professor and his wife, Bodil, weren't at home, and they were safe and unharmed. An alert went out to members of the Holger Club to meet at Jan Andersen's house that evening. After considerable begging, Grethe permitted me to come along, but before we left, my father pulled me aside.

"'You seem to be getting more involved in Grethe's group,' he said. I shrugged it off. 'Not really,' I answered. 'She lets me tag along to some of her meetings.' He locked eyes with me. 'Do you think that I am so out of touch that I don't know what you did last week? When you didn't come home until two in the morning?'

"'You knew?' I said.

"'Grethe is old enough to make her own decisions, and I suppose she has the right to place herself in jeopardy if that is where her passion leads her. I respect that. Denmark would be well-served with more souls like Grethe and Lukas. But you are sixteen. The time has not yet come for you to make such decisions.'

"My father shocked me. Not only was it a surprise that he knew about Lukas's activities, but that he tacitly endorsed Grethe's participation. He never ceased to amaze me. 'Are you saying that I can't go to the meeting tonight with Grethe?'

"He smiled. 'I don't want to quash that homeland spirit. Go, but on one condition; if any retaliatory activities are contemplated, you are to come home.' I agreed.

"Jan Andersen was a little older than most of the members. He had been there from the beginning, when Lukas and Grethe formed the club. He lived in a house in Frederiksberg, a suburb of Copenhagen, with his wife and child. He was a tradesman, an electrician, I think. This evening there were about fifteen of us, and once assembled, Jan called the meeting to order. 'We have learned that the National Socialist Workers Party of Denmark, the Danish Nazi Party, is claiming credit for the bombing of Professor Koch's home. Apparently, Frits Clausen, their leader, has boasted about it. The professor and Mrs. Koch have gone into hiding for the time being,' Jan said to the group, 'and until we are certain it is safe for them to come out, they will stay there.'

"'Do we know the identity of the person who set the explosive at the professor's home?' Lukas asked. Jan shrugged. 'Not for certain. We think it may have been Billy Hendricksen. Somebody said they saw him in the area. As far as we know, he had no business there; he lives on the other side of town.'

"'I thought Billy was in the Frikorps?' another member said. I was unfamiliar with the term and I looked at Grethe. She leaned over and whispered, 'Frikorps Danmark is a military unit which has pledged to fight for Germany.'"

"Free Corps?" Liam says, repeating the phrase phonetically. "I'm not aware of them. That's probably something I should look into."

"Of course," Britta says. "I would expect you to do that."

Liam is taken aback and smiles. "And that I will, but you haven't mentioned it previously. Perhaps the pace of the narrative might pick up a little and—"

"That's enough, Liam," Catherine interjects. "The pace is just fine."

Britta nods. "Frikorps Danmark. Some Danes sided with Germany in the early years of the war, believing that Germany, which was then in total control of Europe, was unstoppable. Many wanted to jump on the bandwagon. Billy Hendricksen was supposedly one, although people said he dropped out when the group was going to be deployed and sent to Russia."

"What about Ole?" Catherine says. "Was he in the Frikorps?"

Britta shakes her head. "Not that I knew. I think he would have been too young. Nevertheless, Jan suggested that somebody follow up on Billy Hendricksen. Then Jan said, 'We have a new assignment, a very important one.' He looked down at me with concern. 'This is highly confidential.' He pointed at me as if to say it's not for my ears. 'She's solid,' Lukas said. 'She was there with us the other night when we secured the shipment. You don't have to worry one bit about Britta Morgenstern.'"

"That must have made you feel proud," Catherine says.

"What was the new assignment, Bubbe? What did Jan tell the club?"

"There was to be another British commando raid on the Atlantic Wall. The best information we had was that the attack would be on the industrial site at Glomfjord, Norway. We knew that the German army stationed in northern Denmark would rush to protect the site. The Holger Club and two other clubs were going to sabotage bridges and roads leading to the coast, making it difficult for the Germans to get to the site and attack the commandos. Indeed, the heavy crate that I helped to bring to Lukas's car contained materials that were going to be used to sabotage Nazi routes to Norway. We were told to listen to the BBC, to listen for 'Greetings for Melody' and we would know the operation was on.

"The message came two nights later. 'Greetings for Melody. Listen Again.' No matter how hard I pleaded, my father would not let me participate. Grethe left with Lukas. They were gone for an entire day and night. Lukas brought Grethe to the house early the next morning. She looked sickly, as she had before. He said the ride back was hard on her, but she said it was just a queasy stomach." Britta stops to calm her lips, which are quavering. She swallows hard. "We lost Jan Andersen and six other members on that mission. They were on their way to set an explosive on the Struer Bridge, a critical path from a Nazi base. They were killed because they were informed upon by a traitor. A squad of German soldiers was waiting for them and killed them on the spot."

Britta stops again. Her jaw will not stop shaking. She takes a deep breath. "They were informed upon because one of the members who was scheduled to go to the bridge let it slip out in a conversation at the Three Bells Bar. It was said that he was talking to a friend he trusted, but that he was careless. There were others standing in earshot, one of whom was Ole Hendricksen."

Catherine, Liam and Emma are stunned.

"At the next meeting of the Holger Club, Lukas was unanimously chosen to succeed Jan as leader of the group. The first line of business was to determine who informed on our operation. We concluded it had been Ole Hendricksen. The other tavern bystanders that night were identified. We knew them all, and none of them would have been so treacherous. Hendricksen was an outsider, rather friendless. How shall I say—socially unwelcome. In a public setting, he would float from one group to another, remaining on the perimeter. That is what the bystanders recall of that evening." Britta pauses again. When she resumes, her voice is tremulous. "When the confidential plan was accidentally and quietly discussed, Ole was slinking around the group and he heard it. That is what the people in the bar remembered, and by elimination, they determined that Ole Hendricksen was the informer."

Catherine sits back. "Well, now we have something. We have an allegation we can put into a pleading."

Emma is hesitant. "We can allege it, but how can we prove such a thing? Bubbe heard it from someone who heard it from somebody else. That's third-party hearsay."

Britta's muscles continue to twitch. She sternly shakes her index finger back and forth. "The proof will be there! It will be there! I am not finished! There is more to come." She pauses and takes a few short breaths. Emma rises and quickly moves around to hold her grandmother. Britta looks up, smiles at Emma and nods. "It will be there, I promise."

Emma looks over at Catherine and says, "Maybe that's enough for today." She helps Britta to rise.

"It will be there," Britta repeats with tears in her eyes.

"I know it will, my Bubbe, but that's enough for today."

"SHE'S RIGHT, YOU know, it's hearsay, many times removed," Catherine says to Liam once Emma and Britta have left. "I'll insert the event in the affirmative defense, and the allegation that he informed on the resistance will allow us to survive for another day, but without more . . ."

"More will come, Cat, I can feel it," Liam says. "She has asked us to be patient. Some facts were given today, and I feel confident that she'll give us more as she goes along."

"I hope so, but if it is the same quality—that is, what she was told or what she heard from someone else—it will be stricken as hearsay."

"What if we can corroborate the hearsay with another witness— maybe one of those bystanders?"

"Well, that is certainly the million-dollar challenge, isn't it? What concerns me much more is the state of Britta's health. You saw her today; she was shaking. She seems to grow weaker by the day, and I believe that the stress of this case is making it worse."

Liam nods. "If she would cut to the chase, just give us the CliffsNotes version of the Henryks bad acts, it would benefit all concerned."

Catherine shakes her head. "It's not going to happen. You and I have already concluded that this narrative is for Emma's benefit, like a Britta Stein memoir. The whole story is going to come out eventually. Of that I have no doubt. If our narrator lives long enough."

CHAPTER TWENTY-FOUR

───◦∞◦───

"GOOD MORNING TO you all," Britta says, and there is a smile on her face. She is feeling better today. Her wardrobe reflects her mood; her light cotton dress has a cheerful floral pattern.

"You're looking chipper today, Britta," Catherine says, picking up her writing pad. "Are we still in 1942?"

Britta nods. "Fall of 1942. It was the morning, I was getting ready for school and Grethe knocked on my bedroom door. Without waiting for an answer, she walked into my room and shut the door. She looked woozy again. Her complexion was green, and I could tell she had lost weight. 'Britta, I need your help,' she said. 'Lukas is supposed to meet me at the quadrangle at noon. He's not answering his phone, so I can't tell him I won't be there. I just don't feel up to it. I don't think I can make it there without throwing up. Can you take him a message?'

"'Grethe, you need to see a doctor. You're sick again and you've been sick a lot. Don't tell me it's just a queasy stomach.'

"She shook her head. 'Britta, please, I just need you to take a message. What is a doctor going to do for me?'

"I started to say something like prescribe medicine or give you an examination, when she blurted, 'Look, I'm not sick. I'm pregnant, Britta.'

"How clueless was I? Sick every morning and I'm not putting two and two together. 'Does Lukas know? Does Mama know?'

"'Lukas knows. No one else. Now you know.'

"'What are you going to do?'

"The corners of her mouth turned up. 'I'm going to have a baby, Britta. That's the way these things work.'

"'I know that, Grethe. Are you going to get married? Does Papa know? When are you going to tell Mama? Has Lukas proposed?'

"'Not yet,' she said. 'We plan on getting married, just not in the middle of a war. We haven't thought everything through yet. Lukas is in his final year at the university. He plans on looking for a better job in the spring. On his bookstore salary, we can't afford a place. If we get married now, we don't have an apartment and we certainly won't live in his dormitory room.'"

Emma's hand is on her forehead. She has a look of astonishment. "So, there is another member of my family that I never knew about? This is *my* family and all these years, I never knew any of this. Now it comes out in the middle of a lawsuit? Why, Bubbe?"

Catherine calms the air with a wave. "It's coming out now, Emma. In her time and she'll tell you when she's ready. Let her be."

"But Bubbe practically raised me. For twenty years we lived under the same roof."

Britta hangs her head. "I'm sorry," she says quietly. "I always meant to tell you everything, but there is pain in this story. I would always think, I'll tell her some other time. And all those years, it didn't just affect you."

Emma is confused. "Well then, who else?"

"Emma!" Catherine says, sternly. "When she's ready." Emma nods and pats her grandmother on the arm. "Okay, Bubbe, your way."

Britta continues. "Grethe was trapped in a dilemma. Babies keep on growing, and your pregnancy doesn't stop for you to solve your dilemma. Back then times were different. It wasn't like today. People didn't just move in together; they got married first. And it was socially awkward, certainly embarrassing, to have a child out of wedlock.

"'You need to get married,' I said to Grethe, and that would have been fine with me; I was crazy about Lukas. He was perfect for her. 'And you need to tell Mama.' I was stating the obvious.

"'We can't get married yet, we don't have anywhere to live,' she said. 'And I don't have the nerve to tell Mama.'

"'She's going to know pretty quick, if she doesn't know already. If it helps, I'll sit with you when you tell her.' She was grateful for the moral support, and we agreed to talk to Mama after Papa left for work. A few minutes later, my father poked his head in the doorway to say goodbye. The two of us were sitting on the bed. He looked at Grethe and raised his eyebrows with that Joseph Morgenstern look that said I know everything. 'I'm off to work,' he said. 'Why don't we talk later?' Oh, I thought, he knows, and there is no doubt.

"He closed the door and we looked at each other. 'He knows,' I said. 'And if *he* knows . . .' Maybe it wouldn't be so difficult to tell Mama after all, we thought.

"As it turned out, she and my father had deduced the situation days ago and had discussed it between the two of them. My mother had three questions for Grethe: when are you going to get married, where are you going to get married, and where do you intend to live? Three questions for which Grethe had no answers. For someone on the road of no return, she had a lot of thinking to do. Mama's first two items posed the unspoken question: church or synagogue? Mama was fond of Lukas, and she knew that he was Lutheran. 'Can you accept that I am not marrying a Jewish man, Mama?' Grethe said cautiously. 'I don't think Lukas plans on converting.'

"'I can accept whatever you two decide,' Mama said, lifting an enormous weight off of Grethe's shoulders. Our mother was a remarkable woman, and Grethe wondered why she had ever harbored fears of her disapproval. Mama surprisingly revealed that she had reached out to the rabbi at the Great Synagogue for his counsel. While he wouldn't officiate a wedding between a Jew and a Lutheran, he thought the rabbi at the Reform synagogue might. Then Mama went to see him, and he consented, if Grethe and Lukas would come to see him first. Problem solved."

"Not entirely," Emma says. "They still don't have a place to live."

"In my mother's mind that was never an issue. They would move into Grethe's room until they got their own place. My mama was only too happy to raise a grandbaby.

"It was an early September wedding, held in the courtyard of the Reform synagogue. There was a late-summer breeze, the leaves had started to turn, and Mama had decorated the chuppah with fall flowers. Of the greatest significance, I was the maid of honor. The wedding was well-attended, though most of the people were from our side of the family. Lukas's family lived on Fyn, quite a ways away."

"Fyn?" said Catherine. "Is that in Denmark?"

Britta smiled. "The island of Fyn is Denmark's most beautiful island, directly west of the island of Zealand, where we lived, across a large expanse of the Baltic Sea known as the Great Belt. You get there by driving over the Great Belt Bridge, one of the longest suspension bridges in the world. The Holstrums lived in the city of Odense, which is also the home of Hans Christian Andersen. Fyn is known as the garden island, because it is so green and flowerful. And there are castles everywhere you look. Positively charming. You should visit sometime."

"I plan on it. So, did the Holstrums come to the wedding over the Great Belt Bridge?" Catherine asks.

Britta nods. "They most certainly did, over fifty of them, including Lukas's sister, Ellen, who was my age. We became fast friends. The wedding was lovely. Grethe, though four months along and showing a bit with a little bump, looked radiant. Mama had arranged for a wonderful feast and we danced well into the evening. When I think back on that day, my father standing proudly in his tuxedo, Lukas and his groomsmen, how happy everyone was . . ." Britta stops abruptly. Once more, her jaw begins to quaver. She reaches for a tissue and looks at her granddaughter. "Had we only known. We had been lulled into a false sense of normalcy, Emma. The great Cooperation Agreement was nothing but a farce. A mere placeholder. In less than a year, everything would change. We'd be scattered to the winds like poplar leaves."

THE GROUP REASSEMBLES after a break and Britta continues. "In the fall of 1942, things began to change. Foretold by the cold winds sweeping down from the North Sea, Denmark's tolerance for the German occupation chilled. Newspapers, a traditionally free and independent voice in Denmark, started to carry stories critical of the Reich. Published news reports on the state of the war, especially the gains of the Allies in northern Africa, Rommel's defeat at El Alamein, and Germany's massive failure at Stalingrad were deemed unacceptable to the German administrators. Father told us that German authorities were demanding the right to manage the content of the news. They insisted on the right of censorship, something that we did not previously have in Denmark.

"Father was required to work late more frequently. There were government meetings well into the night. Relationships with the German ministers were testy. Polite camaraderie, which existed at one time between townsfolk and the German foot soldiers, soured. Soldiers complained to their ministers and ultimately to German plenipotentiary Cécil von Renthe-Fink that they were being selectively denied service from Danish businesses, that they felt unwelcome in shops and restaurants.

"Lukas was away from home more often, and while he wouldn't tell us exactly where he had been, we knew he was on Holger Club business, which meant destruction of German installations and missions of sabotage. Grethe continued to man the radio for coded messages, but she stopped going into the field. From time to time, we'd receive word that resistance groups were having success and disrupting the German forces. German authorities pressured the Danish police to find and arrest the saboteurs.

"The fabric of peaceful coexistence was fraying at the edges. Plenipotentiary von Renthe-Fink sent a warning to the Folketing that Berlin was feeling less secure of Denmark's cooperation. According to my father, the entire concept of a cooperation agreement, where one party is strongly dominant and the other is weak and subordinate, was being tested. It was not long before Berlin decided to make a change. The final straw was something that came to be known as the Telegram Crisis."

CHAPTER TWENTY-FIVE

꧁ꕥ꧂

"Please be seated, Mr. Taggart," Dr. Lundhill says with a rare smile. He produces a document-sized envelope. "I have compiled lists for you, as I promised, with major reference sources. Some of them identify an individual: a curator, a librarian, a docent. Feel free to use my name."

Liam accepts the envelope and slides it into his briefcase. "Thank you very much, I promise to be discreet, especially whenever I use your name."

The professor folds his hands and rocks back and forth. "Don't you have questions for me today, Mr. Taggart?"

"Oh, of course I do, but I didn't want to overstay my welcome, particularly when you have taken the time to prepare this list for me."

Dr. Lundhill spreads his hands. "I anticipated your curiosity and carved a few minutes into my schedule. How are your sessions with Mrs. Stein going?"

"I wish could say they are speeding along. She's methodical. She did tell us that Ole Hendricksen was accused of informing on the Holger Club, resulting in the death of several members."

The professor is surprised. "Well then, that is a significant step forward in your litigation."

"Perhaps. There is a problem proving that statement. I have a lot of work to do. Britta is telling her story in great detail, so maybe she will reveal that Henryks informed a second time. I suppose that informers were common during the occupation."

"Oh, indeed they were. Do you remember when we talked about the Churchill Club? Eight Catholic schoolboys, who named their club after Sir Winston? The members were young, some as young as fourteen. They lived and carried out their string of sabotage in and around the far northern city of Aalborg, where there were Nazi bases. The group managed to steal German weapons, grenades and rifles. They set fires, damaged German vehicles and as I mentioned, blew up a number of boxcars in a guarded railroad yard, all while traveling about on their bicycles. Unfortunately, an informer turned them in to the Nazis in 1942 and the boys were rounded up, tried in a Danish court and sentenced to jail."

"I don't suppose the informer was Henryks or Hendricksen?"

The professor shakes his head. "Indeed not. It was a woman named Elsa Ottesen, a waitress in an Aalborg café. She saw one of the boys steal a gun from a German soldier's coat hanging on the rack, and she turned him in. Informers did terrible damage to the resistance. Nazis learned a great deal of information about the resistance groups from informers or by interrogating witnesses in custody. That's how they brought down the Hvidsten Group, one of the most successful. They would coordinate with the British SOE, to receive crates of explosives by parachute drop. The success of resistance groups and the German administration's failure to contain them was a principal reason for the recall of von Renthe-Fink."

Liam nods. "She has mentioned von Renthe-Fink several times. He was the German plenipotentiary."

Lundhill raises his eyebrows. "At the beginning of the occupation, Cécil von Renthe-Fink was assigned to Denmark with the understanding that he was not to interfere with Denmark's domestic governance. That was the Cooperation Agreement. But as the acts of sabotage increased, as bridges were blown and factories were bombed, as rail lines were damaged and boxcars destroyed, Himmler and the Nazi command became incensed. Then came the Telegram Crisis."

The professor rocks back in his chair. "It was one of those things that would seem to be innocuous, but it enraged Hitler. In September 1942, Hitler sent a telegram to King Christian X wishing him a happy seventy-second birthday. But it was not just a telegram; it was this long windy affair, effusive in an officious sort of way. Clearly Hitler had taken his time in composing such a long and detailed greeting. King Christian's reply was short and impersonal, five words which essentially said, 'Thanks.' Hitler was infuriated. He considered it to be an intentional slight, and perhaps it was. Or perhaps, King Christian received a lot of birthday wishes and this was just one of them. Hitler fumed. How dare Christian reply to him in such a dismissive manner? He was Adolf Hitler, ruler of the universe. Hitler immediately recalled von Renthe-Fink as plenipotentiary, and replaced him with a hard-line Nazi, SS-Obergruppenführer Karl Rudolf Werner Best. He was Heydrich's deputy."

Liam nods. "Ah yes, Reinhard Heydrich, the gentleman violinist. I came upon him in connection with researching Ada Baumgarten. It was a case my wife and I worked a year ago."

"Heydrich was indeed a musician and his father was a conductor, but Heydrich's love of the arts and his gentlemanly manners belied his ruthlessness. He was the political architect of the Final Solution, head of the Gestapo and state security. In Hitler's words, 'The man with the iron heart.' Anyway, with the increasing resistance and the telegram slight, Hitler deemed the situation in Denmark to be serious enough that Dr. Best was brought in to ensure obedience."

"He was a doctor?"

The professor shakes his head. "No, no, in fact he was a lawyer. Years prior, Heydrich had appointed Best to be in charge of training men for the Gestapo. He would tell the trainees that they should all consider themselves to be like doctors sent to rid the country of terrible diseases; and by that he meant communists, Freemasons, churchgoers and, of course, Jews. His Gestapo trainees called him *Doktor* Best; and that's the name that stuck. Everyone referred to him as Dr. Best. Upon taking office in Denmark, the first thing on Best's agenda was a roundup of all the communists he could find. Informers helped him to identify the members of the Communist Party, and they were immediately taken into custody and jailed." The professor nods sharply; a gesture of closure.

Liam picks up his briefcase. "I thank you for taking the time to make out this list. I'm hoping that one of these sources will reveal a link to

Henryks, or Hendricksen. There must have been arrests made of traitors and sympathizers. Britta has maintained that most Danes were loyal subjects, but I have a feeling that there were more Nazi sympathizers than she realizes."

"Oh, quite right. People are surprised to learn that three hundred thousand Danes were active as Nazi sympathizers, not all as informers or traitors, but sympathetic to the Nazi cause. As for the informers, there were many, and the Germans paid them well." The professor rises and extends his hand. "Glad to be of service."

CHAPTER TWENTY-SIX

⸺⊗⊗⊗⸺

"THROUGHOUT THE WINTER of 1942–1943, the resistance campaign intensified, and the successes were dramatic," Britta says as she begins the day's narrative. Britta and Emma had arrived late. Britta fumbled for excuses; overslept, couldn't find the right blouse, coffee machine wasn't working, but in truth, her energy level is down. Catherine suggests that they take the day off and use the afternoon to rest up, but Britta will hear none of it. She pops her finger on the table and says, "Right here, right now; isn't that our marching order?" Catherine looks to Emma for support, but Emma only shrugs. What can she do?

"Acts of sabotage occurred more frequently. The clubs felt empowered by Germany's defeats in Africa and Russia. British and Allied commando units continued their attacks along the Atlantic Wall, relying on Danish resistance fighters for support. As such, Lukas and the Holger Club were busy supplying arms and materials to foreign and domestic saboteurs. Grethe stayed active in the club meetings, but she chose not to go into the field. She was due in early February, and the ice and snow made it dangerous for her to get around.

"Lukas continued to fulfill his managerial activities at the Viking Bookstore. He wasn't making much money, but he offered to give it all to my father as a contribution from the new boarders: Mr. and Mrs. Lukas Holstrum. My father appreciated the offer but urged him to save whatever he could. He and Grethe would need that money to establish themselves once the war ended."

Emma leans forward. She has a keen interest in hearing about the new family dynamics. "How did it work out with a married couple living in the next bedroom," she says with a coy smile.

Britta raises her eyebrows and lifts her chin. "Respectfully," she says. "Nothing less. One knows when to close her ears, and the other one knows when to be discreet. I always felt that the most fascinating aspects of the new living arrangements were the political debates that went on well into the night between Lukas and my father. The Danish population, and Lukas in particular, had been outraged when the invasion occurred, and they resented Denmark's weak capitulation. And after all, my father was a member of the Danish government and partially responsible for the Cooperation Agreement.

"Lukas also took issue with Denmark's concession to join in the Anti-Comintern Pact. 'Scavenius sold us down the river,' Lukas said, referring to the time my father and Scavenius had traveled to Berlin, the time my father almost got arrested. In his criticism, Lukas was not alone. Professor Koch had been a vehement opponent of the Anti-Comintern Pact, which he considered an affirmation of Germany's claim to Aryanism.

"'That was a tense negotiation,' my father said, recalling his harrowing experience with the Gestapo in Berlin. 'Give Erik Scavenius a little credit. He held his own under enormous pressure from von Ribbentrop. Scavenius was able to affirm our red-line demands: no legislation against Denmark's Jews, no obligation to join the German-Japan-Italian Axis, and no obligation for the Danish army to fight against a foreign power. You must agree, it took courage to stand up to the Nazis on those demands.'

"Lukas gave a dismissive wave. 'He didn't stand up,' Lukas said. 'He crawled.' My father smiled. He was there in Berlin, he knew what happened between von Ribbentrop and Scavenius. And he could have set Lukas straight. But my father liked Lukas and he didn't want to crush his spirit or diminish the young man's passion and love for Denmark.

"In many ways, it seemed like my father was enjoying having a son to lock horns with. Not that raising two marvelous daughters was a disappointment, but there seemed to be a connection between Lukas and

Papa, a bonding. What troubled him the most that winter were Lukas's absences, which he knew were dangerous forays into battle zones. My father feared for his safety. As a member of Parliament, he would receive reports on resistance activities from time to time. Many of his colleagues thought that partisans were subverting the delicate relationship between Denmark and Germany.

"My father's misgivings concerning Dr. Best were well-founded. Best received his marching orders straight from Himmler; Denmark was a rebellious little stepchild which did not respect the rules. Best's job was to rein it in, and that meant rooting out saboteurs, which included Lukas and his Holger Club. Best sent several teams of Gestapo agents to attend rallies, lectures and any event where Danish solidarity was endorsed. They were to identify and record the attendees and follow up on them."

"If I may interrupt for just a moment," Liam says. "With all the increased surveillance from the Gestapo, weren't the clubs also concerned about informers like Henryks? Weren't they considered partners of the Gestapo?"

"Hmph," Britta scoffs. "The answer is yes. The Germans were paying for leads and information about resistance groups. As for Ole Hendricksen, he and his family were ne'er-do-wells, always looking for an easy buck. I have no doubts he was hanging around trying to find out who was in a resistance club, so he could sell the information to the Gestapo. After getting burned the first time, the members of the Holger Club took great care not to talk to anyone outside their immediate membership.

"As Grethe's due date approached, she begged Lukas not to go out on assignments. 'Let the others go,' she said. 'I need you here with me. What if I went into labor and you weren't here, and Parliament was in session and Britta was in school? Who would help me?' Lukas agreed. He would only take on a mission if it was urgent and he was personally needed. But, despite Lukas's assurances, Grethe's fears were realized on February 2, 1943."

Gladys knocks and enters the room with a phone message. She is sorry to interrupt but the clerk of the appellate court is calling about a real estate case Catherine is handling. Oral argument is scheduled in two weeks and the justices have received an emergency motion from

Catherine's opponent. Both attorneys must be present before the court tomorrow at ten o'clock to argue the motion. Catherine swears under her breath. This appellate matter has been a nightmare since the day it was filed. Now she will lose a day of preparation in Britta's case, a day she cannot afford to lose.

"I'm going to have to cut this short today," Catherine says. "We'll have an off day tomorrow and we'll resume on Thursday. Britta, I don't need to tell you how important it is to move on to the heart of the matter. I know you want to tell the whole story, but we have ten days left before we must comply with Judge Wilson's order. Please be thinking of how you can separate the wheat from the chaff. Considering the time remaining, be economical; give us what we need."

Britta nods her understanding, but it is unclear that she will change course. Britta is Britta, and it is likely that she will proceed at her pace.

"Emma," Catherine says, "since we're not going to work together tomorrow, I suggest that your grandmother take the day to rest up. We'll see you both on Thursday."

CHAPTER TWENTY-SEVEN

CATHERINE LOOKS AT her watch and then at Liam. Britta is one hour late. No one has called, or emailed, and no one has left a message on the office voicemail. "Give her a call," Liam says. "Maybe she got the instructions wrong. Maybe she thought tomorrow meant . . ."

"Thursday, Liam. We said Thursday more than once."

A few more ticks of the clock and Catherine finally calls out, "Gladys, can you get Emma Fisher on the phone for me?"

Catherine drums her fingers on the table. "I hope Britta isn't sick. You know she isn't well, and she's looked especially fatigued in the last few sessions."

"On line four, Cat," Gladys yells.

"I'm sorry, Catherine," Emma says. "We're trying to get it all together here, but Bubbe's having a rough day. She went out on a long walk yesterday and I think it took a lot of energy out of her. But we're almost ready. I'll drive her down in a few minutes."

BRITTA IS WALKING slowly, one step at a time. Emma has one hand on her elbow and the other wrapped around her waist. Nevertheless, Britta is dressed in her light blue suit and floral scarf, stylish as is her custom. The only exception is the pair of casual flats in lieu of her black block heels. She takes her usual seat at the conference table and smiles weakly. "I think I overdid yesterday," she says. "It was such a beautiful day and I wanted to walk to Belmont Harbor. You know, I used to go there when I first moved to the city. It has always been such a special place for me. In many ways it reminds me of Copenhagen. Staring out at the open sea, there's something so calming; that blue horizon where the water meets the sky." She looks at Emma. Her voice is weak. "I used to take you there when you were young. You and I, we'd watch the sailboats and the seagulls. Just the two of us. Do you remember? You were such a sweet little thing."

"I remember," Emma says softly with a catch in her throat. As do the others, Emma notices the weakened modulation in Britta's voice. Catherine and Liam are still. The room is on pause.

Britta takes a deep breath and shakes away a daydream. "All right, then, full speed ahead. On Tuesday, I told you that Grethe's fears about Lukas were realized on February 2, 1943, because that was the day the baby was born, and Lukas wasn't there. Two weeks earlier, Grethe received a coded message on the BBC radio; a drop was scheduled. This was to be a major operation and Lukas knew it would be a large shipment of weapons. He also knew where the weapons were to be distributed and the sabotage activities that were planned. Because of the scale of the operation, there were to be five resistance groups all coordinated by the Holger Club. They would reconnoiter at the drop site, recover the crates of weapons and transport them to the British commandos who had come ashore and were hiding in farmhouses near the coast.

"Grethe begged Lukas not to go. She grabbed his arms. 'Let Gunnison lead this assignment,' she said, but Lukas felt that such a delegation of authority would be irresponsible. 'I can't leave this mission to an inexperienced member like Knud Gunnison. Since Jan's absence, I have assumed the leadership and I can't abandon that charge. It would put the others in danger.' Despite Grethe's pleas, he left that night. It was January 21, 1943.

"Grethe was worried, but not alarmed when Lukas did not come home the next day. Sometimes those operations took two or three days. When that happened, the group would find a place to hide for a while, often sleeping in cars or trucks. There were times when advance reconnaissance revealed a Nazi patrol in the area, and the drop would be delayed or even canceled. Snafus did occur from time to time. Still, as one day passed into the next without word from Lukas, Grethe's anxiety grew. He should have returned. Someone should have contacted her. Having run out of patience, she called me into her room before I left for school. She was sitting there in her robe, her back propped up with pillows. She looked like she was about to explode.

"'Britta,' she said, 'I need a favor. I'm worried sick about Lukas. He may have been caught in a roundup. If he was, then the Danish police would have him locked up somewhere. Papa might know; sometimes, when there are major political incidents, the members of Parliament are informed. I've tried calling him at his office, but I'm told he is in session. He's not expected back for several hours. I just can't bear not knowing about the fate of my husband. And Britta, the baby's dropped. I can feel it. I know I'm going to give birth any minute. And my husband . . .' She broke into tears.

"I did my best to comfort her. I told her that Lukas had been in situations like this many times, that he was experienced. He would know what to do. Grethe waved it off. She didn't want words of comfort, she wanted action. 'Would you run down to Papa's office for me? Tell him about Lukas and his mission and the fact that I haven't heard from him in a week. Papa may have received news, or he might be able to find out. He has sources. He has contacts in the local police departments. He can find out; I know he can. Help me, Britta.'

"Of course, I would have done anything for my sister, but this was a heavy request. A bitter winter storm was blowing snow all over Copenhagen, and I had been looking for an excuse to skip school and avoid going outdoors altogether. But Grethe was desperate and she had turned to me; what could I do? I grabbed my heavy winter coat, put on my boots, knit cap and scarf and headed out into the blowing storm.

"Though the parliamentary offices were only a mile or so from the house, the walk was brutal, and I was half-frozen by the time I arrived. I went first to Papa's office and received the same response that Grethe had; Papa was busy, Parliament was in session. A serious matter was under consideration; plans were being made to conduct the first general election since the Nazi invasion. It was bound to be a touchy affair. The

Nazi Party was running a slate of parliamentary candidates. I prevailed on his secretary to pass him a note that I had come to see him.

"I waited for a while and finally my father came out to talk to me. He was annoyed. 'Britta, this is not a good time,' he said. 'We're in the middle of debate.' I asked him if he had heard anything about Lukas or a mass arrest. He had not. Grethe said the BBC coded message referenced the coastal area. I asked him if he could contact the police districts in that area. Maybe Lukas was in custody. He groused, said he didn't have time, said he was too busy, but in the end, he gave in. He made a few calls, but they were unavailing. None of his contacts had any information about Lukas.

"When I returned to Grethe and delivered the bad news, I faced another problem. It was all I could do to convince her not to go looking for him herself. Nine months pregnant, in the midst of a bitter winter storm, with Lukas missing for several days and having no idea where he might have gone, she finally conceded that it made no sense for her to lead a search party. My mother tried to calm her and counseled patience. Lukas is a brave and industrious man, she said. We just have to wait and pray for the best.

"But waiting and praying were never Grethe's strengths. In her current condition, she was short-tempered and fresh out of patience. So, she came to me again. 'Britta, you're my last hope. You have to find out what happened to Lukas. No one else will help me.' I grimaced. I knew my father wouldn't approve, he cautioned Lukas not to take risks in the first place. Besides, I had no idea where Lukas could be. Grethe thought that Lukas's mission was near the area where we had received the parachute drop a few weeks ago. That was several hours in a car, and I didn't have a car. So, in the face of all those roadblocks, I looked Grethe in the eye, squeezed her wrists and said, 'I will find him for you, Grethe. I promise!'"

Britta pauses, smiles and gazes around the conference table. "Not too smart to make that promise, was I? But I was determined to do everything possible. She'd have done it for me."

"I am so proud of you, Bubbe," Emma says with her eyes wide open. "I've never known this side of you. You were a daredevil."

Liam blinks. "Never knew she was a daredevil, Emma? Are we talking about your Bubbe, the same person who spray-painted six damning signs on Henryks's wall in the middle of the night?"

"I know," Emma says, "but back then she was only sixteen. Bubbe, if you didn't know where he was and you didn't have a car, how in the world did you intend to keep that promise?"

Catherine is enjoying the exchange. It is clear that Emma is totally captivated by her grandmother's escapades. Catherine is now certain that Britta is achieving exactly what she has set out to do. She is passing along her legacy the only way she can: by narration.

"My first thought was to seek out Professor Koch," Britta says. "He had his finger on the pulse of the resistance. He generally knew what the various clubs were doing. If anyone other than British intelligence knew where Lukas had gone that night, it would have been Professor Koch.

"'Well, hello Britta Morgenstern,' he said when I arrived at his office. 'What brings you out into this storm? How is your sister? Are you an aunt yet?'

"'Any moment now,' I answered. 'Grethe is doing well, and very ready to have her baby. I'm here about Lukas.' Koch nodded. 'I heard the mission was compromised,' he said. 'They were betrayed.'

"'By whom?' I asked. He shrugged. 'No one knows for certain. The rumors say it was the Blue Storm; a National Socialist youth group.' A thought went through my mind. 'Do they wear blue shirts?' He nodded."

Emma perks up. "Ole Henryks's group wore blue shirts."

Britta nodded. "I thought Dr. Koch might know what happened to the Holger Club that night, but again, he just shrugged his shoulders. 'The information is coming to me in pieces. Some were taken into custody, some escaped and went into hiding, and . . .' His voice trailed off.

"'And what else?'

"He lowered his eyes. 'I'm afraid some were shot.' I asked who and he didn't know.

"I kept pressing him. 'Those who were taken into custody, where are they being held?' Again, he didn't know. Perhaps they were handed over to the Gestapo, he wasn't sure. I asked him who would have this knowledge, where could I go to find out, and he shook his head. 'Sooner or later, it will all come out,' he said, 'but as of now, I don't think they have released very much.'

"That was as far as I could go with Professor Koch. My next thought was to contract Knud Gunnison. He was the only other club member with whom I was friendly. If he went on the mission and if he returned, there was a good chance I would find him at home. He might know something about Lukas. It was still stormy, but there was daylight remaining, so I decided to pay the Gunnisons a visit.

"Knud was seventeen. I knew him from school. He lived near the park. I knocked on the door and his mother answered. She held it partially open and looked at me suspiciously. I asked if Knud was home and she froze. 'Why do you want to know?' she snapped. 'What do you want with Knud, and who are you?'

"I was shocked. What an unfriendly woman. Why was she so angry? The storm was blowing hard and Knud's mother didn't have the courtesy to ask me into her foyer. 'I'm Britta Morgenstern,' I said. 'Grethe is my sister and Lukas is my brother-in-law and they are good friends with Knud. I just wanted to ask Knud if he knew where Lukas might be.'

"She sneered at me and shook her head. 'Hmph, Lukas,' she scoffed. 'He's the cause of all our problems. Well, Knud doesn't know anything. And you can be sure that he's not going to have anything further to do with those anarchists.' She raised her voice. 'Do you understand me?' She started to close the door on me when Knud came up from behind. 'She's okay, Mom, let me talk to her.' His mother huffed and left us alone. I stepped into the foyer.

"'I came back two days ago,' he said. 'The mission was a wreck. The Storm informed on us. Three other clubs, over thirty members altogether, stood there at the drop site waiting for the SOE plane. We heard it in the distance and all of a sudden, Danish police, German soldiers and those Gestapo men in plainclothes appeared out of nowhere. The plane approached, circled a couple times, didn't see flares and then flew off. Fortunately, the police didn't know about the flares, and without the proper signals, the plane aborted, so there were no parachutes or weapons for us to worry about. We scattered in all directions, and as we ran, bright searchlights came on scanning the entire area. The police and the military fanned out and many of our members were arrested. Some of us were able to flee into the woods. I was lucky.'

"'Professor Koch told me that some were shot,' I said. 'Is that right?'

Knud nodded. 'There were gunshots. A lot of them. There's just no way of knowing who or how many. We were betrayed, Britta. Some bastards turned us in.'

"'Professor Koch mentioned the Blue Storm Club,' I said, and Knud agreed. 'That's what I meant when I said the Storm. That's Billy Hendricksen's club. They're pro-Nazi.'

"'How would they know about the mission?' I said. He grimaced. 'There were four different clubs joining up on this mission. One of them must have had a leak.'

"Finally, I asked him if he knew any more about Lukas. He spread his hands. 'We were all running. They turned on these blinding lights, there was shouting, gunshots, screaming. Lukas was in front of me, then he was on my left, then he fell. I don't know if he was shot or he just tripped, but I didn't see him after that. I made my way to a barn and hid out there until the next night. I know my mom is angry. She says I could have died, and she's right. She also says we are breaking the Cooperation Agreement. If you ask me, it's the Nazis who are breaking the agreement. I see more Gestapo every day. You see them at all the rallies. You see them hanging out at the university.' At that point, Knud's mother called him. He looked around and with a defeatist sigh, he said, 'My mom, she's really . . . I can't do the club anymore. When you see Lukas, tell him I'm out.'

"I returned to Grethe to say that I was no closer to finding Lukas than when I left the house. I was sorry. She hugged me tightly . . . well, as tightly as she could with that big bundle in front. 'He'll come back to me,' she said. 'I know that he will.'"

Suddenly, there is a knock on the conference room door and Gladys rushes in with an open manila envelope. "This was just served on us by some smart-assed process server," she says. "The punk flips it on my desk and says, 'See you at three.' I wouldn't bother you, Cat, except it's an emergency petition to appear in court before Judge Wilson this afternoon at three o'clock. That's only four hours from now. And there is a notice to produce Mrs. Stein for testimony."

CHAPTER TWENTY-EIGHT

—⚬⚬⚬—

CATHERINE OPENS THE envelope and slides out a set of papers. The room is silent as she sits and examines the contents. With a stern expression, she sets them down on the table before her and turns to Britta. "What did you do yesterday, Britta?"

Puzzled, Britta says, "Nothing really. I told you, I went for a long walk to Belmont Harbor. Overdid it, probably. Why?"

Catherine leans back on her chair; her palm is on her forehead. "This is a petition for an emergency hearing to hold you in contempt of court for spray-painting another Nazi sign on Ole Henryks's property. Let me read it to you. 'At approximately 3:00 p.m., on information and belief, respondent, Britta Stein, in direct violation of this court's injunction order, did enter upon the property adjacent to the front of The Melancholy Dane, and did then and there, with malice aforethought, and in direct violation of this court's prohibitive order, intentionally paint a Nazi swastika, a photograph of which is attached hereto. Plaintiff demands that Defendant Britta Stein show cause, if any she can, why she should not be held in direct contempt of this court for her intentional actions, and upon said hearing that the maximum sanctions allowable be imposed upon her." Catherine slides the copy of the photograph across the table to Britta. It depicts the sidewalk in front of the tavern entrance with a large black swastika, at least four feet wide.

Britta looks at the photo and immediately begins to laugh and clap her hands. Emma cups her face in her hands, repeating, "Bubbe, Bubbe."

Catherine's lips are taut. "Do you think this is a joke, Britta? Obadiah Wilson can, and probably will, sentence you to jail, or at least levy a substantial fine, don't you realize that? All the hard work we've been doing, it might as well be for naught. Even if Henryks was a traitor and an informer, it's all meaningless because you have violated the court's order of protection and committed another criminal act. Any credibility you once had is gone. We talked about your testimony; your word against Henryks's. Well, now you have lost that credibility. You have blatantly and irresponsibly done the most self-destructive thing you could do to your legal position."

Britta stares at Catherine with the hint of a smile. She bites her bottom lip. She holds up both of her palms like a stop sign. "This is marvelous," she says. "It's delightful, delirious and delicious."

"Ach," grunts Catherine. "I give up."

Britta slides the photo back to Catherine. Her smile has broadened "I didn't do this. It wasn't me. I didn't paint that swastika. Don't you see, some other person who obviously knows what a rat Ole Hendricksen is painted that sign. Isn't that wonderful? I can't imagine who it is, but there is at least one other person who knows the truth and intends to stop his charade. I am not the only one who wants to set the record straight." She looks around the table. "I'll accept all of your apologies now."

"Oh, Britta . . ." Catherine is not convinced.

"Wait a minute," says Liam. "This is a photo of a swastika on The Melancholy Dane doorstep. Where is the photo of Britta painting it? When they filed the original lawsuit, they had multiple photos of Britta in her long coat taken in the middle of the night spraying the walls. This looks like a swastika was painted on the sidewalk in bright sunshine. Where is the picture of Britta?"

"Sparks isn't stupid," Catherine says. "He's either holding that photo back to dramatically produce it at the right moment, or he has a witness. There will be some explanation."

"The explanation is that I didn't paint it," Britta says. She taps the table with her index finger. "Catherine, look at me. I am telling you that I did not paint anything yesterday. I took a walk. That's it. There is someone else out there who knows what a fraud Ole Hendricksen is. Don't you think I'm telling you the truth?"

"It isn't me you have to convince; it's the judge. Do you have any way of proving where you were at any given time? Especially at three o'clock in the afternoon?"

Britta shakes her head. "I was on my walk. I suppose you could ask the seagulls. Maybe the totem pole at Addison Street. I stopped there for a bit to rest."

Catherine's scowls. "This is serious business, Britta. I'm not amused. Was the doorman on duty? Did he see you leave the building?"

"Yes, he did. His name is Clarence. He also saw me return a little after four."

"The timing is terrible. Are you sure you didn't see something or meet with somebody to prove you were at Belmont Harbor?"

Britta shrugs and shakes her head. "I stood there watching. All those big beautiful yachts. One of them, a long triple-decker, was pulling out of its slip and going for a cruise. It was poetry, the way it glided so effortlessly. I wished I was on that boat."

"What was the name of the boat?"

"Oh, I can't remember. I don't know if I paid attention to the name." Britta does not seem overly concerned. There is even a touch of giddiness in her demeanor, which perturbs Catherine all the more. She looks to Emma for an answer, but Emma's expression is blank.

She turns to Liam, who appears to be deep in thought. He twists his lips. "Cat, come out and talk to me for a minute."

The two leave the room, walk into Catherine's private office and shut the door. Catherine is beside herself. "What the hell am I going to do at three o'clock? How am I going to defend this? She just doesn't get it, Liam."

"I have a thought," he says. "Yesterday was the first day this week that we haven't all met together. You had an emergency hearing in the appellate court, right? It's public knowledge. Anyone who checks the docket could know that. It was also the first time that Britta decided to go out for a walk alone."

Catherine sighs. "What's your point?"

Liam continues. "We know that Sparks hired that punk Rivers to spy on the office and throw a splash of red paint."

"We don't know that."

"Well, we *think* that. We do know that I ran him down after he dropped a paper bag with a can of spray paint."

"We can't prove that he was working for Sparks. He could be some crazy Ole fanatic."

"But what if Sparks has this guy keeping an eye on what we're doing? What if he has someone watching Britta? He sees that Britta is out for a walk—all the way to Belmont Harbor. Perfect time to paint a swastika. How will she provide an alibi?" Liam shrugs. "Just sayin'. I wouldn't put it past Sparks. You know he'll have a whole bunch of reporters there this afternoon. That's how he litigates."

"I'm not buying it. It's just as likely that Henryks, his kid or one of his barflies is behind it. If it were Sparks, or someone working for him, who stalked Britta and then intentionally planted that swastika for the sole purpose of falsely accusing Britta, Sparks would be disbarred and face serious jail time. He's not that stupid."

"Only if he gets caught."

Catherine shakes her head. "He's a rat, but this is even beneath Sparks. That's a bad theory, but it is possible that it originates at the bar. It's also possible some prankster painted the swastika. Still, I'll bet you that Sparks has a photo or a video that shows Britta clear as day and he'll produce it at the hearing today."

There is a knock on the office door. It is Emma and she has the emergency petition in her hand. "Catherine, I have read through this petition very carefully. May I share a few thoughts?"

"Of course. You know we are very concerned about your grandmother and what she may have done yesterday."

"I know. I don't believe she did anything wrong and I don't believe she spray-painted the Nazi sign, but that's beside the point. I found some irregularities in Sparks's petition that I want to bring to your attention. For one thing, the petition is based on 'information and belief.' A petition for a rule is required to be verified; it must contain the signature of a person who swears under oath that the allegations are true. In this case, the affiant, Ole Henryks, swears that the allegations are true 'to the best of his information and belief.'

Catherine immediately perks up like a Doberman on alert. "Let me see that, please." She scans the document, looks up and smiles. "Good catch, Emma!" Then to Liam, she explains, "It's a defective affidavit. The petition is flawed. Henryks didn't swear that Britta painted the swastika, only that he *believes* she did. Maybe they don't have a picture. Not that I will lower my guard, but I don't think they have any proof.

"Britta, we are about to head over to the courthouse. For a hearing like this, I would usually take days to prepare my witness. We have about an hour. I need you to listen carefully to my instructions. You will be called as a witness and you will be sworn to tell the truth. If you did anything other than walk to the harbor yesterday, as you have told us several times, then you need to disclose it to me now."

Britta shrugs nonchalantly. "There's nothing else. I'm a pretty boring person."

Catherine holds up her index finger to make a point. "Only you know what you did yesterday. I know what you told me, but only you know what you did. Let's leave it at that."

"I feel like you don't trust me."

"I'm doing my job. In a proceeding like this, which is quasi-criminal, you have the right to refuse to answer any question, other than your name. It is a right guaranteed to you by the Constitution."

"I know about the Fifth Amendment. I watch TV. I see those crooks refusing to testify and claiming their Fifth Amendment rights. They are all criminals. How would it look if I did the same thing? Everyone would think I am a criminal."

"I don't care what anyone but the judge thinks, and he is not allowed to draw any adverse inferences from the exercise of your constitutional rights. I will give you a piece of paper to read in the event you decide not to testify. It says, 'I respectfully refuse to answer that question on the grounds that my answer may, in whole or in part, tend to incriminate me.' Do you want to practice that?"

"I most certainly do not. I do not believe that any answer I give will incriminate me and I will not say so."

Catherine's eyes roll up to the ceiling. She exhales a blast of air. "One more thing. There will be a crowd of reporters and court watchers in the lobbies and in the courtroom. There will be video. The reporters will shout out questions at you, like 'Why did you do it?' Do not answer them. They have no right to ask you questions and you have no duty to answer them. The best advice is to look straight ahead and walk into the courtroom. Okay?"

Britta nods. "Okay."

"Any final questions before we head over to court?"

Britta bites her bottom lip. "Am I dressed fancy enough to see a judge?"

Catherine smiles warmly. "You look great."

CHAPTER TWENTY-NINE

———— ∞∞∞ ————

CATHERINE, LIAM, EMMA and Britta enter the lobby of the Daley Center. Reporters with their film crews, sound booms, earbuds, mics and aggressive attitudes instantly descend on them like locusts on a wheat field. As Catherine had foretold, multiple questions, statements and accusations are shouted out and echo off the marble walls.

Though instructed to look straight ahead, pass through the security station and proceed directly to the courtroom, Britta pauses to take in the frenzy. She is dazzled. They are all there because of her and she cannot help but express her appreciation for their interest. Indeed, it was her hope from the very beginning to draw attention to Ole Hendricksen and his wartime betrayals. From beneath her wide-brimmed linen hat adorned with straw flowers, she smiles sweetly and nods to each of the reporters as she passes them, like she would to a classroom full of toddlers. "How are you, dear?" she says to a female reporter who has managed to budge in line close to her. Britta also makes it a point to establish eye contact whenever she can, all of which seems to effectuate a shift in the tenor of the verbal exchanges. The reporters begin to address her more politely. The questions are less accusatory and more inquisitive, often preceded by "Please," and spoken rather than shouted. Though Catherine had counseled against such a parley, Britta seems to be winning the moment.

Liam elbows Catherine. "She may be the most likable ninety-two-year-old in the city," he says. Nevertheless, even though the reporters' questions are more polite, they clearly assume that Britta has painted a swastika on Henryks's property.

Catherine leads Britta to the elevators. When the door slides open, Liam blocks the reporters from coming into the car. Alone for the few minutes it takes to reach the 21st floor, Catherine once again admonishes Britta not to say anything. "You can smile and nod, that's okay, but please do not respond verbally to the reporters. Let's just walk directly into the courtroom and take our seats."

Catherine's instructions are more easily spoken than followed. Reporters are standing outside the courtroom waiting for the deputy to unlock the door so they can jockey for their seats. Catherine steers Britta to a corner of the hallway by the windows, and Emma and Liam take up position as barriers to keep the reporters at bay. Liam leans over to Emma and says, "I guess we'll never know for certain what your grandmother did yesterday, and I hope she's telling us the truth that all she did was take a walk, but I will tell you one thing for sure: she has charmed the pants off these reporters. If Sparks manufactured this stunt in order to generate media publicity, it's going to backfire on him. She is clearly not the demented, crazy, maniacal witch he has characterized. She's a sweet old woman everybody loves."

Emma smiles. "That's my Bubbe."

"In the end," he says, "I doubt it will matter very much what the press thinks. It only matters what the eminent Obadiah Wilson thinks."

Emma disagrees. "In the early stages of the case, you may be right. But if we actually go to trial, potential jurors who have been following the reports in the press will be influenced. Many will come into court with their minds made up."

There is a sudden rush as the courtroom door is opened and reporters scramble through to get a seat. Video and photojournalists are prohibited from entering the courtroom by Wilson's standing order. Catherine, Liam, Emma and Britta hold back until the doorway is cleared and they enter to take their seats at the counsel table. Sparks has not appeared. The first row is reserved for witnesses and, as of yet, it is vacant. There is a low rumble of conversation as everyone gets settled.

The last to arrive, Sterling Sparks makes his grand entrance. He struts in with Ole by his side and the conversations pick up. He is dressed today in a dark gray pinstriped suit, masterfully tailored to his thin body, and complemented by a blaze of colors in his tie and his pocket square. He moves with the grace of a dancer, twirling from side to side to make eye contact with as many as he can. He seats Ole at the plaintiff's counsel table and begins a quick round of handshakes with reporters he knows. He flashes his Colgate smile and chuckles affectionately, especially at the women. For the moment, Sparks is sailing on his personal sea.

All of this prehearing theater plays on around Britta, but her eyes are fixed on Ole Henryks. Her head and shoulders are turned toward him, and her face is locked in a freeze-frame. If her eyes possessed the mythical quality of beaming fire, Ole would be incinerated on the spot. Ole returns the attention with a quizzical look, as if to say, "Why are you doing these things to me? Why don't you leave me alone?" This moment is not lost on the reporters. They scramble to make notes on what they will refer to as "The Face-off." Courtroom artists quickly jot pencil drawings that they will later embellish with watercolors.

The Face-off is not lost on Catherine and Liam either. Britta's stare is not a look that seeks confirmation of her identification. It is a certainty that bespeaks accusation and judgment day. Though proof of the matter—whether Henryks is indeed a traitor, betrayer and Nazi collaborator—will not be reached until trial, Britta has achieved a stepping-stone toward that goal. She has brought Henryks into the valley of confrontation and created substantial doubt of her guilt in the minds of those present, who now have to wonder whether this sweet woman is telling the truth after all. Thank you, Mr. Sparks, for advancing that day and turning those tables, Catherine thinks.

"All rise." The corner door swings open, and Judge Wilson enters, preceded by his clerical staff. His appearance is regal. He scans the room with a menacing look and takes his seat on the elevated bench. "I see that there are no standees this afternoon and for that I am grateful. Let me reiterate my earlier warnings for those who may have forgotten: no pictures, no sound recordings, no videos, no talking." His sonorous baritone comes from deep within his chest, evincing his classical training in voice. As a young man, he considered a career in opera and pursued his studies in New York before the law took him in another direction. The height of his brief operatic career occurred in 1976 when he was the primary understudy for the principal role in Verdi's *Simon Boccanegra*. The Playbills for the two Sunday matinees in which he performed are framed and sitting on a shelf in his chambers beside a flattering review from the *Times*.

Wilson reaches out, opens the case file, removes Sparks's petition for contempt, and places it on the bench before him. "Will the parties please identify themselves for the record," he says.

Sparks jumps to his feet. "Sterling J. Sparks, attorney for plaintiff. I am pleased to be joined today by Mr. Ole Henryks, the plaintiff, who is sitting to my right. It is, of course, my petition to hold defendant Britta Stein in contempt of this court for her intentional and—"

"That'll do," Wilson says without any emotion, and looks to his right. "Ms. Lockhart, for the record, please."

She stands. "Catherine Lockhart on behalf of Britta Stein, who is present in court today." She motions to her left. "I am assisted in this proceeding by attorney Emma Fisher."

"Has Ms. Fisher entered her appearance?"

"Not yet, your honor."

He nods again and says, "We'll note for the record that attorney Emma Fisher also appears for the defendant. May I remind all concerned that I have read the pleading." He tips his head in Catherine's direction. "Is the defendant prepared to proceed?"

"Your honor, all of this came on quite suddenly. We were served at noon today, and we have not had adequate time to respond or prepare. Defendant requests a continuance in order to file her written response."

Wilson shakes his head. "I will certainly allow you to file your written response, and we may end up adjourning to a later date, but I will hear evidence today. On its face, this is a very serious charge. My injunction order was clear. Mrs. Stein was not to approach Mr. Henryks or his establishment. The petition asserts that the defendant intentionally violated that order and painted a Nazi sign on his front steps. Mrs. Stein has a history of painting similar accusations on Mr. Henryks's property. She has admitted so. For that reason, I extended the temporary restraining order when you were last in court. As I recall, Ms. Lockhart, you did not object to the extension."

"That is correct, your honor. With regard to today's petition and its accusations, if an evidentiary hearing were to occur, I anticipate that Mrs. Stein will deny that she violated the order or painted a swastika. But we object to proceeding this afternoon, not only because of short notice but because the petition is defective. If given the right to file our response, we will move to strike and dismiss the petition."

Sparks laughs loudly. "Defective," he says. "Oh, I'm sure. Ha! We attached a copy of a picture of the swastika, Ms. Lockhart, in case you didn't look. It's there in black and white!"

Wilson rolls his eyes and slams his gavel. "Enough, Mr. Sparks. Tell me, Ms. Lockhart, why is the petition defective?"

"The affidavit supporting the petition—"

"Yep," interrupts Sparks, popping out of his seat, "it's supported by an affidavit and it's signed. The original signature is right there on the petition and Ole Henryks is sitting right here in court." Sparks swivels around to smile, nod and gaze at the reporters.

Wilson is peeved. "Mr. Sparks, if you interrupt again, I will continue this hearing for six months."

Sparks quickly sits down. "Sorry, your honor."

"What about the affidavit Ms. Lockhart? Why is it defective?"

"It is based on information and belief. It doesn't swear that the facts alleged are true to Mr. Henryks's personal knowledge."

Wilson raises his eyebrows and studies the affidavit. He turns to Sparks. "She's right."

"But your honor," Sparks says, "he's sitting right here. He'll testify under oath. That's better than a sworn affidavit. He'll take the stand, swear to tell the truth and testify to everything in the affidavit. Besides, the defendant is also in court and she'll testify. I expect her to proudly admit she painted the swastika, just like she boasted about the other Nazi words she painted."

Wilson pulls on his lower lip as he ponders his next move. "I should make you refile," he says. "But then we'd all be back here tomorrow and that would be a waste of everyone's time. I'm deeply concerned that my injunction order may have been intentionally violated and I do want to hear the evidence. Call your first witness, Mr. Sparks."

"I call Nils Henryks."

Ole's son rises from the first spectator row. He is tall, lanky and dressed in a blue blazer over a light blue button-down shirt, open at the collar. He takes long steps and makes his way to the witness stand, where he swears to tell the truth. After a few introductory questions, Nils says, "I was coming to work yesterday about three o'clock. That's the time I usually get there for my evening shift. As I walked to the front door, I saw it on the ground. You could see it from a block away, it was very large. A Nazi swastika on my father's front step."

"Were you surprised?" Sparks asks, and there are several giggles from the spectator gallery.

"Of course I was. I mean, maybe I shouldn't be, because Mrs. Stein has already painted a half-dozen hateful signs, but yes sir, I was." He turns his head to the judge. "My father's no Nazi. He fought the Nazis and helped people escape. I just think this name-calling has got to stop. It upsets him quite a bit."

"Just answer the questions posed to you," Wilson says.

Sparks hands Nils the photograph of the swastika. "Did you take this picture yourself?"

Nils nods. "Yes sir. I took it with my phone and printed it out for you."

"No further questions of this witness."

Wilson looks down at Catherine. "Cross?"

"Mr. Henryks, the swastika was already on the sidewalk when you arrived, is that your testimony?"

"Yes ma'am."

"And I think you testified that you were surprised when you saw it on the ground?"

He snickers. "Well, yeah. Wouldn't you be if it was painted at your law office?"

Catherine is unfazed. "Well, the fact that you were surprised when you saw it on the ground means that you didn't see someone out there painting it or leaving the scene, did you?"

"No ma'am, I didn't."

"Or you would have taken a picture of that person."

"Yeah. That's not all I woulda done."

"We know from prior court proceedings that The Melancholy Dane has security cameras. That's how you identified Mrs. Stein in connection with the other painted statements, am I right?"

"Yes ma'am."

Liam is nervous. He knows where Catherine is going and it's a dangerous path. She is going to ask to see the video of Britta painting the swastika. If they have it, it's good night Britta, but it's better to get it out now during the cross.

"Mr. Henryks," Catherine says, "did you bring a copy of the video with you today, the one showing the person who painted the swastika?"

Nils shakes his head.

"Is that a 'no'?" Catherine says. "You didn't bring any video or photographs showing a person painting the swastika?"

"Don't have a video. The camera is on the side of the building, not in the front. I'm sure that's why Mrs. Stein painted in the front and not on the side."

"So, you didn't see her paint, and you have no photographic proof to offer us today that Mrs. Stein was the person who painted a sign in front of your father's establishment, am I correct?"

"No, I don't, but she did it. 'Cause that's what she does. Who else would defame my father like that?" He points at Britta. "She did it!"

"Move to strike everything he said following 'No, I don't,'" Catherine says.

Wilson nods. "It will be stricken. Anything further, Ms. Lockhart?"

"Nothing further for this witness," Catherine says and sits down.

"Call your next witness, Mr. Sparks."

With the broad smile of a boy about to eat his chocolate cake, Sparks announces, "Petitioner calls Mrs. Britta Stein to the witness stand."

Catherine leans over and whispers, "You do not have to answer any questions at all. Remember our discussion."

Britta nods. "I understand."

Emma helps her to rise from her seat. She takes her by the elbow and wraps her arm around her waist for support, and they walk to the witness stand.

The clerk administers the oath to Britta, but before Sparks can ask a question, Judge Wilson says, "Mrs. Stein, do you understand what this proceeding is all about this afternoon? Do you understand that you are being accused of violating an order of this court?"

Britta nods and as she does the brim of her hat flops up and down. "I do, sir."

"Has your attorney fully advised you of your Fifth Amendment protections against self-incrimination?"

"Yes sir, she has."

Wilson takes a deep breath and says, "Your witness, Mr. Sparks. You may proceed."

Sparks prances up a few paces and says, "Where were you yesterday afternoon at approximately three o'clock?"

"I was at Belmont Harbor, taking a walk."

Sparks stifles a snicker. "Did anybody see you there? At Belmont Harbor? At three o'clock?"

"Oh yes, I'm sure they did. There were many people there."

"What are the names of the people who can testify that you were there?"

"I have no idea."

"I thought so. You say you went to Belmont Harbor; for what purpose?"

"I enjoy watching the boats. One boat, I think it was the very largest boat in the harbor, was gliding out through the channel on its journey. Very picturesque. Lovely."

"Right, lovely," Sparks says amidst a few chuckles. "Would you agree, Mrs. Stein, that you cannot name a single person who could come to this courtroom and verify your alibi that you were watching lovely boats at Belmont Harbor? Agreed?"

Britta shrugs. "I cannot give you a name, but that is where I was."

Liam stands, whispers to Catherine and dashes out of the courtroom.

Sparks continues. "Isn't it a fact, madam, that yesterday at approximately three o'clock, you went to The Melancholy Dane and painted a Nazi swastika on the pavement in front of the door?"

"I did not, nor would I."

"Nor would you?" Sparks laughs out loud, and Wilson slams his gavel. Sparks nods. "I apologize, your honor." Then to Britta he says in a pointed tone, "You confessed to painting six horrible accusations on my client's property, but now you say you would never paint a Nazi swastika, is that what you want us to believe?"

"Exactly. When I painted statements on Mr. *Hendricksen's* wall, they were my words and they were true. When I wrote 'Traitor, Betrayer, Informer' those words were a part of my vocabulary and I used them to express myself. I have never used a Nazi symbol in any expression, because to do so I would have to internalize that symbol; make it a part of my vocabulary. A swastika is the vilest symbol imaginable to a Jewish person. Its use is prohibited in several countries, including Germany, where it is a crime. No practicing Jew would ever choose to adopt a swastika for any personal use whatsoever. It was a sign of exclusion, torture and death. If I had painted that swastika, made it mine for the purpose of expressing my hatred, I would be no better than the Nazis who wore it on their sleeves. I will call Ole Hendricksen a betrayer, a collaborator, and a traitor, and those are my words, but you will never see me use a Nazi symbol; not a swastika, not an SS emblem, not an oak leaf cluster, nor a Totenkopf death's-head. Never!"

Wilson peers down at Sparks. "Anything further, Mr. Sparks?"

Sparks hesitates. He has another question, but he doesn't know how she will answer, and there is a strong possibility that he will get burned again. "Not with this witness."

Liam reenters the courtroom and hands Catherine a note. She smiles. Wilson says, "Ms. Lockhart, will there be a cross-examination?"

"Yes, your honor. Very brief." She walks up to the witness stand and says, "Britta, if I say 'Monica's Island,' does that mean anything to you?"

Britta smiles. "Yes, it does. It's the name of a boat. That is the boat I saw yesterday going on its journey from Belmont Harbor."

Catherine turns to face the judge. "Your honor, if you will give us a short continuance, I will subpoena the harbormaster at Belmont Harbor. He will testify that the fifty-five-foot cabin cruiser, named *Monica's Island*, left its slip yesterday at three o'clock for a trip to New Buffalo, Michigan. He specifically recalls that boat and that hour because it purchased three hundred gallons of fuel before it left."

"It's not necessary to subpoena him," Wilson says and looks at Sparks, who shrugs his shoulders. "Call your next witness, Mr. Sparks."

"We have no further witnesses, your honor."

"You rest?"

"We do."

"Hmm," Wilson says. "I take it Mr. Henryks is not going to take the stand and testify that he saw the defendant painting the swastika?"

"He wasn't there at the time."

Wilson slowly nods his understanding. "Petition denied."

"But your honor," Sparks pleads, "this honorable court is obliged to take into consideration a defendant's pattern of criminal conduct. This court may infer that Mrs. Stein painted that swastika because it is consistent with her past course of conduct."

"Denied." Wilson slams his gavel and stands. He is about to leave the bench, when Sparks says, "Your honor, we do not have a trial date set in this matter. Given the volatile atmosphere surrounding this case, it is essential to convene a trial at the earliest possible moment."

"Volatile atmosphere?"

"Absolutely. My client feels that his life is in danger because of the atmosphere Mrs. Stein has created. Personally, I still believe that she painted the swastika, but if someone else painted it, Mrs. Stein is no less responsible. Her defamatory campaign has turned society against Mr. Henryks, and it's wrong. As I have said many times, the longer this case lingers on the court's docket, the more credibility it gathers and the more it will cause Mr. Henryks to suffer. He is entitled to a quick and public resolution. Either Ole Henryks is a Nazi collaborator, or he is not. Either he is a traitor, or he is not. He is entitled to his day in court. Convene a jury and let it do its rightful fact-finding job—decide once and for all if Mr. Henryks is an innocent victim and if Mrs. Stein is guilty of leveling false accusations. Justice requires that this matter be resolved. We demand an immediate trial!"

Wilson sits back down. He strokes his chin and breathes heavily through his nose while he ponders the dilemma. He has heard Sparks's blustery oratory more times than he cares to remember, but this time, his rants deserve consideration. He tips his head in Catherine's direction. "Ms. Lockhart, how soon will defendant be prepared to try this case?"

"Soon? Not soon. This case isn't even at issue; we haven't filed our answer or our affirmative defense. You gave us thirty days, and they are not due to be filed for eight more days. Thereafter, we intend to engage in thorough discovery as permitted by the rules: depositions, interrogatories, exchange of documents."

Wilson taps his fingers on the file folder. There is a prolonged pause. Finally, he places both palms on the table. "I'll tell you what. We're going to set this matter for status on the day after your pleading is due. At that hearing I will enter a case management order with specific dates. But I can tell you right now, I'm thinking I'll set a deadline of September 30 for completion of all discovery, with a trial a few months thereafter."

"But, your honor, we haven't begun discovery," Catherine says.

"Then you better get to work." Wilson taps his gavel and turns to leave the courtroom. "That will be the order."

The reporters are all standing, gathering up their notepads, getting ready to call in their stories when Sparks turns and loudly addresses them all. His face is red. "She may have been able to slip one by today with that cute boat trick," he says, "but I want you all to keep in mind she was caught and has *confessed* to painting six defamatory remarks on my client's wall. No boats are going to get her out of that. Trust me, in a very few months you will all come and witness a trial, there will be a huge verdict, and the only boat you'll be talking about will be the *Titanic*."

Catherine rolls her eyes. There are chuckles skittering through the gallery. On the way out of the courtroom, several reporters take the time to shake Britta's hand and wish her well.

CHAPTER THIRTY

———— ∝∞∝ ————

"I HAD PROMISED Grethe that I would find out what happened to Lukas, and I had failed. Professor Koch had no information though he had heard that some boys were arrested, and he believed that some were shot. Knud Gunnison told me that Lukas had fallen during the escape, but he gave me no further information. My father had discreetly put out feelers to his law enforcement contacts, but nothing had come of it. Now I was back at home, sitting with my sister in her bedroom, and trying to comfort her. It was the night before her baby was born.

"Suddenly, there was a loud knock on the front door, shattering all of the calm I was trying to create. Then another and another. Hard, frantic rapping. My father rushed to the door and opened it to find two men standing in the hallway. I had a partial view from where I sat on the end of Grethe's bed.

"'Herr Morgenstern?' one of the men said in an imperious, discourteous tone. His accent was decidedly German.

"My father was angry. 'Who are you to come banging on my door like that?' he demanded.

"The man took an identification card from his inside jacket pocket and showed it to my father. It read 'Geheime Staatspolizei,' German for secret state police, which everyone commonly referred to as the Gestapo.

"'What is it you want?' my father asked. 'If this is official business,

you may make an appointment at my office in the administration building, where I keep regular office hours. You have no right to come to my
home.'

"'Really, Herr Morgenstern? I think it is not up to *you* to tell *me* what
my rights are. Where is Lukas Holstrum?' The man's demeanor was officious; he kept his chin in the air and a smirk on his face. His tone was
brusque. I was well-aware of my father's temperament when he got angry, and I knew that they were going to lock horns. These were two
Gestapo agents who were not accustomed to being challenged in their
interrogations, but Joseph Morgenstern was not a man to back down.
He would stand his ground. Knowing that, I was frightened for him.

"The first Gestapo agent, the one who did all the talking, was a short,
stocky man in a long tan overcoat and a brown felt fedora. 'We have
learned that Lukas Holstrum is living in this residence with his wife. Oh
ya, we know that he is here, so do not try to deceive us. We want to talk
to Lukas Holstrum.'

"The agent's loud demands carried into the bedroom and frightened
Grethe. She started shaking. She grabbed my arms and dug in her nails.
'The Gestapo is looking for Lukas,' she said to me in a voice that was part
whisper and part panic. 'This is terrible, Britta.'

"'Maybe it's not so terrible,' I said quietly. 'It means they don't have
him. He's not in their custody and they believe he's still alive. If he was
in prison, or if he had been killed, they wouldn't be here right now.' That
seemed to calm Grethe and she nodded.

"My father had stationed himself in the doorway blocking the entrance into our home like a brick wall. 'Lukas is not here,' he said, 'but
even if he was, the Gestapo has no jurisdiction here and no authority to
confront him at my home or frankly, anywhere else in our country. The
Gestapo does not enter Danish homes uninvited! All criminal and civil
matters are under the jurisdiction of the Danish police and the Danish
courts. I am a member of Parliament and I know the law.'

"The Gestapo agent said something quietly to his associate, and then,
more loudly and sarcastically, he boomed, 'He knows the law, Helmut,
what do you think of that? He knows the law.'

"'I am a duly elected official, a member of the Danish Parliament,'
my father said, 'and I know that we are not in Germany and you can't

come barging into my house. That is the law.' In that regard my father was right. Policies set by the Cooperation Agreement forbade German forces, and especially the Gestapo, from forcing their way into homes or businesses. They were to apply to the local municipal police if they thought there was a crime. My father stood stern and powerful, and I loved him for it.

"'We know who you are, Herr Member of Parliament,' the Nazi said in his pompous tone. 'As a member of the Danish government, you should know that Dr. Best has been assigned here because of Denmark's rampant disobedience. It has allowed anarchists and revolutionaries to run wild and sabotage lawful German operations with impunity. They must be rounded up and punished.'

"My father held up his finger and wagged it back and forth. 'But only by Danish law enforcement personnel, not by you.'

"'Alas, Herr Morgenstern, Danish civil authorities are not doing their job. That is why Dr. Best is now in Copenhagen. The high command in Berlin has sent him here to protect German interests. He is not a man to be trifled with. Dr. Best will make sure that the illegal packs of partisans, like Lukas Holstrum, do not cause any further damage to our interests. *Verstehen?*'

"'Well, if Best has you two running around, I guess he's not doing such a good job, is he?' my father said. 'So, if you've come to bother me at my house, this conversation is over. Good day.'

"The man didn't move. 'We want Lukas Holstrum, Herr Member of Parliament, not you. He is a criminal and a threat to our military operations. He and his so-called Holger Gang have already caused millions of marks in damages. Dr. Best has labeled him a revolutionary and a communist operative.'

"'Good day!' my father repeated, but the agent did not back away. Instead, he shouted over my father's shoulder, 'Lukas Holstrum! Lukas Holstrum, come show yourself! You must come out here for questioning, right now!' The situation was growing more tense, but my father remained unshaken. 'For the last time, he isn't here. Now leave.'

"'Where is he, Herr Morgenstern?'

"My father shrugged. 'I believe it to be an unsolved mystery.'

"There was a pause, and then the agent said, 'Oh, a mystery? Then maybe Holstrum's *wife* will solve the mystery for us. Hmm? That would be Grethe Holstrum, also known as Grethe Morgenstern. Your daughter, I believe? She is the wife of Lukas Holstrum.' He uttered a few short chuckles and then shouted over my father's shoulder, '*Grethe Holstrum! Grethe Morgenstern! Whatever your name is now, Kommen sie, mach schnell!*'

"Grethe and I were locked in a hug, both of us scared to death, but our father was a rock. He put his hand on the door, said, 'Go back to Germany and harass your own citizens. You are in Denmark!' And then he slammed the door in the face of the agent. From out in the hall, the man cursed my father and shouted, 'You will pay for this insolence.' Before leaving, he called from the hallway in a mocking, singsong tone, 'Oh, Grethe Holstrum, Grethe Holstrum, you are in there, and we know you are, and we are waiting for you. You and Lukas. Mr. and Mrs. Holstrum. Believe me, it is only a matter of time.'

"My father came to us and shut the bedroom door. Grethe was a mess; she was shaking and clenching her fists. She was an amalgam of rage and fright. He sat next to her on the bed and she leaned over to cry on his shoulder. 'Don't worry, sweetheart, they are gone now. They're just blowhards. There's nothing to be afraid of.'

"She looked up. 'You slammed the door in his face.'

"He nodded. 'I know, didn't you love it? I'm sure I'll hear about it later. I'll get a memo on keeping up good relations with our German partners.'

"'They threatened me,' Grethe said. 'They said they are waiting for me. I thought the Germans were supposed to leave Danish citizens alone.'

"'They are, but intimidations like this are due to Dr. Best,' my father replied. 'Those men were right about one thing; Best was sent here to tighten the noose. That is why we see a much larger Gestapo presence. Hundreds of agents are being sent here.'

"'It seems like they're so much more aggressive,' Grethe said. 'The Gestapo didn't use to confront Danish people. They just skulked around spying on us and making notes.'

"'You're right. Von Renthe-Fink was a diplomat. He tried to solve problems through negotiation, always abiding by the Cooperation Agreement. Berlin thought he was too lenient. I also believe that the present clampdown is due to the recent failure of the German military. They have suffered critical losses in North Africa, and their attempt to take Stalingrad failed with great loss of life—a huge embarrassment for Hitler and his so-called unconquerable army. Allied bombs are now falling on Cologne and northern Germany. Many believe the war is turning. Berlin is scrambling to keep the lid on a boiling pot, and now they are witnessing an increase in Danish resistance. The acts of sabotage have angered Himmler and the German high command, and then, last November, King Christian's telegram infuriated Hitler. That was the last straw.'

"Grethe began to cry. 'I'm sorry,' she said, 'but this is all too much for me right now. I can feel this baby coming and I'm scared. I need my husband and he's missing. The Gestapo is looking for him and now they want me as well. If I go to the hospital to have my baby, they'll arrest me.'

"My father shook his head and pulled Grethe close to his chest. 'No, honey, they won't. They don't have that authority. When that baby decides the time is right, I'll go with you to the hospital. They won't dare touch us. That would be a clear violation of the status quo, and Werner Best is not about to cause a diplomatic incident. I know that for a fact.'"

Catherine interrupts Britta's narrative. "Was that a fact? Was the Gestapo powerless to do anything in Denmark other than investigate and call the police?"

Britta's partial shrug confirms Catherine's skepticism. "Generally speaking, it was a fact. *Legally,* my father was correct; the Gestapo did not have *legal* authority to arrest Danish citizens or enforce the internal laws. But nothing could be certain during those days. The terms 'authority' and 'power' became more ambiguous as 1943 progressed. It was a year in which everything was turned upside down in Denmark. As the resistance activities increased, Werner Best began to employ the Gestapo as he did in Germany; as a secret police force dispatched to intimidate, infiltrate and arrest anyone determined to be a threat to Germany's military or policy interests. Except, in Denmark the Gestapo was not *legally* authorized to arrest.

"'On those occasions when the Gestapo went too far and Best was chastised by the Danish Parliament, he would merely say that in his judgment, the matter was not internal but one with international implications,' my father explained. 'Best would point to the Cooperation Agreement and say that it was Germany's duty to protect Denmark from foreign enemies and the resistance movement was an arm of the foreign governments. On one occasion he told the Parliament that the acts of sabotage weakened Germany's ability to protect Denmark from a British invasion. And that was how he justified sending twelve armed Gestapo agents to arrest or kill the members of the Holger Club.'

"Grethe wondered how my father knew so much inside information. How could he know what Berlin's instructions were to Dr. Best? My father smiled one of those 'I-know-but-I-can't-tell-you' smiles. He said, 'Oh, let's just say your father is a respected diplomat who keeps his eyes and ears open. Even under the most adverse conditions, there are back channels for diplomats, and we keep them open.'

"Grethe and I had long suspected that our father had established covert alliances with German diplomats. There were times when he would have to step away and take a furtive phone call. If my mother asked who it was, he would brush it off and say it was nothing. 'Folketing business,' he would say. But my father's body language would give him away. We knew that his telephone calls and secret meetings had something to do with the Germans and that he was receiving inside information from someone highly placed. What we didn't know at the time was that his back channel was the German naval attaché Georg Duckwitz. That relationship would later become pivotal.

"Sitting there that night in Grethe's room, with so much tension in the air, I felt the need to lift my sister's spirits. She was about to have a baby and her nerves were frayed. To my way of thinking, it was my job to prevent any negative vibrations from passing through her umbilical cord into my little niece or nephew. 'Let's all make a vow to stay positive,' I said. Grethe looked at me like I was crazy. 'Really, Britta?' she said.

"'Look on the bright side,' I said. 'The Gestapo is looking for Lukas and that has to mean he's alive and safe somewhere. And maybe Lukas also knows they're looking for him, and that's why he hasn't come home or contacted anyone.'

"My father picked up on it. 'I think Britta makes a good point,' he said. 'We have to believe that Lukas is still alive. I haven't heard differently, and apparently, neither has the Gestapo. So, let's all keep positive thoughts.'

"I shot a sister-love smile at Grethe, and she nodded back. We were always a pair, tightly connected. We locked little fingers and we made a pact. We would stay positive and calm; no negative thoughts would be allowed. Ever. That pact lasted for a few hours, or until her contractions started in earnest. By then, calm was out the window. Add to that, she needed to go to the hospital, but she was afraid to leave the house. She was sure the Gestapo was waiting for her, standing under a lamppost, smoking cigarettes, like they did in the movies. My father, as always, saved the day. He dismissed any thoughts that the Gestapo were waiting, but just to be on the safe side, he called his friend, the Copenhagen chief of police, and he and Grethe rode to the hospital in the backseat of the chief's police car, lights flashing."

"Did she have her baby that night?" Emma asks.

"The next morning. A healthy baby girl."

Emma's face lights up. "What did Aunt Grethe name her?"

Britta pauses for a moment, gives a little bite on her bottom lip, looks directly into Emma's eyes and says, "That beautiful baby was named Isabel Holstrum."

When Emma hears that, her expression freezes. "That was my mother's name," she says, then furrows her brow. "But before she married Charles Fisher, her name was Isabel Stein, not Holstrum. Are you telling me that Grethe's baby was actually my mother? Isabel Holstrum became Isabel Stein? *Your* name, Bubbe? And Grethe Morgenstern Holstrum, a woman I never knew, was really my grandmother? And *you* are . . . ?"

"It's a long story, sweetheart. Be patient."

CHAPTER THIRTY-ONE

———◦◦◦◦———

CATHERINE IS STANDING by the side of her bed. A suitcase lies open and Liam is picking out clothes to take to Denmark. "You are not taking that shirt," she says. "It's older than I am, and it has a hole in the back."

"But it's my favorite," he protests. "It's just a running shirt, and besides you won't even know I'm wearing it."

She wags her finger. "I'll know. If you take it, you'll wear it. I can't have my husband running off to Europe with ratty clothes. Everyone will say, 'How could your wife let you travel like that?'" She rips it out of the suitcase and hands him a new T-shirt. "What about your sport coat?"

He shrugs. "I'll wear it on the plane."

Catherine shakes her head. "No, you won't. You'll take it off, rumple it up and put it in the overhead compartment. And then other people will stuff their suitcases right on top of it and it will end up looking like an accordion. Give it to me and I'll fold it for you to put in the suitcase."

He leans over, kisses her on the forehead and smiles proudly. While she finishes packing, he says, "I've made a checklist of people and places I need to see. Professor Lundhill gave me some names; people who work in the museums and the archives. He knows the harbormaster at Copenhagen Harbor. He told me to check the names in the Bovrup Index for collaborators. It's available through the Danish Genealogy Society."

"I remember," Catherine said. "You told me they compiled records of the Danish Nazi Party. You also told me it was online."

"That's partially true. A little more than five thousand Danish Nazis are named and published online. I've reviewed them, and neither Henryks nor Hendricksen is listed. But Dr. Lundhill said there were actually more than twenty-two thousand members of the Danish National Socialist Party, and he thought I might get better access to the Bovrup Index by talking to the society's docent, an acquaintance of his."

"Does Dr. Lundhill have records of the members of the Blue Shirt Club, the one Billy Hendricksen started? Britta said that Ole was a member."

Liam shakes his head. "Not that I know of. I also asked him about the Blue Storm Club. He's not aware of an index that mentions either one."

A sigh escapes Catherine's lips and she stands with her hands on her hips. "Are we kidding ourselves? Are we beating our heads against the wall here, Liam? We have only a few days left until our pleading deadline, we have nothing solid, and you're running off to Copenhagen with nothing but a checklist and a torn shirt? And you don't even speak Danish."

"First of all, you took my torn shirt. Look, if there is something to find in Copenhagen, I will find it. Otherwise, let's hope the wall is soft, 'cause my head is hard. By the way, I think I should call Chick Chaikin to guard the office while I'm gone."

"That's sweet, but we don't need Chick. I don't need bodyguards. We have Gladys. We'll be fine."

Their conversation is interrupted by the ring of the telephone and Catherine leaves to answer it. She quickly returns with a worried look on her face. "That was Emma. She would like to come over and talk to us. I told her it would be okay."

"Did she tell you why? Did she give you any reason?"

Catherine shakes her head. "No, but I've come to recognize different inflections in her voice, and she sounds very troubled to me. I hope Britta is all right."

"I'M SORRY TO bother you at home," Emma says as she enters the foyer. "I had a few thoughts I wanted to share before Liam left for Denmark."

"You could have told me on the phone," Catherine says. "Is it something else; perhaps something more personal?"

Emma nods sheepishly. "It's my grandmother. She's not well. She doesn't want you to know. We've been to the doctor three times since her arrest. Her blood pressure is out of control. This case is taking a toll on her, but she insists on going forward without taking a break. Her doctor has urged her to rest and take it easy."

"That doesn't sound like your grandmother."

"I know. She's struggling to finish her story and give you enough evidence to beat Henryks."

Catherine smiles sympathetically and starts to speak, but Emma says, "I know what you're thinking; why doesn't she shorten it up, why do we need to know about Lukas and Grethe and Professor Koch?"

"We know why," Catherine says. "It's for your benefit. I take it she hasn't told you her life's story before."

"Never. Oh, I've asked Bubbe about her life a hundred times, but she would always change the subject, or just say, 'Not now.' There's pain there, Catherine, and she's never wanted to confront it."

Catherine invites Emma to follow her into the kitchen. "Would you care for a cup of coffee?"

With both hands around a warm cup, Emma speaks wistfully. "The whole time I was in school, my Bubbe lived with us. My mom worked long hours and so Bubbe really raised me."

"Britta never told you that she wasn't Isabel's mother?"

Emma shakes her head. "You saw me; I was shocked when Bubbe said that Grethe gave birth to my mother. What happened through all those years?" She spreads her hands. "I still don't know. Nobody ever told me, not even my mother, who died six years ago. I wonder now if my mother ever knew who her real parents were. I don't think she did. I wonder if she knew about Lukas and Grethe. If she knew, she never told me. She probably thought Theodore and Britta were her parents."

Emma raises her eyes to the ceiling. "As it turns out, Bubbe never had any children of her own. I confronted her earlier this evening. 'Why haven't you been honest with me all these years?' I said." Emma pauses and a tear rolls down her cheek. "I upset her, Catherine. She's not healthy, I love her with all my heart, and I upset her tonight by accusing her of being dishonest. This is the woman who raised me." Emma breaks into tears and leans forward onto the kitchen table. "I had to talk to someone. I'm sorry to have bothered you."

"I'm not bothered, and I'm honored that you came to me. The fact is, she's telling you the whole story now. Isn't that all right?"

Emma nods. "I'm sure that it was the only way she could do it." A slight chuckle erupts. "It's like going through a joint therapy session, like family counseling, isn't it? Life's story bit by bit for my benefit. I know you and Liam have already come to that conclusion."

Catherine smiles and raises her eyebrows. "A long time ago. We refer to it as her memoir."

"But you have a court deadline to plead specific facts and you're letting her proceed at her own pace. You've stuck by her. Is that wise for you?"

Catherine shrugs. "She's the client. She knows the risks. If we don't have proof of specific facts, her defense will be stricken, and the case will go to judgment. It wouldn't be the end of the world. Britta will have passed along her oral history—her memoir—to you. She will have publicly exposed Henryks as a traitor, even though as yet unproven. And there will likely be a million-dollar judgment against her, which will remain uncollectible. I think she has that all figured out."

"And you're okay with that? All your time and hard work in a lost cause?"

Catherine shrugs. "I'm okay with part of what you said. I don't intend to lose."

Liam walks into the kitchen. "Cat, do you know where my brown loafers are?" He looks to the side. "Hi, Emma."

"In your closet, on the floor, I'm pretty sure. Emma, meet the world's greatest detective, who can't find his clothes in front of his face. Nevertheless, he's about to fly to Europe on a fact-finding mission. I've seen him do it a dozen times. He's the best there is."

Emma reaches into her purse and pulls out a piece of note paper. "There are a couple of matters I think would be worthwhile to explore. I jotted them down. Bubbe says that you should look into Margit Simmons and her father's business. Bubbe was unaware that Ole had married Margit. Her father had a business that made a lot of money during the occupation. He could have only done that if the Nazis were buying. She says Ole may have worked there for a time. She also thinks that the picture, the one that's on the tavern wall, where Ole and his father are standing in front of a boat, is significant. Bubbe says that Ole's father was a day-worker. He would not have owned a big fishing boat like that. Bubbe thinks his story about transporting Jewish refugees to safety is a lie. Besides, Jews weren't smuggled to Stockholm, Sweden; they were taken across the sound."

Liam nods. "I know, I've been told that Stockholm would have been too far away. Does your grandmother know the identity of the third person in the picture, the young man standing next to Ole?"

"I don't think she does. She says it's not his brother, Billy."

She hands a note to Liam, on which the words "Henning Brondum" are written. "Bubbe remembers that Henning was a friend of Ole's, and he may have been involved in some organization that was sympathetic to Germany."

"Could that be the young man in the picture?"

Emma shrugs. "Maybe, I don't know. Bubbe didn't recognize the third person. She remembers Brondum being a little older than Ole, and in her words, he was a 'bad apple.' That's all I know." She stands. "Thank you for listening to me. I better go back and make amends with my grandmother." She smiles. "Or my great-aunt. Who knows?"

CHAPTER THIRTY-TWO

"GRETHE AND ISABEL came home from the hospital three days later. It was a joyous day. My mother had decorated the corner of Grethe's room all in pink. Even the bassinet had pink frills. Looking back, I think that my father was the happiest of all. He had a brand-new baby granddaughter, and he couldn't have been prouder. He must have used three rolls of film that morning. Still, there was an uneasiness, a pall that hung over the celebration; family photographs were unfinished without Lukas. It was all the more evident, because no one wanted to address the subject. We had all vowed to remain positive, and speaking of Lukas only opened the wound and made us mindful of the strong probability that he was dead. It became an unspoken rule in the house: don't bring it up unless Grethe brings it up first.

"Knud had told me that the mission was very important to the underground, a major drop of weapons and materials, and for that reason, four clubs, over thirty boys, had been sent out. I didn't know how many had failed to return, nor did I know how to find out. At school, I looked around trying to see who was missing, but there were absences all the time; kids who missed school because they were sick or truant or simply quit. Besides, it was a wet and stormy February, and I missed days myself. From time to time, we'd hear rumors, but that's all they were: unsubstantiated rumors.

"So, with no news and no reasonable way to find out, the Morgenstern family adopted a tacit agreement; we would believe he survived unless we heard otherwise. No news would be considered good news. Besides, we had Isabel and she was the center of our attention. It's amazing how such a little thing can exert such a powerful presence. Whatever tragedies may befall, babies are the embodiment of the phrase 'life goes on.' Isabel filled every room of the house with joy."

Britta pauses her story and reaches out for her granddaughter's hand. "She was like that every day of her life, Emma." Emma nods, wipes away a tear and whispers, "I know. That was my mom."

Britta takes a deep breath and continues. "My father was busy that winter. General elections for the Parliament, the Folketing, were scheduled for March, the first parliamentary elections since 1939, and my father was on the ballot seeking his fourth term. Although he had been elected by a comfortable margin in his three previous campaigns, the world had changed. Previous assumptions were no longer valid. German influence and its effect on the election could not be underestimated and he was deeply concerned about German interference. An election is an expression of freedom, and as such, inapposite to Nazi ideology. Initially, Dr. Best let it be known that he opposed parliamentary elections. 'We are at peace with the status quo under our Cooperation Agreement,' he declared. 'There is no upside to an upheaval in your government.' Best was confident that the German administrators had established workable channels with the Danish government through which he could keep Denmark in line and preserve the fiction of the protectorate.

"As much as SS-Obergruppenführer Werner Best, as he was known in Germany, lobbied against the elections, and for the maintenance of the status quo, his efforts were met with a universal and immediate backlash in Denmark. Danes were unified in their tradition of democracy, and the strong public sentiment insisted upon the elections proceeding as scheduled. It was one of those moments; either the Cooperation Agreement would give way to Nazi autocracy, or Germany would permit the elections to take place in the arrangement that Hitler described as the 'model protectorate.'

"Though it cut against his grain, Best was forced to withdraw his opposition to the 1943 Folketing elections. It seemed as though Denmark's sense of liberty had carried the day, but Best remained unfazed. He believed that the National Socialist Workers Party of Denmark, the DNSAP, could mount a strong campaign and gain a majority of the Folketing seats, especially with his help. The DNSAP put up a slate of candidates and campaigned hard. They were well-financed, and they plastered the city with banners and signs containing wild promises of wealth and fortune."

Catherine raises her hand. "I thought you told us that Nazi membership was insignificant in Denmark."

Britta shakes her head. "That was before the war, in the thirties. After the occupation, Nazi membership grew. There were many, sad to say, who were intoxicated by Germany's military strength. Those who witnessed the German conquests of peaceful countries saw German dominance as inevitable. They sought to join the ranks. Best felt confident that the increase in DNSAP membership, along with Germany's ostensible superiority on the battlefield, would sway the electorate. He boasted about Germany's prominence in Europe and how that would benefit Denmark. He predicted that a majority of the seats would be filled with friendly legislators and Denmark would become a superpower in the European community.

"Best was able to funnel a lot of money and exert a lot of leverage into the campaign. Many shop owners were urged to place campaign signs in their windows. The consequences of refusal were unspoken but obvious. Germany was big business; not only in international trade, but in the local purchasing power of the thousands of soldiers who were stationed throughout the country. A boycott could be disastrous for a small business.

"In fact, the economy became the primary issue in the election. Supporters of the DNSAP boasted that the balance of trade had never been better. Danish factories were running at full capacity. Farm contracts were high. Farmers and ranchers were enjoying record high prices. Denmark was experiencing almost full employment, where a decade earlier it had suffered through the worldwide depression.

"The DNSAP was also peddling fear, a frequent Danish election tactic. After all, Prime Minister Stauning had previously won by running on the slogan 'Stauning or Chaos.' So voters were told that if they didn't elect a DNSAP slate, Germany might pull the plug and Denmark's economy and security would fail.

"Our prime minister was a Social Democrat, the same party as my father. It was a liberal party and it held the majority of seats in the Folketing. The conservatives were next in number. Communists had been banned since 1941. In the 1939 election, the DNSAP ran a slate but received less than two percent.

"As the election approached, my father campaigned day and night. My mother and I were also immersed in the campaign, passing out leaflets at Copenhagen's busy intersections and hosting afternoon tea parties. A few days before the election, when I was standing on the sidewalk passing out flyers to shoppers in front of the Magasin Department Store, Knud Gunnison approached and pulled me aside. 'I'm not supposed to talk to you, you know. My mother would disown me, but I got news about Lukas.'

"I was shocked. 'Is he alive?' Knud nodded. 'Yeah, he's alive, but he's in bad shape. When we were running for our lives and he fell, I thought he might have been shot, and I was right.' Knud looked around to see if anyone was in earshot. He leaned closer to me and whispered, 'He's in a hospital. The Nazis don't know he's alive or where he is, and I hear that they're still searching for him. Don't tell anyone you heard this from me. I could get in a lot of trouble.'

"I grabbed his wrist. 'You have to tell me more. What hospital? Is he in Copenhagen?'

He shook his head and handed me a note. 'This is the name of the hospital, that's all I know.' He was fidgety, and he nervously scanned the area. 'The Holger Club is breaking up; there's only a few of us left, anyway. Without Lukas . . . well, we have no one to lead us. I gotta go. Remember, you didn't hear nuthin' from me.'

"Knud's note read 'St. Vincent Hosp. Fredensborg.' 'Wait,' I said, 'what does that mean, he's in bad shape? How is he? What's wrong with him?'

"Knud shook his head. 'Don't know,' he said, and he quickly walked away.

"I couldn't wait to get home and give Grethe the news. She was sitting in the kitchen nursing Isabel when Mama and I walked into the house. 'He's alive,' I said. 'Lukas is alive!' Grethe burst into tears. 'Where is he?' she said. 'Why hasn't he come home?'

"'Knud said he was in a hospital, that he'd been shot. He said he was in bad shape, but he's alive. That's what's important.' Grethe jumped up. 'I have to go to him. 'What hospital?'

"'He's not in Copenhagen; he's in some hospital in Fredensborg, wherever that is.'

"'It doesn't matter, Britta, I have to go. My place is with my husband. He would come to me if the situation was reversed. If he's been lying in some hospital for five weeks, it has to be very serious. He needs me and I have to go to him.'

"My mother forcibly disagreed. 'Fredensborg is up north, a couple hours on a train. Are you going to drag Isabel up there in March? A five-week-old baby? It's bitter cold. What are you thinking?' She put her hands defiantly on her hips. 'Where would you stay in Fredensborg? Are you going to take Isabel into the hospital? You can't go, it's all a bad idea.'

"My sister stood firm. 'I have to go, and that's it. I can't leave Isabel, I nurse her every few hours, so I have to take her.' But my mother was not going to be any pushover in an argument about her grandbaby. She was not about to back down. 'Well, you can't take Isabel that far in the cold on a train with no place to stay when you get there. That's insane. I'll ask Papa if he can find out about Lukas.'

"Grethe started crying. 'Mama, that's not enough. Lukas is lying in a hospital because he was wounded protecting this country. And he's all alone. Someone needs to go up there, and that someone is me.'

"My mother shook her head. 'I thought you said the Gestapo was following you, Grethe. You were even afraid to go to the hospital when Isabel was born. Papa had to take you in a police car. Are you going to lead the Gestapo right to Lukas?'

"Grethe was defeated, she knew it, and she broke down. 'I can't bear not being with him, not comforting him. He's all alone and I don't even know how he is. He could be dying, Mama.'

"'I'll go,' I said. 'I don't have a baby and I can take a train. I don't care about the weather. Besides, the Gestapo is not watching me. I'll visit Lukas in the hospital, I'll find out how he is, and when he's coming home. I'll call you after I talk to him. I can handle this on my own.'

"Grethe shook her head. 'You're seventeen years old, Britta.'

"'What's that supposed to mean? I'm seventeen and you're all of twenty?' I gave her a dirty look. 'Are you so much older and wiser than me? Are you saying I can't manage a two-hour train ride all by my little self?' Grethe hung her head. 'No, I'm only saying . . .'

"'Good,' I said, 'then I'll leave in the morning.'"

CHAPTER THIRTY-THREE

"In fact, it was an easy train ride. Fredensborg is a small town, straight north of Copenhagen, and I knew next to nothing about it. It happened to be a location for one of the summer palaces of the royal family, built sometime in the seventeen hundreds. Why they chose Fredensborg, I had no idea. There was nothing remarkable about this quiet little town. A few winding streets with a number of small houses and shops. St. Vincent's Hospital was a one-story white-brick building a few blocks west of the royal palace.

"There was a nurse's station in the reception area, and a woman in a light blue gown with a high-brimmed white nurse's cap sat behind the desk. It was a Catholic hospital and I thought maybe the woman was also a nun. I approached the desk to ask about Lukas, but I was mindful not to use his name. Since the Gestapo had come to our home looking for Lukas, I thought maybe they had circulated an alert to hospitals and police stations as well. For all I knew, Lukas wasn't the only person who was injured in the failed mission. So, addressing the nurse, I simply said, 'I understand that you have a twenty-three-year-old patient who has been injured. He's a friend of mine.'

"The nurse looked at me suspiciously. 'I'm not sure we have such a person here,' she said sweetly. 'What is his name?' I thought to myself, how many twenty-three-year-old men could be lying injured in this little hospital, but I figured that's what she was supposed to say. 'I'm not sure of his *actual* name,' I said. 'He goes by the name of Nelson,' which was the only name that popped into my mind at the moment.

"The nurse raised her eyebrows and smiled. She shook her head just a tiny bit. 'I'm afraid we don't have a patient named Nelson.' She didn't send me away, so maybe she knew I was giving her a phony name. 'What is Mr. Nelson's first name?' she asked. Now I was in trouble. 'Just Nelson,' I replied. Her smile broadened. 'Nelson Nelson? Is that his name?' This wasn't going my way at all. I said, 'I could be wrong about the name, but I can certainly identify him on sight. Do you suppose I could just take a walk down the hall and see if he's here?' She shook her head. 'I'm sure you realize that's not possible.' She just stood there with her sweet smile. In this cat-and-mouse game, she was most certainly the cat.

"'Look,' I said at last, 'he's my brother-in-law. I've been told he's here recovering from a gunshot wound. I want to see him, and I want to know how he is.'

"'So, Nelson Nelson, or the name you can't seem to remember, is really your brother-in-law, and you want me to let you roam around my hospital to find him?'

"'That's right.'

"'Not possible. For one thing, we don't have such a patient in our little hospital. I would know. Perhaps he's in some other hospital. I think you should leave now.'

"'I'm not leaving,' I said. 'I didn't come all this way for nothing, and I'm not going to give you his name. And you and I both know why. So, would you please go back into your little hospital and tell the patient who isn't here that Britta has come to see him.'"

Emma laughs and bites her bottom lip. "Bubbe, you did that? Rock on. You were so gutsy."

"That surprises you?" Catherine says. "That she's gutsy? The woman who outs traitors on brick walls in the middle of the night?"

Britta waves it off. "The nurse huffed at me and then left her station and walked away. I sat down in a chair to wait. Either she was going to tell me about Lukas, or she was going to fetch the police. A few minutes later she came out and motioned for me to follow her. We walked down the hallway and into a ward. There were ten beds, all separated by drawn curtains. Lukas's bed was near the rear of the room. She drew the curtain, let me enter and then closed it behind me.

"Lukas lay on his back, his bedsheet and covers pulled up to his chest. 'Britta,' he said in a thin, scratchy voice. His complexion was pale, his eyes were barely more than slits, and his face, neck and shoulders evidenced a loss of body mass. I put on a smile and tried my best to hide what I felt in the pit of my stomach. Yet, there he was, alive and talking to me. He cleared his throat and said, 'How is Grethe and how is . . .'

"'Isabel,' I chimed, in my cheeriest voice. 'Her name is Isabel and she is beautiful. Congratulations, Papa.'

"A wide smile stretched across his face and he teared up. 'Isabel,' he said, and repeated, 'Isabel. I love it. We talked about that name.'

"'You need to see her and hold her. You need to come home. Can you recover at home?'

"He grimaced. 'I don't know, Britta. Have they come looking for me? Sister Elizabeth told me there was a bulletin sent to the hospital asking them to be on the lookout for anyone showing up with gunshot wounds.' He moved his head weakly from side to side. 'I wasn't the only one. They mowed us down, Britta. Several were shot; many more were captured. Sister Elizabeth knows who I am and that I'm hiding. She's a good woman.'

"I smiled. 'She's doing a first-rate job of protecting you, Lukas, you can take my word for it. But yes, they are looking for you. Two Gestapo goons came to the house shouting for you, and also for Grethe, but Papa wouldn't let them in. You don't have to worry about them; Papa says they won't come back. So, when will you come home?'

"He ran his tongue over his lips and cleared his throat. I could tell there was something more than fear of the Gestapo that was keeping him in Fredensborg. 'I have to get better. They shot me up pretty bad, Britta. I took one in the back and some in my legs. I need a little more time before I can travel.'

"'You don't have to worry about traveling. It's only an hour and a half. My father can come and get you and bring you back in a car.'

"He hesitated. 'Not quite yet. I'm still getting treatments. The staff has been great here. I was pretty sick when they brought me in. During the escape, when I was shot, my mates carried me through the woods to a farmhouse. I stayed there for a couple days and the farm woman looked after me, but I had lost blood and I had a fever. She knew I needed medical attention, and she was smart enough to know that the Germans and the police were monitoring the local Jutland hospitals. So, her husband drove me all the way here to Fredensborg. I owe my life to that family. The staff here has been treating me very well. I'm lucky, Britta, don't feel sorry for me.'

"'How long will you stay here? What can I tell Grethe?'

"He swallowed hard and said, 'You can tell her . . . you can tell . . . oh hell, Britta, I can't feel my legs.' Tears rolled down his cheek. 'I can't walk; I can't even get out of this damn bed without someone helping me.'

"I could see that he was weak and pale, and I could deal with that, but the revelation that this powerful young man, this Olympic runner, was now hobbled, it broke my heart. I could not hold back the tears and I reached down and hugged him as hard as I could. 'I'm so sorry, Lukas,' I said.

"Amidst his tears, he forced a smile. 'Damn Nazis. They took away my Olympic Games and now they took away my legs. They just don't want me to run and beat their best runners.' Then he waved me off. 'No pity allowed, Britta. I'm gonna show them all. The doctor says with therapy I could get some feeling back and maybe even walk. He says there are very good physical therapists in Copenhagen.'

"'Then it's settled. I'll go back and tell Papa to come and get you.'

"He pursed his lips and said what was really on his mind. 'What will Grethe say when she looks at me?'

"'She'll say she loves you with all her heart and she has missed you like crazy these past five weeks. You have no idea how hard I've had to work to keep that girl's spirits up. And I know for a fact that Isabel wants to see you too.'

"'Britta, believe me, I'm anxious to get home. They're bringing in a wheelchair for me tomorrow. If I can get around in it all right, then your father can pick me up and take me back home.'

"'Grethe will be so happy. We all will. You'll get therapy in Copenhagen, and if anyone can make a recovery from an injury like this, it would be you. You have the determination.'

"'You're right about that. I am determined to get back as much as I can. I need to get back in touch with my Holger boys. I don't know what's happening with the club or who's organizing the missions. We can't let this setback stop us.'

"I felt deflated. He was lying in a bed, unable to walk, a war casualty, and all he wanted to do was get back into the war. He had a new baby and a beautiful wife. He had his whole life ahead of him. 'I wouldn't say anything about that to Grethe,' I said. 'I don't think that's what she wants to hear right now.'

"'I understand. But there is work to be done and I need to reconnect with my boys.'

"'Does it have to be you? Does it have to be now?'

"He smiled at me and nodded. 'Are the Germans still in Denmark? Have the Nazis been defeated yet? Have we weeded out all the Nazi sympathizers and informers? You know, Britta, it was the Blue Shirts that turned us in. The Hendricksens and the Nielsens.'

"'How can you know that?'

"'I saw them, Britta. When the searchlights came on, I saw them standing behind the Gestapo cars. Clear as day. The two Hendricksen brothers and Kai Nielsen. So, whether I have legs or not, there's work to be done.'"

At this point in the story, Britta pauses, sits back and points her finger at Emma. "That was your grandfather, Emma. He was quite a man."

"My grandfather," Emma echoes softly. "I wish I had known him. And he identified the Hendricksens as informers?"

"Yes, he did," Britta answers, and turns to Catherine. "Isn't that enough to show that I'm telling the truth about Ole? You can put that right in your pleadings."

Emma shakes her head. "We can't use it, Bubbe. You didn't see him. Someone else did and told you about it. It's hearsay. We'd need further proof."

"Well, wait a minute, Emma," Catherine says. "Who says we can't use it? Tell me, what would happen if we allege in our affirmative defense that Ole Henryks, aka Ole Hendricksen, led a group of Gestapo agents to arrest Danish resistance fighters during the war? We could allege all the details that Judge Wilson requires; the date, the place, the wrongful conduct."

"But when it comes to trial, we can't prove it. It's hearsay. It's something Bubbe heard. We don't have any corroboration; no eyewitness, no pictures. It's not admissible."

"Really? Not *ever* admissible? What if Henryks admits in his testimony that it's all true? Is it still inadmissible?"

"No, of course not, but he'll never do that. We'll need proof."

"Sparks doesn't know what proof we have or don't have. My point is this: we have a deadline in four days and we can allege it. It's not false. It just needs further proof."

Emma understands, smiles and nods her head. "Okay, I get it, but we're only kicking the can down the street. We're only buying time."

"Just enough time for Britta to give us further information," Catherine says, "and time for Liam to work his magic and find us something solid in Copenhagen."

CHAPTER THIRTY-FOUR

"TRAVELING BACK TO Copenhagen, leaving him behind in that little hospital, there was a sour knot in my stomach, and it just wouldn't go away. Lukas was unable to walk or even stand, and I had seen him run like a deer. I remembered the day that Grethe and I stood on the sidelines screaming as he won the eight hundred meters in the Danish Olympic Trials. Still, Lukas was alive, and he was determined to regain his strength, so there was reason to be hopeful. If anyone could get back on his feet, it was Lukas Holstrum. I only had to convey that sense of optimism to Grethe. How was I going to do that?

"All the way back, I rehearsed what I would say when I got home. I didn't call Grethe from Fredensborg to tell her about Lukas. She would have wanted all the details, and it wasn't the kind of thing she should hear on the phone. I had to tell her in person, and I had to tell her the whole truth. I decided that it would require the joint effort of my mother and father to tell my sister that her husband, the man she knows as a graceful athlete, a powerful leader in the resistance movement, is now fifty pounds thinner and is unable to stand without help.

"I returned home that evening. My parents were sitting in the front room listening to the radio and Grethe was nursing Isabel when I walked into the house. Everyone turned and looked at me at once, and I totally dropped the ball. No matter what I said, it didn't come out right. I started crying and said, 'He's alive and he's coming home soon, so it really doesn't matter about his legs.' I also blurted out that he was anxious to get back to the Holger Club, which I wasn't going to say at all. I don't know what came over me; I guess I just got flustered.

"Grethe cried when she heard about his injuries, but she was accepting of the disability. That was something I shouldn't have worried about. She had seen Lukas train for the Olympics and she knew how strong his resolve could be. All in all, she took it better than I had expected. For weeks she had been living under the assumption that she would never see him again. Now her husband was alive and determined to rehabilitate as best he could. Returning to the Holger Club, that was another story. 'He is *not* going out on any more missions,' she said. 'If he wants to be an advisor, then that's all right. The resistance can use his leadership. You can be a pretty damn powerful man in a wheelchair. Look at Roosevelt!'

"THE WEEK PRECEDING the Folketing elections was pure mayhem. My father and his Social Democratic Party held rallies, passed out leaflets, and canvassed door-to-door, but that was nothing compared to the DNSAP's campaign blitz. There were nightly torch parades and military marches with dozens of German soldiers in formation, rifles on their shoulders, dressed in full battle gear. They had marching bands and girls carrying banners highlighting the DNSAP candidates, all of which was flooded with a storm of confetti and streamers. Danish Nazi flags, bright red background with a white twisted Nazi swastika instead of a Christian cross, were passed out to the children who lined the street curbs. In the parks and on the busy corners, DNSAP candidates perched like falcons on platforms shouting Germany's praises and accomplishments through megaphones. 'The world's mightiest military.' 'The world's strongest economy.' 'Denmark's most important trading partner and best friend.' Danish citizens were also promised increased wages and a better life through DNSAP leadership. They promised that Denmark would have Germany's full support and protection, and a seat at the European governing council to be formed at the conclusion of the war.

"But between the lines were ominous references to those countries that were foolish enough to reject Germany's generous expressions of friendship. Norway, for example, now flat under the German boot. Danish Jews knew all too well what happened to the Norwegian Jews. Beginning in November 1942, Nazis began to round up the Jews in Norway. They were aided by collaborators and sympathizers. Almost a thousand Jews were sent to concentration camps. And the Netherlands. Oh, the Netherlands. We all knew what happened to the poor Dutch. Formerly a neutral country, just like Denmark, the Netherlands was now under the total control of the Reichskommissariat Niederlande headed by the brutal Arthur Seyss-Inquart and his reign of terror. So, the clear message was, if you don't want to be like Norway and the Netherlands, vote DNSAP!

"My father justifiably feared that the Danish electorate would be swayed, and that the Folketing was destined to become a Nazi rubber stamp. He thought perhaps people in the outlying rural areas would continue to support their incumbent representatives, but voters in Copenhagen and the larger cities were bombarded with this powerful barrage of German propaganda.

"'I'm afraid there are many who see Germany's military conquests and regard Hitler as unstoppable,' my father lamented, 'and they are justifiably afraid. They have seen him steamroll through Europe and they have witnessed his wrath at those who have the temerity to stand against him. They fear that there will be repercussions if the Nazi slate is defeated. And I'm sure there are those who believe DNSAP's economic promises and want a share in the good life. Either way,' my father said with regret, 'I fear our people will be motivated to vote for the DNSAP candidates.' Ultimately, my father was dead wrong about our people, but dead right about the repercussions.

"Two days before the election, my father left to pick up Lukas. In the midst of the electioneering madness, no one would be keeping track of where he went. He was bound to be traveling on campaign business. Likewise, we expected the Gestapo to be so occupied with DNSAP rallies that they wouldn't have time to pay attention to what went on in our house. In truth, I hadn't seen the two Gestapo agents in weeks. Despite Grethe's paranoia, I did not think they were monitoring our home.

"Grethe calculated that it would take four hours for my father to make the round-trip; ninety minutes each way and an hour or so at the hospital, and according to my mother, she checked her watch every five minutes. I went along with my father, not because I would be such a big help, but because I was familiar with the hospital. My father had already made arrangements for releasing Lukas and a wheelchair had been delivered and was available to take him home.

"Sister Elizabeth was sitting at her station when we arrived, and she greeted me with her patented smile. 'Well, if it isn't Nelson Nelson's sister-in-law,' she said. 'Nice to see you again.' My father looked at me with a puzzled expression. I waved it off. 'It's a long story,' I said. We had brought a fresh change of clothes for Lukas, and Sister Elizabeth suggested that she and the staff help Lukas change.

"A few minutes later, Lukas wheeled himself into the reception area. 'He's been practicing,' Sister Elizabeth said. 'He's a very determined young man.'

"'Don't we know,' I replied.

"Lukas reached up and hugged her. 'You've been so good to me,' he said, 'I owe my life to you and the St. Vincent staff. I'm going to miss you all.'

"She had a tear in her eye as well, but she never lost her smile. 'When you get the chance, and when things are safer and quiet down, you come back and visit us, and bring that new baby with you.' Little did she know how prophetic that request would be, and how soon that would occur.

"It was dark when we arrived home. Mama told us that Grethe had been nervous and had scanned the street all afternoon for any sign of the two Gestapo men, but they were nowhere to be seen. As it happened, the homecoming was sweet and without incident. Isabel took right to Lukas, and he to her. The family portrait was complete."

CHAPTER THIRTY-FIVE

"ELECTION DAY, MARCH 23, 1943, started early for us. Mama cooked breakfast before the sun rose; Grethe's favorite—Swedish pancakes and boysenberry jam. We stretched our muscles and gathered around the kitchen table; five of us and little Isabel in her carry-all. Lukas was rapidly regaining his upper body strength. His robust appetite had returned, thanks in large part to Mama's cooking, and he was finding his lost pounds. This particular morning, he attacked the pancakes with a vengeance, enough to make Grethe and me exchange glances and giggle.

"After fidgeting for a while, Papa finally placed his napkin on the table and gave us a look that said it was time to face the music. He gave Mama a kiss and said, 'The breakfast was delicious, but I need to get out to the polling places. I hope things go well for us.' His words were positive, but his tone lacked conviction. Clearly, he was worried about the outcome. As he headed for the door, he stopped to shake a finger. 'Nora, don't forget to vote! We need every single one.' Grethe and I were too young to vote. Lukas wanted to vote, but we were too nervous to let him out in public. We hoped that Papa wouldn't lose by that one vote.

"Mama and I refused to be pessimistic. We held fast to the hope that Papa would be reelected and that the Danish candidates would prevail. We had faith in the stalwart Danes. Although I couldn't vote, I ran after

Papa and walked with him to our polling place. Hand in hand, I was so proud of my father. Whatever the outcome, he was a good man who had served his country well.

"When we turned the corner on Vandersgade, we saw a line of people stretching for blocks waiting to vote. If we were going to lose, it wouldn't be due to a poor turnout. As we approached the line, we stopped short. My father squeezed my hand. It hit us both at the same time; it was the expressions on the faces of the voters. They were not a defeated bunch, not at all. There were no slumping shoulders. There was no cowering. They stood strong and proud, their heads held high, with smiles from ear to ear. My father looked down at me and said, 'Look at these folks. We're going to carry the day, Britta. I can feel it. Just you watch.' And he was right.

"Denmark's voter turnout that day was almost ninety percent, the highest in any Danish Folketing election ever! The three Danish democratic parties carried ninety-four percent of the vote. My father's Social Democrats received the highest number of votes and it was enough to give them sixty-six seats in the Folketing assembly. The Nazi DNSAP, despite all of their money, their rallies and their shows of force, received only 2.1 percent of the vote, which was only enough to secure three seats. It was a total embarrassment for SS-Obergruppenfuhrer Best and the German administrators.

"Denmark celebrated that night. There was a grand party at the Social Democratic Hall. Champagne was flowing, and I was allowed to go. By everyone's account, there had never been such a manifestation of Danish unity. It was a total repudiation of the Nazis and everything they stood for. This was Denmark standing up to Germany, and it wouldn't be the last time. I kept thinking this is exactly what Professor Koch has been preaching all these months; the unity of the Danish spirit. And then I saw him. Professor Koch walked up to us, said 'Congratulations.' We stood there chatting for a few minutes and then he leaned forward and raised his eyebrows. Without putting it in words, he was asking me about Lukas. I nodded. 'Injured, but okay. He's in a wheelchair and getting stronger.'

"Koch raised his glass. 'God bless him. We'll miss him on the front lines, but I'm delighted to hear he's on the mend.'

"I thought to myself, if I know Lukas, you won't miss him for very long.

"The triumph and independence we felt that night, that feeling of standing up to the Nazis, was about to get a dose of reality at my house. Soon after the election, Stefan Munsk, a longtime friend of the family, was a dinner guest. At the time, he was serving as a Danish envoy to Germany, and he had just returned from Berlin. Mama made one of her specialties and Stefan brought his wife, Rena, a quiet woman. Grethe, Lukas and I were there as well. Stefan and Rena hadn't seen Lukas since the wedding, and they were shocked to see him in a wheelchair.

"'My goodness,' Rena said. 'What happened to you?'

"'Bad accident on a bike,' Lukas lied. 'I broke a few bones, but I'm going to therapy and they're helping me.'

"'Well, I hope you get back up on your feet real soon,' Rena said, 'and that you're more careful next time you get on a bike.' Her husband tried to derail her lecture, but she persisted, 'I know how those young boys are on their bikes, Stefan. They can be reckless.' Then pointing at Lukas, she added. 'You have a little baby to raise, Lukas Holstrum, and you cannot be reckless. Promise me, you'll be more careful.'

"'Yes, ma'am, I promise,' Lukas said. 'I'll be more careful on the bike.'

"Initially, the dinner conversation was warm and casual, but I could tell that Stefan was troubled and there was something heavier on his mind. Ultimately, he said, 'Attitudes are changing in Berlin, Joseph. They are not happy with Denmark's election results. They view it as a total repudiation of the Cooperation Agreement.'

"My father shrugged. 'Denmark is a fiercely independent nation, and we strongly defend our democratic values. Germany may not be happy with the results of the election, but we are in full compliance with the Cooperation Agreement, which guarantees our internal sovereignty. It was a fair vote, and the focus was entirely local, not international. These were votes to elect district representatives to the Folketing.'

"Stefan shook his head. 'Berlin does not see it that way. Denmark is a protectorate, and Berlin regards it now as a disobedient child. There have been far too many acts of sabotage, and many have gone unpunished. Their feeling is that the Danish police haven't done enough to curb them. All of this is falling in the lap of Werner Best. He was sent here to impose tighter discipline. Best had assured Berlin that the DNSAP would pick up a substantial number of seats, enough to exert a legislative influence and turn the tide here.'

"'I can't say I feel too bad for Dr. Best,' my father said.

"'Oh, I agree,' Stefan said, 'but now the SS general has his back against the wall and Berlin is expecting him to quell the Danish disobedience. I think we can expect serious demands from Best.'"

Catherine raises her hand and breaks into Britta's narrative. "Lukas and Grethe were sitting at the table. What did they have to say about all this? I'm sure that Lukas had pretty strong opinions."

Britta wags her finger side to side. "These were political discussions between statesmen taking place at our dinner table, and by tradition, they were between the men. Not open to general discussion. It had always been the custom in our house for the children to allow such discussions to take place as though we weren't sitting at the table. We weren't expected to participate; we didn't even react. To all intents and purposes, we weren't there.

"My father didn't seem concerned about 'serious demands' from Best. 'Germany has to recognize that Denmark has a strong national identity. Frankly Stefan, I think they respect our independent spirit and the clear line of our borders.'

"'Do not think that your borders are walls, Joseph. They are lines in the dirt drawn by men, and they exist only so long as men honor them. Hitler has shown, time and again, that he has no regard for borders.'

"'As you know, Stefan, I do not trust the word of Hitler or the Nazis, but they have made it quite clear that their interest in Denmark is limited to preventing foreign alliances, principally with Britain, France and America. I see no indication that they intend to interfere internally.'

"Stefan sighed. 'Open your eyes, Joseph. He has thousands of armed soldiers walking the Copenhagen streets, and the difference between a peaceful occupation and a military takeover is as simple as an edict. Of all people, you and Nora should be terrified of what Hitler is doing to the Jews in his occupied territories.'

"'I have told him that,' my mother brusquely interjected with a slap on the table. 'I am sorry, Joseph, but I must speak. What Stefan is talking about is what we hear at the synagogue, what we hear on your radio, and what is quietly said on the streets. The Nazis call it *Judenrein*—cleansed of Jews. The Nazis want all Europe to be *Judenrein,* and Denmark is in Europe, my dear husband.'

"'Listen to your wife, Joseph. She's a smart woman. I have been in Berlin for over a year now, and I have witnessed firsthand what your synagogue is telling you. Just last November, Alois Brunner, Eichmann's first deputy, was put in charge of Jewish deportations in Berlin. He was told that *Judenrein* was going too slowly. In the next sixty days, twenty-two thousand Berlin Jews were arrested and sent off to concentration camps for so-called resettlement. Just last month, Jews who thought they were exempt because they worked in the German armaments industry were rounded up and put on trains. Many were shot during the roundup. Brunner is a terrible man. On February 22, Brunner reported that the Jewish community had been "liquidated." He used that word, "liquidated." Only eighteen thousand Jews remain in Berlin, only because, for the time being, they serve in various essential work positions. Eighteen thousand, when just ten years ago there were 160,000 Jews in Berlin. I'm afraid they'll all be gone by the end of the month. In March, the Nazis liquidated the ghetto in Kraków, one of Poland's historic cities and home to seventy thousand Jews! Again, they *liquidated* it.'

"I could see my mother's muscles contracting—her neck, her face, her arms. Her hands were clenched in fists. 'Exactly what do you mean by liquidated?'

"There was a quick change of expression as a shroud of despair washed over Stefan's face, and he lowered his eyes. 'I'm sorry, Nora. From what we've heard, they were rounded up and taken to a Polish prison camp and thereafter . . . many were killed.'

"'Killed,' my mother repeated in a state of horror. 'My Lord in heaven, all those people.'

"'I tell you all this for a reason,' Stefan said. 'Goebbels has announced that his country's 'liberation from Jews' was the government's greatest achievement. It is his intent that there be no Jews anywhere in Europe. He is pressuring Dr. Best to register all of Denmark's Jews. Ask yourselves, why would he do that? For what purpose?' Stefan shook his head. 'In the eyes of the Germans, once you are registered, you are distinct, divided from the rest of the populace and more easily subject to their eventual purposes.'

"My father remained adamant. 'Registration would be a direct violation of the Cooperation Agreement. It is clearly stated that no German interference will be imposed on Denmark's treatment of its Jewish population.'

"'Yes, that's true. So what? Does that prevent a unilateral reversal of policy? Hitler is a man of unimpeded power. And he's insane. And that's a dangerous combination.'

"'This is all a nightmare,' my mother said. 'So then tell me, Stefan, what are we supposed to do? Do you recommend that we leave Denmark? Is there someplace safe for us to go? Tell me, Stefan.'

"He shrugged. 'I'm afraid I have no answers.'"

Catherine interrupts the narrative. Sad memories have been percolating and she feels a need to express herself. "In my previous cases with Holocaust survivors, I have personally listened to that dialogue an astonishing number of times. Families reaching that crossroad, considering the dangers, and then consciously rejecting the risk and deciding to stay put. It was the same damn story each time, and as I listened, I wanted to shout at them, 'Leave! Leave now. What is wrong with you? Leave while you have the chance!' I recall Ben Solomon telling me how his family considered leaving Zamość, Poland, when the Nazis had momentarily withdrawn and there was an open escape route. They were going to cross the Tatra mountains into Slovakia, I remember it so well. They had a plan, but they hesitated and found excuses to put off the decision until it was no longer an option."

Britta is looking at Catherine, studying her expression of exasperation, but not in a sympathetic way.

"It was the same with Lena Scheinman's family and her friend Karolina," Catherine says. "Their families were warned to leave Chrzanów, Poland, but they delayed until it was too late. Jacob Baumgarten, a famous violinist, could have taken his family, left Berlin and gone to Boston. He had an opportunity to join the Boston Symphony, but he stayed in Berlin and he was executed." She takes another deep breath and turns to Britta, whose lips have tightened and whose eyebrows have drawn together. Catherine should have picked up on Britta's reproach, but she doesn't, and continues, "I know, it's easy for me to say in hindsight, and it's not fair, I shouldn't judge, but the consequences of staying were dire, yet they each found some reason to ignore the writing on the wall, which to me defies logic and good sense."

Now Britta has heard enough. Her eyes are open wide, and her back has stiffened, and Catherine realizes that she has gone too far and spoken out of turn. Britta says, "Defies logic, does it? Good sense? Do you dare sit in judgment of my father? I suppose, had you been present and seen the future, you would have made a wiser decision, am I right? I suppose if you were there you would have packed up and left everything and everyone you knew—your job, your home, your profession, your elected position in Parliament—and headed off blindly in some unknown direction. Because you were logical. And where would you have gone, Ms. Lockhart? Somewhere else in Europe? At that time, in 1943, Hitler owned Europe—"

Catherine interrupts, "I'm sorry, Britta, I didn't mean . . ."

"Yes, you did. In 1943, Hitler was unstoppable, and yet, he had not chosen to conquer Denmark. For the foreseeable future, we were safe. Jews in every other direction were not. And that's what my father and most Danish Jewish fathers were thinking. He was not reckless, and he was not careless or foolish. He was a member of Parliament with very solid connections, which would ultimately save our lives."

Catherine swallows hard. "I'm sorry. It's my fault, a flaw in my professional character. Lawyers aren't supposed to get emotionally involved, but through our sessions, I feel like I've come to know your family. Each of them. Grethe, Lukas, your father, even little Isabel. I think if I met them on the street, I would know them. I rejoice for them and I fear for them. It's just that I've heard this story so many times, and it tears at my heart. I want to shout, 'Get out! Get out while you have the chance.' Though I have no right to do that."

Britta shakes her head. "Denmark was different."

Catherine sighs. "They all thought they were different. And they all found reasons to stay and they were all killed. And when Denmark was militarily overrun—"

"Well, I don't know your other clients," Britta says. "My family wasn't every other family, and Denmark wasn't Poland or Austria or any other country. Denmark was unique. Our populace was united. Solid. We protected our Jews and we were not about to be dominated by that goose-stepping paper-hanger. That's what my father was depending on."

Emma, who is sitting in the middle of two hardheaded women, quickly places her hand on Britta's arm. "Bubbe, don't get angry, Catherine is on our side. She's just expressing her frustration."

Catherine winces and tries to explain herself in an attempt to diffuse the tension. "I only meant to say that when Denmark was militarily overrun and occupied, that Stefan's suggestion that your family leave might have been—"

"He didn't *suggest* we leave. In response to my mother, he said he had *no answers*. Our country was physically overrun, our streets were occupied, but not our minds nor our spirit. Our cultural identity remained intact, and it would remain so throughout the war. My father's decisions were sound, and the proof of the pudding is sitting right here at this table. Emma and I, we are the proof." Despite Catherine's efforts, Britta's tension is not easing. Her words are delivered in short spurts. She scans the room, her eyes darting here and there, finally coming to rest on Emma. "I think we should go now," she says. "That's enough for today."

"Wait," Catherine says, "I'm so sorry, I don't mean to sit in judgment, and I didn't mean . . ."

Emma waves her off, takes her grandmother by the elbow and walks slowly to the door. "I'll be right back," Emma says. "Give me just a minute."

After placing Britta in the car, Emma returns to the conference room where Catherine is crying. She begins to repeat her contrition, but Emma shakes her head. "Don't blame yourself, Bubbe has had a bad day. Actually, a few bad days. She hasn't been feeling well; her health is failing, she's struggling, and she has no tolerance for her physical limitations. She has always been fiercely independent and now her weakness makes her ask for help. She requires more and more of my help just to do simple tasks, and she's losing her patience. I've moved back in with her. I'm worried about her, Catherine."

"Maybe our sessions are going on too long," Catherine says. "Maybe they are taking their toll, physically and emotionally. Perhaps we should focus on the lawsuit and strive to get to the point more quickly."

But Emma shakes her head. "She won't hear of it. I've raised that subject with her time and again, but she is intent on finishing the story at her pace and in her time. You may have noticed, she's a bit headstrong. I think the problem today is that she felt challenged by your comments. The debate took its toll, and I think she feels drained."

Catherine nods. "That was my fault. Truthfully, I got caught up in the story and spoke out of turn. However, if she thinks my questions are challenging, they're nothing compared to what's coming down the road."

"She's prepared for that. Today, she was challenged by *you* and, given her current fragile state, it threw her off guard. In her mind, you are her champion, her advocate, and if you don't believe in her, well . . . you understand."

Catherine's quickly covers her eyes with her hands. "I'm so sorry."

"It's okay," Emma says.

"No, it's not. I failed. I let my litigator's reflexes get the best of me and overrule my common sense. I can't let Britta lose faith in me because of my insensitivity. I should have seen what you see. You are more perceptive and attuned than I. Emma, you display extraordinary maturity for such a young lawyer. Does Walter know what a gem he has?"

Emma blushes. "You give me too much credit, though I thank you for that. She's my Bubbe; I know her strengths and frailties pretty well."

CHAPTER THIRTY-SIX

"I HOPE I didn't wake you," Catherine says. "What time is it there?"

"It's 11:20 Copenhagen time, seven hours ahead of Chicago," Liam says. "What's the matter? I can tell there's something wrong. How did it go today?"

"Oh, God, not well. For one thing, Britta's health is deteriorating, so much so that Emma has moved in with her. And for another, I made a fool of myself today by attacking my own client, who then terminated the session and went home. Emma says that it was due to Britta's weakened condition, that she's tense and defensive, but I was blind to it, and I'm sitting there battling with her over the soundness of her father's decision to stay in Denmark. She blew up at me, but to tell you the truth, it was my fault. I got emotionally caught up in her story, which I never should have done. I wanted to shout, 'Don't stay in Denmark, Joseph, because Jews will be rounded up and put on trains like the rest of Europe. Get out now!' But Britta said, 'Denmark was different' and I said, 'They all thought they were different, but they made the decision to stay and they were *all killed*.'"

"Whoa, slow down, honey. Take it easy."

Catherine sighs. "Liam, I think that all these Holocaust cases we've been working on the last ten years, they're catching up to me. They haunt me. I see scenes of those Jewish families that we've come to know being rounded up and taken off to death camps. I see their faces and I want to go back in time and shout at them to leave while they still have a chance. And Britta said, 'Well, you weren't there,' and she was right and—"

"Calm down, calm down, Cat. Where are you?"

"I'm still at the office. I've been sitting here alone for a while. I asked Susan to stay a little longer and watch Ben. I'm just not ready to go home."

"Susan's a good nanny, she won't mind. Don't worry about it."

"I know, she said she wouldn't mind. I'll leave in a little while." After a moment of silence, she says, "Britta stormed out and went home. She was right, Liam, and I was wrong. Maybe it was a mistake to take on another Holocaust case so soon after finishing Gabi's case. I think about them in the middle of the night. Don't you? Karolina and Jacob and Frieda and Beka, all those people we've come to know." Catherine breaks into sobs. "Now I'm getting to know Grethe and Lukas and Britta's parents and I'm expecting the worst. I wish you were here."

"I wish I was there too. Do you want to withdraw?"

"No, of course not. How could I do that? I've never abandoned a client in my life, and I'm sure as hell not going to abandon Britta. You know me better than that. I intend to win this case, though right now I don't know how. We have to be in front of Obadiah in three days. All I've got is blue shirts. Please tell me you've found the smoking gun."

"Not yet. I had hopes that Ole would be listed in the Bovrup Index."

"The index of Danish Nazis?"

"Right. Their names were taken right from the DNSAP roles. Unfortunately, neither a Hendricksen nor a Henryks is on the list. But the name Emma gave me on that slip of paper the other day, Henning Brondum, his name is in the index. I asked the curator about him and he told me that Brondum was affiliated with Otto Schwerdt, aka Peter Schafer. He organized a paramilitary group called the Petergruppen—the Peter Group—a counter-resistance group that Brondum was part of. After the war, Brondum was tried in the Danish court as a Nazi collaborator. He was convicted and executed in 1947. I don't know why I was given that paper. What's his connection to Ole?"

"Well, Emma's not sure. She thinks he was a friend. Liam, you need to follow up this lead; it could be a break. Can you get his court records?"

"I'll try. I've checked into Simmons Manufacturing. Assuming that Ole married Margit Simmons, the company was owned by his father-in-law, Ulrid Simmons. They were definitely a supplier of machinery and equipment for Germany during the war."

"Great. Britta thinks Ole worked there."

"But, bear in mind that Denmark was doing a robust business with Germany in almost every segment of its economy. That didn't make them all collaborators or war criminals, nor did it make them Nazis."

"What did Simmons manufacture and sell? It might make a difference if it was military equipment; guns, ammunition, materials used on the battlefield, or used to subjugate the Danish people. Then I could properly allege that Ole was aiding and abetting the Nazi regime."

"I wouldn't do that just yet. It's likely that the machinery and equipment had a military purpose, but I don't have that precise information."

"Liam: three days. That's what I've got. That means I have two days to draft our affirmative defense to bring with me to court on Thursday morning."

"Well, then go ahead and allege he was working for a company that supplied machinery to the Third Reich, just know we may not be able to prove it at trial. Simmons closed over seventy years ago, I have not been able to locate any employment records for Simmons and I doubt that I will. So, you won't be able to prove that Ole worked for Simmons, unless he admits it."

"What about that newspaper, the *Plantagenetic*?"

"Ha. The *Kamptegnet*. It was a dead end. I noticed that it was printed by the Hendricksen Printing Company and thought there might be a connection, but I checked it out. I don't believe that Ole's father owned a company, or anything else for that matter. I think Britta was right when she said he was a drinker and day-worker down at the docks."

"What about the Blue Shirt Club or Blue Storm Club? According to Britta, there were several people who connected Ole and his brother to the Blue Shirt Club: Lukas Holstrum, Knud Gunnison, even Professor Koch all identified Ole as a member and placed him at the scene when the Holger Club was arrested."

"Identified by several people who are now dead and cannot testify.

The bad news is that I haven't come across any records for the Blue Shirt Club or the Blue Storm Club, at least not so far. The curator told me he has heard of the group, but he doesn't know where I could find information about them. But, don't lose hope, Cat, your hubby is hard at work. Get some rest."

"I love you, Liam."

CHAPTER THIRTY-SEVEN

"STEFAN WAS RIGHT. In the late spring and summer of 1943 Werner Best began to tighten Germany's grip on Denmark."

Britta is all business today, as if she knows her time is limited, and she must finish her narrative while her health abides. Still, Catherine thinks she looks unhealthy. She is thinner, and her visage is gaunt. Britta begins the day with an apology for her harsh words and her abrupt departure the day before. Catherine waves it off, insists on shouldering the blame, and the two end up in a warm embrace. All is well.

Britta continues. "The first thing Best did was to implement tight censorship of the press and the radio. The newspapers, fearful of Best's reprisals, became tolerant, and at times even supportive of Germany. Articles appeared harshly critical of the Danish resistance movement. Editorial opinions condemned 'foolish youth whose senseless acts of violence were an insult to the strong political bonds between the two countries.' Citizens were urged to turn in members of the resistance. It was no secret that the German administration was responsible for the shift in editorial comment. Danes had always prided themselves on our freedom of the press and independent editorial content, so the overall effect of the censorship was to strengthen Danish resistance, not only among the saboteurs, but in the attitude of the general public as well.

"Confrontations in public places became frequent. Insults, arguments, even fistfights, erupted between young Danes and German sympathizers. Many of our restaurants and night spots discouraged or even turned away German soldiers. Though the soldiers were a constant source of income, the owners realized that their loyal customers were uncomfortable in the presence of Germans. Many refused to come in if a crowd of German soldiers was present.

"While all this was happening, Danes began to hear of German failures on the battlefield. For the first time, Germany appeared vulnerable. Maybe Hitler had spread his army too thin. Maybe Germany had underestimated its opponents. We found reasons to feel encouraged. In February the Wehrmacht suffered an embarrassing defeat in Russia and surrendered their troops in Stalingrad.

"Then we learned of the Warsaw Ghetto uprising. There had been a quarter of a million Jews locked in that ghetto. Starting in January the Germans began systematically transporting them from the ghetto to the Treblinka concentration camp, where they were murdered. On April 19, Passover eve, the Germans stormed the ghetto attempting to clear it out and send the remaining Jews to Treblinka. But the inmates refused to go and staged an armed revolt. Though greatly overmatched and outnumbered, the revolt lasted an entire month. The world was rooting for Warsaw and we cheered during that month. If those brave people could resist under those conditions, so could we.

"Then we got word that Belgian partisans derailed a train filled with Jews bound for the Auschwitz concentration camp. The Belgians killed the German guards and freed the captives. In May, German and Italian troops surrendered in Tunisia, and the Axis' hold on North Africa disappeared. In June, the German advance along the Russian front in Kursk failed. To the Danes, this all meant that Germany was no longer invincible. It encouraged further acts of sabotage and resistance. Partisan attacks became more frequent and more damaging. Factories that supplied war matériel to the Reich were set on fire. Workers in key industries went out on wildcat strikes.

"Germany was losing its grip on Denmark, and Werner Best requested an increase in Gestapo personnel. They fanned out through the country seeking saboteurs. Suspects were snatched off the street and sent without trial to a prison camp in northern Germany. Gestapo agents, assisted by Danish police, arrested strike leaders. But the harder Best countered, the more resistance he generated. If anything, acts of sabotage increased in number and intensity.

"It was early in the summer when Lukas received a visitor. Larson Starck, the leader of an Odense resistance group, came to the house to ask for Lukas's help. A major operation was being planned in late June. It was ambitious. The objective was to derail a shipment of iron ore bound for Hamburg. The train would have multiple cars filled with ore and oil and would be well-guarded. The operation would be dangerous, but the reward could be great. Starck said that Lukas's leadership would be invaluable. In order to pull off this mission, he needed enough members to establish a manned perimeter, and he needed Lukas's experience in explosive devices.

"When he left, Lukas returned to the living room. Grethe said, 'What was that all about?' Lukas hung his head; he knew this wouldn't go over well. 'Larson is planning a major operation. He has twenty members in his group, but he can't do it alone. This is big, Grethe. Real big. Not only would we destroy the shipment and deprive Hitler of the oil and the ore, but we would effectively cripple the rail route for weeks. I told Larson he could count on us. I would reestablish the Holger Club and give him our support.'

"Sitting in that room, I could see the blood rise in my sister's face. 'And just who is going to lead your Holger Club with you being in a wheelchair?' she asked, though she knew the answer.

"'I don't intend to sit this one out,' he said firmly. 'I may be stuck in this chair, but with a little help I can still get around, and I can organize, and I can make a difference. Grethe, I need you to deliver a message to the remaining members of the club. Tell them I'm setting a meeting at the Viking Bookstore on Wednesday night at seven o'clock.'

"Grethe set her jaw. 'And I need you to stay at home with me and your daughter,' she snapped. 'You're in no shape to lead any sabotage. This crazy operation sounds like a disaster waiting to happen. You think that train won't be well-guarded? The Germans have seen far too much sabotage to let this shipment go unprotected. Troops will be there every step of the way. And they'll be armed. You and thirty country boys aren't going to derail that train. They'll catch you and they'll kill you. And I'm not going to lose my husband. Again!'

"Lukas was trying hard to calm her down. 'We're not going to attack the train. We're going to set explosives and blow up a bridge. There won't be any troops guarding the railroad tracks in a field in the middle of the night.'

"'You don't remember the last time where the Gestapo came out of nowhere with rifles and machine guns *in a field in the middle of the night*? No one expected that either.'

"'We were betrayed. Someone informed on us. That won't happen again.'

"'And you can assure me of that because you know every single person in Larson Starck's club and you can vouch for each one of them, right?'

"'No, but I can vouch for Larson and he's a strong leader. Look, I pledged my support. I have to do this. I need you to get the message out to the Holger Club. Will you do that please, Grethe? Otherwise, I'll have to go myself.'

"'You see how foolish you are. If you go rolling around Copenhagen in that wheelchair, the Gestapo will see you, and they'll pull you in for questioning and you won't come home for twenty days. Or ever. Can't you see what's happening on the streets?'

"Grethe soon realized that her protestations were falling on deaf ears. The Odense group needed help and Lukas didn't want to let them down. His argument finally beat her down and Grethe agreed to spread the word, but as she left, she said, 'You can manage the meeting, organize the operation, pass out the assignments, and plan with Larson, but your involvement stops right there. You're not leaving Copenhagen!'

"On the night of the meeting, Isabel chose to be fussy. Lukas was anxious; he didn't want to be late, but Grethe couldn't leave and Lukas couldn't go without her help. Isabel was taking her time with her feeding—first she would, then she wouldn't, then she wanted to gurgle and coo." Britta smiles. "She was pretty damn cute."

Emma returns the smile. "That's my mom."

Britta continues. "Lukas was losing patience. He had learned how to pace in his wheelchair, back and forth like a tiger on the kitchen floor, and he was driving Grethe crazy. "'Let me go,' I said to Grethe. 'I'll take Lukas and you catch up with us when you can.' The bookstore was a dozen blocks away and I could push Lukas there pretty easily. Grethe agreed and said she would come as soon as she put Isabel to bed.

"The Viking Bookstore was dark when we arrived, but the back door was open. Members of the club were gathering in the back storeroom. I recognized four of the eight from previous meetings. Knud Gunnison was not there, but given his mother's attitude and how nervous he was when he met me on the street, I didn't expect to see him. You couldn't blame him. He was almost killed by the Gestapo in the raid.

"Lukas began the meeting by unrolling a map of Denmark given to him by Larson Starck. He stretched it out on a table and pointed to an area in lower Jutland. 'There is a monthly shipment of Swedish iron ore bound for armament factories in Hamburg. It always travels this route. When it leaves Vejle and proceeds south, it passes a nature park. There are very few towns or railroad crossings in the area and the train picks up speed. There are also several streams and bogs in this region. At this point, right here, there is an iron trestle bridge fifty meters long. The plan is to set explosive charges on the sloping beams under the bridge, blow up the bridge at the precise moment the train is on it, derail the shipment and destroy the southern railroad route, at least temporarily.' As Lukas was finishing his sentence, Grethe walked into the room, stopped dead short and put her hands on her hips.

"'Exactly who is going to plant those explosives?' she asked.

"'We are,' Lukas answered. 'The Holger Club is, along with Larson's Odense group. All of us together.'

"Lukas's words seemed to imply his participation far beyond Grethe's geographic boundary, but she wasn't going to challenge him in front of the club members. At such time as she could get him alone, she'd get assurances that he wasn't planning on leaving Copenhagen, or all hell would break loose.

"'Where are we going to get the explosives?' one member asked.

"'From the SOE, just like before. Larson said his group will be at the drop zone next Monday to meet the SOE flight.' Lukas noticed that one of his members was shaking his head. 'What's the matter, Tommy?'

"'Just like before? That's when we lost two of our members and it put you in a wheelchair. We walked into an ambush. Why will this time be different?'

"'Jesus, Tommy, there was an ambush because we were betrayed. We had a traitor. One of the groups, maybe even ours, had an informer. Look around; you know every one of these guys. We're good here. There's no informers in this room.'

"'Yeah, but I don't know the Odense guys.'

"Lukas nodded. 'I get it, and you don't have to go if you don't want to. Larson Starck has been running his club for a long time and they've done some great work. There are no guarantees, but I trust Larson and his club. It's a dangerous mission, to be sure, but if we're ambushed again, I don't think it will be because we were betrayed by one of our own.'

"The more Lukas talked, the more evident it became that he intended to lead the group on the mission. I could see the tears forming in Grethe's eyes.

"'When are we going?' a member asked.

"'Tuesday,' Lukas said. 'Six days from now. You will have to arrange your own transportation to Vejle, and we will meet up with the Odense group Tuesday at midnight. We'll have to work quickly; the train will be crossing the bridge on Wednesday afternoon.' He looked around the room. 'Who's in?' The members grimaced, shook their heads, let out a groan, but in the end, each of them raised his hand. 'Great!' Lukas said. 'See you all on Tuesday. Remember, not a word!'

"The moment we left the meeting and were on our walk home, Grethe said, 'And how will you run away this time, Lukas? You couldn't get away when you had two good legs.' He looked up at her and said 'Grethe . . .'

"'Don't Grethe me,' she snapped. 'You have a daughter and a wife. You've given enough. You've already given them your legs. Let them do this mission without you. You did your part; you organized it and you've coordinated with Larson. Let him finish it.' Lukas didn't answer. 'Promise me that you'll let the Holger Club go without you,' Grethe said. 'Promise me.'

"'I can't,' he said softly. 'If I don't show, it'll destroy our club's morale and who knows how many others won't go either. I can't pull the rug out from under them, and I can't back out when I told Larson we were in. I'm the leader, I have to go. I know you understand.'

"After we had gone a block or two in silence, Grethe finally said, 'How do you intend to get around? You can't drive.'

"'Tommy will take me. He has a truck.'

"Grethe walked around to the front of his chair, knelt on the sidewalk and put her head on his lap. 'You know I don't want you to go,' she said, and he answered, 'I know.' And she said, 'But if you have to . . .'"

Britta abruptly stops her narration. She struggles for a deep breath. It seems as though she is searching for a word. Emma's eyes are locked on her grandmother, who appears to be in some distress. There is a touch of panic in Emma's voice. "Bubbe? Bubbe, are you all right? Bubbe, can you breathe?"

Britta struggles to respond. "May . . . may I have some water, please," she says with a cough.

Emma reaches for the pitcher and Catherine calls out, "Gladys, call 911; get an ambulance here!"

CHAPTER THIRTY-EIGHT

BRITTA LIES IN the cardiac intensive care unit at Northwestern Memorial. Catherine and Emma are outside her room. The doctor approaches. "Your grandmother is stable."

"Thank God."

The doctor nods. "This is the third time she's been in here this year, but the first time she came in an ambulance."

"Did she have a heart attack?"

"Well, not exactly. It's her congestive heart disease. Her heart is working less efficiently. It's just not as strong as it used to be, but at the moment she's stable. We'll keep her here for a little while. You can go in."

An IV drips into Britta's arm, a nasal cannula is delivering supplemental oxygen and her chest is wired up to the heart monitors. Britta lifts her head and looks sheepishly at Emma. "Like my friend Oliver Hardy used to say, 'Here's another nice mess I've gotten us into.'"

"The doctor says you should eat more and drink more water," Emma says. "I'm going to start making you three meals a day!"

Britta smiles. "I'll get too fat to wear my nice clothes." Turning to Catherine, she asks, "Don't we have to be in court this week?"

Catherine says, "I do, but you don't. In two days, I have to submit our answer and affirmative defense. I think the judge will want to set a schedule for the rest of the case. Of course, Sparks will push for an accelerated case management order and a prompt trial."

Britta thinks for a moment and then says, "I don't want to you object to that. Set the trial as soon as you can."

Catherine disagrees. "We're not ready. We don't have our proofs. We need more time to gather evidence, to put our case together."

Britta's expression is calm and peaceful, but it is determined. "We don't have more time, Catherine. The proof is in my testimony and I need to be around to give it."

Emma doesn't like that answer. "You're going to be fine, Bubbe. You're a fighter. You're the woman who paints walls in the middle of the night. Just get some nourishment and a little rest and you'll be back on your feet as good as new."

"Tell her, Catherine," Britta says. "What happens if I'm not there for the trial?"

Catherine starts to wave her off. "I'm with Emma. Get yourself back on your feet. Let's not have this conversation right now."

Britta won't be put off. "What happens if the case is called for trial and I'm not alive?" she asks again, more directly.

"The case would proceed against your estate, and without a witness we would most likely have to default."

"And Hendricksen would be vindicated?"

"Well, I don't know how much vindication you get against an empty chair, but yes, I'm afraid so. Your testimony is all that we have at this time. We don't have another witness or any physical evidence to show that Henryks is a traitor."

"If Liam finds something in Denmark, could he be a witness?"

Catherine smiles. "Depending on what he finds, but he certainly was not a witness to anything Henryks did."

The nurse returns to the room and says, "We need to run a couple of tests and administer her medication. Could you give us a few minutes? Why don't you two go and get a cup of coffee and come back in a little while."

In the commissary, Emma says, "I think it's a mistake to accelerate the case. Regardless of her weakened condition, she'll want to come to trial and testify. We don't have any admissible evidence at this time other than her testimony. So, she would come to court and with every last bit of energy she would tell her story in front of a hostile courtroom."

Catherine shakes her head. "No, it won't be hostile. The jury would love her, just like we do."

"They won't get to make the decision; it'll never get to the jury," Emma says. Her expression is sorrowful, and her lower lip protrudes. "I love my Bubbe so much, but her testimony won't hold up. Sparks will be on his feet every five seconds yelling 'Hearsay!' So much of Bubbe's story is based upon what other people told her. Lukas *told* her that the Hendricksens were informers. Knud Gunnison *said* he saw Hendricksen with the Gestapo at the drop zone. Britta said Ole was a member of the Blue Shirt Club, but we don't have any proof of the club's existence or that it was a counterinsurgent. I can't let my Bubbe go into court and have every line of her testimony stricken. Sparks will play to the press and make a fool of her and she'd lose the case. That would kill her quicker than a heart attack. We can't let that happen. Please don't accelerate the case."

"I understand," Catherine says, "but she's the client. I have to follow her instructions."

On their way back to the room, Emma says, "All my life I wanted to grow up and be just like her. She's smart, articulate, polished and dignified. Ever the consummate lady, and the strongest person I've ever known. And she goes out in the middle of the night in her overcoat and paints on the wall because she needs to *set the record straight*. We have to protect her, Catherine. We have to preserve her dignity."

"I'll do everything I can."

As they approach the room, the nurse comes out and says, "Did you bring paper and a pen with you? Britta has asked me for paper and a pen. I think she might want to make her last will and testament. You're her lawyer, aren't you?"

Catherine nods. "But I didn't bring any paper."

"I can get you some," the nurse says.

Britta is propped up slightly as she lies in the bed. "Did you bring a writing pad with you?" she asks.

"You already have a will, Bubbe," Emma says. "I made one out for you last year. Remember? You signed it in Walter's office."

The nurse returns with several sheets of white paper. "There is a notary on the third floor. I can call her if and when you want me to."

Britta smiles. "I don't need another will; I need to finish my story. There are things I have to tell my lawyer and my granddaughter, and they will want to make notes."

Emma looks at Catherine and both of them chuckle. "You see what I mean," Emma says.

"LUKAS LEFT FOR Vejle on Tuesday afternoon. Tommy picked him up in his truck and off they went. Although she had tried a few more times, Grethe was unable to dissuade Lukas from going. This was the man she married, and she understood him well. She would have gone with him had it not been for Isabel and her responsibilities as a mother. She had her arms around his neck, and she didn't want to let go. Lukas kissed Grethe and Isabel and left, promising to come back.

"Grethe sat vigil; she had been down this road before. She and I sat in the living room listening to the radio for any news, good or bad. The explosion, if it was successful, would have taken place early Wednesday afternoon, but as of the evening there had been no reports of any acts of sabotage, and gratefully, no reports of partisan arrests. Grethe and I began to worry. Did the mission fail? Were the boys arrested. Or worse? My father had a suggestion. 'The report may have been censored. Dr. Best wouldn't want news of a successful raid broadcast on Danish radio. Why don't we try the BBC?' He turned the dial and tuned into the BBC Danish broadcast. The familiar chimes of Big Ben were followed by 'This is the BBC, London calling, John Christmas Møller speaking. Today British and American bombs rained on German forces in southern Italy. The distant sound of explosions was heard as far north as the Vatican.'

"We listened to the announcer describe war news in one location or another and then he said that brave Danish partisans had demolished a bridge in southern Denmark crucial to the passage of raw materials to Germany. That's how we learned the mission had succeeded.

"The next morning, Danish radio reported that a bridge had been damaged by a gang of young ruffians, some of whom were taken into custody and were being interrogated.

"When Grethe heard that, she broke into tears. She was practically inconsolable. 'I told him not to go,' she said. 'I knew this would happen. He's in a wheelchair, for heaven's sake. If anyone is in custody, it's my Lukas.' Then came a loud knock on the door. My father answered it to find the two Gestapo agents standing there. 'We want to talk to Lukas Holstrum,' one of them said. My father stayed calm and falsely said, 'He's sleeping. What is your business here?'

"'Our business? It is to talk to Lukas Holstrum. Now go get him.'

"My father stood strong. 'I told you, he's sleeping. Now go away.'

"'We don't believe you,' the agent said with a smirk. 'We will see for ourselves.'

"My father stood strong and blocked the doorway. 'We've been down this road before. The Gestapo has no right to come into a Danish house uninvited. And *you* are not invited.'

"A smile stretched the lips of the second agent, and he whispered in his partner's ear. 'Ah,' the agent said. 'Of course. You're telling me that he's sleeping because he's not at home. Am I right? I think maybe he's in Vejle or lower Jutland. That's where he'd be if he was part of the criminal attack on our supply train and the murder of seven German patrolmen.'

"My father shook his head. 'He's asleep in his room. Please extend my sympathies to the Honorable Dr. Best for the loss of his shipment and his seven guards.' With that my father shut the door.

"Late that afternoon, as the sun was setting, Tommy brought Lukas into the house. Grethe fell to her knees. 'Oh, my God, you're safe. I was sure they took you into custody with the rest of the group.'

"'They didn't take anyone into custody,' Lukas said. 'It was a total success. We completed the mission and didn't lose a single man. The bridge was blown just as the train was crossing. Several of the Odense members came out of the forest and held the train guards at bay, while the others dashed back to their cars. A crossfire ensued, and that's when the Germans were shot.'

"The next day, Werner Best demanded that the Folketing take up a resolution for mandatory imposition of the death penalty for anyone convicted of sabotage. The resolution failed. The only affirmative votes were from the six DNSAP members. Still my father cautioned us that the situation was growing more serious every day. Berlin was furious and insisted that Denmark be brought into line. The pressure was on Best and his German administration."

The nurse returns to the room and shakes her finger at Britta. "That's enough for today, Mrs. Stein. Doctor's orders. You need rest and medication."

"But I need to finish my story. You don't understand," Britta says.

"We'll come back tomorrow," Catherine says as she gets up to leave. "You get your rest."

Britta holds up her index finger. "That act of sabotage, blowing up that train, Danes regard that as one of the most effective acts of sabotage in the war," she says proudly. "It caused more damage and created more disruption than other acts of sabotage."

Catherine raises her eyebrows and smiles. "Was it Denmark's greatest show of resistance in the war?"

"Oh no," Britta says. "I will tell you that tomorrow."

CHAPTER THIRTY-NINE

BRITTA IS IN a sitting position when Emma and Catherine enter her hospital room. Her tray of food has been pushed to the side. Remnants of scrambled eggs remain on the plate along with two pieces of dried toast, though the corner of one has been nibbled. The two small pancakes, packaged syrup, black currant jelly and orange juice are untouched. The little silver pot of coffee is empty.

"Good morning, Bubbe," Emma chirps brightly. "You're looking good today."

Britta scoffs. "I look like the wrath of God. My hair is a dreadful mess."

Emma chuckles, cuts a piece of pancake, dips it in the syrup and tenders it to her grandmother. In return, she gets a look that says, "Absolutely not." Emma presses on. She waves the fork back and forth in front of Britta's face. "C'mon, Bubbe, just one bite. Here comes the choo-choo train."

Britta opens her mouth, accepts the forkful and makes a face. "I need more coffee," she says. "And be ready to take your notes.

"As the summer of 1943 progressed, so did the Danish resistance. The movement, which had started with the youth clubs, like the Holger Club, now reached a cross-section of Danish society. Food shortages, especially in fruits, vegetables and paper products, became commonplace. One could never count on her local grocery store having what she needed. Textiles, bicycle tires, nylons, sewing machines were scarce. Danes resented the imposition and the hardship caused by the shortages. After all, these hardships were foisted upon us and we were not a country at war.

"A large plant, manufacturing airplane parts for the Luftwaffe, was burned to the ground and the British phrase 'Do it well; Do it now' was painted on the charred beams. Wildcat strikes popped up in several cities where plants, formerly producing consumer products, were filling orders for Germany. Factory workers resented the increased German surveillance. The Gestapo seemed to be everywhere. They didn't have the authority to arrest, but they would urge Danish policemen to randomly arrest Danish citizens on suspicion of one thing or another.

"Toward the end of July, my father's friend Stefan Munsk and his wife, Rena, once again joined us for dinner. You may remember, Stefan was a Danish envoy to Berlin and he always seemed to have inside information, but because of the civil unrest that summer he had been recalled. As a courtesy to my mother and Rena, there was a general agreement not to discuss politics at the dinner table. However, when the dinner was finished, my father and Stefan retired to the living room for brandy and cigars, and the debates began. My father was in a good mood. 'It appears that the mighty Third Reich is coming apart at the seams, fraying at the edges, as it were,' Papa said. 'The Reich is back on its heels: Russia, North Africa, the Atlantic and,' he paused, took a sip of brandy and said with a grin, 'and of course, here in Denmark.'

"'Perhaps,' Stefan said as he lit his cigar, 'but make no mistake; Germany owns Europe. The army is still strong, the country is wealthy and Hitler is ruthless. Denmark would be well-advised not to test his resolve. Especially this month.'

"'This month? What do you know that you are not telling us, Stefan? Who have you been talking to?'

"'Hmm,' he said as he took a draw of his cigar, 'only to Hermann von Hanneken, general of the German infantry, proud wearer of the German Cross of Gold for repeated acts of bravery, and now serving as supreme commander of German land forces in Denmark.'

"'You've spoken to General von Hanneken?'

"Stefan, pointing his cigar for emphasis, said with a tinge of self-importance, 'I have. He is pushing for all Danish forces to be disarmed. He doesn't trust us, can you imagine? I was there when he said to Best, 'Look at the violence, the rise in criminal sabotage, and you Werner are unable to control it. If the Allies were to land in Denmark tomorrow, could we trust the Danish forces to honor the Cooperation Agreement?'

"My father shrugged. 'Just talk.'

"'No, Joseph, it's gone further than that. Von Hanneken has drafted plans for disarming our army and he wants our navy disarmed as well. He hopes to implement his plans in September.'

"My father was shocked. 'I thought Best was in charge.'

"Stefan shrugged. 'They are in conflict, but Best does have an ally. Wurmbach is also opposed to von Hanneken's plan.'

"'Are we talking about Vice Admiral Wurmbach?'

"Stefan chuckled. 'The senior German naval officer in Denmark. Do you know any other Wurmbachs?'

"That comment made my father laugh and the two of them refilled their brandy snifters. At that point, Lukas entered the room. 'Join us,' my father said, and he offered Lukas a brandy. Stefan continued, 'Wurmbach argues against taking over the Danish navy at this time. He says that the Danish navy is cooperative and performing duties that the German navy would otherwise have to assume. Both Best and Wurmbach believe that this so-called Danish unrest is overblown. Just isolated incidents here or there, a smattering of malcontents, and not a coordinated movement at all. And to tell the truth, I am inclined to agree with them. You must admit that true civil unrest would be an act of national suicide. Germany can stomp its big black boot on us on a moment's whim. I think our people realize this. The Danish people want to cooperate.'

"My father's eyebrows lifted. 'Stefan, you've been out of the country for some time, you may be a little out of touch with what the Danish people want. What do you think, Lukas? Is Danish unrest overblown?'

"'No,' Lukas said. 'If anything, it's understated. Our people are supportive of partisan activities and it is inevitable that acts of sabotage will only increase as the occupation continues. The Danish people are fed up with Germany and they want them to leave. They want to be neutral and run their own lives like they have done in every other European war.

Take my word for it, there will be more explosions, more fires, more damage.'

"'Really,' Stefan said with a smile, 'and how would you know this, young man? Are you a member of one of these partisan groups?'

"Lukas tapped his wheelchair. 'No sir, I'm hardly in any condition to go running around with those loyalists. I just hear things, you know. I work in a bookstore and people come in, browse the books, and they talk. From what I hear, there is general dissatisfaction with the occupying forces and there is strong support for the loyalist partisans. I predict there will be hundreds of acts of sabotage before this occupation is over. Only from what I hear, of course.'

"'Well,' Stefan said, 'we know that it's common for eggheads and revolutionary types to hang out in bookstores, don't we? I hope you're wrong, because if there are hundreds of acts of sabotage, the hawks in Berlin will prevail and there will be serious reprisals brought upon the Danish populace.'

"As it turned out, both Lukas and Stefan were correct. There were other acts of sabotage, followed by swift reprisals. On July 28, just a few weeks after our dinner, a disenchanted Danish dockworker set an explosive device and blew up a German freighter in the Odense harbor. The Germans had wanted to guard that ship, but were persuaded to allow the Danish dockworkers to manage their harbor. That changed after the explosion. Admiral Wurmbach quietly began to formulate his plans to take over and disarm the Danish navy.

"German reprisals intensified. Random arrests increased. There were unexplained murders of clergy, poets and writers. As a consequence, Danish workers rebelled. They went out on strike. There were demonstrations in the streets of several towns. Acts of sabotage happened in broad daylight. There was a general air of revolt, and it all led up to the crisis at the end of August."

Britta's nurse returns to the room, checks the monitor and her IV, and says, "Mrs. Stein needs medical attention right now. Her doctor is coming in a few minutes. I think we should give her some time to rest, don't you?"

Emma and Catherine gather their things to leave. Britta says, "Wait. Catherine, please, may I have a minute?" She motions for Catherine to come closer. "Emma, would you give me a moment alone with Catherine, please?"

Emma steps into the hall, and Catherine moves up to the head of the bed. Britta whispers, "Are you going to court tomorrow?" Catherine nods. "Then you must do whatever it takes to get the case to trial at the earliest possible date. Do not object to a motion to expedite."

"It's not that simple," Catherine says. "The judge undoubtedly has other cases scheduled for trial. Sparks has the right to take depositions, subpoena witnesses, file motions. Besides, I have to tell you that Emma is diametrically opposed to advancing the case for trial until you have completely recovered and are healthy enough to sit through what is bound to be a grueling trial."

"There is a lot that Emma doesn't know. My condition is worse than she thinks. I've tried to hide it from her."

"She knows more than you think, Britta. She's very perceptive. Let me ask you, given your condition, why risk your health by proceeding with a trial? Henryks isn't worth it. What does it matter if he gets inducted into some make-believe hall of fame?"

"It matters to me. When I finish my story, you'll understand why. I never knew that Ole Hendricksen survived the war. I surely didn't know that he lived in Chicago. Not until I saw the article in the *Tribune*. I need to finish what I started, Catherine. Most importantly, Emma needs to know about her mother and the family from which she is descended. One needs to know and appreciate her heritage. And Hendricksen needs to pay for what he did to us. Trust me, he's a worm, and he'll crumble in a trial."

"He won't crumble unless I have the evidence to confront him. So far, we're not there. I have to file our defenses tomorrow, I can fill in the blanks later, but I have to have the outline headings. What can I accuse him of?"

Britta nods. "He collaborated with the Gestapo to inform on members of the resistance. He betrayed Jewish families to the Nazis. He and his friends were members of counter-resistance groups. During the exodus, he acted to prevent Jews from escaping."

Catherine writes down the points and says, "What evidence will we have in support of those accusations?"

"My testimony," Britta says firmly with a raised chin. "And the admissions you can elicit from Hendricksen. And whatever your husband can bring us from Denmark. Most of all, we have your skill as a lawyer."

Catherine closes her notebook. "Right," she says softly.

Britta's lips tighten. "I hold him responsible for what happened to my family, and he will pay dearly with the unmasking of his fraudulent reputation. We will win this lawsuit because it is just."

Catherine nods her head; she understands. "When you painted Hendricksen's walls, you knew this would be the consequence. You expected him to sue you, didn't you? You actually wanted this lawsuit."

"He had to stand trial for what he did. A public trial and condemnation. I certainly couldn't bring a suit against him for being a Nazi collaborator seventy years ago, could I? He had to be the one to bring the suit, and he took the bait."

"Yes, he did. To get him into a public courtroom and on the television every night, *he had to sue you,* and you had to raise his nefarious conduct in an affirmative defense. All in all, that was brilliant."

"So, my young friend, he will be tried, and he will be judged. It is his just reward. And I need to be there to see it. Don't object to a motion to expedite." She reaches out for Catherine's hand. "And my granddaughter must know her family's story. She has a right to know on whose shoulders she stands. It will help to define her life."

Catherine has a lump in her throat. "What if all this proves too strenuous for you, Britta? You're in a hospital now. What if you succumb to the . . . ? How will Emma know her story then?"

"In the top drawer of my bedside table, there's a notebook. I have written it all out. Everything that happened."

The doctor enters the room, looks kindly at Catherine and tips his head toward the door. Britta squeezes Catherine's hand. "Our little secret," Britta says.

"LIAM, THIS WAS a very hard day for me. Britta is more ill than we believed. I hope you have something good to tell me."

"I love you; how's that?"

Catherine chuckles. "It's perfect. I was hoping for something a little more, but that will do."

"Are you going to court tomorrow?"

"Yes, I am. Our affirmative defense is due and I'm going to file it in open court."

"What are you going to say?"

"I am going to allege that Ole was a member of a Nazi-sponsored counterinsurgency group—the Blue Shirts aka the Blue Storm—that he personally informed on resistance fighters causing the arrest and death of partisans, that he informed on Jewish families and that he worked for a company that manufactured products for the Germans."

"Well, as to the products, you're on solid ground. They were ball bearings and turrets used in German Panzer tanks. That's what the Simmons Manufacturing Company made and shipped. I don't have the employee records, but I think you can get Ole to admit he worked for Simmons, and they made war machinery to Nazi specifications. As to the assertions about the Blue Shirts and the betrayal, we have no corroborative proof—it's all hearsay."

"Hell, Liam, the whole damn thing is hearsay, but I can *allege* hearsay. If, at the end of the day, that's all I have, it will be stricken, but I can allege it in my affirmative defense. It will get us past tomorrow. Sparks doesn't know what evidence I have. Besides, there are exceptions to the hearsay rule. Ole could confess. Britta says he will crumble under cross-examination and maybe he will. Maybe he'll blunder into making admissions. The ball bearings and turrets will be useful. Do you have proof of that?"

"I do, but I have more. I'm working on a couple of leads, I can't say for sure that they will pan out, but let's go ahead and allege them anyway. Allege that Hendricksen was part of a group of Nazi sympathizers that tried to sabotage the Jews' escape in October 1943."

"Liam, Ole has publicly stated that he and his father helped to transport Jews to safety. He has a picture of the boat on his tavern wall. The *Perlie B*."

"I have a meeting with the harbormaster tomorrow. If he confirms my suspicions, he'll tell me that the boat belonged to someone else. And I have a theory about who it belonged to. If I'm right, it's a blockbuster. It ties in with Ole's membership in Nazi-sponsored organizations and also to the sabotage of Jewish rescue operations. I could be wrong, but go ahead and allege them anyway. Worse comes to worst, you won't be able to prove them, but my gut tells me I'm right. By the way, I was able to obtain Ole Hendricksen's birth certificate with the names of his mother and father, just in case he says that he's Ole Henryks and not Ole Hendricksen."

"Great work."

"Do me a favor, if you can. The night Sparks threw that big shindig for Henryks at The Melancholy Dane, Ole Appreciation Night, there were several reporters, and they made video recordings. Would you see if you could get a copy?"

"Sure. What do you have in mind?"

"I'll tell you when I get back."

CHAPTER FORTY

⸺◦◦◦◦◦⸺

"I STOPPED BY the hospital this morning," Emma says as she and Catherine enter the elevator on the ground floor of the courthouse. "There's really no change. They said they'd like to keep her for a day or two longer."

"Did you feed her breakfast?" Catherine says with a wink.

The door opens on the 21st floor. There is commotion in the hallway and Catherine sighs. "I wish I could just come to the courthouse and practice law without having to deal with a mob of reporters, but here they are, gathered like teenagers outside the stage door of a concert hall." Catherine nods to Vera Paulson, who wanders over with her cameraman.

"Can I get a few clips for the noon broadcast?" Vera asks politely.

She's one of the few who conduct themselves with civility, Catherine thinks. "Sure," she says.

"By the terms of the last court order, your client, Mrs. Stein, is to provide details about how Mr. Henryks was a traitor and a Nazi collaborator," Vera says. "Are you prepared to do that today, or will you be asking for a continuance?"

"There will be no continuance. We will be filing our affirmative defense this morning, with all the appropriate factual details."

"Details that show how the words painted on the wall of The Melancholy Dane tavern were true?"

"Were and are. Mr. Henryks was in fact a Nazi informant, a traitor and a collaborator. He betrayed his Danish people and, specifically, Jewish families. As you know, truth is an absolute defense to a lawsuit for defamation, and we intend to win this lawsuit."

Hearing those words, other reporters rush over with their microphones and video cameras and circle around Catherine and Emma. "We understand," Vera says, "that Judge Wilson will enter a case management order this morning which will set a firm trial date. Are you going to suggest a date? Will it be far in the future?"

Nick Donnegan, a brash reporter from ABC, steps forward. "What do you think?" he says to Vera. "She'll ask for a date five years from now. This case'll never go to trial because these two people aren't going to live long enough. We're all wasting our time here."

"No one required you to be here," Catherine says. "I'm sure that Judge Wilson will set proper deadlines in accordance with his schedule and the rules."

"Where's your client?" Donnegan asks with a grin. "Is she out painting buildings this morning?"

Emma lurches forward. "You're not funny, Mr. Donnegan. She happens to be in the hospital. She's ill."

Donnegan snickers. "I guess that's what she gets from running around with a spray can in the middle of the night in her nightgown defaming restaurant owners."

In a flash, Emma's hands shoot out, slamming Donnegan in the chest and knocking him backward. "She wasn't in a nightgown, you prick. And she wrote the truth."

Catherine quickly grabs Emma and guides her toward the courtroom. "He's not worth it, Emma," she says. Donnegan stands up, brushes himself off, smiles and says, "You got some temper there, little lady. You should see a shrink; get some anger management."

As Catherine and Emma are arranging their files on the counsel table, they hear more commotion out in the hallway. "The eminent Mr. Sparks must have arrived," Catherine says. A few moments later, Sparks enters the courtroom with Ole Henryks by his side. A rush of reporters follows him in and jockeys for seats.

Catherine stands, walks across the room and hands a document to

Sparks. "This is a copy of Mrs. Stein's affirmative defense which we will tender to the court this morning."

Sparks accepts the document and lays it on the table without looking at it. He is smartly dressed in a three-piece charcoal suit that shimmers in the courtroom lighting. "Where is Mrs. Stein?" he says. "She didn't come to confront her archenemy today?"

"Her attendance is not required. This is a routine call."

Sparks points to the reporters in the gallery. "Nothing about this case is routine, Catherine. You know I will be pushing Obadiah for an early trial date. I presume you will oppose that."

From behind them, Ole shouts, "What the hell? What are you trying to do to me?"

They turn to see Ole reading the affirmative defense. He is standing at the counsel table and the papers rattle in his ancient hands. He waves them in the air. "This is a bunch of damn lies. You can't let them file this, Sterling." Sparks rushes over to the table. He takes the document from Ole and helps him settle back into his seat. There is a rumble of conversations in the gallery.

Sparks picks up the copy of the affirmative defense and takes his time reading the document. "Seriously?" he says to Catherine. "You intend to prove that Ole materially interfered with the escape of Jewish families from Denmark? That he was a member of a Nazi-sponsored organization that informed upon the Danish resistance? That he worked for a company manufacturing and shipping weapons to Germany, that they were manufactured in accordance with German specifications? You have proof of all this?"

"Most certainly we do. I wouldn't allege it if I couldn't prove it." Upon hearing this discourse, there is a loud exchange in the gallery.

"Lies!" Ole shouts. His face is red, and tears are flowing freely. "Sue her, Sterling. Sue her for writing those lies. Add her to the lawsuit. Lockhart is defaming me the same as her client."

Sparks taps him gently on the shoulder. "Calm yourself, Ole. Statements in a judicial proceeding are privileged; we can't sue Ms. Lockhart. But she and her client will have the sorriest day of their lives when this case comes to trial."

"All rise," announces the clerk as the corner door opens and Judge

Obadiah Wilson takes the bench. He looks down at Sparks. "I see you've brought your fan club with you today." Then to the gallery, he says, "Usual warning. No noise, no photos, no recordings." He nods to his clerk. "Call the case."

"Case number 18-L-20998, *Henryks v. Stein,* continued by previous order."

Sparks, Catherine and Emma approach the bench and identify themselves for the record. Catherine hands a copy of her pleading to the judge. "Mrs. Stein's affirmative defense, your honor," she says, "with factual detail in accordance with your order."

Wilson scans the document, raises his eyebrows and says, "My, my, my."

"It's scandalous," snaps Sparks. "Where's the proof of these outrageous accusations?"

"I suppose you'll find out when she answers your interrogatories and sits for her deposition, Mr. Sparks," Wilson says calmly. "Isn't that the way these things usually work in our profession?"

Sparks is just warming up. He begins to pace back and forth in front of the bench. He has his index finger ready for emphasis. "Don't you see what she has done?" he says. "She has compounded the harm brought upon Mr. Henryks. It is not enough to falsely claim in generalities that her spray-painted words are true, she has now made it ten times worse by specifying conduct she cannot possibly prove."

"Well, we do not know that at this stage, do we, Mr. Sparks?" Wilson says.

Sparks points to his client, who is sitting at the counsel table shaking his head and mumbling. Then he speaks to the entire courtroom in a heightened tone. "Member of a Nazi-sponsored organization? Making weapons for the Nazis? Preventing Jews from escaping? Informing? Betraying? Your honor, these horrific accusations are hanging in the air for all to see and consider until the day comes that they are proven false and blown away. But every day between now and then is a day that Mr. Henryks must live under a cloud of infamy. You know what will happen," Sparks says as he waves his arm at the reporters sitting in the gallery. "All these fine ladies and gentlemen of the media will now go out and repeat these accusations, even though they are lies, because that is their job.

Breaking News! Can't you see it? Millions of listeners and viewers will form their opinions long before we get the chance to disprove them. We must prevent this perverse abuse of our legal system. I respectfully move that you place defendant's affirmative defense under seal, strictly protected from public view. Further, I move that you issue a gag order to all present today in this courtroom, strictly prohibiting them from disclosing what has been said and heard in this room today. That is the only way to protect a good man's reputation."

Judge Wilson sits silently while he ponders the motion. He taps his fingers on the top of his elevated desk. He breathes deeply through his nostrils. There is not a sound in the courtroom. Finally, he stands and announces, "The court will take a short recess. In the interim and until I rule, there will be no public disclosures of anything that has transpired this morning. No texts, no calls. I prefer that everyone just stay put, unless there is a prior commitment or a personal need." He turns and leaves the courtroom.

Sparks walks over to Henryks, who says, "Thank you, Sterling. Well done."

Thirty minutes later, Judge Wilson returns, and his clerk slams the gavel. "Court is back in session. Come to order."

Sparks immediately steps forward, "Your honor, if I may add one more thing . . ."

Wilson holds his palm up like a stop sign. He solemnly shakes his head. "No, Mr. Sparks, I'm ready to rule. While I respect your concern and that of your client, we have a strong tradition in this country and in our state. Our founding fathers determined that, unlike the star chambers and secret courts of prerogative that existed under old English common law, our courts would be open and public. That is carved in stone in the Constitution. In Illinois, our statutes provide, 'All records, dockets and books required by law to be kept by court clerks shall be deemed public records, and shall at all times be open to inspection and all persons shall have free access.'"

Wilson continues, "The First Amendment to the United States Constitution provides that 'Congress shall make no law abridging the freedom of the press.' While we have on rare occasion allowed certain court filings to be placed under seal—health records, children's identities, Social Security numbers and the like—the threshold is very, very high. Our Supreme Court has held that the mere fact a person may suffer embarrassment or damage to his reputation as a result of allegations in a pleading *does not* justify sealing the court file. Accordingly, your motion must be denied."

Henryks jumps to his feet. "That's not fair. They will write all these lies. Sterling, you have to do something. File an appeal."

Judge Wilson nods slightly. "You may indeed appeal my ruling."

Sparks shakes his head. He knows that an appeal will take months if not years, and will most likely be unsuccessful. "Your honor," he says, "because of the damaging content of Mrs. Stein's affirmative defense, we demand that this court set an immediate trial date. It is only fair to Mr. Henryks that the allegations against him not be allowed to linger unopposed. We do not think there is a shred of evidence to support such baseless claims and we insist on the opportunity to dispel them at the earliest possible date."

Wilson is inclined to be sympathetic to Sparks's request, with limitation. "Given the gravity of the situation," the judge says in his deep voice, "I am persuaded to enter an expedited case management order. All depositions and written discovery must be completed within three months. Motions for summary judgments are to be filed within three weeks thereafter. I will set a pretrial conference for a date five months from today."

"Five months!" Sparks says. "My client has to live under this cloud of shame for five months? And how long after that will the trial be? I'm sorry, but that's far too much time. I will waive my right to take Stein's deposition. I will waive my right to file interrogatories or request production. I will even waive my right to file a motion for summary judgment, even though I'm sure I would win it. I will waive all these rights to proceed to an immediate trial where we will show the world that Mrs. Stein has absolutely no evidence, and we will once and for all end her outrageous attacks against my client. It is only fair. I demand a trial in three weeks!"

The gallery gasps. Judge Wilson smiles. "You demand, do you? Well, you can waive *your* rights, you can't waive the defendant's rights. Ms. Lockhart has a right to conduct her discovery. My scheduling order is actually very generous to you, Mr. Sparks."

Emma elbows Catherine, leans over and whispers in her ear. Catherine nods. "Your honor," she says, "may I have a moment with my co-counsel?"

Catherine and Emma step to the side. "He's playing right into our hands," Catherine whispers. "That's exactly what your grandmother wants."

Emma nods. "You should have seen her this morning. I don't think she'll be able to withstand months of discovery. As much as it grieves me to say, my Bubbe may not even survive ten or twelve months."

"Right now, her testimony is all we have," Catherine says. "You know as well as I, that much of her testimony is based on what other people told her and it's hearsay. It will be stricken."

Emma agrees. "I do know that, but Sparks doesn't. If we had to answer interrogatories and submit Bubbe to a deposition, Sparks would find out we don't have solid evidence. He'd be able to file a motion for summary judgment and it would be granted. Henryks would walk away with a judgment against my Bubbe, and she'd never even get to tell her story to a jury. Sparks is a fool. He's offering to give up his rights without knowing what kind of evidence we have. *Or don't have!* I think we should agree."

Catherine grimaces. "I'm still hopeful that Liam will come up with something. He's never failed me. If we had another six months, that would give Liam plenty of time to gather evidence. But you might be right; Britta's health is our primary concern. It's a tough decision."

"You're the boss, Catherine," Emma whispers, "but I say we honor Bubbe's request. If nothing else, she'll get her day in court."

They return to the judge; Catherine speaks. "Your honor, I wish to dispel the erroneous notion that Mrs. Stein wants to delay this proceeding. Let's also dispel the notion that Mrs. Stein is afraid of a trial. On the contrary, she is anxious to show that her words are true. If Mr. Sparks is so eager to proceed to trial that he will waive all his rights to discovery and to pretrial motions, then Mrs. Stein will do the same. We agree to an immediate trial."

The courtroom explodes. Comments fly from the gallery. "Did you see what Six-o'clock just did? He pulled a fast one on Lockhart that we've never seen before." "Six-o'clock does it again." "Sparks is masterful." The clerk repetitively slams his gavel. "Order," he shouts. "Silence."

Wilson is confounded. "This case gets more curious every day. Well, if that is the joint request of the parties, then the court will honor it and we will proceed to trial three weeks from today. Court is adjourned."

Reporters flock around Sparks. He is relishing his stardom. As Catherine and Emma leave the courtroom, the reporters shake their heads. One of them looks at Catherine, snorts and says, "She just doesn't get it."

Vera Paulson is in the hallway waiting for Catherine. "I've been covering this beat long enough to know that you just scored," Vera says. "It was the waiver of his motion for summary judgment, wasn't it? You're worried about the strength of your evidence."

Catherine smiles. "You'll never hear that from me."

"Is that why your husband's in Copenhagen; digging for evidence?"

"How do you know that?"

Vera smiles and bites her bottom lip. "In my business, you have to stay alert. Someone saw him at the airport."

"Can I ask for a favor?" Catherine says quietly. "Just between you and me?"

"You bet. I'd love to see the day Six-o'clock gets clocked. What do you need?"

"A copy of the video taken at Ole Appreciation Night."

Vera nods. "I'll get you a copy. Now tell me, what's wrong with Mrs. Stein?"

"Not for public knowledge, but she's ninety-two and she has heart problems. She's in the cardiac ICU."

"Tell her I wish her the best."

CHAPTER FORTY-ONE

―⊗⊗⊗―

"You got your wish, Britta," Catherine says. "We go to trial in three weeks."

A smile forms on her lips and Britta says, "Thank you." She is slightly inclined in her bed. Wires and tubes connect her to the ICU equipment. "I have the two best lawyers in the world."

Emma stands quietly by the side of the bed. A tear runs down her cheek and she flicks it away. She has never thought of her grandmother as a frail woman. In Emma's eyes, her Bubbe has never aged. She is ever strong, ever dynamic and ever elegant. But now she lies in a form-less hospital gown on a bed with metal side rails, wearing no makeup, her hair in disarray, a nasal cannula delivering supplemental oxygen, and she looks a thousand years old. Only her smile is recognizable, and when it appears on her dried lips, it comforts Emma.

"How did you manage to have a trial set so soon?" Britta asks.

Catherine shrugs. "As it happened, Mr. Henryks was so put off by our accusations that he instructed his attorney to demand an immediate trial."

"Ole was always the biggest fool in town." Britta points to her bed's remote control. "Can you lift my head a little? Did you bring your note-pad?"

"Bubbe, we have a little time now. The trial won't begin for three weeks. Why don't you rest, get your strength back, and we'll resume again when you get home?"

"No time like the present," she says. "As long as my mind is sharp—and it is—let's forge ahead." Catherine and Emma exchange glances, shrug their shoulders and take their seats by the side of the bed. Britta has spoken.

"Before this damned inconvenience put me in this dreadful hospital, we were talking about how the tensions were increasing throughout the summer of 1943. By August, most Danes were fed up with the Germans treating us like we were their wards. Mr. High-and-Mighty, Dr. Werner Best, felt that he had the right to tell us how to run our country. So, he would issue his orders left and right, and, in turn, we would flout them. Sabotage became so common that not a day would pass that we didn't hear of a fire, or a bombing, or a derailment.

"The more we asserted our independence, the harder Best and his administration retaliated, which caused us to rebel even more. It was a vicious cycle. The German presence in our communities was repugnant to us. We had declared our neutrality, just like our neighbor Sweden, but Germany treated us differently. Germany dearly depended on Sweden for raw materials, oil, ore and manufactured goods. Germany didn't *need* any Danish products. They only needed Denmark as a passageway, a staging area and a buffer. We were a strategic landmass. Nothing more.

"So, our response to Germany's oppression was to block the passageways. We blew up the railroads. We set explosions to blow deep holes in the roads. We set fires to German installations. The workers in factories that supplied goods to Germany went on strike. Street demonstrations turned into protest marches which inevitably wound up in more violent sabotage. In the end, Germany lost patience with our defiance.

"In August, in the heat of our protests, Best sent out a call for more troops. Berlin dispatched thousands of infantry troops to General von Hanneken. Twenty-nine hundred more Gestapo agents were sent to Best. But the saboteurs were not dissuaded, and the acts of defiance continued. As August drew to a close, Best demanded that Danish authorities halt all strikes, protest marches and acts of civil disobedience, or the consequences would be severe.

"My father was rarely home during those days. It seemed like the

Folketing was in session every day and night. He was always running from one place to another trying to stay a step ahead of the next conflict. Wisely, he reconnected with his friend Georg Duckwitz, the German naval attaché. Georg was a German, but a good man. At one time he was a member of the Nazi Party, but he became disillusioned by their policies and resigned. In 1939, when he was working for a maritime shipping company, he agreed to take an assignment in Denmark as the German naval attaché.

"Georg was a good friend to the family and always a source of inside information for my father. He lived in Lyngby, a northern suburb of Copenhagen, in a beautiful white-brick house. We were invited there on several occasions.

"Georg held an important position in the German legation. He was in charge of commercial shipping. As such, he worked under Admiral Wurmbach. You remember, I told you last week that Wurmbach had proposed taking over the Danish navy when saboteurs bombed the German freighter in Odense harbor. He didn't do it at that time, but he kept those plans on his desk. In late August, Georg told my father that Wurmbach intended to execute those plans, but he didn't know exactly when."

"My father passed that information along to Admiral Vedel, head of the Danish navy. Vedel had heard those rumors himself, and was making preparations in case Wurmbach decided to go ahead. As you can imagine, during that chaotic period there were rumors galore. Plans and preparations were always being made, but we continually hoped that things would sort themselves out. After all, the Cooperation Agreement was still in effect.

"Everything came to a head on August 28. Best was fed up with civil disobedience. Fully buttressed with a fresh supply of troops, he delivered a formal ultimatum to the Folketing. 'The Government of Denmark has shown its inability to control the street violence and the criminal acts of sabotage,' he wrote. 'Accordingly, on behalf of the German administration, I am declaring a state of emergency. Henceforth, labor strikes are strictly prohibited. Strikers will be jailed. Anyone providing financial support to a striker will also be arrested. Persons committing acts of sabotage will be tried in German military courts and if found guilty, sentenced to death. Demonstrations are outlawed. Public gatherings of more than five persons are prohibited. A curfew of 8:30 p.m. will henceforth be enforced throughout the land.' Possession of firearms and explosives was also prohibited and they would be confiscated where found. Finally, Best demanded that the Folketing establish special tribunals to hear cases of violations of these orders and to carry out the sentences.

"My father called us all together that afternoon before he left for the Folketing session. We sat there in the living room: Grethe, Lukas, my mother and me. Oh, and of course, Isabel. 'I think you should know what's going on,' my father said. 'We must be cautious about what we do and where we go.' Those comments were clearly meant for Lukas. My father told us what Best demanded of the Folketing and that he expected the Folketing to reject the demands. 'If I know my fellow members, they will never accept those terms. I think we should anticipate difficult times ahead. The streets are now full of angry German soldiers led by angry German officials. We must be as careful as we can.'

"My mother was furious. 'What happened to the Cooperation Agreement; the promise not to interfere in our internal domestic affairs?' she said. My father just shook his head. 'Right now, we can't risk violating Best's orders,' he said. 'I urge you all to stay in the house as much as possible.'

"Predictably, Lukas voiced his opposition. 'I am the manager of a bookstore,' he said. 'The owner is out of town and I have responsibilities. I can't stay in the house; I need to work.'

"My father, who was no one's fool, shook his head and sighed. 'Lukas, we all know that selling books isn't the only thing you do in that bookstore. Best's decree now makes sabotage punishable by death.'

"'Best's decrees won't stop the saboteurs; I can guarantee it,' Lukas said. 'I know for a fact that the Odense club is planning a major operation in Aalborg.'

"'Lukas!' Grethe snapped. 'You promised.'

"Lukas raised his hand. 'I know, I know. I promised I wouldn't go out on any more missions and I'm not going on this one. The Holger Club is not involved. But Larson's bunch will blow apart the Nazis' northern communication center.'

"My father sighed. 'It'll only make things worse.'

"'What is the Folketing going to do?' my mother asked. 'What is the official response going to be to these unlawful demands?'

"'I'll tell you later this evening. There is a special session called for seven o'clock,' my father answered, 'and you can be assured that the debate will be raucous.'

"'I hope the Folketing doesn't let them push us around,' Lukas said. 'They have no business in our domestic affairs and no right to run our criminal courts. That agreement is written in stone. Speaking for my generation, we will never stand for it.'

"My father nodded and said, 'I think most of my parliamentary brothers agree with you.'

"That night, the Folketing met and roundly rejected Best's demands, declaring them to be an unlawful usurpation of domestic authority. Best then prepared an order to dissolve the Folketing, but before he could issue it, the members all handed their resignations to King Christian X and our government was dissolved. Best then declared that Denmark was 'enemy territory' and he instituted martial law. Thousands of German troops flooded our streets. They were now in control.

"Now that the lines had been drawn, Admiral Wurmbach decided it was time to implement his takeover of the Danish navy. In his capacity as naval attaché, Georg Duckwitz received that order and secretly informed my father. Late that night, my father left the house and met with Admiral Vedel. Vedel had feared that action would be taken against his navy, and he had a contingency plan. He called it Operation Safari, a plan to prevent Germany from seizing Danish navy ships. When Vedel heard the news, he gathered his staff and implemented Operation Safari. They sent the code 'KNU' to all of the captains of the navy vessels. The captains all knew what to do. They were to immediately cast off, leave the Denmark harbors and head directly toward Sweden. If they were stopped or if they couldn't make it to Sweden, they were instructed to scuttle their ships—sink them to the bottom of the sea, rather than give them over to the German navy.'"

Britta starts to cough. She tries to catch her breath, but her spasms won't let her. Her coughs come rapidly and from deep inside. Emma dashes out to get the nurse. Britta points to her water cup and Catherine holds it for her while she sips through the straw. Emma returns with the nurse, who assesses the situation and says, "So, we're having a bit of a cough, are we? Can you take a breath for me?"

Britta is partially successful. "Just relax," says the nurse calmly. "Take shorter breaths. That's better."

Soon, Britta is out of her crisis. She looks at Catherine and Emma, who stand at the end of her bed. "Quit your worrying," she says. "I'm fine." The nurse brushes her hands together and smiles. Britta points to Catherine's writing pad that sits on the table. "Time's a-wastin'," she says.

Catherine gives her head a quick shake to make sense out of what just happened and picks up her pen.

"Operation Safari," Britta says. "It failed. Only four of our navy ships made it to Sweden. Out of fifty-two. That's how dangerous escape across those waters would be. German destroyers roamed the sea between Denmark and Sweden. Thirty-two ships went down to the seafloor. The rest were seized by the Nazis and converted into German battleships."

"That's enough for today," the nurse says emphatically. "She can tell you her navy stories tomorrow. Now we're going to rest." Britta starts to protest, but Emma and Catherine gather their things, kiss her goodbye and leave the room.

"How DID IT go today?" Liam asks.

"Eventful. Britta had another setback. Her condition remains serious. I think we allowed her to work too hard today and it took its toll. But we are progressing. From what I understand about Danish history, we are close to the end of her story."

"Any more details on Ole Henryks, and why she says he was a traitor?"

"No." There is disappointment in Catherine's voice. "Wish there was."

"Well, hang in there, I think I'm on to something. Did you get the copy of the video from your reporter friend?"

"It was delivered to the office today; I haven't watched it. Why is Ole's party so important?"

"If I recall, he made some statements that should be helpful. I'll let you know when I get back and I have a chance to view it. I was down at the harbor today. If I'm right, it's a solid find for us. I have an appointment at the courts tomorrow. I hired a lawyer who can help me research the old dockets. Maybe there are transcripts. I don't know. How did it go with Obadiah this morning?"

"Trial in three weeks."

"What? How can you possibly complete your depositions and interrogatories in three weeks?"

"No depositions, no interrogatories. No discovery at all. Straight to trial."

"And Sparks agreed to this? He has no idea what you will introduce into evidence."

"Well, when you put it that way, neither do I. But Judge Wilson was suggesting a trial in January, and if you saw Britta today, you would say 'the sooner, the better.' In her present condition, she is totally unable to endure the strain of litigation. Who knows what the future holds? Besides, Henryks went ballistic when he read the affirmative defense and demanded an immediate trial. I merely accommodated him."

"Somehow, I think you plan to do more than merely accommodate him," Liam says.

CHAPTER FORTY-TWO

―⊛―

"SHE HAD A restful night," the nurse says to Emma and Catherine. "If she continues to improve, we think we can move her to a regular room. But please, can I ask you not to overdo today? Break up your sessions; let her rest."

"You should tell that to my grandmother," Emma says, and the nurse nods her head. "I know," she says. "She's a tough one."

Emma smiles. "Can we go in now? Is she ready for us?"

The nurse chuckles. "Is she ready? She's been asking about you from the moment she woke up."

"Bubbe, you're looking good this morning," Emma says. "I brought you a donut. Maple frosted. The doctor says you're supposed to eat."

Britta scrunches her nose.

"And a cup of real coffee," Emma adds, holding out a cup, which brings a smile to Britta's lips. A few minutes of small talk and Britta is ready to work.

"OPERATION SAFARI WAS a failure, Admiral Wurmbach's plan to take over our ships essentially destroyed our navy. General von Hanneken disarmed our army, and as we headed into September, we had no armed forces at all. Our national government had dissolved, and martial law had

been imposed, but local and municipal governments were left function-
ing. The Germans left our police force intact, but it was subject to the
instructions issued out of Dr. Best's office. Everywhere you looked there
were squads of soldiers. Curfew was strictly enforced at eight-thirty, but
exceptions were made for factories, and for shops and restaurants. Especially those that served German customers. Lukas, because he managed the bookstore and had to close up, and because he had to wheel
himself home, frequently came home after nine o'clock.

"Day-to-day activities continued as before. Children went to school,
buses ran, people were free to attend religious services. In Denmark,
ninety percent of the country was Lutheran. Almost eight thousand of
us were Jewish and there were no laws or prohibitions against practicing
our faith or attending synagogue. There was no discernible discrimination, but that was false security. A mirage. Everything was about to
change.

"Werner Best was a Heydrich disciple, pure Gestapo through and
through. He was even called *Doktor* Best, remember?"

Emma nods. "I remember. He told his Gestapo trainees that they were
like doctors trained to rid the world of disease, like the Jews."

"That's right. From the moment he was assigned to Copenhagen, he
was anxious to impose racial laws similar to Germany, Poland, Austria
and every other country Germany had conquered. Best abhorred the freedom Jews enjoyed in Denmark and was angry that Germany permitted
it. Jews weren't required to register, their property wasn't confiscated,
their licenses weren't taken away, they weren't forced into ghettos, nor
were they ever rounded up or sent to slave labor factories or concentration camps. Best was always in favor of subjugating Denmark's Jews, but
his hands were tied by the Cooperation Agreement and Hitler's desire
that the two countries coexist amicably.

"Once martial law had been declared, Best saw an opportunity to put
his racist plans into effect. On September 8, he secretly sent a telegram
to Hitler. He said that the country was entirely under his control, there
would be no effective dissent, and therefore, he was seeking permission to round up the Jewish population and clear them out of Denmark.
Confident of Hitler's response, Best called Georg Duckwitz into his

office two days later. He told Duckwitz that Jews were going to be taken into custody, loaded onto German freighters and merchant ships and transported to ports where they would be transferred to trains for their final destination. As naval attaché, Duckwitz was put in charge of logistics. He was ordered to begin planning the transports as smoothly and as quickly as possible.

"Duckwitz was shocked. He questioned the wisdom. Remember, Duckwitz was an educated man, well-regarded by Berlin. He pointed out that there was no Jewish uprising nor any threat to the German administration in Denmark. Why take action that is sure to alienate the rest of Danish society?

"But Best was a hard-liner, a Heydrich clone. 'All Europe is to be cleansed of Jews,' he said. 'That was the decision at Wannsee. Aktion Reinhard.'"

Emma asks, "Bubbe, did Georg Duckwitz tell the family about this conversation with Best?"

Britta shakes her head. "Eventually, but not at that time."

"Hmph," Emma scoffs. "Some friend."

Britta glares at Emma. "Don't be so quick to condemn. I wouldn't be sitting here if it wasn't for Georg Duckwitz. And neither would you. Duckwitz was a hero. The opposite of Hendricksen, who was a traitor."

"I sure wouldn't mind hearing about how Hendricksen was a traitor," Catherine says with a smile.

"I'm getting there. Be patient. When Duckwitz left Best's office, he decided to do something. Because of his years in the Reichsleitung, the executive branch of the Nazi Party, he had credibility in Berlin and with Hitler himself. He was one of the few who could request and receive an audience with Der Führer. So, Duckwitz flew to Berlin and met with Hitler in an effort to prevent the Jewish deportations.

"Duckwitz believed that he could appeal to Hitler's logic. Hitler prided himself in accomplishing such a wonderful Cooperation Agreement with Denmark. He boasted about it. It was a political masterpiece, a model protectorate, he said. He regarded Danes as brother Aryans. In his mind, he was protecting Denmark from invasion while preserving its culture. Duckwitz played to Hitler's ego. He pinned his hopes on the idea that

Hitler would not be inclined to create national resentment over a few thousand Jews. He was wrong. Hitler rejected the plea, refused to over-rule Best, and Georg flew home.

"About this time, Stefan was once again a dinner guest. He was no longer assigned to Berlin, and he had no inside information, but he expressed his worries about us. 'They're basically running our country now, Joseph. What is to stop them from issuing their racial laws and registering all the Danish Jews?'

"'What would you have us do, Stefan?' my father said. 'Where would you have us go? Denmark is basically an island. The seas surrounding Denmark are full of Nazi warships and U-boats. We saw what happened to the Danish navy when they tried to sail across the sound to Sweden.'

"'What about my cousin Natalie in Stirling, Scotland?' my mother said. 'We could go there.'

"My father shook his head. 'How? My fishing boat is too small. It couldn't safely hold five adults and a baby for the many hours or days it would take to sail around Denmark, out into the open Atlantic and then to Scotland. It's just not an option.'

"'But you've spent many years down at the harbor,' she countered. 'You know so many of the captains. In a pinch, wouldn't one of them take us?'

"'If there was an order for all Jews to report, to be collected and trans-ported, would you really ask someone to risk their life violating that order and sail out through a naval blockade to smuggle us somewhere else?'

"She grimaced. 'I guess not.'

"What my father, my mother and Stefan didn't know at that dinner, was that Georg Duckwitz had one more card up his sleeve. He secretly scheduled a meeting in Stockholm with Per Albin Hansson, the Swed-ish prime minister. He flew there for the professed purpose of discuss-ing passage of German merchant ships, but that was pretextual. No one suspected that he was doing anything else. Meeting with Hansson in the Riksdagshuset, the Parliament house, under the veil of confidentiality, he disclosed Best's plan to arrest all of the Danish Jews and send them to concentration camps. It was Duckwitz's belief that Best intended to make the arrests on September 30 and October 1, 1943.

"'Those are the dates of the Jewish holiday of Rosh Hashanah,'

Duckwitz said. 'Best knows that Jewish families will be attending services and having holiday dinners in their homes. He has asked for and received an extra commando force of eighteen hundred Gestapo for the purpose of arresting Jews in Copenhagen's Great Synagogue and in each of their homes. I don't know if it is possible, but if Jews are able to escape Denmark and make their way to Sweden, will they find sanctuary here?' Hansson assured Duckwitz that Sweden would welcome Jewish refugees. 'We welcomed nine hundred Norwegian Jews fleeing the Nazis last year,' he said, 'and we will do the same for Denmark's Jews.'

"Duckwitz returned to Copenhagen on September 28. He immediately sought a meeting with my father and Hans Hedtoft, former leader of the Social Democratic Party. Duckwitz disclosed Best's plan to arrest the Jews on September 30 and October 1. He also told them of his meeting with Prime Minister Hansson and Sweden's offer to grant sanctuary to Jewish refugees. 'In fact,' Duckwitz said, 'Hansson told me that there are several resorts and hotels along the western shore that are vacant and accessible now that the summer season is over. Hansson said that Jews would be welcome to stay there until they are permanently settled. Of course, getting to Sweden would be quite the task. Joseph, your people must be warned. They must take any measure they can to survive.' Duckwitz stood. 'In any event, I leave it to you to get the message out. I have to get back to the office. You didn't hear any of this from me. I wasn't here tonight.' And he left.

"There wasn't much time for my father to act. Decisions had to be made on the spot; who to contact and how to spread the message. Hans said he would contact Marcus Melchior, chief rabbi and spiritual leader at the Great Synagogue. My father was a close friend of C. B. Henriques, leading member of the Board of Deputies of Danish Jews. 'We can't stop with just the Jewish community,' Hedtoft said. 'All of Denmark must be alerted if we're going to save our people.'

"Lukas, who had been sitting with Grethe and me in the kitchen and eavesdropping on the conversation, wheeled into the room. 'I can help,' he said. 'I will get the word out to our network of partisans.'

"'What about Bishop Damgaard?' Grethe said. 'Doesn't your mother know him pretty well?'

"'Your mother knows the Bishop of Copenhagen?' Hedtoft said. 'He's the most powerful religious leader in Denmark. If he decides to help, he can reach millions of Danes.'

"'My mother knows him and so do I,' Lukas said. 'I'll go see him first thing in the morning.'

"Hans stood to leave. 'The clock is ticking,' my father said. 'Rosh Hashanah starts tomorrow night.'

"'Right,' Hans said. 'I'll go see Marcus tonight.'

CHAPTER FORTY-THREE

———◦∞◦———

"THE NEXT MORNING, Lukas called and made an appointment to see the Bishop. It was not easy. The receptionist initially told him that the Bishop was very busy, that he should consult with his parish pastor. 'Sorry,' she said, 'but the Bishop's schedule is full.' Lukas dropped his mother's name and said that the meeting was an emergency. Hearing that, she squeezed him in for a 'brief meeting' at the noon hour.

"Frederik's Church, called the Marble Church by locals, is an impressive structure with a large green dome. It is located in the Frederiksstaden district of Copenhagen, across the street from the royal palaces, and not too far from our home. We left in plenty of time, Grethe, Lukas and I, for we didn't dare be late. The streets were quiet for a Wednesday morning. If there was a major Nazi operation planned, it was not evident on the streets of Copenhagen. There were scattered groupings of soldiers and smaller pairings of men in long trench coats who I assumed were Gestapo, but Grethe thought I was being paranoid.

"As we passed the canal, I saw Ole Hendricksen standing with a group of his friends. Lukas saw him too. 'That's the rat who betrayed us to the Gestapo the day I got shot in the legs,' Lukas said. 'Knud saw him too, clear as day, standing with them and pointing us out.'"

Emma looks at Catherine. "Direct identification. Betrayer, informer, collaborator."

Catherine nods. "Right. All we would need is Lukas."

Britta continues. "As we approached the church, I heard someone yell from behind, 'That's him. That's Lukas Holstrum. He's right there in the wheelchair.'

"I turned around to see Hendricksen with a group of men, the ones I supposed were Gestapo. They came over and stopped us. One of them said, 'Papers, please.'

"'We don't have any papers,' Lukas said. 'This isn't Germany. We don't need papers here.'

"'Are you Lukas Holstrum?' he said. Lukas said that he was. 'Then you are to come with us. We have questions. Come along.'

"Grethe protested, 'You can't arrest him for no reason. You're not the Copenhagen police. This isn't Germany; you have no authority here.'

"The man snickered and said, 'Well, that's where you're wrong. Germany has declared martial law. Now come along, Lukas Holstrum.'

"Where I got the nerve, I don't know," Britta says, "but I spoke up. 'You can't take him, he has an appointment with the Bishop of Copenhagen. That's where we are headed right now.'

"'She's right,' Grethe said. 'If you make him miss his meeting, there will be questions asked. One doesn't just fail to appear for a scheduled appointment with the Bishop of Copenhagen. He will want to know why we didn't make our appointment and we will have to tell him that you arrested us for no reason. The Bishop will want to know why you interfered in church business. There's no doubt that you will have to answer to him. This will probably create quite an incident.'

"'It's true,' Lukas said, 'if you don't believe us, just come to the church and see for yourself.'

"The second man pulled on his partner's sleeve and whispered something to him. It was enough to change his mind. 'You can go for now. We will talk later. Perhaps when your meeting *with the Bishop* is finished.'"

Catherine asks, "Was Ole there the entire time?"

Britta tips her head. "I think so, but I can't say for sure. I know he's the one who pointed us out to the Gestapo. I saw him and I heard him yell."

Emma pumps a fist. "That's not hearsay; that's eyewitness testimony."

Catherine agrees. "Yes, it is. Though it may be inconsequential, Ole is clearly an informer. It's just her word against his, but it will get us to the jury. There will be no default judgment, and she'll get to tell her story."

A beatific smile settles on Britta's face. "Sweet music," she says. "And more to come."

The nurse enters the room to check Britta's vitals and at her stern suggestion, the group decides to take a break.

"Dr. Hans Fuglsang-Damgaard, Bishop of the Church of Denmark, rose to greet us as we were shown into his office," Britta says after the break. She has had a cup of coffee and is raring to go. "He was majestic in his appearance.

"'Thank you for seeing us on short notice,' Lukas said. 'My mother sends her regards.'

"'And how is Joanne?'

"Lukas nodded. 'She is well. Thank you for asking.'

"'Tell her I wish her the best. I will try to find time to visit her. Now, what is the emergency that brings you young people to see me this morning?'

"'Your Eminence, we have just learned some shocking news and I don't know whether you've heard about it yourself.'

"The Bishop smiled. 'Well, I haven't really heard anything shocking today, but maybe you can tell me.'

"Lukas's face was dead serious, and the Bishop took note. 'It's not just shocking, it's unbelievable, but given the times, I'm afraid it's true. The German administration, through Dr. Best, has plans to arrest every single Jewish person in Denmark and transport them all to a concentration camp.'

"The Bishop raises a skeptical left eyebrow. It is obvious he finds this proposition to be incredible. He shakes his head. 'That would be a violation of every agreement we have with Germany. I'm afraid it sounds preposterous.'

"'I beg your pardon, Your Eminence, but is the present state of martial law preposterous? Is a dissolved Folketing preposterous? Are thousands of Nazi soldiers and Gestapo men in our streets preposterous? This illegal roundup is set to happen over the next two days!'

"'How do you come by this information, Lukas?'

"Lukas hesitated. He would have to breach a confidence. He looked to Grethe and she nodded. He had no choice. 'Georg Duckwitz told us last night. He went to Berlin to try to convince Hitler to cancel the decree, but Hitler refused.'

"'Georg told you that?'

"'Yes, sir. Mr. Duckwitz just returned from Sweden where he sought the assistance of the Swedish government. Joseph Morgenstern, Hans Hedtoft and the three of us all heard him last night. He was in our living room. And he told us to get the word out. People should be warned. I told him I would try to talk to you, that you could get the word out better than anyone.'

"The Bishop was stunned. 'This is planned for tomorrow, you say?'

"'The mass arrests are to commence over the next two days,' Grethe said. 'They are the two days of Rosh Hashanah, the Jewish celebration of the New Year. Best knows that all Jews are likely to be at home with their families or at the synagogue.'

"The Bishop rose from his seat. 'I will do what I can,' he said. 'Thank you for telling me.'

"'One more thing,' Lukas said. 'Mr. Duckwitz is taking a big risk. He asked that we keep his identity a secret.'

"'Understood.'

"WE ARRIVED HOME a little after three p.m. 'How did it go with the Bishop?' my father asked. We shrugged our shoulders. 'He said he would do what he could, whatever that means. He didn't believe us at first. Then Lukas told him that the information came from Georg.'

"'Oh, Grethe, we swore not to divulge his identity.'

"'I know, but he wasn't going to believe us. We told him that Georg's identity was a secret. What happened with the rabbi and Mr. Henriques?'

"'They were shocked as well. The rabbi will make an announcement at services tonight, although he doesn't really know what to tell people.

What guidance can he offer? He said he would pray for an answer.' Then my father motioned for Grethe, Lukas and me to come closer. 'I've decided we're going to make a run for it. Where and how, I do not know, but we will not be here tomorrow when the Gestapo comes. I want you to gather essentials, whatever you can easily carry, keeping in mind we have a baby.'

"My mother walked into the room. She looked beautiful. She had on her black brocade dress, her hair was up and styled, her makeup was expertly applied. Her strand of pearls sat perfectly around her neck. My eyes opened wide. 'I thought Papa said . . .'

"'I have dressed for services,' she said, 'as did my mother before me, as did her mother before her. No Nazi is going to change that. Services begin at sundown and we will be walking. I suggest you go get ready.' And I did, and I was proud to do so.

CHAPTER FORTY-FOUR

———◆◆◆———

"THE GREAT SYNAGOGUE was filled to capacity, but that was not atypical for Rosh Hashanah. Those Jews who were devout and attended services regularly, and those Jews who only came twice a year, all made it a point to be in temple on this High Holy Day. Pre-service conversations were lively in the sanctuary while people were taking their seats and exchanging wishes of *Shanah Tovah* and Happy New Year. In such a festive setting, it was impossible to imagine that some sick mind desired the total destruction of this community, or that there was a death warrant pending.

"Rabbi Melchior solemnly stepped up to the bimah and the sanctuary grew silent. He lit the holiday candles and, knowing what he knew, he paused to swallow hard before reciting the *Shehecheyanu*, the traditional prayer of thanks to God for watching over the congregants and enabling them to reach this season. Then he stopped.

"'Ladies and gentlemen, my Jewish brothers and sisters, my *Danish* brothers and sisters, we have no time to continue prayers. I must make a sad and tragic announcement. It has come to my attention that the Nazi administration has called for a pogrom. We have learned from absolutely reliable sources that it is the secret intent of the Nazi administration to arrest every single Jew in Denmark and transport us to camps in Poland and Germany.' He held his hand up to stifle the shrieks and shouts that ensued. He looked sternly at his congregants, many of whom were in denial and disbelief. 'It is not a crazy rumor; it is a fact,' he said. 'They intend to come for you during the days of Rosh Hashanah when you are at home. You must all leave now, go to your homes and make immediate plans to hide and protect your families. They will come for you tomorrow. Do not be at home when they come.' More shouts and shrieks, and the rabbi called for silence again. 'We have also learned that Sweden has adopted a policy of sanctuary for all who can get there. Go now, protect your loved ones, and may God be with you.'

"At the same time as Rabbi Melchior was giving his address, Bishop Damgaard was preparing a pastoral letter in his office at the Marble Church. Copies of that letter would be rushed by theological students to every church in the diocese. Every bishop and every pastor was directed to read a copy of the pastoral letter during Sunday worship.

"I have committed to memory the content of the pastoral letter:

> *Because the persecution of Jews conflicts with the understanding of*
> *justice rooted in the Danish people and settled through centuries*
> *in our Danish Christian culture, irrespective of divergent religious*
> *opinions, we shall fight for the right of our Jewish brothers and sisters*
> *to keep the freedom that we ourselves value more highly than life.*

"Christian churchgoers would be urged to give shelter, food, money and assistance to all Jews trying to escape the Germans. Though the pastoral letter was meant to be read during the upcoming Sunday service, its content was leaked out to the community. Within hours, Danish Christians were ready to help in any way they could.

"OUR FAMILY ARRIVED home from synagogue and immediately made plans to leave. 'Where will we go?' my mother asked. 'We're not taking that baby out into the sound on your raggedy fishing boat.'

"'The objective is to get to Sweden,' my father said, 'but I agree, not in my boat. We will have to find a captain. I know many of them, but the harbor is controlled by the Germans at this time. The harbormaster answers to Admiral Wurmbach.'

"'I have a suggestion,' Lukas said. 'Until you figure something else out, at least for the time being, why don't we hide in the back room of the bookstore? It's just a storeroom. No one knows it's there. I can assure you that Germans don't shop at a Danish bookstore. As long as I've been working there, I've never waited on a German customer. I'll have Tommy bring our supplies and Isabel's cradle in his truck.'

"My father smiled and patted Lukas on the shoulder. 'Thank you, my son, that's a fine idea.'

"We each packed a bag with essentials, and we left the house that night believing we would never return. On our walk to the bookstore, we noticed that the streets were busier than usual, but I shouldn't have been surprised. People like us were leaving Copenhagen in the middle of the night by car, by bicycle, and on foot. When we turned the corner, a taxi driver saw us and pulled up alongside. 'You don't know me,' he said, 'but I would like to help you, if I could. Where are you headed?' That was to be the most oft-repeated phrase in Denmark for the next week and a half.

"We arrived at the bookstore just before the hour of curfew. Lukas cleared out a section in the storeroom. There was a door to the back alley that locked from the inside and a door to the front of the store. During nonbusiness hours, Lukas kept the bookstore's street door locked. It was our intent to stay hidden in that storeroom until my father could arrange passage to Sweden. Lukas and Tommy brought supplies later that night: extra clothes, shoes, bedding, Isabel's bottles, formula and baby food. We thought we'd be okay for a little while. We were wrong.

"The next day was September 30, the first day of Rosh Hashanah and the first day of the Nazi pogrom. Lukas went out in the morning and came back with pastries, coffee and tea. He told us that the streets were filled with Gestapo and German trucks. 'There are multiple men in plainclothes whom I have never seen before. Dozens of them. They are definitely Best's legions. They're walking in groups of three or four and knocking on the doors of houses and apartments. They have lists. They're shouting out names.'

"'Did you see them taking people into custody?' my father asked.

"'No, I did not. I see them knock on a door, shout out a name, no one answers and they leave. They are not breaking down the doors or destroying houses, but I have seen them try to force some locks.'

"'Duckwitz told us that Best wanted the arrests to be conducted without damage or civil disturbance. He doesn't want the world press to see upheaval in his "model cooperative protectorate." Obviously, our people are hiding, but I don't know how long they can hold out. They've got to get to Sweden somehow.'

"Lukas shook his head. 'Right now, it would be pretty hard. There are Gestapo and soldiers everywhere.'

"'How do they know who is Jewish?' my mother said. 'How do they have lists? There has never been any census that identified people by religion. Denmark never wanted to know how you worship or if you worship. Jews never had to register like they did in the other countries. There have never been any yellow armbands for Jews to wear, or Stars of David painted on store windows. How did the Nazis get the names and addresses of Jewish families?'

"My father shrugged. 'The synagogue would have names and addresses in their files. I don't know if Rabbi Melchior had a chance to destroy those files before the Gestapo entered his office.'

"Lukas sneered. 'Not just the synagogue. Informers, that's how they know. People like the Hendricksens. The Gestapo pays informers, although I think Ole and William Hendricksen would do it for free.'

"From our hiding spot in the back, we heard people come and go into the store all during the day, though Lukas said business was quieter than usual. Street traffic was minimal. It seemed that all Copenhagen was aware of some kind of nefarious activity and was staying off the streets. Lukas brought us lunch and dinner and the six of us spent the second night of the Jewish New Year in the storeroom of a bookstore.

"'How long do you think it will be necessary to stay here?' Grethe asked.

"'Until I can get down to the harbor and talk to one of my friends,' my father said. 'Lukas will tell us when it is safe for me to leave.'

"'That could be quite a while,' I said.

"'Well, at least we'll have plenty to read,' my mother responded, in one of her rare attempts at humor.

"On October 2, Lukas reported that the Gestapo was having very little success at ferreting out Jewish families. 'There is far more Nazi activity on the streets today,' he said when he returned with our lunches, 'but I hear that they are not finding any Jews at home. They are all in hiding, just like we are. I saw Ole Hendricksen when I came out of the sandwich shop, but I don't think he saw me.'

"Unfortunately, he did. Later that afternoon we heard the bell over the front door jingle and Lukas say loudly, 'Ole Hendricksen, what are you doing in my store?'

"'It's not your store; it belongs to old man Finkel,' he said. 'Maybe I'm looking for a good book. You know, a book on *places to hide*.'

"'Is that right? When did you learn to read? You're not welcome in here, so get out and take your two friends with you.'

"Another voice was heard. 'Lukas Holstrum, how nice to see you again,' the voice said in a strong German accent. 'Where is your wife and your Jewish family?'

"'Far from here,' Lukas said. 'They left two days ago. They probably saw you coming to their house and scooted out the BACK DOOR. Why don't you ask Ole? He and his sister Elizabeth seem to know everything.'

"My father looked at me and Grethe, nodded, and tilted his head toward the back door.

"'I don't have a sister Elizabeth,' we heard Ole say. 'What are you talking about?'

"After a moment we heard a man say, 'What's behind that door, the one in the corner?'

"'Books, supplies, I don't know,' Lukas answered calmly. 'Mr. Finkel keeps it locked. I don't have a key.'

"Hearing all this, we grabbed the baby and as much as we could carry in our arms, quietly opened the back door and walked out into the alley. My father had absolutely no idea where we would go, but I did.

CHAPTER FORTY-FIVE

"IT WAS MID-AFTERNOON when we exited the back door of the storeroom and walked out into the alleyway: me, my father, my mother and Grethe with Isabel in her arms. Each of us was holding a bundle. Make no mistake; we looked every bit like the classic picture of refugees on the run. If we were spotted by the Gestapo or an informer, we'd have been captured, loaded into a truck and taken away. And we knew it.

"My father suggested that we take back streets toward a small residential hotel where he knew the operator. We needed a safe and secure place to stay until we could figure out our next move. But the hotel was several blocks away and the risk of exposure was considerable. My father, as a prominent member of Parliament, was a recognizable figure. Maybe not to the Gestapo but certainly to local residents, some of whom had turned informant. Hendricksen had already taken the Gestapo to Lukas. The last thing we heard as we were walking out the door was the Gestapo agent saying, 'Lukas Holstrum, you will now come with us. We have questions and you will give us answers.'

"We proceeded down the side street, anxious and afraid. Walking as a group of runaways in broad daylight, it seemed as though any minute we'd be stopped. As those thoughts were going through my mind, a woman came out of building right in front of us. She stood there looking at us, sizing us up, and as we approached her, she said, 'Jewish? Are you Jews?' My father looked at her but did not answer. She took that as an affirmation and nodded. 'Yes, you are. You are Jewish,' she said, and she opened her door. 'I am a friend, do not be afraid. Come this way. Hurry.'

"Her apartment was on the second floor of a four-story building that was at least eighty years old. The stairs creaked as we ascended. The doors, transoms and woodwork were dark walnut, and the hallways had that musty scent of old wood and carpeting common in old apartment buildings. She opened her door and waved her hand quickly, ushering us in. 'You will be safe here,' she said. 'There are no Jews in this building and no reason for the Germans to come here.'

"'There are five of us, maybe six,' my father said.

"'We will make room,' she said. 'I am Rosalyn.' She shrugged. 'Just Rose.' She showed us to a back bedroom. 'This used to be my son's room. It will be crowded for you, but you can stay as long as you need.' She looked at Isabel and smiled. 'How old is this precious thing?'

"'She's ten months; her name is Isabel. I am Grethe, this is my father, Joseph, my mother, Nora, and my sister, Britta. I'm afraid my husband, Lukas, has been taken by the Gestapo.' Grethe's eyes filled with tears and she began to cry. And so did Isabel.

"'My, my,' Rose said, taking Isabel in her arms. 'Such tears, little one. Does she eat solid food yet? Cereal? Mashed vegetables? I'm very good at making mashed peas and carrots. My son loved them.'

"'Rose, thank you so much for your generosity,' my mother said. 'We will leave as soon as my husband can make arrangements, but we are forever grateful for your kindness.'

"Rose brushed it off. 'I am a Danish woman, no more, no less. You would do the same.'

"THAT NIGHT I took my father and Grethe aside. 'I know what Lukas was talking about when he was arrested. His words were meant for us.'

"My father nodded. 'I know. He told us to go out the back door. That was a good warning.'

"I shook my head. 'That's not all. He talked about Ole and his sister Elizabeth, remember? And Ole said he didn't have a sister Elizabeth?'

My father nodded. 'Well, that was a clue for us. Lukas was telling us that he wants us to go St. Vincent's Hospital and Sister Elizabeth will hide us. And he will know where to find us. We know her. She will help.'

"My father realized I was right. 'How are we supposed to get all the way up to Fredensborg?' he said. 'It's thirty miles away and I'm sure the train stations are filled with Gestapo agents and their spies.'

"'What about Tommy?' Grethe said. 'He would take us.'

"'I don't know how to contact him.'

"'I know where he lives,' Grethe said. 'I'll go there tonight.'

"That was a bad idea, and everyone knew it. Isabel needed her mother. The Gestapo had long ago been alerted to Grethe, and they had her husband in custody. With Grethe in their clutches, they could get Lukas to say anything. My father couldn't go, he was too recognizable to be on the streets. It fell to me to contact Tommy. I left a little before ten o'clock.

"Tommy's house was five miles away and I didn't get there until after midnight. The neighborhood was quiet, the lights were all off in Tommy's house and I hesitated before knocking. I didn't know who lived in the house with Tommy, or who would be at home. To tell the truth, I wasn't positive I had the right address. What if Grethe was wrong? I knocked very softly at first. Then louder. A young woman came to the door in her robe, opened the door a crack and looked at me for an explanation, as if to say, 'This had better be good.'

"'Is Tommy home?' I said.

"'I should hope so. Who are you?'

"'Britta Morgenstern, Lukas Holstrum's sister-in-law.'

"She swung the door open and stepped aside with a look that said, 'I should have figured.' She gestured for me to take a seat in the front room and said, 'I'll get him.' A moment later, he came out in his T-shirt and pajama bottoms, rubbing his eyes. 'Britta? What's happened? Where's Lukas?'

"'The Gestapo. They took him for questioning this morning. We need your help.'

"'Where is your family? They're not still in the bookstore, are they?'

"'No, we're staying in a woman's apartment. She rescued us off the street this afternoon. We need you to drive us up to Fredensborg as soon as possible. Can you do that?'

"He nodded. 'I have to work, but I can take you tomorrow night.' He got dressed, grabbed his jacket from the front closet and said, 'Come on, I'll give you a lift back to wherever you're staying.' He turned his head toward his bedroom and shouted, 'Marta, I'm going to drive Britta home; I'll be back in a . . . I'll be . . . be . . . be . . .'" Britta stops suddenly.

Emma jumps to her feet. Britta is blinking her eyes, giving her head a quick shake, as though she could clear away a cobweb. She tries to speak but she has difficulty forming her words. She can't seem to articulate. She tries again. "Tommy drive . . . Tom . . ." Her jaw is moving erratically. Finally, her head flops back and her eyes roll upward.

"Bubbe!" Emma screams. "Bubbe!"

Catherine dashes out of the room and returns in an instant with the nurse, who immediately calls in a code. As they wheel Britta's bed out of the room, she is attended by two other nurses. Emma is hysterical and Catherine wraps her arms around her.

TWO HOURS LATER, Catherine is on the phone. "They don't know exactly," she says. "They think she may have had a mini-stroke, the doctor called it a TIA. It's related to her congestive heart disease. She's sedated. Emma is staying by her side. I'm going to go back over there in a few minutes."

"I'm so sorry," Liam says. "You've been telling me that her health is failing, but I hoped that she would have been strong enough . . . Damn, I guess the case is over."

"That's the last thing I'm thinking about right now, Liam."

"I know, I'm sorry, I didn't mean it that way. It's just that the last several weeks have been so focused on finishing her narrative and preparing for a trial that . . . I'm sorry. I'll come home tomorrow."

"Did you finish your work? Do you have some evidence of Ole's betrayals? Can we prove anything at all? If Britta doesn't recover, you're all we have."

"I've got some. Didn't you say that Britta had a notebook? Doesn't it have the whole story in it?"

"You can't read a notebook to a jury, Liam. It's not testimony."

"Well, you can get a continuance, right. If she's too ill to come to court? Sparks can't object to that, can he?"

The conversation pauses and Liam listens while Catherine sobs. "I'm not thinking about a continuance, or about Sparks or anything else, Liam. All my thoughts are with Britta and Emma. Right now, I couldn't care less about this damn trial."

"All right. All right. I have one more appointment in the morning and I'll take the evening flight home. How is Ben doing? I miss him."

"He misses you too. Susan has been very generous with her time and has been practically living at the house during these past weeks."

"Tell her I'll be home soon. I love you."

"Love you too."

CHAPTER FORTY-SIX

———⚬∞∞⚬———

CATHERINE ENTERS THE CICU, where Britta has been for the past week and a half. Today she is raised to an inclined position, she is awake, her eyes are open, but she is minimally responsive. She has limited movement of her left extremities. Her speech is labored and barely understandable, as though her tongue is five sizes too large. Emma sits by her side. "Little bit by little bit, she's coming along," Emma says with a smile. "She's breathing better today. Her oxygen level is good, her heartbeat is stronger. The doctor said it was a transient stroke and he expects her to get better."

"It is progress, for sure," Catherine says. "It seems difficult for her to speak."

Emma sadly nods her head. "Speech and mobility. But it's been less than two weeks since her crisis. The doctors say that they don't know how much or how quickly she'll recover, but I know my Bubbe; she's strong and she's determined. There's no one like her. She'll be fine. She's come a long way in the last week and a half. If anybody can, she can. I know she understands every word we're saying, even if she doesn't immediately react. Cognitively, she's right there. She'll be back to her old self in no time; just watch."

Catherine believes it is wishful thinking, but says, "I'm sure you're right, Emma. There's no doubt." Then moving closer to the bed, Catherine says, "How are you feeling today, Britta? Every day a little stronger, right?"

Britta manages a tiny smile. She looks at Catherine and opens her mouth. She is trying to say something.

Catherine leans over. "What is it, Britta? What do you want to tell me?"

Britta runs her tongue across her lips and struggles to say in a breathy voice something that sounds like "Oh-mook."

A light goes on. Catherine knows exactly what Britta is trying to say. "Notebook? Is that what you mean, Britta?"

Britta closes her eyes and tries to smile. She gives a slight nod.

Catherine stands and turns to Emma. "All these weeks, as I'm sure you know, your grandmother has been telling you the history of your family. Much of what she's told us is not necessary for the trial. We all know that. It's for *you*, Emma. She wants you to know your heritage; your aunts, uncles, grandparents and, most importantly, your mother. She wants you to know who you are. It is your Bubbe's way of making sure the family will live on in your heart. In her present condition, she can't do it. But there is a notebook; she's written it all out. It's in her night-stand. Get it and finish the story on your own." Turning to Britta, Catherine says, "Did I say that right?"

Britta nods.

Tears are flowing down Emma's reddened cheeks. Her sobs make it difficult to talk. "But I don't want to read the story, I want Bubbe to tell it to me. If I read it myself, it won't be the same. Let's wait; she'll get better."

Britta shakes her head and tries to say something.

"Can I make a suggestion?" Catherine says, after a bit. "You'll probably think I'm silly."

"Believe me, I won't think anything you say is silly," Emma says.

"I was thinking, if you go get that book and bring it here, I will read it out loud, and you and your Bubbe can listen together. Maybe she'll even give us a comment every now and then, if she's up to it. She has tried so hard to give this story to you, and there's probably not much left. What do you think?"

"I think you are an angel from heaven."

EMMA RETURNS WITH the book late that afternoon. Catherine thumbs through the notebook and seems to find the place where Britta has stopped.

Britta's Notebook

I got into Tommy's truck and he drove me back to Rose's apartment. It was after one o'clock when I arrived, and my family was fast asleep in the little bedroom. My mother and father were snuggled up on one side of the bed. I don't know whether they had intentionally left the right side for me, but I took it. Grethe and Isabel were curled up in a big chair. I managed to get a few hours sleep before Isabel decided everyone should get up. Rose made breakfast for us all—eggs and pancakes and oatmeal and fresh juice—without ever a thought that she was doing something special. She was a Danish woman taking care of Denmark's children. We came to learn that there was a Rose on every street in every town in Denmark, something the Germans wholly underestimated and could never comprehend. In all the countries they conquered, they never encountered such a unified spirit. Hal Koch was right on the money.

Rose went out for a while in the afternoon and when she returned with a bag of groceries, she said, "I've never seen so many soldiers and foreigners on our streets. They're looking for Jewish families, but they are failing. They stand at the doorways yelling names, but no one comes out. They stop people on the street and ask for identification, but none of the people are on their lists. I also have to tell you that there are many Danish citizens protesting very loudly. There are signs in shop windows criticizing the German administration. There are even articles in the paper expressing support for our Jewish citizens. I must admit it brings a smile to my lips and warmth to my heart to know that my friends and my townsfolk are standing up for what is just and right. I have friends that have taken in a family, the same as I have. All Denmark must be doing the same. The Germans are very frustrated. When you go out, please be careful. They are everywhere."

During the couple of days we spent with Rose, my mother and she became fast friends. Though from different backgrounds, they were alike in many ways. Each loved to cook. Each was a devoted parent. Rose had lost a child and her husband to disease when the plague came through in 1918. Her remaining son had moved away. My mother sensed her loneliness and vowed to spend time with her when the war ended and we returned.

After dinner, we bundled our things and waited for Tommy. I sat by the front window watching for his truck. When he didn't come by eight o'clock, we started to worry. The curfew was still in effect, though it was randomly enforced. Tommy worked for a plumbing company and could fudge an excuse for being out past curfew. But by ten o'clock, we were certain that our plan had been compromised for some reason. Something had happened. Tommy wasn't Jewish and there was no reason for the Gestapo to detain him, unless they somehow got information about our escape, maybe even from Lukas during his interrogation. It made me sick to think what Lukas must be going through. We put our bags down and prepared to spend another night in Rose's apartment.

At midnight, Rose came into the bedroom and told us to crowd into the closet; there was a knock on her door. She wasn't going to answer it. I asked her to look out the window. She came back and said there was a red truck on the street. "Is it a large red truck with doors on the back?" I said. Rose nodded. It was Tommy. We all exchanged hugs with our new friend and lifesaver. "Promise me," Rose said, "that you'll come back and see me when this is all over."

"We'll throw a grand dinner at my home—wine in the goblets, fresh flowers on the table—and we'll each prepare a special dish," my mother said. With that, we walked out into the night and climbed into the truck. Tommy normally kept his truck full of tools and materials, but for this occasion, he had emptied the inside and put blankets down for us. We settled in and headed north toward Fredensborg.

"I didn't know if you were coming," I said to Tommy. "You were four hours late and I was worried that something bad had happened."

"Sorry," Tommy said, "but I stopped by your house to get the baby's bag, like you asked me to. It, uh, it took me a long time to find the bag." My forehead furrowed. Four hours to find a bag? That didn't sound right.

"The bag was right by the front door," Grethe said. "What aren't you telling us?"

Tommy hesitated, and finally said, "Lukas is there. In the house. He's in pretty bad shape. The Gestapo beat him up."

"Why didn't you bring him?" Grethe said.

Tommy shook his head. "I shouldn't have told you; he made me promise not to. He said he needs a couple of days to rest. They also busted up his wheelchair and I have to fix it. He can't get around."

Grethe was beside herself. "Damn, Tommy, why didn't you come and get me earlier? I should be with my husband. He needs me. Turn the truck around. Let's go back, pick up Lukas and take him with us to Fredensborg."

"No," Tommy said, "he made me promise. He'll kill me if I bring you guys back there. He says that's just what the Gestapo wants you to do. That's why they beat him up and left him in the house with a busted wheelchair. They want you to come for him. He's bait. If you go back to get him, they'll arrest you and your whole family. Besides, I need time to fix his chair. I'll bring him up to you as soon as I can. Maybe two or three days."

Grethe was not satisfied. She did not want to hear logical or sensible solutions. In fact, she did not want to hear anything; she wanted to be with her husband. "I need to be by his side. I should be tending to him; he's hurt, and my place is with him."

"You won't be tending to him if the Gestapo get their hands on you and cart you away. Before you know it, you'll be in some concentration camp. Then what are you going to do with your baby? I'm telling you, these goons are everywhere. I'll take care of Lukas, don't worry. He's a tough guy. I'll bring him up to Fredensborg in a couple of days."

Tommy took the back roads all the way to Fredensborg. We didn't arrive at St. Vincent's until almost four o'clock in the morning. The night was pitch black. No moon. All during the ride up there, I kept thinking of all the things that could go wrong. We had never checked with Sister Elizabeth before leaving Copenhagen. She could have moved away. The clinic could be closed. The clinic could be full. The clinic could be unwilling to take us in. Still, we couldn't stay in Copenhagen. We had to go somewhere safe to hide while my father figured out a way to get us to Sweden.

Tommy pulled the truck into St. Vincent's small parking lot. "I think we should wait until morning before trying to go in," I said. "If I was Sister Elizabeth, I'd be sleeping at four a.m." Everyone agreed that was a good idea, except Tommy. "I can't stay," he said. "I have to work. If I'm not on the job site by eight, I'll get sacked."

Since I knew Sister Elizabeth, I suggested that I go in first and talk to her. As I approached the door, more fears crept though my mind. What if Nazis were stationed there now? What if they had taken over the hospital? What if Sister Elizabeth wasn't willing to hide us? Maybe she didn't want that responsibility? Maybe it was too much of a risk for the hospital? We weren't sick; we weren't hospital patients. I felt like panicking. What made Lukas think that this was a good idea? I turned around and looked back at the truck. There was my vagabond family. They were counting on me.

The front door was locked. What could I do? I knocked. I waited. I looked back at my family. I knocked again. Finally, an older woman came to the door. I didn't recognize her. I asked for Sister Elizabeth. This was my first hurdle. After all, she could say, "Who?" or "She's not here anymore," or who knows what?

"What is your name?" the woman asked.

"It's Britta. Please tell Sister that I am Nelson Nelson's sister-in-law. She'll know."

The woman gave me a funny look. "I think she's sleeping. Can you wait until morning?" I shook my head and pointed at my family standing next to the truck. She nodded and walked away.

A few minutes later, Sister Elizabeth appeared in a robe, rubbing her eyes. She smiled at me. "Hello, Britta, do you need a place to stay?" Second hurdle cleared.

"I do. And my mother, my father, my sister and her baby. Lukas sent us to you because we need—"

"I know what you need," she replied. "Get your family and follow me."

She took us through the ward and back to an examination room where we were each given patient gowns. The hospital was busier than before. All of the beds in the ward were filled, and they had cleared out the sunroom and the lunchroom for additional beds. "It seems as though we are facing an epidemic," Sister said with a wink. "I have heard that there are four hundred cases of serious illness in Denmark that require immediate hospitalization. All quite suddenly. Isn't that strange?"

"Has the Gestapo come this far north?" my father asked. "I thought maybe they were only concentrating on Copenhagen. We're hoping to find passage to Sweden."

Sister Elizabeth nodded. "Then you are here for the *Elsinore Sewing Club*. You and everyone else in this clinic. I'm afraid the Gestapo has sent its agents throughout Zealand and I assume throughout all of Denmark. You may stay here until the Elsinore Sewing Club has a place for you."

My father nodded. "We thank you. I hope we won't be long. Where is the closest harbor?"

"Are you not listening to me? The closest harbor is Elsinore."

My father slapped his forehead. "I understand. The Elsinore Sewing Club. Of course." She nodded. My father was familiar with Elsinore Harbor; he had sailed out of there before. It was only a twenty-nautical-mile journey across the Øresund to the Swedish city of Helsingborg. If the wind, the currents and the waves cooperated, you could make the trip in a fishing boat in under two hours.

She led us back into the converted lunchroom that would be our quarters for the time being. "They came through here yesterday, two or three cars of Gestapo men. And it's just a matter of time until they come again." She handed registration cards to my father. "We'll need false identities for each member of your family. If any of you have a medical condition or you need medication, put that down as well. We've told the Germans that there is influenza in the region. Every patient and every visitor must wear a face covering. It also serves to hide your identity."

"Do we need to do anything special to join the Sewing Club?" my father asked.

Sister Elizabeth smiled. "I'll activate your membership. When the time is right, I'll let you know. It will be on short notice so be ready."

While we were talking, we heard a loud conversation coming from the reception area. "Wait here," Sister said. "I'll be right back."

When she returned, it was clear to me that she had received bad news. "The church in Gilleleje, a fishing village north of us, had been hiding eighty Jews in the cathedral attic," she said. "Eighty men, women and children. They had come from all over northern Zealand seeking shelter, trying to escape the Nazi deportation order. In accordance with the Bishop's letter, and like churches all over Denmark, the Gilleleje church had taken in these frightened souls and was safeguarding them. Last night, the church was suddenly surrounded.

Nazi soldiers stormed the church and lined everyone up while the Gestapo walked back and forth matching them to their lists. Two of the church's deacons protested and were beaten. They loaded all of the families into their trucks and drove them away. Eighty innocents."

"How did they know the families were there?"

"No doubt they were betrayed by informers, paid or unpaid. Please excuse me, Lord, but may all such demons roast in hell. Little children, mothers and fathers, people who never did anyone harm. Can you imagine? They were huddled in an attic like little bunny rabbits hiding from the wolves." She blotted her tears and then turned to us. "We do what we must. We will do our best to protect you, but the wolves will come back. If you hear four bells it is a warning; they are here. Cover up. Look sick. The wolves are afraid of illness."

She motioned for us to follow and said, "Come this way." Each of us was assigned to a bed and before long, each of us had a medical chart listing our condition as serious and likely contagious.

Catherine closes the book and lays it on the table. "That's enough for today," she says. "It's late, Liam is coming home tomorrow night and I have things I have to do. I haven't seen him in days and I'm hoping, like the Wise Men, he'll be bringing gifts from afar."

"Didn't Liam tell us to allege that Henryks was an informer, that he manufactured weapons for the Nazis and that he interfered with the Jewish escape?" Emma says.

"He did, but I'd like a lot more detail than that. At the time, he said he was still digging, so hopefully he'll have found something. Meanwhile, we have our pretrial conference in three days. You need to think about that, Britta. It would be a good time to ask the judge for a continuance until your health has improved. He'd most certainly be obligated to grant it. I think it's practically a necessity."

Britta shakes her head. She mouths the word "No."

Catherine gathers her things and turns to leave. "Just think about it, Britta," she says again.

Emma follows Catherine out into the hall. "Do you have a moment?" she asks. "I know you want Bubbe to give you permission to continue the case. You think that she's not healthy enough to come to court."

"She's not."

"But her health could improve."

"In less than a week and a half? Seriously?"

"I know my Bubbe; she's tough, but that's not entirely it. She's worried about how much more time God will give her. She needs to confront Hendricksen while she's still alive. It's an obsession with her, in case you hadn't noticed. I know deep down she fears that she might not survive a continuance, and that Hendricksen would be vindicated without a fight. Bubbe can give testimony that he was an informer. She can tell the court what she's been telling us. Win or lose, she will have had her day in court. She will have told her story to the public. Can't we give her that? That might be her last wish."

"She can't testify from a hospital bed."

"I disagree. Technically she can, and it can be broadcast to the jury. Besides, don't the rules allow us to present her testimony on video?"

Catherine smiles at Emma's knowledge. "They do. The rules permit a party to present a witness's testimony in a video evidence deposition if the witness is unavailable to come to court, but Emma, your grandmother is not even healthy enough to give an evidence deposition. She would have to testify from her hospital bed just as though she were in the courtroom; direct examination and cross-examination by Sparks. And you know that Sparks will be incisive, aggressive and just plain mean. Your grandmother is not in command of her speech and she is definitely not strong enough to endure an hour or two of contentious testimony. In her present condition, I would be afraid of what that would do to her."

"But isn't that her decision?" Emma says. "What if that's what she wants? Doesn't she have a right to make that decision for herself?"

Catherine knows she's right, but fears the whole thing can go wrong. "We'll talk more about it tomorrow."

CHAPTER FORTY-SEVEN

———❊———

BRITTA HAS BEEN raised to a sitting position. She is off supplemental oxygen and there is better color in her complexion. She is alert and happy to see Emma and Catherine. She is better now than she has been for the past two weeks, although her ability to articulate words has not improved very much, nor has her mobility.

Emma looks at her food tray. "You didn't finish your breakfast, Bubbe. Do you need me to feed it to you?"

Britta sticks out her tongue. Emma laughs. It is good to see her grandmother in better spirits. The nurse has informed them that Britta will be transferred to a regular room later in the day.

ONCE SETTLED, CATHERINE opens Britta's notebook and continues:

Britta's Notebook

Lying in St. Vincent's Hospital was a test of our patience. One day rolled into the next and we waited for word from the Elsinore Sewing Club. Nevertheless, the staff of the little hospital could not have been more charitable nor more warmhearted, expecting nothing in return. My father, who had managed to bring a supply of money with him, made a generous donation to the hospital.

Sister Elizabeth told us that the harbormaster, a man named Simon Svedsted, has a condition that "affects his eyesight." He says he does not see well in the predawn hours when the Elsinore Sewing Club is most active. According to Simon, fishermen are transporting Jewish families to Sweden in the dark of night up and down the coast. Simon is not the only Danish harbormaster who looks the other way. Still, the voyage is a risky venture. The Øresund is full of Nazi patrol boats.

On our third day, we heard four bells: a "Gestapo alert." Everyone knew what to do. The hospital staff moved through the ward whispering, "The wolves are here. Cover up." Masks covered our mouths, and we pulled the sheets high onto our faces. Two Gestapo agents walked slowly and menacingly through the ward, stopping now and then to stare at a patient, as if they could tell a person's religion from the medical chart or a partial view of their face. From the ward, they proceeded into the lunchroom where we were lying. One of the men stopped in front of my bed. He said to Sister Elizabeth, "It seems like your patient population has grown, madam nurse. As I recall, this used to be a room for lunches. Now there are so many sick patients. How do you account for that?"

"Influenza," she answered. "Or it might be tuberculosis, the symptoms are similar. If I were you, I'd cover my face." She pointed at Grethe. "This one especially is very sick." Hearing that, Grethe started coughing, a racking cough that she had perfected on days she didn't want to go to school. Out of the corner of my eye, I could see my mother shivering in the bed next to me. She was probably shivering from fright, but it appeared that she was feverish. The man put his hand over his nose and mouth and quickly backed up. His wrinkled forehead conveyed an expression of utter disgust. "What about this baby?" he said, moving over to Isabel's crib. "Who does it belong to?"

Sister Elizabeth shrugged. "We don't know. She was dropped here three days ago. She had spots all over. We think she has a bad case of *German measles*. Have you had them? If not, I wouldn't pick her up. The disease can make you impotent."

He took a quick step to the side, tugged at his partner's sleeve and said, "Wilhelm, let's go. There's nothing here." Then to Sister

Elizabeth, he said, "We're leaving for now, but if we find out you are hiding Jews, you will be arrested along with them, and you will suffer their fate, and this facility will be shuttered."

"Of course," Sister Elizabeth answered calmly. "I would expect nothing less. I'm not a fool."

Two days later, Tommy returned to the hospital. He walked in and asked the nurse at the front desk for permission to see Grethe. He was told that there was no Grethe in the hospital and it was too late for visiting anyway. He was being turned away, when Sister Elizabeth saw him. 'I know who he means,' she said, and she brought him back into our room. Grethe was overjoyed to see him, but the mood was short lived. Tommy came alone.

"Why?" Grethe cried. "Why didn't you bring Lukas?"

Tommy shook his head. "He's not up to it yet. I'll bring him up here when he's feeling a little better. He's still suffering from the interrogation. The Gestapo were pretty rough on him. He'll be okay, but right now he can't travel."

"Tommy, tell me the truth. What's really wrong with my husband?"

"That is the truth. You know, that bastard Hendricksen flipped on you. He knew that Lukas lived with a Jewish Parliament member and his family and he told the Gestapo. That's why Ole brought them into the bookstore. They came to get Lukas. I have no doubt Hendricksen is a paid informer. During the questioning, the Nazis kept asking Lukas where you and your father went, but he wouldn't tell them. They kept hitting him. In his stomach. In his head. Lukas has real bad headaches now, and he's spitting up a little blood. He needs to rest. He'll be okay, but he can't travel yet."

Grethe was reaching the limit of her tolerance. Her nerves were shot. "Tommy, you don't understand, we're waiting to go to Sweden. We could be on a boat any minute now. Lukas won't know how to find us. He's hurt and I have to be with him. Please go get him and bring him to us."

Tommy shook his head. "Grethe, it's you that doesn't understand. He's in no shape to travel. He can't even sit up in his chair. It's going to take time. When he's better, he'll book passage to Sweden. He's not a Jew, he can go anytime. He said he'll find you."

While they were talking, Sister Elizabeth came in. "Tommy, how many people can you fit in your truck?"

Tommy shrugged. "I don't know; you mean if we squeezed them in?"

"That's exactly what I mean. Can you fit ten in at a time, if they're all standing up or squished together?"

"Maybe. It'd be pretty uncomfortable."

"The Sewing Club says there are two fishing boats waiting for us in Elsinore Harbor. It's nine miles away. Can you make two quick trips?"

Tommy smiled. "Right now? Sure."

"Wait," Grethe said, "he has to go get Lukas. We have to wait for him. We can't leave without Lukas."

"There's no time, Grethe," Sister Elizabeth said. "We have heard that the Gestapo is coming back here. They are suspicious of our increased population. Right now, we have an opportunity to clear out twenty people."

"Then I can't go," Grethe said. "My place is with my husband."

Tommy shook his head. "That's a bad idea. You have a chance to escape deportation; you need to take it."

Sister Elizabeth brought out the first ten patients. They had changed back into their street clothes and were stepping up into the truck. Grethe kept arguing with Tommy and my father. She was begging Tommy to go back. She didn't want to leave her husband, especially when he was badly injured and needed her care. But her pleas were falling on deaf ears, and she knew it. Twenty people stood a chance of escaping the concentration camps, but they had to move right then and there. There was no time to get Lukas.

The first group pulled away, and half an hour later, Tommy was back at the hospital. He reported turning the passengers over to a captain on one of the fishing boats. He saw them getting on board. Now Sister Elizabeth brought out five patients. One of them was a little girl, no more than five years old. She handed her to me. "Take her with you," she said, "she has no one. Hold her hand." I took the hand of the very frightened little girl and told her that everything was going to be okay. I would take care of her. We all climbed into

Tommy's truck; my mother, Grethe with Isabel in her arms, and me with my hand around the wrist of a scared little girl who told me her name was Celia.

The level of fear felt by all of us was manifest on the ride to the harbor. Some were shaking, some were weeping, and some were gripping their companions so hard that their knuckles were white. We knew the Gestapo was in the area headed to the clinic, and at any moment we could be pulled over and taken away. There were no guarantees that the Elsinore Sewing Club would have a boat waiting for us in the harbor, or that the Germans weren't also waiting at the harbor. Fifteen minutes later, Tommy pulled into the harbor lot. A large yellow fishing boat named the *Lily Francis* was waiting at the pier, engine running. The gangplank was down, and the group quickly lined up to board. My family was the last in line.

The passengers were being guided onto the deck and then down into a lower holding area where the fishermen normally kept their catch. The hold was covered with a large gray tarp. Standing at the dock, Grethe was crying hysterically. Every fiber of her being was ripped in two directions at once.

"I can't leave my husband," she said over and over. "Tommy, please take me back with you."

Tommy immediately held up his hands. "You don't want to do that, and Lukas wouldn't want you to do that either. The city is crawling with Gestapo. They know Lukas is home, they put him there, and they'll keep checking to see if any of the Morgensterns return to him. If you show up, they'll arrest you. It's a death sentence, Grethe."

The ship's captain was waving his arm. It was time for us to board. My father helped my mother onto the boat. Grethe and I were next, but Grethe froze. She took a deep breath while she made her decision. She kissed Isabel on the forehead. "God, forgive me," she said, and she handed the baby to me. "Goodbye, my precious love. I have to go to your father. God willing, I'll see you again very soon." She looked at me with plaintive eyes and said, "Britta, once again I need you. I can't take Isabel with me tonight. Tommy might be right about the Gestapo, and I can't risk it for my baby. Take care of her until I see you again." She jumped out of line and ran straight for Tommy's truck.

My father took Celia's hand. As the boat pulled out, I saw Grethe standing next to Tommy, waving goodbye.

The captain pulled in the lines and we cast off, sailing into the night. The sea was black, the sky was black and there was a black hole in the hearts of my family. We knew the risk Grethe took, and that ultimately it was her decision. We prayed for her safety and that she would join us in Sweden at some time in the future. We wouldn't allow ourselves to consider the possibility that we'd never see Grethe again. I looked at little Isabel in my arms and I wondered what the future held for her. Whatever was down the road, she was now my responsibility.

We were gliding along in total silence. Everyone's nerves were on edge. I was giving Isabel her bottle when I felt the boat slow down. All of a sudden, there were flashing red lights and crisscrossed beams of bright white searchlights lighting up our boat like it was carnival time at the Tivoli. A siren sounded. A loudspeaker ordered us to heave to. Some of the women cried. I felt fright in the pit of my stomach. We were told to come up to the deck. So much for hiding. We climbed up and saw a patrol boat with armed soldiers all dressed in black. Our captain called us all together. "Your journey with me ends here," he said. "Everyone must now line up and get ready to transfer to the other boat." All our escape plans led us to this, I thought.

A plank with rope handrails was leveled between our boat and the patrol boat and we did what we were told. As we stepped onto the deck of the patrol boat, the captain said, "You have entered Swedish waters. You are now the guests of the Royal Swedish Navy, and we will escort you the rest of the way. Let me be the first to say, welcome to Sweden."

CHAPTER FORTY-EIGHT

"How is Britta today?" Catherine asks as she arrives in the hallway outside Britta's new hospital room. The question is essentially rhetorical and both of them know it. They speak quietly. Inside the room, a doctor is attending to Britta.

"Basically unchanged," Emma says. "She's in a regular room now, but they still have her wired up. Her mobility is still diminished, especially on her left side, and her speech is impaired. But she does seem a tad stronger today. She's angry. She resents being sick, and she has no patience for her slow rate of recovery."

"Maybe the impending trial is too much pressure for her," Catherine says. "We could do something about that."

"I know, but she doesn't want us to continue the trial date. In some ways, I think the trial is giving her energy. It has focus. It's become her mission."

"Is her speech any clearer? I'm asking that because we have decisions to make. This afternoon we'll be sitting in Judge Wilson's chambers for the pretrial conference. We'll be talking about stipulations, witnesses, jury instructions and the like. Right now, your grandmother is lying in a hospital bed. Her ability to communicate her thoughts is impaired. Focus or not, isn't a motion for a continuance the responsible thing for us to do? Even if it's against her wishes?"

"It's a question that turns upon an uncertain future," Emma says. "I tend to agree with you. In her present condition Bubbe cannot contribute. But she does not want us to continue the case; she's made that clear. She wants it heard in her lifetime."

"But trial is set to begin in ten days."

"Who knows what she'll be like in ten days? My incredible grandmother could recover. Her speech could come back." Emma lowers her eyes. "I know, that's fanciful thinking. The smart thing is to continue the case for a few months. By then, she might be strong enough to come to court and take the witness stand. If that happens, then we made a great decision even though it was against her instructions."

Catherine smiles. "Okay then. So, are you going to come back here and tell her that you continued her case?"

Emma winces. "I think I would leave that to you."

Catherine nods. "Right. So, let's consider it from Britta's point of view. What if she doesn't get stronger, or, as she fears, she doesn't survive? In that event, in, say, six months from now, the trial would proceed against her estate and, in her absence, most likely Henryks's testimony would be unrebutted, a judgment would be entered, and he would be vindicated. Isn't that her concern if we get a continuance?"

"Of course it is. If we go against her wishes and she doesn't make it to the trial, we will have betrayed my Bubbe."

"That's right."

"I don't think I could live with the guilt."

"Okay then. Let's consider an alternative. What if we did an evidence deposition to preserve her testimony and we ask for a continuance, hoping for her recovery? If she recovers, we'll disregard the deposition and she'll testify in person. If not, we'll play the video. The deposition could be filmed right here from her hospital bed. She'd still have her day in court, in a manner of speaking."

Emma doesn't like the suggestion. She tips her head toward the hospital bed. "How can she do a videotaped deposition? She can barely speak. How effective would her answers be? How well could she stand up to Sparks's cross in her current condition?"

Catherine concedes, "True. A video deposition could turn out to be a disaster."

"And she wouldn't be confronting Hendricksen, would she? She'd be testifying to a court reporter in her hospital bed, dressed in a hospital gown, hooked up to machines in a hospital room. Are you going to tell my Bubbe that she's going to be filmed and shown to a jury in that condition? Are you kidding? Do you know how long she takes getting dressed in the morning, just so she'll look perfect to come to your office and sit in your conference room? She'll never go for that."

"Well," Catherine says, "I have another idea." A wily smile appears on her face. It's obvious that Emma is about to see the devious side of attorney Lockhart.

"What am I sensing?" Emma says. "What do you have up your sleeve?"

Catherine wiggles her eyebrows. "There's a play here, Emma, if we can pull it off. On most lawyers, I wouldn't try it, but Sparks is so brash, so overconfident and so enamored of his abilities, it might just be the right move. Maybe it's our only move. Let's go to the pretrial conference and tell Judge Wilson that we're ready for trial."

Emma is puzzled. "Is it Liam? He came home last night, didn't he? Did he bring us the smoking gun?"

"My hubby, the world's greatest detective, did bring us some pretty good stuff. Is it enough to carry the day, to prove that Hendricksen is a Nazi collaborator? I don't know. Maybe not. But when we add that to Britta's knowledge, what she's seen and what she's heard, I think a jury could be persuaded. Besides, she'll get her day in court and she'll confront Hendricksen."

Emma's forehead is furrowed. She doesn't see where this is going. "Whatever you're thinking, Catherine, you are way ahead of me. You just said that Bubbe can't testify. She can't articulate her thoughts well enough, and even if she could testify, her testimony is generally hearsay. Am I right?"

Catherine holds up a hand. "Does Sparks know that? Does Ole Hendricksen know that? They don't know how well she speaks. They didn't take her deposition, so they don't know what she's going to say. They're not aware that much of her testimony could be hearsay. And remember, it's not hearsay if she has corroborating evidence to back it up, or if Hendricksen admits it on the witness stand."

Emma is still baffled. "But we don't have corroborating evidence to back up her statements."

"They don't know that either. They didn't force us to produce our evidence, so they don't know what we have. I may be able to get Britta's testimony in, but not through Britta. I'm going to try to put it in through Ole, word for word."

"And you're going to get him to say that he was a traitor and an informer?"

"Well, that's the million-dollar question, isn't it? Ole knows he was a Nazi collaborator, he knows he was an informer, he just doesn't know how we're going prove it. He'll look up and see Britta sitting there and he'll assume that she will soon take the stand. He'll assume that she will testify that she saw him bring the Gestapo, that he turned in Lukas, that he informed on the Holger Club. And he knows that it is all true. So, he'll either panic or he'll try to outsmart us. Either way, he has to lie. But when liars start to lie, bad things happen to them. They stumble. They make up stories that are easily disproved. Britta won't agree to a continuance, so I think that's our best shot."

"But Catherine, he won't see her there. Bubbe won't be sitting in court. She's in the hospital."

Catherine takes a breath. She exhales. "That's the loose end. She's sitting up today. She seems a little stronger. Maybe by next week, she'll be well enough to sit in a wheelchair, just long enough to make an appearance in the courtroom. She wouldn't have to do anything other than just sit there for a few minutes and then leave. If she can't appear, then we'll have to do our best without her."

Emma bites her bottom lip. She's in awe of her co-counsel. She loves what she's hearing. "I hope she can make it. If so, she'd get to see you confront Ole in open court. I'd pay big money to see that show."

Catherine smiles. "Okay, that's the plan. It's risky. It'll take some maneuvering, but I say we give it a shot. Let's go see how your grandmother's doing today."

"HELLO, BRITTA," CATHERINE says brightly. "How's my favorite client doing today?"

Britta nods and says something that sounds like "Just dandy."

"This room has a better view. I can see the lake."

Britta makes a face. "Ach."

"Emma and I are going to court this afternoon for our final pretrial conference. We intend to tell Judge Wilson that we are ready for trial. Is that okay with you?"

Britta smiles and nods sharply. "Good," she says in a muddled voice. "I wan go t trial."

Catherine glances at Emma, who is also smiling. "Do you think you could get into a wheelchair, Britta? Have you done that yet? Did they bring you up here in a wheelchair?" Britta shakes her head. "No."

"Whenever you feel up to it, you should ask your doctor or your nurse if you could go to the courthouse in a wheelchair. They may not want you to go."

Britta nods. "I . . . will go."

Catherine reaches over to the table and picks up the notebook. "Let's get back to Denmark. Time's a'wastin', as someone once told me.

Britta's Notebook

The Swedish navy patrol boat brought us into Helsingborg Harbor. We were filled with conflicting emotions. We had left our home, our businesses, our schools and our loving Danish community. We were sad and we were angry. Yet, there was goodness in the world. We were rescued and cared for by Rose, by Sister Elizabeth, by the Elsinore Sewing Club, and by the Swedish Royal Navy. And now, Sweden was providing food and shelter for us. There were no Gestapo here, no Nazi soldiers and no Dr. Best. There were no wolves waiting for us in Sweden.

Over the next several days, seven thousand two hundred Danish Jews were ferried across the Øresund by Danish fishermen for Swedish sanctuary. Almost every Jew in Denmark. A little over four hundred didn't or couldn't make the journey, for one reason or another. In an extraordinary feat of national unity, ninety-five percent of our Jewish community was saved from deportation to the Nazi concentration camps and certain death, all by the collective effort of their

Danish countrymen. No other country in history had ever accomplished such a miracle.

An expat community of resident Danes and Danish refugees had quickly assembled on the Swedish coast. Temporary rooms had been found for us and the other refugees. Our family, which now included little Celia, was taken to the Grand Hotel. The rooms were lovely, and the people were gracious, but we worried about Grethe and Lukas. How would they ever find us?

The Danish expats, which now included several thousand non-Jews, formed a representative body and my father and Hans Hedtoft were happy to participate in the group's leadership council. Indeed, Hedtoft would become Denmark's prime minister in 1947. The community gradually moved south and settled in the Swedish city of Malmö.

As the weeks passed, we kept up a normal life, not knowing when or if we would ever return to Denmark. My father got a job in an accounting firm, and my mother worked part-time in a bakery. That left me to watch Isabel and Celia, and as you know, I became Isabel's mother.

Emma interrupts the reading. "Is that why my mother's maiden name was Isabel Morgenstern?"

Britta nods. Her facial expression is sad; she is close to tears. "Easy . . . tha Holstrum."

"What happened to Grethe?" Emma asks. Britta points to the notebook.

Britta's Notebook

It was early in the spring of 1944 and we had been in Sweden for six months. My father had been inquiring through his political channels trying to find out what happened to Grethe and Lukas. We learned that four hundred and seventy Jews did not escape. They were arrested by the Gestapo and transported to the Theresienstadt concentration camp. We didn't know if Grethe was in that group.

"Were they killed in the concentration camp?" Emma asks.
Britta shakes her head and points to the notebook.

King Christian found out that the arrested Jews were being sent to a concentration camp and he protested. The German administration refused to even consider his protests. So, King Christian appealed to his close friend, King Gustav of Sweden, to intercede. As if Sweden had not already done enough, King Gustav and his prime minister, Per Hansson, filed a complaint with the Reich Chancellery, to Hitler himself. They said they had been informed that four hundred seventy Danish citizens were arrested and sent to a death camp, all in violation of the Cooperation Agreement for the model protectorate. Was that true? If so, it was a very serious violation.

Hitler did not want to alienate King Gustav. He needed Sweden. Hitler sent word back to King Gustav that he was mistaken, that the Jews were sent to a beautiful village he had made for them in Czechoslovakia. The king did not believe him, and Hitler offered to prove it. 'Send the International Red Cross to Theresienstadt and they will report back to you on how well the Jews are being treated.' A date of June 23, 1944, was set for the inspection.

In the interim, the Germans fixed up Theresienstadt to look beautiful—they planted grass, they made fake stores, a fake bank. They had music playing. When the Red Cross came, they were totally fooled. They reported to Gustav how well the Jewish prisoners were being treated. At the end of the war, most were released. Fifty-one died.

"Was Grethe in that group, the four hundred that survived?" Emma asks.

Britta shakes her head. "No."

Catherine looks at her watch. "Time for us to go, Emma. Pretrial starts in half an hour."

CHAPTER FORTY-NINE

―⦊⦉―

THE 21ST FLOOR hallway holds only a smattering of reporters this afternoon. There will be no courtroom shenanigans; the pretrial conference will be held in chambers. Still, a few reporters mill about outside Judge Wilson's door hoping to land a quick statement or two from an attorney on the way in or out. They can always depend on Sparks for a snappy quote. Vera Paulson wanders over to Catherine and Emma. "Word on the street is that Britta Stein is still bedridden in the hospital," she says. "Are you seeking a continuance?"

"How do you know that?" Emma says.

"Oh, honey, everyone knows. You can't keep secrets in this town."

Catherine steps in. "Vera, I'm not sure what we're going to do yet and that's the truth. We'll have to see what happens this afternoon in our conference."

Vera pouts. "I thought we were friends, Catherine. You're not coming to court without a plan. I know you have a plan. What is it?"

Catherine smiles. "Buckle up."

The general commotion picks up a bit as Sterling Sparks comes out of the elevator and struts down the hall. A few smiles, a few boasts, a wink at Janie, and Sparks heads into the courtroom. According to Wilson's standing pretrial order, clients are required to be present in case there are decisions that need client approval. Ole walks in with

Sparks and takes a seat in the courtroom. His jaw is set. He is ready for the face-off.

"Where is Mrs. Stein today?" Sparks asks, feigning surprise. He knows the answer. Catherine ignores the question and arranges her papers.

Wilson's clerk enters the room, announces the case and states that the pretrial will be held in the judge's chambers. "Attorneys only," he says, and Ole retakes his seat. Sparks says, "I'll come out in a few minutes, Ole. I'm sure this won't take long."

OBADIAH WILSON IS sitting at his desk in his corner office. Behind him through the plate glass windows, the Chicago skyline forms a majestic backdrop. There are mementos on his desk and on his bookshelves: leadership awards, civic honors, pictures with the high and mighty. Framed photographs of his grandchildren. In the center of his credenza are the two framed Playbills from the 1976 Metropolitan Opera's production of *Simon Boccanegra* in which he sang the principal role. In moments of stress, Wilson stares at those Playbills and wonders what life would have been like had he stayed on that track. He gestures with an open hand to Catherine, Emma and Sparks to be seated in the three chairs before his desk.

Sparks takes his seat and immediately speaks up. "I know that Ms. Lockhart is going to ask you for a continuance this morning, your honor. Her client is not here today, in violation of your standing order. She's going to claim that her client is ill and in the hospital. Now, I'm not casting any aspersions, but I've seen that trick pulled many times. People check themselves into a hospital to avoid going to court and facing the music. If Lockhart's going to ask you for a long continuance, it proves what I've been saying all along: that they want to kick this can down the street until both parties are dead. I want to know if Lockhart has brought a doctor's note with her this morning."

"It's *Ms.* Lockhart," Catherine says curtly. "And I have not."

The judge puts his reading glasses on, opens his calendar and turns the pages. "I heard that Mrs. Stein was ill," he says. "I don't have another opening for a trial until next January. I can put you in the week of January 22."

Sparks jumps to his feet. "That's months away. I told you she'd do this. My client is ninety-five years old and he'll have to live with these false accusations for another seven months! That's extremely, severely prejudicial to my client."

Wilson disgustedly shakes his head. "She's in the hospital, Mr. Sparks. With a heart condition that she didn't fake, am I correct, Ms. Lockhart?"

Catherine nods. "We hope for the best, but that is her current condition."

"Well," Wilson says, "here's what we'll do: I'll give you the January date. If one of my scheduled trials settles, I'll give you both a call and if Mrs. Stein's health has improved, we'll slot you in. I think that is fair to both parties. As for today, why don't we go ahead with the pretrial while we're all here. Fair enough?"

"Actually, that wouldn't be fair to Mrs. Stein," Catherine says. "I'm not ready for this pretrial conference today through no fault of my client. Normally we would sit here and exchange witness lists and pre-mark our exhibits. I'm unprepared to do that because my client is lying in a hospital and can't work with me. Additionally, the rules give Mr. Sparks the right to seek an order requiring me to produce my client at the time of trial for testimony, and I can't guarantee that I can do that. I can't tell you when I will have my witness list or exhibits ready for a second pretrial conference."

"I don't care!" says Sparks with a sneer. "I don't need to see her witness list or her pre-marked exhibits, and I'll waive my right to an order that Mrs. Stein appear at trial. The only reason that I would call her is to prove that she *wrote* all those despicable and defamatory signs on my client's property. I don't care *why* she wrote them, or *how* she wrote them, or what hobgoblin came to her in the middle of the night and instructed her to paint those lies. I only need to prove that the words are hers and that she painted them."

"Oh," says Catherine, "in that case, we'll stipulate to the signs, your honor. We don't deny that Mrs. Stein wrote those words. As to the court's suggestion, I do think it's fair. Both the plaintiff and the defendant are in their nineties, and we don't know how many more days God will grant them. A long-term continuance may not work. Especially for Mrs. Stein, whose health condition is perilous. As long as I have Mr. Sparks's waiver of witness lists and pre-marked exhibits, I propose that we not give up our trial date next week in the hopes that Mrs. Stein's health improves. Next week, if she's not any better, then we can do what you suggest and wait for an opening."

"Agreed," Sparks says quickly.

Judge Wilson raises his eyebrows. "Under the circumstances, with the agreed stipulation, and barring notification from Ms. Lockhart that Mrs. Stein is not well enough to proceed, we will keep our trial date next Monday as scheduled."

Sparks leaves the courtroom with a Cheshire grin and the reporters flock around him. "Trial next week, folks. Lace 'em up," they hear Sparks say. Emma and Catherine stroll over to the elevators. "So, we followed Bubbe's instructions and didn't continue the case. And Sparks is going to trial next week, and he doesn't know who our witnesses are, and he doesn't know what our evidence will be," Emma says quietly. "That was masterful."

Catherine shrugs. As the elevator doors open, Vera catches up with them.

"Sparks says you're going to trial next week. Is that right?" Catherine nods. Vera smiles. "That was your plan all along, wasn't it?" Catherine winks and holds her finger to her lips.

Two DAYS LATER, five days until trial, Catherine and Emma are sitting with Liam in Catherine's office prepping for trial. Several documents and booklets are spread on the conference room table. Much of it consists of materials Liam has brought with him from Denmark. "I don't read Danish," Catherine says. "We need to get all of this translated right away. This registry from the Copenhagen harbormaster, the one identifying boat BC2342, has it been authenticated?"

Liam taps on the corner of the document. "That is the government seal. The document is authenticated, but I don't know what it says either. Something to do with the city of Copenhagen and the authority to operate the harbor, and that it is an official government document. I've been told that the information on the two pages concerns the ownership and disposition of boat BC2342."

"Were you ever able to get the employee roster from Simmons Manufacturing?" Catherine asks.

Liam shakes his head. "I don't think it exists anymore, so I don't think we can prove he worked there. But I was able to obtain information about the products manufactured and sold by Simmons to Nazi Germany. Like I told you, they manufactured ball bearings and turrets to German specifications for use on the Panzer tanks. They also made the swivels that supported the machine guns on the hoods of the tanks."

"How do we prove that?"

Liam takes out another sheaf of papers. "These are official records from the German archives. They were developed postwar to identify companies that supported the Nazi war effort. They were sent to me by Gunther Strauss. Do you remember him?"

"Is he the lawyer in Berlin?"

"Right. He helped us when we were litigating Gabi's property in Italy by producing the official trust records for VinCo Winery that proved the beneficiaries were former Nazi officers and their sons. Last week, Gunther sent me copies of pages from the postwar trials. They clearly show Simmons was a supplier of war materials, and again, those are official government documents, and they have been authenticated."

"Did you find any records of a Blue Shirt Club or the Blue Storm Club?"

"No. There were lots of teenage clubs in those days; some were saboteurs, some were sympathizers, and I assume many were just social clubs. Not that many clubs are officially identified. I did bring you authenticated court records from prosecutions of other clubs and club members."

Catherine turns to Emma. "I need to know what shade of blue the boys in the Blue Shirt Club were wearing. Let's take an assortment of blue paint samples and see if Britta can remember the color of the shirts. You saw her this morning, what's the word on her condition?"

"Determined. She had the nurses put her into a wheelchair and push her around the fifth floor twice before I got there. After a while, I took her for a ride myself. With help, she can get in and out of the chair but it's hard for her. Her left side is useless."

"How is her speech?"

Emma grimaces. "Very slow and deliberate, but better. Sometimes it's not easy to make out what she's saying." Emma shakes her head. "Words don't sound like they should. It's hard for her to articulate, but she's trying."

"Will the doctors release her for Monday?"

"It doesn't seem likely."

"In the event she is released and can come to trial, we need to prepare her. Let's do that tomorrow."

CHAPTER FIFTY

———— ∞∞∞ ————

BRITTA IS SLEEPING when Emma and Catherine arrive. "I can tell you, your grandmother is pretty bossy," the nurse says. "She's demanded to be wheeled around the fifth floor twice already today. I believe it has tired her out. She wants to do too much. Remember, she is recovering from heart failure and a stroke."

"She wants to go to the courthouse in five days," Emma says. "Do you think she'll be discharged by then?"

"To go to a courthouse? No. I would be surprised if she was discharged to go to a rehabilitation facility in five days."

"Hello, Emma," Britta says slowly. "When . . . did you . . . come? I . . . sleeping."

"We just arrived, Bubbe. How are you doing today?"

She makes a fist. "Great." She tips her head toward her wheelchair and says, "Ride?"

"Maybe you've had enough for one day, Bubbe. Don't push it."

Britta pouts. She holds up a finger and circles it around to indicate another whirl around the fifth floor.

"Maybe in a little while," Emma says.

"Can we talk about the Blue Shirt Club for a minute?" Catherine says. "You said you saw Ole running around in a blue shirt."

Britta nods.

"And he was in a club with other boys who all wore the same blue shirts? You're certain?"

Britta glares.

"Okay, you're certain. Short or long sleeve?"

She points to her arm right above the elbow.

Catherine shows her a copy of the photograph of Ole standing with his father and another boy at the Copenhagen harbor. The photo is in black and white. "Is Ole wearing the shirt in this photo?"

Britta squints. "Could be."

Catherine produces color charts that Emma picked up from a paint store showing a variety of blue shades. "Do you think you could tell me which shade of blue those shirts were?"

Britta studies the paper and points to a sample. "This."

Catherine circles the color and hands it to Emma. "When we're done, I'd like you to take this to the office and hand it to Gladys. Tell her I need a short-sleeve shirt dyed in this color blue."

Once again, Emma is puzzled. "We have no corroboration that the Blue Shirt Club betrayed the Holger Club, or that it engaged in any anti-resistance activities. In fact, we have no evidence that Hendricksen was even a member of the Blue Shirt Club."

"Ole doesn't know what we have." Catherine picks up the notebook.

Britta's Notebook

Throughout the summer of 1944 and into the fall, we cheered for the Allied advances in Europe from our Jewish expat community in Malmö, Sweden. My father had acquired a shortwave radio and we kept up with world affairs the best we could. We were living in a rented apartment, one bedroom with a pull-down Murphy bed. My father had steady work from the accounting firm, and my mother worked twice a week in the bakery. I spent a lot of time with Isabel. She was growing like a sunflower, looking every bit like her mother. Celia, the girl that accompanied us from St. Vincent's, lived with us for a while until we connected with her aunt in Malmö.

The summer was full of walks to the sea and outings with my friends. Several of my high school friends lived near us. All in all, it was pleasant enough, but Grethe's absence hung over us like a black cloud. We hadn't heard a word from her in over a year. Had she gone into hiding? Did she and Lukas ever make their way back to St. Vincent's? We still held on to the possibility that she had survived and would come knocking on our door, but we knew it was a long shot.

One season turned into the next and as 1945 progressed, it became obvious that Germany was losing the war. We listened intently to the BBC. Like before, we'd gather in the living room around the radio. Two-year-old Isabel would walk into the living room, point at the radio and say, "BBC time." We heard how the Russian army had retaken Warsaw in January, had liberated Auschwitz and was now fifty miles from Berlin. American troops continued to advance from the west, crossing the Rhine and taking Cologne. The Allies relentlessly bombed German cities, and the ancient city of Dresden was essentially destroyed. As March drew to a close, General Eisenhower issued a demand that Germany surrender.

On May 1, 1945, the BBC broadcast a bulletin that Adolf Hitler had committed suicide with his wife in their underground bunker. On May 2, the BBC interrupted its broadcast to report that German troops in Italy had surrendered to the Allies.

On the evening of May 4, as we gathered to listen, we heard an excited announcer say, "This is London, the BBC, broadcasting to Denmark. At this moment, it is being announced that Montgomery has stated that the German troops in the Netherlands, northwest Germany and Denmark have surrendered. This is London. We repeat: Montgomery has just now announced that the German troops in the Netherlands, northwest Germany and Denmark have surrendered."

My mother picked up Isabel, said a prayer and twirled her around. Five years of occupation were over. There was dancing in the streets of Malmö. We could all make plans to go home.

A large flotilla was arranged to bring us back to Denmark. Plans were announced in Sweden and in Denmark. We boarded our boats in Malmö Harbor, said goodbye to our Swedish saviors and headed for Copenhagen. It was a longer trip than the one we had taken in 1943. The crossing was farther south, where the Øresund was broader. On our way across the sea there were many animated conversations.

It had been eighteen months. What should we expect? What will our city, our homes look like? Will they still be there? As the harbor came into view, we saw thousands of people standing on the beaches. They were there to welcome us back home, cheering and waving red and white flags. Our country's flags. Their Jewish brothers and sisters, their *Danish* brothers and sisters, were returning home safe and sound.

We walked from the harbor toward our home through streets filled with celebrants. In an unprecedented gesture of kindness, the citizens of Copenhagen had taken care of our homes for us in our absence. They had kept them neat and secure. Many people found that their houses had been regularly dusted and cleaned, and the tables were set for their return. There was never a doubt in any of their minds that we were an integral part of our nation's community, and that we would return. Never had I been so proud to be a Dane.

We held little hope that Grethe and Lukas would be waiting for us and, sadly, we were right. Our house was empty; there were no signs of Lukas or Grethe. Like so many other Jewish homes, our house had been loved and cared for in our absence. There was a vase of fresh flowers on the dining room table with a note that read, "Welcome home, Morgensterns. Your friend, Rose."

I sat with Isabel in Grethe's room for a time. She was only two and would probably not remember, but I wanted her to see her mother's room as it was when she was born. We would make it into a little girl's room for her soon afterward. I sat there and cried. What was it all for? Millions dead, families destroyed. Cities burned. For what?

About a week after we returned, we had a visit from Tommy. He had put off visiting us because he was embarrassed. He felt responsible for Grethe's fate. Against his better judgment, he had driven her back to Copenhagen, to Lukas, on the night we sailed for Sweden.

"I should have never let her back into my truck," he said. "We stood there on the bluff overlooking the harbor and she told me that she had to go home and take care of her husband. She wanted to care for him, get him healthy and then bring him to Elsinore. I knew at the time how bad Lukas was. The Gestapo had beaten him so badly, I knew he'd never be the same, that his chances of recovering were poor. But I didn't have the heart to tell her. I just couldn't. But I should have."

Tommy stopped and swallowed hard. "She just loved him so much. She thought she could nurse him back to health with the power of her love. And she tried, Lord a-mighty, how she tried. But he died about three weeks after she returned. I told her then that I would drive her to Elsinore and get her on a boat, but she insisted on giving Lukas a proper burial.

"Lukas Holstrum's funeral was a beacon for the Gestapo. Out in the open, and in the middle of his service, they came into the church and took her away." Tommy hung his head. "So, in truth, I am responsible, and I feel so bad. She was such a good person, full of love. She told me she was grateful that she had been able to comfort Lukas in the last days of his life."

Catherine closes the book.

Britta places her hand on top of the notebook. Her eyes are full of tears. She speaks slowly and deliberately, making sure to state each word clearly. "For many years . . . I thought about . . . Ole Hendricksen. I . . . cursed him. He . . ." She runs her tongue over her lips. ". . . brought Gestapo to bookstore . . . for Lukas. H-he . . . caused their deaths. If not . . . for betrayal . . . my sister would've survived." Britta stops. She takes a sip of water. "Years passed. Ole long out of my thoughts. I saw . . . newspaper. Honored. A war hero." She scowls. "I couldn't let that go."

CHAPTER FIFTY-ONE

EMMA AND CATHERINE arrive in courtroom 2103 at 9:45 a.m. without their client and without the usual boxes of trial paraphernalia one would expect on the day of a trial. The gallery, packed since the doors opened at nine o'clock, is buzzing: "Look, Stein's not here." "She's not coming." "I wouldn't either, would you?" "What do you think is going on?" "Obviously, Lockhart's going to ask for more time."

Catherine and Emma take their seats at the defense table. Catherine turns to Sparks and says, "Good morning, Sterling."

He sits with Henryks at plaintiff's counsel table, leaning back in his chair. His legs are crossed and he drums his well-manicured fingertips on the tabletop. "No client today, Catherine?"

"She's in the hospital."

Sparks scoffs. "You might have given me the courtesy of a phone call. You could have spared me the wasted trip down here with Mr. Henryks."

"I'm not asking for a continuance, Sterling."

"You're going to proceed to trial without a client?"

Catherine shrugs.

The corner door opens. "All rise. This branch of the Circuit Court of Cook County is now in session, the Honorable Judge Obadiah Wilson, presiding. Case number 18-L-20998, *Henryks v. Stein*. Case on trial." The judge steps up to the bench, everyone retakes their seats and the courtroom becomes quiet. Wilson looks down at the defense table, sees Catherine and Emma sitting calmly and quickly grasps the situation. No one has approached him for a continuance. He shifts his gaze to Sparks. "Is the plaintiff ready for trial?"

Sparks pops up. "We are, your honor. With or without a defendant."

"Ms. Lockhart, is the defendant ready for trial?"

"She is."

"Well, this should be interesting," Wilson says to himself. Then to his clerk, "Call out the first jury panel."

"It took three hours to pick the jury," Catherine says into her cell phone. "Emma and I are going downstairs to grab a bite. Opening statements will commence at two p.m. Are you coming down?"

"Wouldn't miss it," Liam says. "I just stopped by the office to get the blue shirt from Gladys, but it's not ready. She can pick it up at four o'clock."

"That's okay, we won't need it before tomorrow. On your way down, would you stop by the hospital and check on Britta? I know she was planning on wheeling around this morning, but I'd like to know how strong she really feels. How long can she sit up in a wheelchair?"

"If she says she's feeling all right, do you want me to bring her to the courtroom this afternoon for opening?"

"No. First of all, she'll lie to you. Get the information from her nurse. I don't need her this afternoon anyway."

Court resumes and it's time for opening statements. The jury is admonished that the lawyers' statements are not evidence; the evidence will come later. Sparks stands and strides assuredly toward the jury box. He gives his suit jacket a light tug. "Ladies and gentlemen of the jury, and may it please the court. My name is Sterling Sparks and I am honored and privileged to represent that fine man over there, Ole Henryks. For ninety-five years, Ole has enjoyed an impeccable reputation. For many years he has been an impresario here in Chicago. He owns and operates a five-star restaurant called The Melancholy Dane. For those of you who don't immediately get the connection, the name is a reference to Shakespeare's Hamlet. It is not meant to signify a sad dog." Sparks chuckles at his joke. "There is a sign hanging in The Melancholy Dane. It says, 'Nobody goes away hungry or thirsty or without a smile on their face.' It's a jolly place, owned and operated by a jolly man. That's Ole's reputation.

"Of equal or even greater importance, Ole was a hero during World War II in his native country of Denmark. You will see a photograph of Ole standing next to his father in front of a boat that the two of them used to transport Jewish families across the sea to Sweden to escape the Nazis. You can imagine the bravery it took to save those people. In consideration of that bravery, Ole is being honored by the Danish-American Association of Chicago and is going to be inducted into their hall of fame. That too is Ole's reputation."

Sparks swings around to confront his opponent. He points his finger like a spear. He loves that move; it's dramatic. It usually makes the defendant squirm. But today, his opponent is not in the courtroom. He points at Catherine and Emma. "The woman that those two lawyers represent, who is not in court today—you can draw your own conclusions—has seen fit to trash Ole's reputation. On purpose. Mrs. Britta Stein, a woman that Ole doesn't even know, snuck around in the middle of the night and painted the most hateful, caustic, insulting language on the walls of Ole's restaurant for six nights in a row." Sparks holds a piece of paper and reads from it: Liar, Traitor, Betrayer, Informer, Nazi Collaborator, Nazi Agent. "That's what she wrote on Ole Henryks's wall.

"And ladies and gentlemen, she won't deny it. She can't deny it. We have her legal stipulation that she wrote each and every one of those words. Those words, by themselves, are so mean, so damaging, that the evidence will show them to be defamatory per se. When words are defamatory per se, the law does not require us to prove any special damages. Damage to Ole's reputation and standing in the community is presumed. If I prove to you that the words are defamatory per se, I don't have to prove that my client's reputation has been damaged. The law presumes that for me.

"To tell you the truth, my job in this case is so simple, I shouldn't even charge a fee." Sparks covers his mouth in a cutesy gesture and says, "But I might anyway." He turns to face Catherine and Emma and holds out his hand. "I don't have to prove anything because Mrs. Stein has done it all for me. She has admitted everything."

Sparks leans on the jury rails. "Ladies and gentlemen, at the conclusion of this case, I will talk to you again. At that time, I will ask you to award my client, Ole Henryks, his just compensation for the damage done to his reputation. Not that any amount of money can compensate Ole for what he has had to endure, and the amount is entirely up to you, but I will suggest that an award of five million dollars would be fair." Sparks spins around and struts back to his seat.

"Ms. Lockhart?" Judge Wilson says.

Catherine rises and walks confidently to the jury. Her head is held high. Her demeanor is dignified. She is all business. "Ladies and gentlemen of the jury, your honor, Mr. Sparks, Mr. Henryks, Ms. Fisher, may it please the court. Mrs. Britta Stein is ill today and regrets that she is not in attendance. She has asked us to proceed anyway. The words that Mr. Sparks read to you, they are indeed damning. And it is true that Britta wrote all those words, and we do not deny it. Damning, yes. Insulting, yes, but Mr. Henryks has sued for defamation, and in this case, we will prove to you that those words are not defamatory. They are not defamatory per se, they are not defamatory per quod, they are not defamatory at all. Why? Because those words are true, and truth is an absolute defense to a suit for defamation.

"Now, I will tell you that Britta had a legal right to speak and write those words, but she did not have the right to spray them on Mr. Henryks's brick wall. She violated a Chicago municipal ordinance, for which she has paid a $750 fine. You might criticize her for that, but this case is not about damage to a brick wall. The paint has been washed away. There is no damage, and Britta is not charged with damage, and that is not a part of this lawsuit in any way. Britta Stein is charged *only* with defamation. So, the *only* issue for you to decide is *not* whether Britta wrote those words—she did—but whether the words are *true*. Because if they are, they are not defamatory, and you must find in favor of the defendant.

"In the United States, our First Amendment guarantees us the right to speak the truth. And to write the truth. Even if it is on a wall. We will prove to you in this courtroom that the painted accusations are true. Mr. Henryks was in fact a traitor. He collaborated with the Nazi regime in Denmark. He informed upon Danish freedom fighters and upon Jewish citizens. He betrayed the Danish people. He betrayed my client's family. At the end—"

"I did not!" Henryks screams. He stands at his seat and points a bony arm at Catherine. "You are a liar. I was never any of those things."

The gavel slams several times. Sparks gently directs his client down into the chair. Judge Wilson raises his eyebrows.

Catherine turns toward Henryks and says calmly, "Yes, you did. You assisted and collaborated with the Nazis and we will prove it to this jury. You turned upon your native country in favor of a murderous foreign adversary, and we will prove it to this jury." Catherine returns her attention to the jury and says, "Remember, your job is to determine one thing and one thing only: Are the words true? Did she write the truth? At the conclusion of the evidence, I will ask you to find in favor of Britta Stein and dismiss this case."

The courtroom is silent as she returns to her seat. Emma is in awe; her eyes are as big as half dollars. There are murmurs and rumbles skittering through the gallery. The gavel slams again.

Wilson turns his eyes to the jury. "Ladies and gentlemen, we're going to break for the day. We'll begin with our testimony at nine o'clock tomorrow. Please do not discuss this case with your fellow jurors or anyone else. Stay away from the newspapers and the television. Their opinions are unimportant, and often wrong. It is you who will be deciding this case."

CHAPTER FIFTY-TWO

A STERN LOOK from Judge Wilson immediately silences the anxious gallery on the morning of the second day of *Henryks v. Stein*. "Good morning Mr. Henryks, Mr. Sparks," he says. Then redirecting his attention to the defense table, he says, "Good morning to you, Ms. Lockhart and Ms. Fisher. May I inquire on the health of Mrs. Stein?"

"Thank you for asking, your honor," Catherine says. "She's still in the hospital, but she seems to be doing better. She's very eager to receive our accounts of the proceedings, which we pass along to her every time we get a break."

Wilson gives a quick nod. "Very good. Anything more before we summon the jury?" Seeing no response, he nods to his clerk.

"All rise for the jury." Twelve jurors and two alternates file in and take their seats. They are also eager for the proceedings and the testimony to begin. Wilson says, "Mr. Sparks, you may call your first witness."

As everyone expects, Sparks calls Ole Henryks. After the routine preliminary questions, Sparks says, "Ole, have you been honored recently?"

"Yes, I have. The Danish-American Association of Chicago has recognized my accomplishments in Denmark and also here in Chicago for the many civic causes that I've sponsored. They voted me into their hall of fame. I'm Danish, you know, by heritage." He stares at Catherine with narrowed eyes and curls his lip. "They want to honor me for being a war hero. Second World War, you know. I saved the lives of Jews."

"How did that make you feel, Ole, to receive an invitation to a hall of fame?"

"I felt like it's a crowning achievement to a lifetime of service. I am proud of what I've done in my life and obviously the association feels the same way. That is the good reputation that I have enjoyed." His jaw begins to shake. He purses his lips, turns his face to Catherine and raises his voice. "That is, until her client sought to destroy it for no reason."

Sparks approaches the witness stand, showing deep concern. He will milk this emotional outburst for all it's worth. "Calm down, Ole. Take a sip of water. Do you need a break?" Henryks shakes his head. Sparks continues softly, "Now I know this will be extremely painful for you, but I need you to tell the jury what happened last March 14."

"The day started out like any other. I came to The Melancholy Dane, about six o'clock, and saw right away we were getting a pretty good crowd. I thought to myself, something must be going on. Some of my regulars started saying to me that they were sorry. Others said, 'What's this all about?' I asked them, what do they mean? They say, it's about the Nazi sign painted on the side of my building. I went out and took a look, but there was nothing there. They said they saw it on TV. I asked my son and he said yeah, it's true. My son, Nils, he always opens the bar. When he came in the afternoon, he saw the words 'Nazi Collaborator' spray-painted on the side of my building. *My building.* Calling me a Nazi!" Henryks stands, his face is red. He shouts, "A goddamn Nazi!"

"All right, all right, you need to settle down, Mr. Henryks," Wilson says. "Let's take a break." Looking straight at Sparks, he says, "You have to calm your client down, Mr. Sparks. We can't have these outbursts."

"Calm him down?" Sparks says with his hand on his heart. "It's not his fault. It's Stein's fault. You can see what her defamatory words have done to Mr. Henryks and his reputation."

Wilson stands and slams his gavel. "The jury will disregard counsel's remarks; they are not evidence, and clearly out of line. Mr. Sparks, I caution you against doing that again or I will call a mistrial and recommend you for discipline. You know better."

CATHERINE SHOOS AWAY reporters in the hallway. "No interviews during a break. There is a witness on the stand."

Emma pulls her aside. "What do you think?"

"Aside from having a jury watch a ninety-five-year-old man crumble into a hysterical crying fit, it's what we expected. It's heavy-handed, but that's basic Sparks. He's managing his direct reasonably well, though I suspect some of the jurors can see through the theatrics. Still, watching an old man have a meltdown is never good for us. I anticipate we'll have two or three more. It certainly raises the bar for our defense. Hearsay identifications won't carry the day."

"Bubbe saw Henryks bring the Gestapo to confront her and Lukas outside the Lutheran church. Bubbe heard Henryks bring the Gestapo into the bookstore when they arrested Lukas. Those are firsthand identifications. Not hearsay."

Catherine nods. "I agree. But she'd be testifying to what she saw and heard from behind a door seventy-five years ago, and neither of those actions is unequivocal. Not enough to label Ole a traitor. He'll try to explain them away. We'll need more. Ole is going to have to help us out."

"I have faith in you, Catherine."

Catherine notices that everyone is starting to file back into the courtroom. She whispers to Emma, "If your grandmother is healthy enough, we may need her tomorrow. I want you to go to her condo and get whatever clothes she would want to wear to court. And her makeup. Tell her that I don't want her here to testify; I just want the jury to see her. It's too easy to convict a ghost. And I want Henryks to see her too. That should send chills up his weepy spine. Of course, I only want her here if she's up to it. Make sure you clear it with her nurse."

HENRYKS RETAKES THE STAND. "At first, I thought it was some punk kid who painted 'Nazi Collaborator.' Just a one-time shot. But then the next night 'Traitor' was painted. Then 'Betrayer.' Now people began to ask me what the hell is going on? I even had some old friends of mine question me. You know, what did you really do during the war, Ole? I thought you were a hero? I had to explain myself. Who knows what they think today? All these years I've led a good life . . ." Henryks can't go on. He sobs loudly and turns his head. His reddened eyes hold pools of tears. It is excruciating to watch. Sometimes the jurors avert their eyes.

"We put a camera on the wall," he says when he resumes. "The next night, when she came to write 'Informer,' we filmed her." He shakes his head. "I came to this country in 1947. I was twenty-four years old. I made a good life for myself and my family. Seventy-one years in the U.S. No trouble. Why does some woman I don't even know have to come and do this to me now? Why, Sterling? Why? I don't even know who she is." He hunches forward and covers his eyes.

Judge Wilson is forced to call another recess while Henryks composes himself. When he retakes the stand, Sparks has an oversized exhibit. He has enlarged the black-and-white photo of Henryks, his father, and another young man standing by a boat, affixed it to a poster board and set it on an easel. "Do you recognize that photo, Ole?"

Henryks smiles broadly, the first time all week. "I should say I do."

"Tell us about it," Sparks says.

"That was the night the Jews were all running away, trying to escape. The Gestapo wanted to catch all the Jews and send them to one of their prison camps. But all of the rest of us, we hid the Jews. In the middle of the night, we put them in our fishing boats and sailed them to Sweden." He points at the photo. "That was our boat. We rescued forty Jews."

"What would have happened if you got caught by the Nazis?"

"Are you kidding?" He draws his index finger across his neck like a knife. "They'd have killed us on the spot. They were ruthless, those Gestapos."

"Weren't you afraid?"

"Nah. We did it because it was the right thing to do. We were tough."

Sparks stands still in the middle of the courtroom. He's letting the testimony sink in. Then he turns to the judge and says, "No further questions, your honor."

Wilson turns his attention to Catherine. "Cross-examination, Ms. Lockhart?"

She stands. "I have no questions at this time."

There are multiple gasps from the gallery. "No questions?" "Is she nuts?" "After what he said?" "She's throwing in the towel."

Wilson looks at Sparks. "Call your next witness, Mr. Sparks."

Sparks is caught off guard. "I, uh, I didn't expect, uh, to need him so soon."

The judge is peeved. "This is your case, Mr. Sparks. Are you prepared to proceed?"

Sparks is rattled. The gallery loves it. Any action is good action. "I'm going to call Nils Henryks, your honor. Ole Henryks's son. I just need a few minutes to get him here. He's probably at the restaurant."

Wilson exhales loudly through his nostrils and addresses the jury. "Well, ladies and gentlemen, it appears that this is a good time to get your lunch."

NILS HENRYKS, THE tall, slender, balding son of Ole Henryks, takes the stand with a pleasant smile and swears to tell the truth. "Calling your attention to March 14, please tell us all what happened that day."

"I came to work that day, like always. I open the place every day. I mean, it's my dad's but I run it. I saw the words 'Nazi Collaborator' painted on the south side of our building. I didn't know what that was all about. I didn't think too much of it. I went and got some paint remover and scrubbed it off. Then I opened the bar."

"What did your father have to say about that?"

"I didn't tell him. Why bother him with stupid stuff like that?"

"But he did hear about it that day, didn't he?"

"Yeah. Some guys told him they saw it on TV. One of the stations must have filmed it in the afternoon before I got there. My dad was pretty upset. You know, he fought the Nazis."

"But that wasn't the end of the painted words, was it?"

"Nope. The next day I saw 'Traitor' and I washed it away. But it was on TV. Then the next day was 'Betrayer' I think. Then 'Liar.' That's when I decided to put up a camera. That night it filmed a woman in an overcoat spraying the wall at three-thirty in the morning. 'Informer,' she wrote. I took the video down to the precinct and showed it to the desk sergeant. They said they'd send a car over the next night. She had just finished writing 'Nazi Agent' when they arrested her."

"How many of those filthy, defamatory words made it to TV?"

"All of them, I think."

"From what you have observed, Nils, how has all this affected your father?"

"Really tore him up. He's been depressed since then. I worry about him. It's not like he's a young man who can brush it all off. He takes it seriously. It's done a number on him. It's a real shame."

"Yes, it is," Sparks says solemnly. "No further questions for this witness, your honor."

Nils starts to leave the witness stand when the judge says, "Hold on, Mr. Henryks. Any cross-examination, Ms. Lockhart?"

"Yes, your honor," Catherine says. She places the poster and easel up in front of the witness stand, facing the jury box. "Mr. Henryks, do you recognize this photograph?"

"Yes, ma'am, I sure do. It hangs on the wall behind the bar."

"Has your father ever told you who the people are in that picture?"

Nils smiles broadly. "Only about a hundred times. That's my grandfather Viktor and my father Ole. And that's my grandfather's boat that they used when they rescued the Jewish people."

"And the third person, the young man standing next to your father? Who is that?"

Nils shrugs. "I'm not real sure, I think my father said it was Henry, one of his friends in Copenhagen."

"Could that be Henning?"

"Yeah, could be."

"Henning Brondum?"

"Yeah, I think that's right."

"Thank you. No further questions."

Nils gives his father a hug on the way out of the court. Judge Wilson says, "Call your next witness, please, Mr. Sparks."

Sparks stands, scans the courtroom as though he is looking for someone, and then says, "I don't have another witness."

"Does the plaintiff rest?"

Sparks seems unsure, but says, "Yes. The plaintiff rests."

"Will the defendant have witnesses, Ms. Lockhart?"

"Yes, your honor, we most certainly will."

Wilson rises, slams his gavel and says, "Court stands in recess until tomorrow morning when we will hear the defendant's case."

CHAPTER FIFTY-THREE

———❦———

CATHERINE AND EMMA are seated at the counsel table, engaged in quiet conversation. To Emma's right are two boxes they have wheeled into the courtroom. The gallery is anxious for the morning's proceedings to begin, but not nearly as anxious as Catherine, who keeps looking over her shoulder. Someone is not there. She is plainly nervous. Sparks and Henryks have yet to arrive and their counsel table is empty. Emma is equally nervous. It is nine o'clock and she knows they are a bit out on a limb. They have taken a chance. They did not issue a notice to appear. The court clerk peeks into the courtroom, sees that the plaintiff's table is empty and closes the door. Finally, Sparks and Henryks arrive. They walk quickly and confidently to their seats, nodding to members of the press as they pass. Catherine looks at Emma and breathes a sigh of relief. "Phew! He's here. Risk averted."

The judge enters, asks the attorneys if there are any matters to discuss before bringing in the jury, and hearing none, instructs his clerk to summon them. As they file in, the jurors scan the room to see who the witnesses will be. There is no one sitting with Catherine and Emma. Catherine studies the jurors' faces. She thinks they look at Henryks sympathetically. Too sympathetically for her liking.

"Ms. Lockhart, you may call your first witness."

"May it please the court, defendant calls Ole Henryks."

Ole is shocked. He jumps out of his seat and looks down at Sparks. "I already testified," he says. "What's she doing? Is this legal?"

Sparks nods and smiles. "It's legal, Ole. She can call you. Go ahead, you'll do fine."

Ole heads up to the witness stand, takes his seat and nods to the jury with a look that says, "Didn't we already do this?"

Catherine steps toward the witness stand. She has a document in her hand. "Would you state your name, please?"

"Ole Henryks, same as it was yesterday." He smiles at the jury.

"Mr. Henryks, you swore to tell the truth this morning, didn't you?"

"Yeah, so?"

"Well, I just asked you for your name."

"And I told it to you. Ole Henryks."

"Was your father's name Viktor, and your mother's name Marion?"

"That's right."

"Were you born on March 15, 1923, in Copenhagen, Denmark?"

"Yeah."

"I have here a birth certificate for a boy born to Viktor and Marion *Hendricksen*, whom they named Ole Hendricksen." She shows it to Ole, who takes his time reading it.

"So, let me ask you again, Mr. Hendricksen, what is your name, and this time please tell me the truth."

"Well, now it's Henryks. I changed it."

"Did you change it legally? Because I haven't been able to find any court records of a name change, here or in Denmark."

"No, I just go by Henryks. It's shorter, you know?"

"When did you decide to go by an alias? Was it when you entered the United States in 1947?"

Ole shrugs. "It could have been."

"So then, did you lie to the U.S. Immigration Service when you entered the country in 1947?"

"I didn't lie to nobody."

"Did you come to the U.S. with your wife, Margit?"

"That's right."

"Did you tell the immigration officer that her name was Margit Henryks?"

"She said that. And it was Henryks. I might have changed it before, when I was in Denmark."

"Not Margit Hendricksen?"

"No."

Catherine hands him another document. "Mr. Hendricksen, I am handing you a Danish marriage certificate from June 12, 1946. Can you tell me the names of the two individuals who appear on this marriage certificate?"

Henryks squirms a little. "Ole Hendricksen and Margit Hendricksen."

"Did the two of you lie to the U.S. Immigration Service?"

"It was her idea. Start fresh in America."

"Mr. Hendricksen, did you two change your names because you didn't want anyone in Denmark to be able to find you in the United States?"

"That's ridiculous."

"Your wife's maiden name was Simmons, wasn't it. And you were working for her father's company in Copenhagen, am I right?"

"Yeah. Margit Simmons. I worked there from 1943 to 1945."

Emma takes a breath. "Point for our side," she says to herself.

"Both you and Margit worked for Simmons Manufacturing, didn't you? Was that how you met?"

"No, I knew her from school. She got me the job at Simmons. She was working in the office; I was working on the assembly line."

"Margit was the daughter of the owner, and she also had an ownership interest in Simmons Manufacturing, didn't she?"

"Maybe."

Catherine picks up a paper that appears to have military vehicles depicted, then looks back to the witness. "You were manufacturing turrets, I believe?"

"Yeah, I think so."

"These were turrets to be shipped to Germany, weren't they?"

"I suppose so. Almost everything Simmons made was sold to Germany. Lots of Danish companies did business with Germany, Miss Lockhart. Farmers, dairies, cattlemen, windows. It was no crime."

"But not all those dairies and cattlemen manufactured and shipped military war materials or arms to Germany, did they?"

He shrugs. "I don't know."

Catherine consults the paper in her hand. She lets it flop forward so that Henryks can see the military vehicles pictured on the document. "But *you* and your wife did. You made turrets to hold machine guns on German tanks, didn't you? And at the time you were making these turrets to hold machine guns for the Nazi army, Germany had already declared Denmark to be enemy territory, hadn't it? Remember that? Martial law?"

"I remember, counsel."

"After the war, were there war trials held in Denmark for Nazi collaborators? Were they prosecuted in the Danish courts?"

"I don't know. I didn't stay in Denmark. My wife and I moved to America."

"Is that why you and your wife moved to America and changed your name to Henryks? Were you afraid of being prosecuted as a Nazi collaborator? Was Simmons Manufacturing a corporate collaborator?"

"Not true."

"Did you believe that Danish authorities would come looking for Ole and Margit Hendricksen, both of whom made and sold weapons and war materials to Denmark's enemy?"

"Total nonsense."

"Is it? Was Margit's father, Johann Simmons, the other owner, prosecuted and convicted for collaborating with the Third Reich?"

"It was different. He was always coming and going to Germany and he had contacts with the German army."

"Contacts with the Wehrmacht, the army that you were manufacturing and shipping weapons to? Wasn't it your job to manufacture weapons to German specifications?"

"I was on the assembly line."

"You were more than that, weren't you? Was the husband of the owner's daughter just a mere assembly line worker?"

"I was more like a supervisor."

"So, in 1947, when the war trials were going on and your father-in-law was being convicted, you and your wife came to America under an assumed name to avoid being charged as Nazi collaborators, is that all true?"

"No. Wrong. I was never charged with anything."

Catherine walks back to the counsel table and puts the document down. Emma looks at it. It's a page from a toy catalogue showing plastic replicas of Nazi tanks. Standing at the table, Catherine turns and asks, "Mr. Hendricksen, were you a member of the Blue Shirt Club, or as it was sometimes called, the Blue Storm?"

Ole shakes his head and looks at the jury. He spreads his arms. "What are you talking about now? A blue shirt what?"

"I'm talking about the Blue Shirt Club. Were you a member?" She reaches down into a box and takes out a short-sleeve blue shirt.

Ole's jaw drops. "Where did you get that?"

Catherine savors the moment. The deception worked. "Let me repeat my question. Were you a member of the Blue Shirt Club?"

"Yeah, as a kid, a long time ago. There were lots of clubs in Denmark."

"Like the Holger Club?"

"Yeah, like the Holger Club."

Suddenly, there is a rumble of muffled conversation. Everyone's attention turns to the courtroom door, where Liam enters with Britta and pushes her up to the counsel table. She is dressed in a black knit dress. There is a light gray wool shawl covering her neck and shoulders. Her makeup hides her otherwise pale complexion. Her head is held high. She sits erect. Her composure is solid.

Ole's shock is appreciable. His nerves are on display. There is an observable twitch. He looks at Sparks plaintively and says, "Sterling?"

"Your honor," says Sparks, "may we have a short break?"

Wilson shakes his head. "No, not now." He nods at Britta. "Good morning, Mrs. Stein," he says. "Continue then, please, Ms. Lockhart."

Catherine picks up another sheaf of papers and approaches the witness. "Mr. Hendricksen, was the Holger Club one of the Danish teenage clubs that was engaged in resistance activities? Anti-Nazi activities? Sabotage of Nazi installations?"

"Some clubs were. I'm not real sure about the Holger Club."

Catherine looks through the papers she is holding in her hand. She flips a couple of pages, seems to find what she is looking for, and says, "Calling your attention to January 22, 1943. Did you and the Blue Shirt Club have occasion to be in Jutland that night?"

Ole's eyes lock on Catherine. He doesn't know what she has in her hands. He scoffs. "How would I know that? January 1943?" He utters a nervous chuckle. "I don't remember, counsel, what I was doing in January 1943."

"Let me try to refresh your memory. On that night, near the town of Vejle, a British plane was dropping arms and explosives by parachute to members of the Holger Club to distribute the weapons to the British underground and Danish freedom fighters. On that night of January 22, 1943, did you and other members of the Blue Shirt Club lead the Gestapo to that site to arrest the boys of the Holger Club?"

"No," he shouts. "That's a lie."

"Did you inform the Gestapo that the weapons drop was going to take place at that time so they could arrest the Holger Club, and did you personally lead them to the site? Did you betray the boys in the Holger Club?"

Henryks stands and points at Britta. "She's lying," he screams. "She's the liar. She and her brother-in-law, Lukas Holstrum. They're both liars. I didn't have anything to do with that roundup. It wasn't my fault that Holstrum got shot running away. You can't blame that on me."

"Mr. Hendricksen, I didn't say anything about Lukas Holstrum, or that he was shot, or that he was running away. Obviously, you knew those things because you were there."

"I was not. You tricked me."

"And while we're on it, I'm a little confused, Mr. Hendricksen. I thought I heard you testify yesterday that you didn't know Britta Stein. I think your words were, 'I don't even know who she is.' But yet you know that Lukas Holstrum is her brother-in-law?"

Henryks utters a nervous chuckle. "I meant I didn't really *know* her. I mean, I knew who she was, but we weren't friends or anything."

"Speaking of Lukas Holstrum, did you bring two Gestapo agents to the Viking Bookstore to question Lukas Holstrum on October 4, 1943?"

"He wasn't Jewish, you know. I didn't bring Nazis to a Jewish family like you claim. They wanted information from Holstrum about Jews who were hiding. So I didn't inform on any Jews." He nods in satisfaction.

"Was Lukas Holstrum's family Jewish?"

"His married family, but they weren't there in the bookstore."

"Mr. Hendricksen, I submit to you that they were there, hiding in the back room, and they heard you say you wanted a book about hiding."

"A lie! Another bald-faced lie! She's lying, can't you see that? How could I know her family was hiding there? Obviously, they were hiding somewhere. They were all hiding somewhere. All the Jews. Hiding like little mice in a cupboard."

"And you thought that Lukas could tell the Gestapo, after a little persuasion, where his family was hiding, didn't you?"

"Nonsense. Maybe the Gestapo thought that, but how could I know what Holstrum would or wouldn't tell them?"

"In October 1943, was the Gestapo paying informers to tell them where they could find Jewish families?"

"I didn't take any money."

Sparks closes his eyes. That was a terrible answer. Things are going badly. He stands. "Break, please, your honor?"

Wilson raises his eyebrows. "All right. Ten minutes. Mr. Henryks, you are not to speak to anyone during the break."

"How are you feeling, Britta?" Catherine says quietly. Liam and Emma are keeping listeners at a distance. "Better," Britta says. "Nice to get out of . . . hospital."

Catherine notices that her speech is improving. "Did they discharge you?" Catherine says.

Britta has an impish smile. "Not exactly. I discharged me. I couldn't miss this."

"Your presence has rattled him, Bubbe," Emma says. "He's stumbling all over himself. Catherine is doing a masterful job."

Catherine shrugs. "The truth has a way of wiggling out."

Britta reaches out and squeezes Catherine's hand. "Thank you for what you have done."

"Don't thank me yet. I don't know if we have enough to convince the jury."

THE GAVEL SOUNDS the resumption of the proceedings and Henryks retakes the stand.

"Mr. Hendricksen, I want to call your attention again to the photograph on the easel. You identified your father and yourself. There is a third person, who appears to be a young man like yourself. Who is that?"

"I don't remember. Probably one of the guys I hung around with."

"And it's your testimony that the three of you on this very night transported Jewish families to Sweden in that very boat."

"That night and the nights after."

"Did you call that boat the *Perlie B* and tell people that you led Jewish families to that boat?"

"Right. The *Perlie B*. Perlie Bjorn was my grandmother."

"Your son, Nils, testified that the other young man in the picture was named Henning."

Henryks leans forward. "No. He said Henry, and you said Henning. You tricked him like you trick me."

"Is the other man in the picture Henning Brondum?"

"I had a friend Henry Wolf, you know. That's probably him. I don't know any Henning Brondum."

"Mr. Hendricksen, please look at the photograph again and read the numbers and letters on the side of the boat you call the *Perlie B*."

"BC2342."

"What do those numbers stand for?"

"You have to register your boat in the Copenhagen Harbor. There is a fee."

"Precisely. I believe it is your testimony that your father owned this boat, is that right?"

"He did, named after his mother. And we rescued Jews in that boat."

Catherine hands a document to Henryks. "Mr. Hendricksen, this is a registration form from the Copenhagen Harbor for the year 1943. Do you see the registration for boat BC2342?"

Ole finds it on the page and scowls. "It says it's owned by Henning Brondum. But I don't know him. I mean it's possible that we were standing in front of someone else's boat when the picture was taken. It's a long time ago. I could have forgot the numbers."

Catherine nods to Emma, who turns on her computer at the counsel table. "Your honor," Catherine says, "we are going to play a short video clip which will be displayed on the monitors."

Wilson nods. "Go ahead."

The clip begins. It is a crowded party at The Melancholy Dane. Catherine lets it run for a minute or two and then pauses it. "Mr. Hendricksen, can you tell us what is going on in this video?"

"Yeah. Of course I can. That was a party thrown for me at my tavern. It was called Ole Appreciation Night. You can see all the people that were there to appreciate me. They did it to show their love after Mrs. Stein wrote all those terrible lies about me."

"There were many speeches that night, weren't there? Including one by you?"

"Yep. There sure were."

"Let's play the second clip," Catherine says.

All eyes are on the video monitors. A major is giving a toast. He says, "My uncle and Ole would share fascinating stories of Copenhagen back in the day. They talked about the resistance, they talked about fighting the Nazis, they talked about saving lives. Oh, those were the days. My uncle Ole and their buddy, Henning Brondum, like the Three Musketeers." Then the picture shifts to Ole Henryks, who says, "Henning, ya, we had a club. There were others. My friend Kai Nielsen. It was good times; when we were young. We went fishing; Henning had a boat."

The courtroom is silent. Henryks jumps to his feet in the witness box. "Sterling?" he says. "We need a recess. We need a break right now. I need to talk to my lawyer."

"No, Mr. Henryks, not now," Judge Wilson says.

Henryks appeals to Sparks, who shakes his head. Then to the judge, he says, "I need to use the washroom."

Wilson rolls his eyes. "Very well. Mr. Sparks, you will stay seated. My clerk will accompany Mr. Henryks to the bathroom. We will stand in recess for ten minutes."

Catherine says, "One question, if I may before we break, your honor." He nods. "Henning Brondum didn't rescue any Jews, did he, Mr. Hendricksen? He turned them over to the Gestapo, didn't he?"

"No, I don't know."

"He lured them to that boat and then turned them over to the Germans, didn't he? On that night in 1943."

"I have to use the washroom."

"WHERE ARE YOU going with this?" Britta whispers to Catherine during the break. "The evidence must be pretty damning."

"Nothing I have is as damaging to Ole as what he has just done to himself. He has validated an accusation that I could not possibly prove."

The gavel signals the return of Henryks to the witness stand and Catherine steps forward.

"Mr. Hendricksen, when you talked about the club that you had with Henning Brondum and Kai Nielsen, the club that you were referencing that night in your restaurant, that wasn't the Blue Shirt Club, was it?"

Henryks slowly shakes his head. He looks beaten. "No, it wasn't. Henning was not in the Blue Shirt Club."

"That's right," Catherine says. "What was the name of the club that he and Kai Nielsen formed?"

Henryks hesitates. He takes deep breaths. The jury's eyes are locked on him. There is no escape. "Sometimes it was called the Brondum Gang. Other times it was called the Peter Group. Petergruppen."

Catherine is holding another document. "Am I correct that the Petergruppen was sympathetic to the Nazis in 1943?"

It's over and Ole knows it. He nods. "It was created by the German administration in Denmark. They named the club after Peter Schafer, the German who formed it."

"Am I also correct that the Brondum Gang, or the Petergruppen, was a counter-resistance group?"

"Yes."

"Did it fight Danish resistance efforts?"

"I think so."

"Isn't it a fact that on the night of the exodus, Henning Brondum lured Jewish families to his boat, BC2342, and then turned them over to the Gestapo?"

"I know you won't believe me, but I didn't do it personally. I never turned in people, I never went on any of those raids. But they did; Brondum and Nielsen and others. They attacked the Danish freedom fighters. They led Jews to the Gestapo. But they were only my social friends, I didn't go on any of their raids. Not me, you have no proof."

"In 1947, were seven members of the Petergruppen, including Henning Brondum and Kai Nielsen—your social friends, your Three

Musketeers—were they tried in a Danish court, convicted and executed for war crimes?"

Ole hangs his head. The courtroom is deathly silent. He says, "Yes, they were."

"And is that why you and your wife, Margit, came to America and changed your name?"

Ole nods.

"No further questions, your honor. The defendant rests."

Wilson looks at Sparks, who is hunched over his papers. "Any redirect of this witness, Mr. Sparks? Will there be any rebuttal?"

"No, your honor."

"Then the evidence is closed. We will hear final arguments tomorrow morning."

CHAPTER FIFTY-FOUR

"Ladies and Gentlemen of the jury, Judge Wilson, Ms. Lockhart, Ms. Fisher. May it please the court." Sparks is dressed for closing argument: a light gray suit, colorful tie and pocket square and white monogramed shirt. Nevertheless, the gloom of the previous day hangs over the room. There is an absence of energy. The bell has sounded. The round is over. Still, Sterling Sparks will lie down for no man. Or woman. He confidently addresses the jury.

"Ladies and gentlemen, we are not here to prosecute anyone for war crimes. This is a civil case against the defendant for defamation. You don't have to like anyone or dislike anyone. You just have to follow the law. That is what you've sworn to do.

"Six times Mrs. Britta Stein has written the most heinous accusations known to modern man," he says forcefully. "She has accused Ole Henryks of being a Nazi and collaborating with the Nazi regime against Denmark during the war. She doesn't deny it. Indeed, she stands by it. Ole has sued her for defamation. As we have said, the words themselves are defamatory. The plaintiff's burden in this case is to prove to you by a preponderance of the evidence that she has *written* those words for the public to see. We have satisfied our burden. The case would be over, but for the affirmative defense raised by Mrs. Stein." He looks across the room to the defense table, where Catherine, Emma and Britta are seated.

"For her affirmative defense, Mrs. Stein says she is not liable to Ole because her words are true. Because truth is an affirmative defense, Mrs. Stein and her legal team must prove to you, by a preponderance of the evidence, that each of the words she wrote are true in fact. I submit to you: she has not done that.

"Oh, she has raised circumstances, scenarios from which she urges you to draw conclusions. She has laid down pieces of a puzzle in the hopes that you will take the final leap and supply the missing pieces. That you will supply the missing facts, the facts that Ole was a traitor and a collaborator. But that's not your job, it's hers. Where is the *proof* of the missing facts? Where is the proof of betrayal? You heard testimony that Henning Brondum and Kai Nielsen were executed as war criminals and collaborators. And they may have been friends of Ole. But Ole was never arrested or prosecuted. He said he didn't go on raids with them. Where is the proof that he did? Ms. Lockhart asks you to make that leap just because he was their friend. She wants you to supply that missing evidence. But ladies and gentlemen, evidence is her burden, not yours, and she has not met it.

"She has not proven that Ole informed. No witness has come forward to say that. She has not proven that Ole collaborated. No witness has come forward to say that. Think about this trial. The defense has not supplied a single witness. Where is the eyewitness testimony? Where is her case? If any of those horrible accusations were true, wouldn't you have heard from a witness? You didn't see a single witness. Lacking such direct evidence, you must find for the plaintiff." He nods and sits down.

JUDGE WILSON KNOWS that Sparks's case has disintegrated, but he has seen juries do strange things for strange reasons. He nods to Catherine. "Ms. Lockhart?"

"Ladies and gentlemen of the jury, Judge Wilson, Mr. Sparks, Britta, Emma, may it please the court. Mr. Sparks has asked where our witnesses are. He said, 'You didn't see a single witness.' Catherine smiles. "He was wrong. You did see a witness. An eyewitness. His name is Ole Hendricksen. Did Ole Hendricksen lead the Gestapo to arrest the members of the

Holger Club resistance group on that hill in 1943? Of course he did. He knew too much, didn't he? Things that he wouldn't know unless he was there. His was the eyewitness testimony. He knew Lukas Holstrum was shot running away. He volunteered that and never did explain how he knew. But we know how he knew. He was there.

"Ole Hendricksen brought the Gestapo to arrest Lukas Holstrum at the bookstore and then he volunteered that they were really there looking for Britta's family that was *in hiding*. Like 'little mice in a cupboard,' remember? When asked if he was informing for the Gestapo and taking money, he said, 'I never took any money.' He didn't deny informing, just taking money. He admitted to supervising weapons manufacture for the army of a foreign adversary; Denmark's enemy. That is collaborating with the enemy and traitorous by definition.

"He did not rescue people in his father's boat. It was Henning Brondum's boat, and Brondum was a traitor and a collaborator. Brondum didn't rescue Jews, he led them to the Gestapo. Perhaps Hendricksen's relationship with Brondum and Nielsen is the most significant and damaging admission in his testimony. You saw him brag in the video about the club he was in with Brondum and Nielsen. 'Henning, ya, we had a club.' Remember those words. That was his confession to being a member of the Brondum Gang, the Petergruppen, founded by the Nazis to conduct counter-resistance sabotage on behalf of the German administration. He admitted that he and his wife fled Europe, secretly changed their names, and immigrated to America rather than face prosecution either for selling armaments to the Nazis or for being a member in the collaborationist Brondum Gang. Or both.

"Ole Hendricksen was not a war hero. He was a traitor. He was a Nazi collaborator. He was an informer and a betrayer. He was a man who made a choice when the Nazis came to Denmark. He bet on the wrong team. I will admit that it was sad for us all to witness Mr. Hendricksen publicly coming to terms with his fake persona, but we are compelled to conclude that his reputation was built on lies and falsehoods and finally exposed.

"Britta did not take the stand. I did not call her, and Mr. Sparks did not call her. I suppose we will never know what motivated her to write those words at this particular time of her life, but her motivation is ir-relevant. The only issue for you to decide, as I said at the outset of this trial, is whether the words she wrote are true. Damning though they be, they are true. You must find for the defendant."

CHAPTER FIFTY-FIVE

———— ∞∞∞ ————

BRITTA IS BACK in her hospital room. She is seated in her wheelchair, staring out of the window at the park below. Emma sits beside her with a comforting hand on her grandmother's arm. Britta's mood is contemplative, not at all what Emma expects. "Bubbe, you should be celebrating. The jury returned a verdict in your favor in less than two hours. You were vindicated." Britta smiles and nods.

At that moment Catherine and Liam burst into the room and close the door. Catherine unwraps a bottle of Champagne and pours some into four plastic flutes. She raises hers and says, "A toast to my hubby, the world's greatest detective, without whom we would have never won this case."

Liam shakes his head. "All praise goes to the world's greatest attorney." He smiles and looks around the room. "She paid me to say that." Catherine elbows him.

"I will definitely raise my glass to the world's greatest attorney," Emma says. "What an education I received in trial management. Catherine saw the play and executed it perfectly. Proof of his betrayals, his traitorous acts, his membership in Nazi-sponsored organizations, none of which could have gone into evidence without Ole's confession on the witness stand. Catherine engineered it perfectly. She led him right down the path and he never saw it coming."

"They say that cross-examination is the crucible of truth," Catherine says. "People think it's easy to lie, but it's not. One lie begets another and eventually the truth bleeds through." Catherine raises her glass again. "But here's where the praise belongs: to my powerful and determined client, Britta Stein. What a remarkable, detailed memory! What strength of purpose! To the world's greatest Bubbe, and the world's greatest storyteller."

Britta breaks into a smile, though one side of her mouth rises higher than the other. She takes a small sip of Champagne, licks her lips and says, "Don't tell my doctor . . . or my nurse. Or the woman . . . Emma has hired . . . to live with me." She shakes her head. "Apparently . . . my independence is a thing of the past."

"That will be the day," Catherine says with a laugh.

"I must say this case opened my eyes," Liam says. "What the people of Denmark did during the war is inspiring. One of the most interesting things I did while in Copenhagen was to visit the Danish Jewish Museum. It's a beautiful structure. The corridors and walls are laid out to spell the Hebrew word 'Mitzvah,' which I am told refers to deeds done in order to fulfill commandments."

Britta nods in confirmation. "And at . . . Yad Vashem . . . in Israel . . . there's a section which honors . . . Righteous Among the Nations . . . those people who risked their lives . . . to save Jewish people during . . . Holocaust. Soldiers, priests . . . nurses, government officials. Georg Duckwitz . . . He is honored. And there is one area . . . a tree . . . planted in a garden . . . along with a replica of a boat . . . dedicated collectively . . . to the people of Denmark."

After a short pause, Emma says, "You know, Six-o'clock was actually a gentleman at the end of this case. He came up to me and said he wished me the best, that I was a fine lawyer, and that I was learning from a *great* lawyer. He said, 'Catherine Lockhart was the better man today.'"

"Better *man*? Hmph," Catherine says.

The door opens, the nurse steps into the room, takes a look around, smiles, says, "I didn't see anything," and leaves.

Emma giggles. She raises her glass. "Bubbe, it took seventy years, but the truth prevailed. You set the record straight and you avenged your family. You achieved justice for them. Victory is sweet."

Britta shakes her head. She does not agree. "No, Emma . . . this was a hollow victory . . . I derive no pleasure from it . . . It doesn't bring back my sister . . . or reverse history. Ole Hendricksen got . . . what he deserved." She shakes her head again. "But he's just a pitiful old man . . . whose debts have come due. He was an unprincipled young man . . . but not a demon. Unlike the Nazis he worshipped. He was not banal . . . he had no personal agenda. He was just a mindless follower . . . in search of approval." She curls her lips. "What he did to my family . . . and to others . . . is unforgivable. But he didn't bring the war to Europe. He didn't invent Nazism." She points a finger. "He was a hanger-on . . . looking for acceptance . . . at the expense of his morality . . . Even with a judgment against him . . . he will never see it that way . . . But he was no war hero . . . that's for damn sure . . . and I wasn't going to let him get away with it."

"Amen," Catherine says.

Britta holds her glass and takes a small sip. "Please join me in a toast . . . to my sister, Grethe . . . who possessed more inner strength . . . than men like Hendricksen could ever imagine. And to her husband, Lukas . . . a true war hero . . . who protected us all to the very end . . . at the cost of his life." Tears fill her eyes. "To my mother and my father . . . may they rest in peace. To Isabel, of blessed memory, the lovely daughter Grethe and I shared." She lifts her glass a little higher and turns to her right. "And finally, here's to Emma, the brilliant young attorney . . . who is now the repository of the Morgenstern family legacy. Carry the torch proudly, my worthy granddaughter."

"Worthy indeed," Catherine says. "What a phenomenal co-counsel. What a great second chair. I'm not trying to steal you from Walter, that wouldn't be nice, but if at any time you decide that big-firm legal life isn't for you . . . well, you know where I am. We could sit down and talk. Right after Liam and I get back."

"Get back?" Liam says.

"Tuscany, my dear hubby. Did you forget? We have a date with Aunt Gabi."

ACKNOWLEDGMENTS

Defending Britta Stein is a work of historical fiction. I've always believed that writing historical fiction is a little bit like cheating. The setting has already been written for me. It's history. My job is to create characters and a plotline to weave into that backdrop. In that regard, I need to say that the principal characters portrayed herein are imaginary and do not refer to any actual persons, living or dead. Britta, Grethe, Emma, the Morgenstern family and Lukas Holstrum are all products of my imagination. Similarly, Ole Hendricksen, his wife, Margit, and his son, Nils, are fictional and do not represent any person. To my knowledge, there is no tavern named The Melancholy Dane, and if there might be in some location, the use of the name in this story is unintentional and is not meant to refer to any existing establishment. Similarly, to my knowledge, there is no such association as the Danish-American Association of Chicago. It is my fictional creation. Nothing in this story is meant to refer to an existing Danish American association in any location. Likewise, Simmons Manufacturing is fictional and not meant to refer to any company called Simmons.

While the Circuit Court of Cook County is an institution where I have spent the better part of my forty-nine years of litigation practice, Judge Obadiah Wilson is a fictional character and is not meant to refer to any judge, living or dead. Catherine Lockhart and Sterling J. Sparks are fictional characters and do not refer to any specific attorney I have known, though in many respects they are amalgams. If you are an attorney and you see yourself in Sterling J. Sparks, I am sorry. Truly. The reporters are all fictional.

The marvelous story of Denmark in World War II is factual and occurred as described in the story. What the people of Denmark did when they received word of the Nazi deportation orders was unique in World War II history. As a country, they came together to hide, protect and ultimately rescue 7,200 of their Jewish brethren from certain death. They are indeed honored as an entire country at Israel's Yad Vashem Holocaust Museum in the garden of the Righteous Among Nations.

Though Joseph Morgenstern is a fictional character, he is representative of a Danish Parliamentarian in that period. The parliamentary elections of 1943 are accurately reported. Thorvald Stauning, Hans Hedtoft and Erik Scavenius were, in fact, all Danish prime ministers, who acted as portrayed in the story. Georg Duckwitz was the German naval attaché who, at great risk to himself, divulged Obergruppenführer Werner Best's order to round up and deport all of Denmark's Jews on Rosh Hashanah. Duckwitz did in fact travel to Berlin and attempt to convince Hitler to revoke Best's order, and upon failing to do so, he did travel to Sweden and met with Prime Minister Per Hansson to secure sanctuary for Denmark's Jewish refugees. Although he did not divulge the secret to Morgenstern, Duckwitz did tell it directly to Hedtoft, who then spread the word through Rabbi Melchior and Hans Fuglsang-Damgaard, the Bishop of Copenhagen. The pastoral letter sent to all churches in the diocese on the day before the scheduled roundup is quoted accurately.

Sister Elizabeth and the St. Vincent's Hospital are fictional but representative of hospitals throughout Denmark that did provide shelter and a hiding place, quite often citing the German measles on the medical chart. The Elsinore Sewing Club is historically accurate and did provide passage for Jews during the exodus. Hal Koch was a professor of church history and a proponent of Danish unity. He is quoted accurately in the story.

The bravery of the youth resistance clubs in Denmark is legendary. The Churchill Club and Hvidsten Club were authentic and their exploits